BREEDS 3

Also by Keith C. Blackmore

Mountain Man
Mountain Man
Safari
Hellifax
Well Fed
Make Me King
Mindless
Skull Road
Mountain Man Prequel
Mountain Man 2nd Prequel: Them Early Days
The Hospital: A Mountain Man Story
Mountain Man Omnibus: Books 1–3

131 Days
131 Days
House of Pain
Spikes and Edges
About the Blood
To Thunderous Applause
131 Days Omnibus: Books 1–3

Breeds
Breeds
Breeds 2
Breeds 3
Breeds: The Complete Trilogy

Isosceles Moon
Isosceles Moon
Isosceles Moon 2

The Bear That Fell from the Stars
Bones and Needles
Cauldron Gristle
Flight of the Cookie Dough Mansion
The Majestic 311
The Missing Boatman
Private Property
The Troll Hunter
White Sands, Red Steel

BREEDS 3

Keith C. Blackmore

All rights reserved. No part of this publication may be reproduced, stored in a retrieval system, or transmitted in any form or by any means electronic, mechanical, photocopying, recording, or otherwise without prior written permission from Podium Publishing.

This is a work of fiction. Names, characters, places, and incidents are either products of the author's imagination or used fictitiously. Any resemblance to actual events, locales, or persons, living, dead, or undead, is entirely coincidental.

Copyright © 2016 by Keith C. Blackmore

Cover design by Alexandre Rito

ISBN: 978-1-0394-8349-1

Published in 2024 by Podium Publishing
www.podiumaudio.com

BREEDS 3

1

Not a breeze brushed the bay, leaving the sea as flat as a sheet of steel.

The night waned, but the sun hadn't yet breached the trees behind the little green bungalow. Ross Kelly, contemplative and relaxed from a solid night's sleep, sat on his front deck, high on a hilltop, and faced the water. A blue winter coat protected him against the cold as he shifted in an old lawn chair. Steam curled off the cup of coffee in his left hand. The occasional gull drifted through his line of sight, and he watched it without thought, just appreciating the animal for what it was.

Ross Kelly smoothed his thick black beard. He studied the water, scanned its opaque surface in the pre-dawn light, and sipped his coffee. Gifts. All gifts. He'd received his own that year, mere months ago. His life had changed big time, in most cases for the better.

Black ducks, three of them, swam close to the rocks in search of breakfast. They floated perhaps a kilometer away from Ross's hillside perch, mere specks on the water, yet he spotted them without squinting. He held his breath, focused on his hearing. Wood creaked. A muffled *pop* issued from inside his house. A car approached in the distance. Perhaps a kilometer away. Ross took a hit off his coffee and rubbed his nose.

Gifts.

Of sight and of hearing. All his senses, really. His eyesight had improved to a degree he'd never thought possible. He felt wonderful. Better than wonderful. The slow advance of arthritis in his fingers and knees had halted and receded to nothing. If he went for a hike, the hike usually became a run, and he could cut through deep woods for hours without stopping. He felt healthier, stronger, faster than when he was twenty-two. And his skin! When he looked in the mirror he saw a man ten years younger. The bags under his eyes had retreated, a couple of scars had disappeared, his teeth had stopped aching, and even his hairline's slow withdrawal had stopped and even gone on the offensive. He kept his hair buzzed short for ease of maintenance, but it didn't stop the folks of Amherst Cove from commenting on his apparent renewed vitality.

Ever since that night all those months ago, Ross Kelly's health had improved dramatically. Frightening, really, if one didn't know why. Ross knew. He'd been lectured. Doug Kirk had warned him, warned him that there was a dark side to such abilities. And Ross had felt those particular urges ever since taking down his first moose with his bare fangs. The softest whisper at the back of his mind informing him that there was better game afoot—plentiful game if he dared hunt it. Ross didn't dare. Did everything to keep from daring. The craving wasn't so bad in the mornings, as if it was still asleep, but during the day it awoke.

Kirk had lectured him about that as well.

Ross recognized its danger. His appetite was a concern but, thus far, still in its infancy. He'd only been a *were* nine or ten months, but the hunger would grow. Kirk told him it would. Moses Morris advised him to give in when the impulse got too strong, and that got both wardens cursing at each other in an argument. Not that Ross would ever give in to such a carnivorous itch. He preferred Kirk's advice. Eat rare steak, pork, anything to take the edge off. Eat it raw if the cravings were really bad. Gorge himself if he had to. Or go out at night and hunt down an animal. That usually did the trick.

So Ross did that.

The moose helped. Even that bear he'd devoured 'til his gut nearly burst. He could never eat all the meat he procured, so he stored the remainder away, much to the wardens' amusement. If anyone came into his home and looked into his freezer, Ross would have a lot of explaining to do. Not that anyone visited him, except Alvin.

Ross felt a pinch of resentment then, of feeling boxed in despite his new powers. More than anything, he wanted to help his neighbors and friends of Amherst Cove avoid the ailments of old age. He couldn't, however. The wardens had made that clear. They'd also made it clear that, within the next five years, he would be leaving the little village and moving to another part of the island. Somewhere far away, where no one would know him and he'd live the next twenty years or so under a new identity. That wasn't something that Ross looked forward to. He loved Amherst Cove. Loved the people. At one time he'd been faced with the possibility of moving in search of work. Now, however, he hated the idea.

Ross's eyes moistened, as they usually did when he dwelled on such thoughts. Some fucking werewolf he was.

Kirk had told him he could return to Amherst Cove after a time, perhaps fifty or sixty years later, but Ross wasn't sure about that. Most of the folks he knew would've passed on then, and just gazing at their houses, perhaps owned by sons or daughters, or perhaps boarded up and empty, would tear his guts out. That was the idea behind the move, Kirk explained, so that there'd be fewer living friends to recognize Ross.

That summoned a deep breath. Ross followed it with a shot of coffee. He dreaded such an encounter, where he might have to deceive a young boy or girl grown into adulthood, or a senior defying the eternal and living well past a hundred years. That was going to kill Ross, to see those people much, much older while he remained youthful and pretending to be another. The very notion was reason enough to leave and never return.

Gifts. Terrible, terrible gifts.

Thick clouds blanketed the sun, rendering the shoreline in a heavy shade. Ross frowned, took another hit off his coffee, and watched the feeding ducks. The car he'd heard approaching was closer, stopped and idling, and Ross looked to his right, down the length of his driveway hemmed in by yellow grass.

A van had stopped at the top of the hill, the driver dithering at a fork in the road. Ross had seen the same hesitation many times before. It didn't make a difference if the driver took the right or left road down the slope. The lanes eventually reunited at the bottom of the hill.

Ross didn't mind the clueless drivers, as long as they didn't pull into his driveway and ask for directions. He didn't really like being disturbed so early. Later would be fine, but not right now.

With that thought, he returned his attention to the bay's gray water, flat and stolid. November had embraced the island, and Ross's thoughts turned to Christmas. Across the bay, the waterline fused with the shore in a low-lying patch of fog. Rooftops poked through the gauzy ribbon. Neighbors would be rising within the hour, firing up their woodstoves, and the hills would come alive with the rush of cars.

Ross thought of Kirk again, his recent phone call, and the man's apology. Kirk always seemed to end a conversation by apologizing, for changing Ross into a werewolf. It had been the only way to save his life. No matter how often Ross assured him that he harbored the warden no ill-will, Kirk still apologized, and that touched the Newfoundland man.

Ross frowned as guilt twisted his innards. Kirk had been honest with him, but Ross hadn't reciprocated. He'd done something Kirk might not approve of and it bothered him greatly. He'd have to contact the Halifax warden soon and explain his actions, why he'd done it, and take whatever punishment befitting his new station in life. He hoped Kirk would understand. Ross didn't really have much of a choice in the matter. It had been a matter of life or death, and he was still inexperienced, drunk off his newly acquired powers.

Or maybe he would just say he'd been drunk. That might float better.

A metallic click from the direction of the van pulled Ross out of his thoughts. The van remained idling at the head of the diverging roads, its side door slightly ajar.

Well, shit, Ross thought.

Odds were he was going to get visitors. He took another shot of coffee and looked back over the bay.

The air screamed and sizzled a split instant before Ross's scalp exploded. He flopped onto the wooden deck, coffee mug falling with a clatter, and landed ass up. For a brief moment his body shivered. Just a moment.

A second shot drilled a hole through Ross's rib cage, flipping him onto his side to face the road.

His quivering stopped.

A third shot took him through the heart, as did the next two, fired within a span of seconds.

Then the shooting stopped.

The van door opened wide and a man stepped out, dressed in a gray winter parka and black denim. Black hair had been shaved to just a prickly shadow. He looked left and right and judged that he was alone. He marched down Ross Kelly's driveway, purpose in his stride, to the tune of the van's idling. A few pebbles rustled in his passage.

The black-haired man stepped onto Ross's deck, his boots loud on the fitted planks. He stood over his victim and pulled out a handgun with an attached suppressor.

He straightened his arm and shot Ross five more times in the chest.

The van's engine thrummed.

The black-haired man altered his aim and fired one last round into the dead man's head. He lingered then, inspecting the kill while concealing his weapon with his tall frame. He located the brass casings from where they'd rolled on the wood and made quick work of picking them up. Once done, he turned and waved to the van.

The nearby houses (there weren't many) remained quiet and sleepy.

The van reversed and backed into Ross Kelly's driveway. The rear doors opened and three more men jumped out, all similarly dressed for the cold weather.

They carried large tanks of gasoline.

As the body and house were liberally doused, the black-haired man stood back and watched. At one point he regarded the peacefulness of the bay, while pungent fluid glugged and splashed in the background.

As the crew retreated to the van, someone flicked a match into the bungalow's doorway.

The fire got the black-haired man moving.

Halfway to the van, he reached into a pocket and retrieved a cellphone.

*

In another white van, parked along an empty back road hidden by trees, a burly man answered his phone. The leather coat he wore creaked as he brought the phone to his ear. His dark complexion appeared sleepy, further darkened by a thick goatee that hung off his chubby face like a dirty shovel. He listened, squinted at the brightening Nova Scotia sky, and soon broke the connection.

He fit a headset to his thick skull, taking a second to get it comfortable. The strengthening sun glared through the window as he pinched the accompanying mic and brought it in close to his mouth.

"All go," he said.

2

The morning peeked brightly into the cabin, but Morris didn't feel its cheer. Chills seized him instead, and he interpreted the cold as a warning that he should've been gone long ago. After the incident with Bailey, it took him three days to make his way back to Pictou County, riding buses down to Yarmouth and doing a milk run tour back to his territory. He needed to get home, needed to get some quality thinking done. Last night he had an overwhelming urge to call Douglas Kirk for a talk, but in the end he did not. Kirk would only verbally wrestle with him over the phone, call him paranoid and leave him questioning his own thoughts.

What Morris needed was proof.

Proof that the elders were indeed out to kill him. And Kirk.

He had eventually returned to his cabin in the countryside, isolated and peaceful, and, thanks to Bailey, ventilated. Morris had nailed a thick quilt over the wreckage of his picture window, cursing Bailey with every nail he pounded home. Goddamn fucker just *had* to bust through his window like a twisted sidewinder missile. Morris was so fucking glad the *were* was dead.

That morning, with the cover over the window, an irresistible urge to leave had taken Morris. He didn't know where he'd go, but staying in Pictou County didn't sit well with his guts. The road called him, so perhaps he'd heed it, maybe lose himself in a big city (cement shitholes that they were) and make his way west. Or north.

But he'd get out of Nova Scotia. Quiet-like.

The only thing troubling him that morning, however, was whether or not to inform Kirk.

The Halifax warden had shown a considerable, if not surprising, amount of balls for a vegan. Not many would have survived the horrors of Borland's pack or come through the unhinged ferocity of Bailey, but Kirk did. Kirk did in aces. Morris wasn't one to powder asses, but he gave credit where it was due, and Kirk had demonstrated that, despite his penchant for dicking around with morals, he carried a sizeable pair of dog balls. Even waved them in a person's face when things got dirty, when it came down to the crunch of bone. Not the best humper to have at one's back, but acceptable, once you got past all of his fucking moping.

At seven-twenty in the morning, Morris still wasn't sure of calling Kirk or not, so he busied himself with gathering up the few belongings that mattered and stuffed them into an army duffel bag. Spare jeans. Sweaters. Underwear. His badge, the silver Bowie knife. Once finished, he went to the freezer and frowned at the frost-covered roasts. There was some good eating there, but all of it too damn long to prepare. And he wasn't overly fond of gnawing on a beefcicle. He decided to leave the food, skip breakfast, and head out to the highway. Find a restaurant far away. Bailey's crotch rocket awaited, parked on the front lawn where he left it, and Morris had even located the keys.

But should he call Kirk? That was the question.

Morris cracked open a morning beer (no way he was leaving those behind) and drank deeply, if not pensively. In the end, he decided not to call his old friend. Not today. Maybe later. When Morris hit Montreal or somewhere. He'd sniff out and buy a prepaid phone, make the call, and dump the device immediately after. Maybe he'd buy two disposable phones.

He tipped the can back, downed another mouthful, and stopped with a lurch. Beer dribbled into his beard, but Morris didn't feel it.

He looked to the front door.

Then he heard it again, the distinct scuffing of boots on a dirt road.

Morris sniffed the air and crept to his picture window, jabbing two fingers into a crease and pulling the quilt back a crack. He couldn't smell shit but his ears still worked fine. His ears were working incredibly well, in fact.

Morris finished his beer and placed the empty can on the floor. He went to the front door and opened it a sliver. The soft rustling of fabric teased his sensitive hearing and he scanned the forest surrounding his home. A single road, its length concealed by the woods, lay empty. The wind blew away from him, robbing him of scent.

Not that he needed it.

A figure gradually came into sight, hiking up the road. Morris opened the door a little wider, seeing it was a small woman with a backpack. He relaxed somewhat, remembered his beard, and wiped himself clean.

The woman, a short brunette with her face glazed in make-up, stopped at the mouth of the road. She studied the cabin in turn, her mouth slightly open as if in wonder of what she'd found. After a few seconds of indecision, she adjusted her shoulder straps and walked forward, designer boots scuffing along Morris's lawn.

She stopped before the front deck, eyeing the open door.

"Anyone home in there?" she asked, her voice creaking like a bullfrog's tenor, and not in a good way. As if she couldn't be bothered with putting any more wind into the question. Morris suspected she was very good at whining.

He opened the door with two fingers.

"Oh, Jesus." She flinched and retreated a step, ready to bolt.

Morris had that effect on women.

But she recovered and even took a moment to compose herself when he didn't charge after her. She smiled prettily, brightening her half-assed attempt at make-up.

"You're on private property," Morris told her, getting a not-so-subtle whiff of her god-awful perfume, which smelled like the sweat off a dead man's piss sack.

"Oh yeah?" she asked. "Yours? Sorry about that. I figured it was with the road and all. I was camped out overnight, near the highway."

"Camped out?" Morris asked dubiously. "In November?"

"Well," she granted with a shrug, "camped out in my car. Damn thing died last night on the road and I don't have a cellphone. So I was stuck out here."

"You're stuck out here?"

"Uh-huh. In my car. All night. Doors locked and me in the backseat."

"All night?"

"Yep. You okay there, buddy? Or you just like repeating shit? Lord help me if you got a banjo in there. Anyway, yeah. Freaky, huh? And the only station I could get on the radio was a crackly one with electric yodelers singing rock songs and callin' it country. I'd be seriously pissed off if I didn't have alternative music with me. As it was, I'm only a little pissed off, but a whole 'lotta bewildered. No one drives along these hick roads or what?"

Morris considered that, taking his time in answering, which had a visible effect on his visitor.

"Not that you're a hick," she quietly pointed out. "You're not. At least, I hope you're not. Even though I'm wondering what that smell is, which makes me think of carbonated moose ass. Ah. Can I use your phone?"

"What makes you think this hick has a phone?"

"Well... do you?"

"I do."

"Then you're not a hick," she smiled. "Unless it's one of those old-fashioned lap phones with the fat ass and the dial that purrs when you stick your finger in."

Morris frowned again, but in mild amusement.

"You have one of those?" She brightened, hopeful. "Well, awesome if you do. I was just shittin' ya from before. You don't smell like moose ass. I don't even know what that smell is. I like those old phones, too. Got character. So anyway… can I use it?"

"I guess. Can you?"

"Sure thing." She smiled again and wiggled fingers as if casting a spell. "These do magic. All the time."

"Who you gonna call this early?"

"Roadside assistance. The automotive equivalent of a defibrillator. Or a polar bear dunk. I need a man to get my machine back on the road. Or a woman. I like women folk, too."

Morris eyed the road behind her

She turned around as well. "See something?"

"No," Morris said and closed the door. He got his phone and brought it back, opened the door just a crack and judged her again.

"You some kind of recluse or something?" she asked pointedly. "Or just fucked-up in a retarded kinda way? 'Cause you're really starting to freak me out here."

Morris opened the door wide enough and held out the phone halfway. "Here."

She studied him with a screwed-up hitch of her mouth, then the phone, then him again. "What's with that?"

"With what?"

"Holding it out like that, like you want me closer. You got lots of practice luring kids into the backs of vans or something?"

Morris waggled the phone.

"You're not going to grab me or anything?" she asked plainly. "We're a long way from the highway. I'm not a beauty or anything, but I bet I'm plenty hot enough for your gonads to start warming up the butter. You better not grab me. I'm warning you. Else I judo-toss your ass onto the front lawn."

Morris actually smiled. "Judo-toss, eh?"

"On the front lawn," she jabbed a thumb over her shoulder. "Your front lawn. Think about it."

"I'm a pretty big guy."

That earned him a roll of the eyes. "And I'm a five-foot pushover, is that it? Jesus Christ, I should've expected this. You're right. How could my five-foot fuck-all female frame ever be a match for your big-assed hairy masculine self?"

Morris extended his arm a little further, opening the door that much wider.

"You're like a hairy fucking bush turtle stickin' its neck out," she scolded in that whiny, can't-be-bothered bullfrog pitch.

"Take the phone."

"Thank you, superior male," she said. "I'll certainly allow you to impregnate me at your leisure. For sure. Bitch."

She snatched at the phone, knocking it from his hand.

"Well, shitfingers," she cursed and bent at the knees to retrieve it.

Morris watched her go down, smiling at the effort, and lifted his eyes to the treeline.

A bullet drilled him right above the nose, blasting out the

back of his skull in a spatter of pulpy matter. The impact blew him into the cabin where he landed on his back. There he lay, eyes open and staring with all the glassy indifference of a broken-down slot machine.

A shadow crossed his still frame.

The woman loomed over him and inspected the kill.

"Got you on the first shot," she muttered and shifted, extending a gun in her hand. "Greasy-assed, shit-monkey biker prick."

She fired five times, each shot an exclamation point of flame, hesitating only to adjust her aim. Two bullets went into Morris's head, destroying his face and bouncing what remained of his skull off the floorboards. Three shots blew apart his heart and chest. The gunfire echoed in the morning stillness, the harsh smoke causing her to squint.

The woman hefted the cellphone and waved at the distant treeline, signaling the coast was clear.

Three gunmen emerged. She paid them no further attention as she deposited Morris's phone in a pocket and took out her own. A number was speed-dialed.

"That's two," she reported and hung up.

*

Not a minute later, within the white van, the burly man made another call.

3

The phone on Kirk's coffee table buzzed about in a spastic whirligig amongst a collection of empty beer bottles. The commotion jerked him from a drunken sleep nowhere as deep as he wanted. He sniffed hard and felt a gelatinous chunk nail the back of his throat, which initiated a frightening fit of coughing and heart-felt hoarking. He sat up, red-faced, and barked a few more times while holding onto his couch for support. His copy of *Salem's Lot* had fallen from his chest and landed on the floor, the page lost.

That put a sick-dog frown on his face. Kirk looked from the book to the phone, the device still grinding away on his coffee table. He eventually picked it up without checking the number.

"Yeah," he answered, in nothing resembling a question.

No answer.

Kirk scratched at his head, his beard, and worked his way down to his balls. "Yeah, this is Kirk."

Nothing.

But there was a presence on the other end of that

connection, an awareness that Kirk sensed and immediately disliked. He recognized badness, knowing badness as certainly as a person tasting sour milk.

"Hello?"

Whoever had called him wasn't feeling particularly sociable. Neither was Kirk. He snapped the phone shut and placed it back on the table, regarding it with distrust as if the infernal piece of plastic was the communicative equivalent of a Ouija board. Kirk rubbed his beard and then his pajama-clad thighs, waiting for the phone to do jumping jacks right there. It didn't, of course, but that didn't alleviate the growing sensation of *verboten* in his guts.

The phone's timepiece informed him it was seven thirty-two. In the morning.

Too early for this shit, Kirk thought. He stood and stretched long and hard, enough to expose a hairy midriff. He studied the number of dead soldiers on the table, then the ones remaining in the nearby case. He took a moment to count, and saw he was two bottles shy. Another fucking morning mystery. At this rate he could go for a morning piss and discover his dick missing and not bat an eye.

Fridge, he realized, thankful for solving one of those puzzles. He winced, tasting that morning-after, blasting-tarp dryness associated with stale beer. Kirk zombie-shuffled from his living room into the kitchen. It had only been a few days since his place had been infested with company, most of it unwanted, and now that his domain was once again his, he discovered it to be emptier than it had ever been.

All because of her.

Kirk stopped, sighed, and pulled open the refrigerator door. Finger-drummed as he inspected the sparse contents. He downed a pitcher of water, drinking straight from the plastic lip, then pulled out a two-liter carton of orange juice, which stretched his stomach to uncomfortable limits. He finished, burped loudly, and kicked the door closed.

The phone attracted his groggy attention once more.

He crossed the floor and picked up the device.

Private caller.

You fucker. That did nothing for his curiosity. Kirk fumed and discovered he had other, more immediate concerns. He shambled towards the washroom, intent on choking some porcelain. Maybe even do an impression of a mother bird feeding her one chick.

Twenty minutes later he emerged from the can, feeling somewhat better, and returned to his couch. Morning light glowed around the curtained window, wanting to be let into the apartment. Kirk didn't want to let it in, wished to remain in the dark for a little while longer. So he sat, hands clasped between his knees, and stared at his damn phone for a few minutes more, losing himself in a morning stare.

The musical *ding dong* of the doorbell disturbed him, though it was far more preferable to a heavy knock. Kirk picked up his paperback and dropped it on the table, then rose and stumbled with a curse toward the door. He hoped it wasn't the apartment manager. Not this early. If it was, he'd haveta go all angry squirrel on his ass.

His hand stopped midway to the first lock. Kirk frowned and leaned into the door to use the peephole.

One guy, dressed for winter. Carrying a clipboard and looking far too sunny to deal with.

Kirk released gas and leaned against the doorframe. It was far too early to deal with visitors. He debated answering the door, when a second *ding dong* nudged him. That deepened his scowl. The guy with the clipboard looked like a fucking ding-donger. He'd probably stay outside and ring that set of chimes all morning long. Just to piss off anyone hiding inside.

Kirk knew the type.

"Yeah?" he reluctantly asked through the door.

"Mr. Kirk?"

"Yeah."

"Sir, I'm here to check for radon in your apartment."

"Radon?" Kirk's forehead wrinkled in puzzlement.

"Yes sir."

Kirk glanced behind him. "There's no radon here."

"I'm sorry, sir. You wouldn't be able to detect it without the proper equipment. It's a colorless, odorless, tasteless gas, but dangerous if you're exposed to it for a long period of time. There've been reports in the lower condos and we've detected significant levels. Enough to warrant a full check of the building. We're going through all the units today and taking readings, seeing just how far it's gone."

Radon?

Kirk ogled the guy through the peephole a second time. He looked way too earnest.

"It'll only take five minutes, Mr. Kirk."

"Can you come back later?"

"'fraid not, sir."

"I'm not presentable."

"Not a lot of people are at this hour, sir."

"I mean, I'm really not presentable."

The guy paused. "I'm good with it, Mr. Kirk."

Grudgingly, Kirk hesitated. He considered his gloomy apartment reeking of beer, bad breath, and morning afterdump, which was probably more dangerous than any radon.

You asked for it. Taking a diver's breath, Kirk undid the locks and opened the door.

The service guy smiled pleasantly. Kirk disliked him immediately. He allowed the far-too-early visitor to enter.

"Nice morning out there," the guy said in a not-so-subtle hint at the closed curtains.

Kirk wanted to tell him to fuck off. Instead, he mumbled, "Yeah."

"This won't take long."

"Mm."

The guy wandered deeper into the apartment, inspecting the floor and ceiling as if fearing a cave-in. *Radon.* Though still half-cut from the night before, Kirk wondered if he would be able to smell any such gas. *But you couldn't smell that shit*, a voice reminded him. *Odorless, remember?*

Right, he answered himself. Ruminating, he closed the door.

The service guy turned around in the hallway, right at the juncture to the kitchen and the living room. The dim bulb overhead contorted his features, deepening his eyes sockets and polishing his bald head. He looked like a creepy plastic doll.

"This won't take long at all." The guy smiled and produced a suppressed gun from behind his clipboard. The radon man fired as Kirk instinctively dodged right, blowing a hole through Kirk's shoulder and speckling the door behind him. Kirk rebounded off a wall and surged forward as the gunman fired a second time. The bullet cut past his left ribs and punched a wall in a puff of gypsum.

Kirk one-armed the gunman, grabbing him about the throat, and heaved him into the ceiling. The head broke through in a loud *crump* of plaster, slamming solid beam. The gunman dropped in a dust cloud and Kirk leaned against the wall for support. He spied the gun, the make unknown to him, and the suppressor meant to lessen the noise.

His left shoulder screamed at him. Kirk whimpered, knowing he'd been shot by silver—one never truly forgot the unmistakable lick and burn of that hated metal—and inspected the ragged hole in his t-shirt and flesh. A sickening, knee-weakening blast of pain overtook him when he prodded the bleeding wound, his shoulder lifeless at the very joint.

The gunman stirred.

Kirk soccer-kicked his head.

The warden growled, clenched his teeth, and relied on the wall for balance as he struggled to lock his front door. As he reached for the chain, the room whirled on him, spinning and tilting, and he fell forward, smashing his face into the door. His cheek smeared blood all the way to floor.

Get moving, he ordered himself.

"Shot me with silver." Kirk staggered past the dead gunman, ignoring the foot-sized indentation in that hairless profile. He made it to the washroom without passing out. He grabbed a towel and pressed it into his wound, hissing at the contact.

"Jesus Christ," he muttered, red-eyed and whimpering at the blazing, ball-shriveling acidic burn of that despicable metal, like being branded by a fire-bathed iron. He pulled the towel away and saw roses soaking well into the material. *Just fucking great.* Kirk pawed at a nearby cabinet and pulled out more towels to press against the wound. The pressure dropped him on the toilet. He waited until the dizziness passed, watching the hallway, noticing a set of unmoving boots and bare ankles.

"The fuck you get silver?" Kirk growled in misery, riding a fresh wave of agony that almost clawed him unconscious. "Oh sweet Jesus. Oh Jesus Christ. C'mon superhealing. C'mon, kick in. Kick in, goddamnit. Where are ya?"

He waited for the pain to reside, but it never did. At least not on a level that he was aware of. Kirk sat and panted and squealed and cursed, wanting the pain to be over, wanting it *all* to be over.

There's meat in the hall. A voice whispered at a safe distance. *Fresh off the truck.*

Kirk considered the dead man. Actually considered it. So much that he rose from the toilet seat and staggered to the bathroom door. He leaned against the frame and studied the corpse as if evaluating where to take the first bite. One bite would be enough. Just one quick and nasty mouthful.

His shoulder demanded him to eat.

Kirk dropped to his knees, looked to his wound, then the ceiling, and then the hairless face before him.

Who was this dead prick?

He reached out and shoved the guy away, jamming him against the baseboards. The warden crumpled against the opposite wall and regarded the door.

Was he alone?

Gritting teeth and sweating a fragrant mix of beer and fear, Kirk got to his feet. He wasn't about to chow down on a body in his home. That was a mess he would never be able to clean up. Kirk staggered to his curtains and stopped at the corner. He pulled one back, far more than he intended, and peered into the parking lot.

Crack!

The glass popped inwards in a spider's hole, missing him by an inch and scaring the unholy squirts out of him. He flung himself into the corner.

Crack! Crack!

The curtain tented with each impact, allowing brilliant fingers of light into the room. Kirk held himself upright with one arm, his back pressed flat against the wall, and stared at the bright intrusions.

The gunman wasn't alone.

Moaning, Kirk stumbled through his living room and crushed two toes against the coffee table.

The pain was breathtaking. Supernova-sized. He dropped to his knees.

"*Oh... sweet...*" Kirk croaked and clawed at the carpet as if searching for car keys. He whimpered, sniveled, and choked back a sob. His fingers brushed metal and he looked to see the radon man's gun.

Setting his jaw, Kirk grabbed the weapon in his right hand, thankful that it had been his other shoulder taking that goddamn silver bullet. He stood and made it to the kitchen counter, grabbed at the bowl with his truck keys, and willed his blasted shoulder to life.

A violin screech of pain canceled that idea.

Kirk awkwardly deposited the keys in the pocket of his red plaid pajamas, went to the door and managed to look out the peephole. He threw open the locks, swearing on the chain's refusal to slide and drop on three successive attempts, and finally got the door opened on the fourth try.

Kirk stuck his head out like a prairie dog on speed, ready to bolt for deep earth.

The hallways were empty.

He considered strapping on his boots, but that would have taken far too much time, so he got moving, barefoot, past the silent apartments in the hall. Visions filled his head, of neighbors pressing their heads against their doors or muting the morning news. The imagery distracted him somewhat from his excruciating shoulder. Just a fraction. When a part of one's body has been dipped into molten lava, a person has a hard time convincing the rest of himself it's just that one part.

Speed-walking as if he had an undetonated missile shoved up his ass, Kirk made a straight line for the nearest stairwell, wondering if he was going to pass out in the hallway. He shuffled past the elevator fast enough to start a carpet fire, seeing lit numbers halfway to his floor and rising. That truly got his ass moving.

His right shoulder slammed into the stairwell door and clanged the metal slab off the wall. He then shoved himself inside, holding on to the railing as he descended.

Six levels. That was all he had to go. Six floors down. *Not so bad*, he thought through the blinding light needling his brain. *Not so bad at all. I can do this.*

The realization of leaving his wallet in his apartment clubbed him like a mallet, halting him on the third-floor landing. Somehow, he managed not to swear aloud, vacillated and deemed it too dangerous to go back.

The first-floor EXIT door loomed ahead, and Kirk could've barked a cheer right there. He stopped at the barrier, stuck the gun between his knees, and cracked it open.

Footsteps slapped the stairway above his head.

With a moan, Kirk hurried into the lobby, past a wall of mailboxes, and huffed it towards the glass double doors where the sun did what it could with a gray morning. He made it through the main entrance, swearing on how the doors opened *inwards* and not out, resulting in the loss of seconds.

Cold air slapped Kirk's face and he took in a lungful. He darted to his left, pebbles stabbing at his feet, and zeroed in on his truck. He lurched past a series of cars and pivoted to the left, skirting between parked vehicles, reaching for the door of his Durango.

The high-pitched shriek of a bullet split the air a microsecond before he was blasted from his feet. He landed face-down on the pavement, just beneath the driver's side of his pickup. Time slowed. The morning held its breath. Kirk was dimly aware of two things. A second firestorm in his tortured shoulder and a whip lashing across the thick of his back.

He rolled over and crunched into a sitting position.

A man huffed it around the corner of a nearby SUV. The stranger carried a silenced gun in his right hand. His face full of stern concentration.

Until he spotted Kirk—

—who fired from the ground, blasting a hole in the killer's head and knocking him off his feet. Kirk didn't care if the guy was a man or not. The silver bullet stopped him all the same.

He pulled himself up using the truck for support and opened his door. Thank God he never locked the thing. Kirk secretly hoped the truck would be stolen—the vehicle looked like it had been shat out of the seventies. He tossed the gun on the passenger's seat and climbed aboard.

The rear window exploded, showering him with crystals and spiking his system with adrenaline.

Kirk ducked, got the key into the ignition on the first try, and put the truck into reverse. He stomped on the gas. The truck blasted out of the parking space, doing forty and scraping the swinging driver's door along the length of the parked SUV.

The reversing pickup rear-ended a pair of shooters

arriving late on the scene, sandwiching the men against the hood of a much newer truck, their screams cut horribly short by the crunch of metal against metal. Torsos flopped forward and back.

Kirk sat up, his head much clearer, and slapped the machine into drive. The lurch slammed his door for him. The bodies behind him dropped from sight.

A guy stepped out of the building's main entrance, leather-clad and scowling. His arm rose and aimed a black pistol.

The Durango's passenger-side window blew apart. Kirk hunched up, shying away from the shots. The truck screeched as he made a hard left and then over-corrected, hauling the vehicle back the other way. The bed left-hooked a sedan's fat ass, twisting the car in its painted slot and knocking out an indicator in a spray of red shards. Shots twanged into the truck's tailgate, the metallic stoppage ringing out like a war pick chipping away at an anvil. A bullet bit a chunk out of the passenger seat's headrest, and something zinged across Kirk's eyes, close enough for him to bat lashes.

He stomped on the accelerator.

Tires shrieked as Kirk swerved into traffic like a four-wheeled torpedo, undoubtedly causing multiple heart attacks. Another screeching of rubber, marking asphalt. Drivers collapsed upon their horns. Kirk gained control of the truck's fishtailing, focused on the road ahead and steered into a lane. More cars screeched around him, and one vehicle blasted through a bus stop shelter with spectacular results.

Pedestrians scattered like gray-suited pigeons as it rained glass and debris.

Driving with one hand, Kirk pushed himself back and grimaced with the pain. The zip across his back stung like a foot-long papercut. His left arm was a bloody slab and his toes had set up a campfire below. He gasped and checked his driver's mirror.

No siren.

No signs of pursuit.

Traffic whizzed by. He alternated between lanes, bare feet aching and freezing while he worked the pedals. *Sorry, baby girl*, Kirk projected to his truck.

Had to be fucking November. He grimaced and pulled around a metro bus. He checked his gas, saw it was good, and settled in, concentrating on steering despite the blazing wrecks of his shoulder, back, and toes.

Then it hit him.

Where the hell was he going?

"Holy shit," Kirk whispered, wishing the pain away so he could think. He had no boots, no winter clothing, no coat, and no money. The rear window had been blown out and the cold gnawed through his bloody t-shirt and pajamas. His wallet was back at the apartment with all his plastic and fabricated identities. It was probably no longer there; whoever had gone to his place might very well have grabbed it before running. Or gone back after he shot out of the parking lot.

And who the fuck were *those guys anyway?*

He spotted an off-ramp and drove for the lane, merging

with traffic with ugly insistence and wondering if his taillights had been blasted along with everything else in his life.

The question came back to him—where was he going? He had half a tank of gas, no money, and no phone, but he did have every loose rock in creation sticking out of the bottoms of his all-too tender feet.

And… he was still alive.

Thank you Lord Jesus.

Overcoming the urge to speed through the city streets, Kirk focused on blending in until he realized where he was. As far as he could tell, no one pursued him. Ten minutes later, he stopped the Durango at a semi-full parking lot in the shadow of the McKay Bridge. Small tugboats sailed the river before him. Buildings that might've been apartments rose at his back. Kirk waited, listened, and when his pulse rate returned to just above normal, he plopped his head on his steering wheel. His left arm hung and dripped. He felt sick, perhaps from blood loss, maybe from the receding adrenaline from his system. His consciousness circled him like water swirling around a drain. A fence of unburdened elm trees hid parts of the waterfront, but the sweet tang of brine and bilge wafted through the truck, hitting him with all the force of cheap smelling salts.

Part of him believed the acetylene burn of his gunshot wounds was lessening. They still hurt like a sandpaper fuck, but at least he could think coherently. To a point, anyway.

Silver.

They had fired silver at him. No one used silver bullets

unless they knew what he was. They obviously knew *where* he was. And there was a whole team of them blasting away. *Take your time*, he told himself. Think it through. He remembered the shots peppering his living room window. At least three shooters, perhaps even four or five if the pair he squashed into the parked truck was with the team.

If they weren't…

A bleary-eyed Kirk sighed and glanced around to see if anyone was nearby. The parking lot was devoid of people, so he lowered his head into the crook of his arm.

Despair welled up inside him.

*

In the cabin's living room, a phone rang. The burly man with the grim reaper's beard and dark complexion answered. He sat in a chair, the armrests digging into his sides, and stared at a wall. He grunted twice at the incoming report, seeing possibilities, gauging probabilities.

The call lasted only ten seconds.

"All done?" the woman called Emma asked, or Em as she warned her companions to call her. She leaned against a wall with her arms folded. Beside her, two men zipped up the leather body bag of the very dead husk once called Moses Morris.

The brute—whose name was Enzo Barronni—regarded her with a look bordering on whether or not he should kill her. Or, at least, that was how Em interpreted the expression.

"No," he said.

"No?"

He didn't repeat himself.

"So… what do we do?" she asked, taking care not to be a smartass. Not around Enzo Barronni.

He didn't immediately answer. There weren't many that got away with that around Em. "We wait," he released when he was ready.

Not the words she wanted to hear. Em looked out the front door of the cabin, past the white van parked on the lawn, and settled on the solitary road that stretched off into the woods.

She dared not ask how long.

4

When Kirk opened his eyes, he realized he'd passed out on his steering wheel. The violent shivering had revived him. A freezing wind blasted through his shattered windows and he huddled down. His arm remained unresponsive despite how hard he willed it to obey. The bleeding had at least ceased, which was a plus, but the truck's interior below his arm looked as if he'd slammed the door on someone's throat.

"Fuck me," Kirk breathed and acknowledged the fire in his toes. His shoulder and the trench across his back had noticeably lessened. If he was lucky, he figured he'd be pain-free by night, or sooner if he could get something to eat—which wasn't going to happen considering his finances.

The gun rested in the passenger seat, sticky with blood. He left the weapon there, wanting no part of the thing. He believed it was a Glock, or some variation thereof, but wasn't sure. Pistols weren't his thing. They weren't any *were's* thing, as the elders prohibited their usage.

The men trying to kill him were using silver rounds; thus, they knew he was a *were*.

And they knew where he lived.

His innards clenched at the thought that Morris had quite possibly been right. That the elders wanted to kill him.

Holy shit, he mused darkly and pulled the Glock into his lap, careful not to further aggravate his back. The damn thing might have been flayed to the spine. He studied the weapon, wondering just how to release the magazine from the grip. There were buttons on the side, so he nudged them one way, then the other. He'd watched enough movies to know he was in the right area, anyway. Unless the movies were wrong, somehow. Or he had a different kind of gun.

One flick of the thumb and the magazine spat into his hand.

Kirk withdrew the case and lifted it. The topmost bullet was silver. Raw and uncovered, the metal made his jaw ache.

He replaced the magazine, tossed the gun onto the passenger seat, and cringed as the weapon left his hand. The gun bounced on the cushion with the barrel pointed at him. Kirk exhaled and swore, making a mental note to *not* throw around firearms inside his truck. All he needed was to shoot his own nuts off.

A smile appeared on his bearded chops, but his humor faded fast.

The elders wanted him dead.

Kirk gripped the steering wheel and stared into space. If they wanted him dead, it was only a matter of time before it was so. The realization numbed him. The only authority he'd ever known had apparently signed off on him. There was a chance he was mistaken, but Kirk remembered the conversation he'd had with Morris only days earlier.

The elders want you and me dead. And it's because of what we did on the Rock. Because of what we ate and what we are.

Morris's phantom voice uneased him. After a minute of brooding, Kirk eased back, taking the pain, and started up the truck. He was bootless, moneyless, driving a shot-up pickup that might've been gored by a tractor at one time.

There was only one place to go.

Pictou County.

*

The drive through Halifax was a nervous one. Kirk expected either to be pulled over by the police or shot at by his unknown hunters. Stopping at red lights was the worst, since anyone behind him could get a good look at him and his damaged ride. At one particular traffic stop, a young woman ceased talking on her phone and gawked in horrified wonder. Kirk hunched over the steering wheel and angled his face away, hoping she wouldn't snap off a picture. When the light turned green, it took every ounce of self-control to not stomp on the accelerator. After that, traffic remained smooth as he headed out of the city, but the interest remained like a bad rash. Drivers glanced his way. A couple even flicked their headlights at him.

I know, I know, Kirk projected. *I look like shit.*

The highway was a thankful stream of streaking vehicles, so he put the pedal down without fear, aiming for Morris's place. The wailing of his wounds had dropped two or three degrees more. His broken toes ached, and his shoulder still refused to work, but he could tolerate the pressure against his back a little longer. November, always a bitch, had dropped the temperature to well below zero, so the wind chill lashed him with unwanted attention.

Houses below off-ramps scrolled by and disappeared. The forest thickened. The sun beamed on merrily enough, but without a lick of warmth. Kirk tried not to dwell on the cold. He had much worse things to worry about.

In time, he hit cabin country.

Kirk slowed to make the turn onto Morris's dirt road, an unmarked, forested cave that any other driver would outright ignore.

Gravel crackled underneath the tires, the sound oddly comforting. At least he was here, off the highway and out of sight.

But then Kirk was falling.

The truck bounced through the first pothole, snapping his mouth shut and flinging him towards the ceiling. He slammed against his seat, too numb to do anything but take it. He braked, wondering if he'd been shot at or just fallen through the earth's mantle. The truck rattled on, rising and falling as if he'd turned onto abandoned railway tracks.

The road smoothed out somewhat, giving him hope that the worst was behind him.

Then he hit the second pothole.

The hole was, in reality, a portal to the center of the earth. Or so it felt. Kirk experienced a split second of weightlessness, where the left side of the vehicle tilted, just before the tire's steel rim hit dirt and rebounded high enough to climb out. The impact jangled him merrily, from ass to teeth and everything in between, and still the truck functioned, even after that brutal pitfall.

Trembling, Kirk stopped his machine. He calmed himself, taking a few seconds to pity his truck. The day had been far too hard on the old iron horse. He intended to talk to Morris about his road. Kirk might even make him pay for his next vehicle, a fucking moon buggy if he was going to camp out in the Pictou warden's territory.

Sunlight speckled the road's darkest sections, enticing him to take another run at it. Once ready, Kirk eased the truck forward and the pickup responded, chugging and bouncing like a trooper. He checked his remaining side mirror often, expecting to see important parts littering the dirt behind him. Tree limbs reached out and clawed lines in the vehicle's sides. The road narrowed to almost a footpath, forcing Kirk to slow down. Rocks with spade-like edges protruded through the gravel. He took care avoiding those, steering into foliage and shoving the forest back.

As deplorable as the road was, Kirk decided he wasn't going to mention it to Morris. Relief welled up inside the Halifax warden, glad to have completed the trip without any further incident, and without drawing the attention of the police. He also dearly hoped Morris had some spare clothing that might fit him.

The road widened and the Pictou warden's cabin came into view. Kirk drove onto a lawn of dry leaves and braked, eyeing the home with a relieved smile. Never in his life had he been so happy to see the hillbilly's habitat.

A huge quilt hung in the picture window, nailed to the upper frame to block the wind, but other than that, Morris's cabin looked wonderful. Better than wonderful. *Holy shit*, Kirk thought, he just might volunteer to cook supper for the cantankerous bastard.

Shifting into park, Kirk slumped and relaxed. He looked to the cabin and then the dashboard clock, noting the time. Ten twenty-nine. Not bad, all things considered.

To his unease, Morris didn't appear on the front porch. Kirk waited seconds, the soft running of the engine the only sound at the scene. He stared at the door, willing it to open, but it did not. Bailey's motorbike, still untouched, was parked not far from Kirk's truck. He lingered on the bike before glancing around the rest of the property.

Tire tracks, flattening the frost-stiff lawn, caught his attention.

The pickup continued to idle, waiting for its master to make up his mind.

Kirk hunched over the steering wheel, following the tire trail with his eyes. Morris had yet to appear on his porch, spouting off a few choice sailor curses. Kirk dearly wanted to hear them. Wanted to shout a few of his own right back at his fellow warden.

The tracks went around the cabin's corner, disappearing from sight.

As far as Kirk knew, Morris didn't own a truck.

A droning grew in his ears then, an unchecked ringing similar to microphone feedback. And just underneath that eerie sound, Morris whispered.

I think once he was done with me, he was going after you.

Then the voice was gone, swallowed up in that white noise. Kirk strained to hear, his fingers tickling the ignition keys. The quilt hanging in the window didn't move. Tree tops swayed and shushed for silence. Sunshine highlighted the tracks leading around the house, bleaching all other colors. Some leaves scuttled as nimble as crabs along the grass.

And still no Morris.

But his voice whispered again, somewhere just behind Kirk's ear.

I think once he was done with me…

The last word brought on a stab of dread, one much too strong for the warden to ignore. He fumbled for the gearstick as a single, undeniable thought pierced him.

Morris.

Morris was dead.

And Kirk had driven up like a wailing five-year-old who had cut his knee and gone running home to mother. Out of the corner of his eye, the quilt rippled around the edges. Kirk resisted turning his head, tracking the flutter. A crack appeared along the window frame. A hint of a shadowed face peeked out, keeping to the shade so as not to spook the target.

The face didn't belong to Morris.

Kirk shoved the truck into drive. He hit the gas just as the first gunshot screamed through his driver's window in a violent snowstorm of glass. The silver bullet zinged along the base of his skull, just missing its target. The Durango hopped forward and he jerked the wheel to avoid crashing into a tree. More bullets shrieked around the truck as it whipped around the cabin's corner, several ricochets missing Kirk's bouncing head a second time.

A van. A white van was parked behind Morris's home, its rear end almost filling the backyard. Kirk steered around the parked hog and floored it just as several men burst out of the cabin's back door.

Men with weapons.

Automatic gunfire ripped into the tail of the faithful Durango, punching jittery lines of braille into the gate as Kirk whipped around the cabin's far corner. Bullets sizzled around his bobbing head as he struggled to keep aware of where he was driving. His windshield exploded and raining glass bit into his brow like teeth. The truck circled the next corner, god bless its unleaded heart, and surged ahead in an unexpected, fuel-injected burst of speed, aiming for the open mouth of the dirt road.

A rush of hope gushed through Kirk.

Holy shit.

He was going to escape this deathtrap.

Then the bullet storm struck.

A spray of silver comets ripped into the truck's rear, lasering past his ears. The ceiling board dropped and hung loosely over his skull. Kirk ducked, glimpsing knobs and dials before he ate dash. Bullets pinged and ricocheted through the empty space. The truck bounced as if on a dirt trampoline. Automatic gunfire chewed on the Durango's ass as he pulled away.

Then nothing. The shooting ceased.

Kirk ripped away the ceiling liner and suddenly discovered that the road turned sharply out of sight just ahead. He pushed himself up, turning the steering wheel as the truck careened forward.

He made the turn.

But straightening out was another matter.

The Durango skidded, fishtailed as if just released from a sportsman's hook, and clipped a low-hanging bough. Tree limbs whipped the shattered windshield and clawed for Kirk's face. Wood crackled and snapped. Kirk ducked again, losing further control of the truck but not the accelerator.

That he regrettably stepped on.

When the truck roared over the strips of protruding rocks, it wasn't any surprise to hear both front tires deflate in explosive fashion. Kirk thought he'd been shot by a double-barrel shotgun.

The truck veered hard to the right, plowed through a wall of brush, and smashed its grimacing grill into a birch tree trunk. Meat, metal, and glass flew forward. Kirk shook like a rat in a shoebox, his face scrubbing against the dashboard and leaving pieces.

The world went dark.

Then light.

Then crazy.

Gauzy steam drifted from the truck's wrecked front, and it took Kirk a few seconds to realize what he was looking at—the buckled, naked ceiling of the Durango's cab. A row of pebbly teeth was all that remained of the windshield.

Blood ran into his eyes and he felt as if he'd just head-butted a tank. He attempted to lift himself up and immediately stopped when new and exciting pain sparkling along his back and ribs told him to stay right where he was. He tried to clear his eyes and discovered in dreamy horror that a section of his scalp had blinded him. He pinched the sliver of skin, lifted it away and slicked it back. He proceeded to wipe his eyes clean. Once vision had been restored to a degree, Kirk inspected himself over a drunken pout, seeing his t-shirt bloodied anew and his pajama bottoms also heavily doused. The steering wheel was above his left hip. He pushed against the column and wormed his way free, squeezing himself into the passenger side. Somewhere in those seconds, his scalp flap half-blinded him again. Kirk slicked it back once more, blinking away the dribbles of red that found his eyes. His feet touched his headrest, the cushion reduced to a ragged metal plate. Sponge foam littered the interior like white guts splashed with scarlet.

Pressed against the passenger door, Kirk peeked over the backseat and looked back the way he'd come.

The Durango's headlong charge had mowed down some of the younger, smaller trees and snapped the branches off the bigger ones, creating a wide swath of destruction all the way back to the road some twenty feet away. Kirk's eyes widened at the sheer destruction his old dog had done.

His dismay fizzled.

The path left by the smoking truck would be found any minute.

Oh Jesus. Kirk squirmed and inspected his predicament.

Thick woodland surrounded him. The pickup's engine had permanently mated with a tree. He'd just peeled himself off a dashboard. Cuts and bruises covered his shivering arms and added sick sensations to his other hurts. His shoulder and toes remained fucked-up and his head probably resembled a ruptured punching bag.

Kirk took a breath, a deep one, and forced the change.

His jaw locked up before freeing with an audible click. His fingers clamped onto plastic edges. His blood quickened, heated, and threatened to ignite his arterial network. His skin tightened and popped sweat while his temples rang like church bells. Clothing stretched and split along seams and Kirk pushed, pushed as if forcing a medicine ball through a pee hole, knowing he had little time to transform. Internal pressure increased. Organs were unpleasantly shoved around and squished into strange places. His eyes bulged. Fleshy matter split apart and spurted onto seat fabric. Blood plopped in creamy congealed clumps. Nausea consumed him, hot and colon-twisting, and he gulped down air as the pleasure-pain sensations from growing and contracting increased in tempo.

Kirk didn't worry about any of that.

He was past worrying.

The mass of a huge wolf, three hundred pounds plus and some seven feet long from tip to tip, squeezed its hairy mass through the destroyed windshield. The beast pulled itself free of the semi-crushed cab and slipped onto the wrecked hood. Kirk growled, muzzle splitting into a snarl, and stopped upon hearing an engine somewhere beyond the truck.

He leaped from the hood and landed on four paws. His injured shoulder shook ominously at the impact, but held. The bone had mended well enough to use, much to his relief.

Kirk heard a metallic click, somewhere behind him.

But instead of attacking, he scampered off into the woods.

*

Six gunmen jumped out of the white van and advanced upon the wrecked pickup. Camouflaged winter gear covered their frames while black balaclavas concealed their faces. They crept forward in a wide line, filling the path cleared by the Durango. Red dots roamed over the smoking metal carcass.

A dark shape vaulted through the underbrush, fleeing the scene of destruction. Three gunmen turned and fired. The barrage lit up the forest, shattering the silence. Light chased the escaping werewolf and shredded vegetation. The shooters advanced, standing tall and firing from the shoulders, tracking their target. Splinters burst from tree trunks and leaves drizzled the air.

Magazines were emptied.

Two gunmen lifted their laser-sighted MP5s but didn't fire, resigned to watch the beast disappear into the surrounding woods. A third man straightened, sighed, and lowered his weapon. He pinched his headset's microphone.

"He's changed and gone. Just saw him run off."

There was a pause.

"Get back here," Barronni ordered on the other end.

The gunman didn't like the sound of that.

*

Back at the cabin, Enzo Barronni stood next to the quilt-covered picture window. He placed a forearm against the wall and rested his head against it. The big man's shoulders heaved but he said nothing. A wary Em watched him the whole time. Seconds passed, long and uncomfortable. She could barely contain her curiosity, but she didn't want to break the quiet. Not around him.

Finally, he regarded her with black eyes that might have been cut from a shark's head. Irritation furrowed his hairy brow.

His phone buzzed and he answered it. "Yeah."

He listened, eyes downcast. "No. We missed."

They missed, Em corrected in silence. If she'd had her big gun with her at the time, she sure as hell would *not* have missed. She would've shot the fucker's pecker off and made him howl before drilling him five times more.

"You know where the cabin is?" Enzo asked into the phone, his sleepy eyes narrowing. "Then get here when you can."

He hung up and studied Em stoically. "Two's fucked-up pretty bad. Barely got away before the cops arrived on site. It'll be a chore to get out of the city so we're on our own for a while."

"Two fucked-up and got fucked-up," Em said, hoping her snark wasn't too offensive.

Annoyance flashed in Enzo's eyes, like a dying fire getting a fresh shot of air.

Em decided to keep her mouth shut.

Barronni studied his phone and jabbed a thumb into its face, speed-dialing a number. His shoulders slumped when he put the device to his ear.

"We missed Douglas Kirk," he said. He directed his attention to the floor.

The phone whispered.

"All right." Barronni broke the connection and considered Em with that same black-eyed, no-nonsense expression of neutrality that always managed to unnerve her. She forced herself not to look away, even though her forehead begged to be scratched, even though her eyes were drying out.

"There's a lake nearby," Barronni stated. "Claymore, I think. Cabin country. When the others get back here, you take them and head over there in the van. Go in quiet but be ready."

"What about the civilians?"

"Be discreet, if necessary."

"Management pissed off?"

Barronni blinked as if just waking. "Yeah. They're pissed off."

"Two outta three ain't bad," Em offered, inwardly swearing at her dickhead brain for uttering such a line.

"I'll wait here," Barronni stated. "What's left of Two is on its way here. When they arrive, we'll follow along the highway. Just in case he tries to change back and hitchhike."

"With his junk hanging in the wind?"

Barronni glared with all the intensity of a poorly fed boar.

Em took the hint and got moving, glad to be excused. Barronni creeped her out without breaking a sweat. She went out the front door and waited for the remainder of her own team to return in the van. The van had all the heavy fun stuff.

Douglas Kirk, she thought and looked to the bright sky.

He was the one who got away.

But Em hadn't flicked her hook into the water just yet.

5

After an hour of bounding through wiry, frozen timberland, Kirk reached the weekend retreat known as Claymore Lake. He halted at the cold water's edge and lapped up his fill with his front paws dipping. His shoulder, thank God, had stayed together long enough to get him out of danger, and his fur had kept him warm. Now he needed to find a place to think and rest, even better if he could locate some food and clothing. He lifted his head and took stock of his surroundings while waves lapped against a rocky shore. Houses ringed the body of water, some built on rises, others built deeper amongst the trees. The properties varied in size and style, but they all looked like second homes to Kirk, the nearest to his right some thirty meters.

He could almost smell the money.

There was no scent of dogs on the cold air, or any other animal that might cause a scene, so Kirk crept through the undergrowth, pushing through tangles of brush and keeping the lake on his left. A short crawl later, he pushed his muzzle through a wall of bushes and beheld a two-story cabin. A sizeable satellite dish sprouted from one corner of the lawn, resembling a white mushroom shorn in half, while just past that, a work shed with a pair of wheelbarrows lay out front. Brown vinyl siding, a white trim, and the faintest whiff of an uncleaned barbecue grill sifted past his nose. A huge pair of patio doors faced the water, presiding over a grand deck and fashionable furniture.

The place looked and smelled empty. Kirk liked.

He circled the dwelling, staying hidden in the forest curtain until he spotted the front door. His shoulder, while functional, ached dearly, with every step threatening even more suffering if he didn't stop soon. A nervous Kirk followed the pathway leading to the entrance, crouching low to the pavement to avoid detection.

After making sure he wasn't being watched, Kirk reverted back to his human suit. He let the change flow unhurried, knowing his body needed time to readjust his organs. The process drained him of his remaining strength, and when it finished he slumped and lay gasping, as if he'd just collapsed after a marathon. His hurts had lessened considerably, even his shoulder, and when he stood, he discovered his broken toes had mended.

The front door was locked. Kirk took two steps back and studied the wood cabin. A small window to the right, just past the deck's railing, caught his attention.

"I'm real sorry about this," he said.

A long shovel rested in the deck's corner, the handle made of hardwood. Kirk took it and smashed out the window. He cleared the frame of the glass, raking the handle around the edges, and when it was cleared he gathered up the doormat and lined it around his makeshift opening.

A minute later he was inside.

The interior was only a few degrees warmer, but it blocked the biting wind. Kirk pulled the mat inside and slapped it across a washing machine. He left the laundry room smelling of fabric softener and stepped into the main living area, closing the door to prevent any further invasion of winter air. A huge, open living space stretched out, surprising him with the ample space. The cabin hadn't appeared so big on the outside.

Bare-assed and brazen, Kirk shuffled past a luxuriant living room complete with a stone fireplace, the hearth scorched and black. A big-screen TV, plush leather sofa set, wide rugs, and a coffee table that might've been cut from some monstrous redwood were laid out in precise lines, crisp edges. A rustic saloon bar took up a back corner, but a drink wasn't on his mind.

Kirk stopped on a rug, his feet very much appreciating the gesture, and eyed the kitchen. He found orange and tomato juice, half a dozen eggs, bread, some apples, and an assortment of jams in the fridge, and half a block of mild cheese on a shelf. Not bad, but Kirk was disappointed. The freezer contained three packs of processed wieners and some flattened hamburger patties whose texture resembled brains.

Kirk frowned at the beef, but he'd eaten worse. And it was all food. At least he hadn't broken into a weekend getaway owned by vegans.

He fired up the stove and cooked up a hearty breakfast.

Eggs, wieners, and brain patties, washed down with a carton of tomato juice, orange juice. Several slices of toast also went down, painted with jam and butter.

Finally able to relax, Kirk studied the cabin's interior. It truly was a hidden castle, cold at first, but warming up to him. A set of bare, wooden stairs just next to the laundry room led to a second level with an overhang and railing, providing open views down into the living room and through an overhead bank of windows pointed towards the lake. Natural light flooded the space, and he took a few seconds to count the windows.

He counted fifteen when, mid-chew through a strawberry jam sandwich, he stopped and considered his naked ass.

Later, in a master bedroom, complete with an en suite and foot-warming rug, Kirk found one side of a walk-in closet sparsely filled with men's clothing. His luck surprised him considering the morning he was having. He grabbed a pair of jeans and held them to his waist.

Holy shit.

Apparently a fat-assed ogre owned the place. Whoever the guy was, he had an impressive waistline of at least sixty inches. Kirk placed the jeans against his own lean midsection and cringed at the size difference. He continued rummaging through some drawers, cocking an eyebrow at sets of skimpy fishnet stocking underwear for guys and even skimpier, multi-colored man-thongs. An ordinary pair of blue pajama bottoms with a drawstring seemed out of place in the collection. The bottoms billowed about his legs and ankles once he pulled them on, but it didn't impede his movement. He pulled the jeans on over them, and feeling creative, used the string from the bedroom window's venetian blinds. *Beggars can't be choosers and all that*, he figured, looping and tying off the drawstring. Summer socks went up to his ankles and no higher, but the real fright came when he pulled three t-shirts off their hangers.

Each one displayed jaw-dropping offensive slogans.

The first one read *Goddamn My Shit Stinks!*

The second one read *I'm Shy, but I got a HUGE dick!*

The third was, when compared to the first two, rather polite. It read *It Swings to My Knees*.

The clothing did nothing for Kirk's morale. In fact, his desperation spiked when he discovered there wasn't another stitch in the closet.

Holy shit, he blurted in horrified wonder and rooted through the remaining drawers. There was nothing else. If he didn't wear the clothes, he'd freeze. And if he wore the t-shirts, chances were he'd freeze anyway, but slower.

"Fucking unreal," Kirk grumped and pulled on the t-shirts, putting the least offensive *It Swings to My Knees* on last. He covered that one up with a thin, sky-blue bathrobe, reducing the lettering to simply *I win*.

Which was fine with Kirk.

Jeeeesus, he groaned as he studied himself. He was looking for warmth and got the freak show. Just his luck he broke into a place with only summer clothing on hand. Dressed as he was, he wouldn't have to worry about any killers finding him. The boys with the extra-large butterfly nets would surely scoop him off the streets before then.

Shaking his head, he moved out of the bedroom, avoiding all mirrors.

On his way downstairs, Kirk hesitated. He picked up a nearby notepad and pen and, in uppercase letters, wrote:

I'M SORRY FOR BREAKING IN BUT IT WAS NECESSARY. THANK YOU FOR THE FOOD, DRINK, AND CLOTHING. I DIDN'T TAKE ANYTHING ELSE.

Dropping the pen on the kitchen table, Kirk read his words and sighed. The note was placed beside the pen, in clear sight.

How long could he stay, he wondered, before the owners returned? It was Monday, and the Claymore Lake community appeared vacant for the time being.

Then he thought about the death squad still on his tail.

And Morris.

Well... damn.

Moses Morris. Kirk wasn't a hundred percent sure if the man was dead or not, but now that he had time to think about it, wherever Morris was, he wasn't there willingly. The warden would not take kindly to having his den occupied by a group of *were*-hunting gunmen. Perhaps he was on the run as well? Kirk rubbed his beard then, wondering who to contact. The elders came to mind. He wouldn't mind calling them up and hearing what that whispery voice had to say. Matter of fact, that didn't seem like a bad idea at all. Go straight for the jugular. Perhaps it was a mistake. Perhaps those gunmen didn't want him. Maybe he'd just driven up the road at the worst possible time and the shooting started...

Kirk wandered to the sofa and shook his head. No, none of that made sense. Not after the morning he had. He glanced around the cabin and searched for a phone or a computer. No luck.

There had been two squads of gunmen, one for him and one for Morris. The bunch hunting him had screwed up, narrowly, but did the team at Morris's cabin get their target? Kirk remembered the guy who'd knocked on his door, remembered how professional he'd been, right up until he pulled the gun. The bastard had waited until the door was closed, to ensure maximum privacy. Cool and well-planned.

That hooked in the fabric of Kirk's mind. They were well-planned. Thoughtful, even.

And they were still out there.

The chill returned, despite Kirk's interesting layers of clothing. Smart operators would deduce that he had changed back into his human form by now. And that he'd be bucknaked when he did.

Smart operators would then anticipate him looking for clothes.

And if they weren't too concerned with knocking down Morris's door, chances were they would head in the same direction as Kirk did, aiming to check on the nearest communities.

Claymore Lake.

The sound of a distant engine froze Kirk. In a blink he was at the rear door, peeking through a peephole.

He waited.

And waited.

The engine faded and the driveway remained empty, but Kirk didn't relax. He couldn't relax. Though he needed to rest and allow his body to regenerate in relative peace, he couldn't chance it here. Kirk backed away from the door, deciding it best not to linger. Not in Claymore Lake. Perhaps not even in Nova Scotia. Not anymore.

Having made his choice, he threw the remaining brain patties into the frying pan and while they were cooking, he tore through the house. The owner had stuffed an old hockey bag into a laundry room cupboard. Into this, Kirk loaded whatever remaining food the cabin possessed. He filled a plastic jug with water and tossed in a bottle of Captain Morgan's rum along with a bottle of Jack Daniels, taking care to distribute them on either side of the bag. He located a ski mask, which may or may not be a blessing, as well as mittens, and a pair of leather boots that were a little too tight about the toes. Swearing, he pulled off his three layers of ankle socks and hauled the boots on anyway.

The thought of searching for valuables hit him, but Kirk dismissed it. He wasn't going to take any more than needed. The bottles of rum and whiskey weren't necessary, but he figured, where he was headed, he'd need that little extra internal burn. Probably be grateful for the bottles when he got around to taking the first sip.

A few final supplies went into the hockey bag and when he thought himself ready, Kirk clomped across hardwood floors towards the deck exit, intending on making his escape. He hesitated at the patio doors, looked around as if wondering if he'd missed anything, and decided he had not.

With the exception of the window he busted, a few dirty pots, and some missing clothes, the place wasn't in too bad a shape.

He, on the other hand, figured he might attract the attention of any surveillance satellites wandering overhead.

"Sorry for the window," he whispered to the cabin. "I'm going now. Thank you."

Even though the note was on the table, saying the words gave him a little peace.

Kirk wasn't surprised when the downstairs closets had no jackets. So he slung the hockey bag across his bathrobed back, hearing a protesting tinkle and slosh from the bottles therein, and fitted the ski mask over his face. He grabbed a pair of ski poles and peered out the door.

Wind blew on the lake, ruffling its pale surface. Not another soul in sight, on this side of the water or the other.

Kirk waddled outside and sealed the cabin behind him.

The wind remembered him from earlier and whipped at his face, seeking skin. It quickly slipped through the layers, but he forced himself to forget the cold. *Civilization or off-grid*, Kirk thought, surveying the lake. Cabins as majestic and inviting as the one he'd just violated dotted the shoreline, their windows like staring eyes.

The treeline beckoned.

Kirk marched for the woods as the sound of lapping waves filled his ears.

Rum and whiskey sloshed on his back.

6

Branches raked Kirk's sky-blue robe, which failed to protect him from the weather, but, thankfully, the vice-like squeeze the boots had on his toes distracted him from the cold. He tried not to think of either as he hiked through the bush, hoping he didn't leave too big a trail to follow. The idea was to emerge on a highway somewhere far away from Claymore Lake. He chugged over the uneven landscape, his supercharged healing factor suppressing the dreadful arthritic ache of the silver's after-effects in his shoulder.

It was tiring. Punishing.

Walking in the Nova Scotia wild got him sweating and calmed his rattled nerves, but also gave him plenty of time to dwell on the plans of the elders. He shoved the thoughts away, deciding it best to concentrate on moving forward, losing himself in the forest. Every now and then, however, the elders came back, whispering why they wanted him dead.

Kirk figured he knew. His *were* healing ability was a boon, but the reoccurring urges to eat other *weres*? Not so much. He'd become a monster amongst monsters.

Reason enough to put him down right there.

The landscape rose and fell. The thickets surrounding the cabin had opened into unevenly spaced firs with ample room to pass between them. A thick roof of boughs cast the land in shadow. Kirk double-timed it, wanting to place as much distance between Claymore Lake and Morris's cabin as possible.

It wasn't long before he heard the windy hissing of speeding traffic.

The highway glared under an afternoon sun. Vehicles sped along in multicolor flashes. Kirk stopped just at the forest's edge and soaked in that last bit of shadow, fearing the great open strip before him. The treeline had been cleared some twenty meters back from the pavement, creating a no-man's land of yellow grass straddling the highway.

There was nowhere to hide if the need arose. Not even a dip or a rock.

Kirk weighed his options. Speed was key. He'd have to assume his hunters were determined and that they were already tracking him. Their silver-loaded weapons very much disturbed him. What were the chances they'd be on the highway? Then there was the question of his appearance. The only thing missing was a shopping cart.

Decision made, Kirk stepped into the light and marched through ankle-high grass to the road. When he reached the pavement, he stayed on the shoulder and turned west. Head down and shoulders slumped, he trudged forward, knowing full well how he looked. With the oversized bathrobe, slung hockey bag, and baggy jeans, most motorists would probably speed by. With his mask down, no one would recognize him, but odds on getting a ride also diminished. He decided he'd take his chances. He stuck his thumb out, turned and walked backwards, and started counting cars.

Thirteen whizzed by. Some drivers ignored him completely, others considered him a roadside oddity.

"Yeah, yeah," Kirk muttered, even though he was sweating underneath all his layers. His shoulder worked but still bothered him, and so did his tightly packed toes.

The sun blazed at his back. Every now and again he glanced over his shoulder, just to check on where he was going. The wind increased and whipped past his frame, hollering as if he were deaf. Kirk kept his attention on the cars, looking for guns and faces lighting up with recognition. He glanced down at his robe and noticed that the neckline had opened even more, changing the *I win* to a cringe-worthy *I Swing*.

That got covered up right quick.

Memories flowed, and he recalled another time, a younger time. Walking along the roads in the early morning, following a set of swaying hips made ghostly by a lingering fog. She dressed in denim even then, telling him that she didn't wear girly clothes much. Little details like that came with a carefree smile and sometimes, if he was lucky, the smile would be directed at him.

The image brightened his spirits but only for a few seconds. Kirk knew where the memory would take him. The trick, when thinking of Carma, was to know when to shut the valve off.

More cars whizzed by while his cramped feet grumbled louder. He considered kicking off the boots and continue walking in socks. That would really give drivers something to talk about. It might even work in his favor, but he doubted it.

Fifty-eight cars.

Fifty-nine was a white knight of a pickup. The driver, topped off with a ball cap and sunglasses, was all teeth as he yakked away on a cellphone. His grinning face flickered from his side mirror to the road and back again, like a bobble head needing to be stilled.

Kirk's outstretched arm faltered. Unease flared. He didn't care for motorists who talked and drove at the same time.

The driver noticed Kirk, just the slightest turn of his head, but the warden saw it all the same.

Sunglasses and teeth made it clear what he thought of hitchhikers.

Maybe he did it for shits and giggles, or maybe he harbored a deep-rooted dislike for highway walkers. Whatever the reason, the pickup driver gunned the engine and aimed for Kirk, crossing the white line and charging into cyclist territory.

Kirk jerked himself back as the pickup zipped by, the air blasting him. The truck veered back onto the highway with a victorious toot-toot of a horn.

Standing on frozen grass, Kirk steadied himself with the

ski poles and glared after the vehicle speeding away, hoping maybe the driver's head might explode. He doubted the asshole even stopped talking on his cellphone. Maybe, if Kirk was lucky, he'd meet up with the bastard at a roadside service station farther up the line. If he did, he vowed to set that phone to vibrate and shove it up the driver's ass.

A horn caused him to jump again.

A large white truck—one for delivering furniture—slowed onto the shoulder. Tires crackled on pebbles. Two men crammed into the cab stared at Kirk. They pulled up beside him and the passenger window descended.

"You all right?" a young man asked, perhaps in his early twenties and cultivating a shadow of a mustache.

Kirk nodded.

"Saw what that dickhead did," the guy said. "Some people's children. You see some pretty dangerous shit on this strip and not enough cops."

"It's been that kinda morning," Kirk said, his weariness coming through more than he liked.

The young guy looked to the driver and then back. His eyes ran over Kirk's outfit.

"It's been a rough morning," Kirk said, cutting off the questions. "I'd rather not talk about it."

The guy nodded, understanding the sentiment. "Where you going?"

Good question, Kirk thought. Where was he going? "Truro."

"We're headed that way. Need a lift?"

"Sure. Thank you."

"You sure you're okay?"

Kirk lifted his ski mask, revealing a faint smile. "I'm good. Like I said, just a rough morning is all."

"We don't have any room up front, but if you don't mind riding in the back, we'll take you to Truro. We're passing through there."

"That'd be great, thanks."

The guy got out of the truck. He was dressed from neck to ankle in a gray-green coverall, with a red badge over a chest pocket that read *Milton's Home Furnishings*. Kirk followed the Milton man to the rear doors while traffic continued to shoot by, with some cars channeling war drums through their stereo systems.

"There's no heat back here but you'll be comfortable," the Milton man said as he undid the doors. He pulled them apart to reveal a complete living room, all coated in plastic, filling the back of the truck.

"Wow," Kirk whispered, very much impressed. "This is better than home."

The Milton man smiled. "That's a six-thousand-dollar furniture set. Brown European leather. Sectional and recliner. Got end tables back there as well but stay away from those if you don't mind."

"I don't think I'm worthy."

"Not about being worthy," the Milton man smiled. "Just be careful on the plastic is all I ask. Try not to tear anything. And watch your boots."

"I will."

The furniture man gestured and Kirk climbed into the

back. He dropped his ski poles and hockey bag on the floor and gently sat down on the sofa's edge.

"All good?" the Milton man asked.

"Oh hell yeah."

"Where do you want to get out, exactly?"

"How far you going?"

"Ah, we're delivering this to Brookfield, so we'll be driving on by Truro."

Brookfield. That was on the 102 and heading south, back into Halifax. Truro didn't exactly seem far away enough.

"Let me off anywhere on the other side of Truro if you can," Kirk said.

"The other side of Truro?"

"Yeah. Just before you make that south turn. If you can."

"Oh, we can do that. Not a problem."

"Thanks."

The Milton man smiled in understanding and closed the door. A single glass portal was set into the wall just behind the cab, which supplied the only light in the square cave. It also allowed the guys to check on the furniture. Kirk ran a gloved hand over the plastic, marveling at the leather softness underneath. He sat back and tried to relax.

The truck pulled back into traffic.

An hour later, the bulky truck decelerated, waking Kirk from a semi-doze. It was cold and he shivered at the lack of heat. One of the Milton men rapped on the glass window and twirled a finger. Kirk raised a hand in thanks. Time to walk.

When the truck stopped, he stood and studied the living room set, knowing he'd probably never experience such luxury ever again. The rear door opened, flooding the interior with light, and the Milton man withdrew as if releasing a trapped animal.

"Thanks for this," Kirk said and hopped down.

"Not too uncomfortable for you?" the guy asked.

"That was better than my apartment."

The Milton employee chuckled. "Where you going?"

"Ah, Calgary," Kirk said.

"On foot the whole way?"

"Hadn't fully figured that out yet," the warden admitted. "But yeah, I think so."

"Be careful, then. I've been at this job for only a year, but I know the highways can be weird and wonderful. Keep your eyes open, okay?"

"I will. Thanks again."

Another warm, sympathetic smile, and the Milton man walked away in a drift of exhaust. Kirk watched him go. A door opened and slammed, and the truck indicated its intention to join traffic. The movers rumbled back into that multicolored river and immediately headed for an exit indicating the 102. The truck curled downwards and away, and soon disappeared underneath an overpass.

Kirk saw the Halifax County sign. To his left, the outer fringes of Truro sat brightly. He'd driven through there a couple of times, but never stopped. He wouldn't be stopping this day, either.

Calgary. He'd just said that to make the furniture guy feel better, but the word resonated. *West.* Kirk hefted the hockey bag over his good shoulder, grimaced at the weight, and adjusted the strap until it was bearable. He gripped the ski poles and got marching.

Head west. Stay off-grid, take the back roads, and make tracks away from the east coast. They'd be on his trail, but at least he had something of a head start. And it was a big country. Very easy to lose oneself in, as long as one was careful. Even dressed as he was.

Kirk nodded affably in Truro's direction.

He hoped he could return there someday. Maybe stay overnight. When things were calmer.

On that note, a white van approached, speeding towards him with a heat seeker's intensity. Kirk froze, immobilized by the charging vehicle. Two men occupied the cab, both wearing sunglasses, and both focusing on the hitchhiker standing on the side of the road.

Warning klaxons went off in Kirk's skull.

But the van blasted by him, not altering its course in the least. A decal plastered on the backdoors told him to DRINK DECAN RED! The van dipped down a slope and five more cars followed it west.

Kirk bent over to hold his knees.

In time, he checked the rest of the oncoming traffic, all the while attempting to steady his nerves. The van got to him. Scared him. He needed to move and get out of sight.

With that, he turned his back on the town and marched. Every ten paces or so, Kirk glanced nervously over his shoulder.

A crow-shaped strip from a blown-out tire marred the gravel shoulder, and he nudged it with his ill-fitting boot. A crosswind slashed at his face until he pulled his ski mask back over his head, knowing he lessened his chances at getting a ride. Sweat started to flow again, soaking into damp undershirts. He didn't care. And he didn't bother with hitchhiking.

The temperature hung around zero while he trudged along, shivering every now and then. He stayed a step away from a ditch, which gave him some degree of security. If someone charged him in a car, he'd dive into the thing and let the car roll by.

Another bout of shivering, more frequent as the day progressed. Kirk wished for a parka. And a shower.

The sun rounded the sky overhead, studying him with bright-eyed indifference. Open fields spread out on either side of the highway, some plowed, some covered with wild grass, all collared by thick walls of trees. Plastic bottles and a few beer cans littered the ditches, placing a frown on his face.

The flat expanse stretched out before the warden, with only bags of garbage and the occasional road sign marking progress. Vehicles streamed by and Kirk gave them a wide berth, wary of their intentions. He rested once, under the awning of a few scruffy trees, a good distance back from the highway. There he dug out his water jug and downed half the contents before drawing a hand across his face.

Traffic buzzed. Windshields reflected a descending sun. Night was only a short hour away.

When he resumed his trek, he didn't return to the road

but marched along the edge of some farmland. The grooved patches eventually grew into thick woods. A dirt road materialized along the way and ran parallel to the main drag, some forty feet from the asphalt. Cars and trucks continued to pass by and he sensed each driver watching him, wondering where he was heading. That made him move a little faster. Some of those drivers had cell phones. There was a small chance someone might find him interesting enough to take a picture or even record.

That uneasy feeling gripped him once more. He hoofed it down and up the sides of a shallow ditch, staggered for balance when he rose, and hiked the short distance to the forest. He felt better upon entering the treeline. Kirk paused, hidden amongst the foliage, and stared back at the highway. None of the traffic whipping by slowed down, searching for where he left the road, and that made him feel even better. He retreated a little further into the evergreen screen and, eventually sat, the ground chilling his butt. The hockey bag came forth and he fished out a plastic baggie. He ate two fried brain patties from a stash of eight. These he placed between a couple slices of bread and, with a little ketchup from a squeeze bottle, an early supper was ready. The food was cold, but it went down, and he was thankful to have it.

West, he thought, the word ringing in his ears. West was turning out to be too damn far away.

When he finished eating, Kirk rose, trembling, and draped the hockey bag over a shoulder. He gripped his ski poles and checked on the sun. There wasn't much time left to the day. He considered taking the dirt road for speed but decided against it, preferring the concealment of the woods.

Head down and bowed over, he got moving.

Off-road, the uneven earth quickly punished his feet and lean frame. The hockey bag, though hanging off his good shoulder, still tormented the one poisoned by silver. The forest he hiked through was much denser than the previous one, with tangles that whipped his knees and thighs. Every now and again he staggered, caught by an unseen rut. He aimed curses at his luck in clothing and the mounting pain in his feet. City life might have softened him somewhat, but the lack of layers and cramping footwear were killing him. The boots tormented him more, and he considered changing into a wolf. That wouldn't do, however. He disliked the idea of changing over. Besides, changing into a wolf would allow him to cope with the woods but he'd have to leave everything behind, and the idea of transforming back a second time without any nearby clothes didn't appeal to him. Not in early winter weather. He didn't want to break into another cabin and raid another summer wardrobe.

So he pushed on, the sounds of the highway receding with every step. He used to love hiking in the woods, used to love camping overnight. Used to. One time.

Until this whole *were* bullshit trumped everything else.

Kirk halted that train of thought, before it carried him to places best left in the past. He wondered about Moses Morris, and if he'd somehow escaped. He hoped the biker warden had.

By evening, with the sun departing an indigo sky, he scrambled down a gulley shadowed by tall fir, towards a stream with waters like black glass. He splashed through, hissing at the icy stabs leaking through his boots.

Well fuck, Kirk swore at the water's contact. *Not waterproofed either.* He trudged onto dry land and shook out his legs as if he'd just pissed himself. How the hell could a person afford a second home on a lake and *not* own a pair of half-decent waterproof boots? It amazed him. Feet freezing and sloshing, Kirk's misery deepened another notch.

"Fuck," he repeated aloud and forged ahead, into the deepening gloom.

His boots farted wetly with every step, his feet morphing into irregular blocks of ice.

The land sympathized with him, and to make things somewhat better, the tangled brush thinned out into wide halls of fir and the occasional patch of birch. Kirk crossed paths with an old dirt road, running north-south. He thought it was a trail for snow machines at first, but soon realized his mistake. Pushed off to the side and abandoned amongst the bushes lay a rusting hulk of a truck, the evening shadows tethering its metallic hide to undergrowth. The paint had long since been scrubbed free of the ancient, two-door heap. None of the windows were intact, perhaps smashed out by baseball bats or rocks. Kirk never did understand why people did that.

He stopped at the unwanted wreck. The box was a rust pit wired with fallen branches, while the interior appeared relatively intact. Half the cushions had been shredded, yellow sponge hanging over the seat, but the passenger side appeared fine. Kirk tried one door, then the other, both refusing to budge. He cleared the box of dead brush and heaved in the hockey bag and ski poles. The door handle rattled when he gripped it and planted his aching feet.

Kirk wanted that door open. The cab would serve as shelter until morning.

He yanked, with everything he had.

And ripped the metal handle free.

The momentum flung him backwards, where he landed on his ass in a surprised huff. He sat there for a moment, staring, and snorted.

Should've been smarter than that.

With a groan he regarded the ruined door. Kirk crawled up on the hood and slunk through the missing windshield. He settled in, cringing at the distressing rip of seams in the seat, and checked himself. The hockey bag was just an arm's reach away through the rear window, but Kirk decided to let it be. He propped himself up against a door and, with the exception of his feet, felt comfortable.

Except for the escalating shivering.

Straining, grunting, Kirk pulled off the cramping boots and dropped them on the truck's floor. The smell of wet leather wafted richly as he kneaded his tortured feet. The ripped driver's seat caught his attention, and after a quick prodding, he leaned back and inserted both feet into the ripped cushion, sighing at the spongy warmth.

Not bad, and certainly a relief to get the boots off.

Just like a big old oven mitt, Kirk thought. Things were improving. If only the seat heaters worked.

With nothing better to do, he decided to eat. He needed the calories for repairs.

Another pair of hamburger patties went down with the last of the sliced bread. A few sips of water from the plastic jug completed his supper and got him thinking about a medicinal shot of forty proof.

A bottle of Captain Morgan soon followed.

The first tentative taste screwed up his face, as did the second one. The third shot wasn't a kitchen party either, nor the fourth, but Kirk soon appreciated the glow lighting up the launch pad of his stomach. In short time, the cold didn't bother him so much. He studied the captain's face, smiled back in the growing dark, and settled in for the night. The wind rose, and branches rustled overhead.

Within that rusty shell, Kirk sat nursing his bottle with his ski mask rolled above his upper lip. The rum's magic spread through his limbs, and he welcomed the respite. Thoughts of why he'd been marked for death caused him to scowl in resignation. He was doomed. Royally fucked. He didn't know the resources of the elders, but they had mustered two groups of killers to off him and Moses.

Moses. You poor bastard. I hope you got out in time.

The night deepened and Kirk's visibility retreated. He sat and stewed, partaking of the captain's comfort. He was increasingly glad he'd brought the old sailor along. Borland probably drank plenty of rum in his day, and that got Kirk thinking about the old dog.

How did the Newfoundlander manage to… do… what he did? How had he managed to retain his human form, but access nearly all the powers of his *were*-blood? Ever since Kirk and Morris took the bastard down, the question of how he'd managed to do it stumped Kirk. He suspected he was missing something. Some key he hadn't yet considered. Then there was Bailey. Bailey, whose head had been blasted off with a shotgun. His head had grown back, and he had come out of it even stronger than before. Was there a connection between Bailey and Borland? Kirk suspected there was, but damn if he could figure it out.

Part of him wondered if he could become such a... wolf-thing.

The rum sloshed and Kirk steadied the bottle in his mittens. He then reached through the window, pulled the hockey bag close, and searched it by feel alone. After locating the ankle socks, he struggled with getting all three pairs on, and then returned his feet to the cushion cavern.

The surrounding woods occasionally creaked, shifted, and even snapped. Kirk sniffed, finding nothing amiss, and gave the bottle a fond pat. He wished he had something to read, wished that the something came with a built-in night light. His eyelids grew heavy. The medicinal sips of rum stopped. His final few acts before calling it a very bad day was tucking the bottle between his thigh and the seat, and rolling the ski mask down over his face. Arms were folded and hands stuffed into armpits.

Jesus Christ, Kirk thought. *I woke up on my couch this morning.*

He sighed, and settled back.

Sleep took him quickly.

He dreamed of Carma, of chasing her through a midnight forest in great moonwalking bounds. He couldn't see her face, but he knew it was her, knew her scent. She was a wolf, with fur the color of sun-brightened snow. As a man he pursued her, though this wasn't a problem to him. He closed the gap between them, pounding over her path, hands reaching as he drew near. The ground warmed his feet. Trees whipped at his face. She leaped over a wide gully and he followed, landing close behind her on the other side.

He grabbed for her tail, only to watch her spring away with a burst of speed. He struggled to close the distance, though his feet, which were now paws, had turned to lead.

Far ahead, Carma's voice echoed as if she was right in his ears.

Kirk smiled in his sleep.

She growled again, a base, throaty thing, which puzzled him a little. Her glowing form pulled even farther away, disappearing between the trees.

The dream world trembled and its features fell away, replaced by the sound of glass and cloth being dragged across metal. Kirk woke, blinked, and sensed a presence in the back of the truck. Some alien mass filled the rear box. Bad air and dried shit assaulted his senses. A mass of fur pulsated and bulged through the opening once barred by the rear window. Fabric ripped.

Kirk's eyes widened.

A black bear was poking around his hockey bag, smelling the brain patties stashed within the troublesome material. The animal cursed and groaned with impatience, turned and shamelessly shoved its furry ass deeper in the empty window frame.

"*Hey!*"

The great beast snorted and flinched, pulling its ass free as if sitting on an electrified shitter. The truck lifted as the animal fled from the box and into the night. Kirk watched the thing disappear amongst the trees, hoping that its smell would follow suit. It did not.

"Fuckin' bear," Kirk grumbled, staring hopelessly at the hockey bag's shredded hide. He lifted it to his nose and cringed.

"You pissed and shat on my gear?" he asked in growing disbelief. "You *pissed*. And *shat*. On my gear!"

And, after a few follow-up searches, had apparently eaten the last of the hamburger.

"You furry *bastard*," Kirk fired at the animal.

Not happy in the least, he shook the significant pile of scat free from the bag's exterior, heaving it into the night. A bear-sized load of urine had soaked the cloth, the damage notable. The beast had clawed one end of the hockey bag open, turned, and cut loose on the other. Kirk pulled the bag into the cab and dumped the remains on the floor.

Bear slobber soaked the remaining food and fabric.

"Great," Kirk sighed in disgust. "Just great. You furry-assed fucker, you." He looked out the back window. "Stay the fuck away. Just stay the fuck outta sight. Goddamnit."

The forest became quiet.

He kept guard, wary but drifting, only to open his eyes to morning sun.

7

Just an hour after Kirk had broken into the lakeside cabin, a white cargo van crept into the Claymore Lake area, driving up the dirt road and meticulously checking every dwelling. Em sat in the passenger's seat, scanning for their quarry. Three additional gunmen waited in the back. Two of them sat near the van's rear windows, while the third man sat directly behind Em, looking over her shoulder.

"Stop here," Em ordered the driver. The van halted, rocking on its suspension, and she quickly got out. Most of the weekend cabins were empty, but she still intended to check every one.

She zipped up her coat and headed towards a driveway curving around a clump of trees. A cabin's profile came into view, a single-log bungalow with a nearby shed not ten feet from the front door. Or side door, as Em wasn't sure which was which. She was distinctly aware of gunsights following her, knowing the guy who sat behind her in the van—an ex-soldier named Jude—would cover her until no longer necessary. The van's tires crackled on crushed stone as it crept a little farther along the road, keeping her in view as she proceeded to the main entry.

A door mat read "WELCOME" in weaved black and brown. Em stopped and rapped on the door. While she waited, she studied the lawn and the nearby bushes, so neat and trimmed. She wouldn't mind having a similar place when she retired. Not quite as mundane, however, but close.

The door opened. A guy appeared, perhaps in his late fifties, with a *yee-ha!* beard hanging off his chin and a t-shirt that read *I like Sloppy*. Questionable stains spotted the fabric. He ogled her in surprise, as if she'd caught him doing weird things with hamsters, and a hand lifted to one of his two impressive sideburns that resembled exploding tires caught in a freeze frame.

"Yes?"

"Hi," Em said shyly, summoning the charm. "Um, I was in the neighborhood—I'm not from around here—and, anyway, I noticed that this area is really, really nice, but I didn't see any signs for a town name or anything. I mean, I'm so impressed that I'm thinking about buying some property around here if there was any available. Can't do that unless I have a name, though."

She ended with a frayed note of regret and a smile. The little-girl act turned her stomach every time.

"Oh, ah," Old Sloppy smiled and suddenly was aware of his attire. He utilized the door to partially cover himself. "This is Claymore Lake. Yeah. Nice area. Really nice. Quiet. A little rowdy on the weekends. Well, sometimes. I mean I can hear the neighbors if they really—"

"How many places are around here?" Em asked with school-girl innocence, hating how sugary the question came out.

"Oh? Ah, maybe about thirty or forty? Maybe." Old Sloppy smiled wider, showing teeth that hadn't been tended to that day. "It's a nice area. Friendly people. Even nicer when you get to know them."

"Oh, that's nice," Em said brightly, reeling back the snark. "No weirdos, I hope. I put up with them every day. I used to work in a bank and you get them all the time. Constantly staring at my boobs. Women, too."

That rattled Mr. Sloppy, who blinked and visibly rebooted. "Ah, oh, that's, ah, yeah. Sorry to hear that. Banking isn't a bad job, though. Ah, I have a sister who's in accounting."

"You do? That's the place to be."

"I know," he nodded emphatically. "Makes me wish I never took up truck driving."

"So any weirdos around?"

"Ah," Sloppy scratched an ear. "Not really. Most folks I know around here are pretty decent. Normal folks."

No such thing as normal, Em thought. *Only conformity.* "Is it noisy during the week? I was thinking about writing a book up here."

"Ah no, no, not too noisy at all," Sloppy answered. "Well, except on weekends, like I said. There can be a few parties where the noise gets a little out of hand. But that's not—you can certainly get a book or two done up here. Place is pretty quiet during the week."

"I guess most folks go back to the city or…"

"Yeah, most do. Most do. Some hang on like myself, if, you know, they're not busy or on vacation. What have you."

What have you, Em thought wryly. "Any properties for sale? I really like the A-frames."

"Ah, Bob and Kate Carol are thinking about it. You got a computer?"

Before Em could answer, a voice called out from behind Old Sloppy. "Roger?"

Old Sloppy turned around and a petite woman, well-groomed, appeared in the doorway. She slipped an arm around old Roger and studied Em.

Em turned her charm on full blast, smiling until her cheeks ached. The lady, probably Roger's age, was a stunner, and Em was momentarily bedazzled by her good looks.

And the shirt that read *I like Sloppy, too*.

"Olivia," Roger addressed, draping an arm around her shoulders, "this young lady is interested in buying some property up here."

"Oh?"

"I certainly am," Em remarked, really feeling the burn in her chops.

"Oh well, I'm Olivia Cruise and this is my husband Roger…"

Ten minutes passed before Em could escape the meaningless conversation. Ten full minutes she'd have to erase from memory by smoking something clinically proven to kill brain cells. She'd gotten everything she'd wanted to know about the area, even informed the Cruises (they owned their own trucking company) that she'd been taking an extended tour of Claymore Lake. That was one drawback of being so interactive with the locals—once in the mode, you had to observe and adhere to social protocol.

In the end, when Em said she had to get going, Olivia extended her hand, wished her well, and even gave Em a suggestive double squeeze, which only brightened Em's façade upon contact.

The people you meet in cabin country.

"Well?" Jude asked, the man responsible for shooting Morris. His high-powered carbine pointed at the van's floor. "Learn anything?"

"More than I want to know. You think anyone would notice if we kill everyone around here?"

Jude frowned. Jude had no sense of humor.

"I don't think anyone would," Em thought aloud. "Seriously. Not in the least. Driver—drive on. Those freaks didn't see any other freaks wandering around. We have thirty to forty houses in the area, most of which are probably empty. Get moving. If he's here, we'll find him."

But Em had a feeling Douglas Kirk wasn't around. Em believed Douglas Kirk was off the reserve and running, running as if hell itself was scorching the hair off his ass. And in a way, it was. If he managed to get out of his own place and narrowly escape the second attempted hit back at Morris's, Douglas Kirk might very well have realized that there were people out to kill him. Em didn't share any of that with Jude, however, or anyone else on her team. She knew Jude preferred a positive attitude while on the job.

She'd worked with him enough times over the past seven years to know that much about the guy. That, and he had no fucking sense of humor.

The van slunk along, avoiding pot holes where it could, dipping dangerously where it could not. Some of the cabins were concealed farther back from the main road, making a check both easy and somewhat awkward. Not everyone would be quite as accommodating as the Cruises. Em could handle them, though. There wasn't much she couldn't handle—other than being hit on by older women who wore suggestive t-shirts. She'd been doing this job for seven years, contract by contract, putting down werewolves wherever they could find them. She didn't join up because of some personal traumatic experience—there was no sob story that had compelled her to rid the world of a supernatural evil. Truth was, a guy she once worked with, a contractor of questionable practices who regularly took on work where people got shot or stabbed or poisoned for cash in return, just out of the blue mentioned a much bigger opportunity that might interest her.

Big money, he'd said.

But big risks.

Hunting down werewolves. Usually in human form, which Josh—her old partner—took the time to explain. Nailing them in human form was the safest way to bag one of the bastards. And he was right. No one and their dog wanted to face a fully changed, usually pissed off werewolf. The things were damn-near unstoppable killers, which, in a way, made them so much fun to put down. At least for Em. And the team—always a team—knew who was masquerading as a person, so all they had to do was show up and shoot the target in the face. Repeatedly. And the heart. With silver. It took silver to put them down. Just like the movies.

The thing Em had always wondered about, and questioned Josh about when he was still alive, was... how did they know their targets were actual werewolves? Seriously? As far as she could see, they were popping ordinary people in their homes. Given, some of them certainly *looked* like animals. Old Mr. Sloppy himself, Roger Cruise could've been on a werewolf movie poster. And silver bullets, while extravagant, were just as deadly to a regular person. Josh, however, had insisted they were werewolves and, truthfully, when he was handing over big manila envelopes filled with brown hundred dollar bills, Em didn't care. She'd go along with the fantasy. Hell, she'd shoot the fat asses off leprechauns and ambush woodland fairies if the cash was there.

It had also been equally curious that the team assigned to a hit never came across a werewolf on their own. It was always Josh getting a phone call from a mysterious contact who always knew where the target was, name and address included. So there was some serious doubt on Em's part for the first two years. As far as she was concerned, in that period of time, she was executing about three to five unsuspecting civilians a year and getting paid for it. It just took a phone call to get on a target. Usually the most contracts came in October, which was fine with her. More cash. Sometimes even a big, wet bonus.

A great job, in her sociopathic mind.

Until one day, she discovered firsthand that werewolves were indeed real.

One job. Five years back. A hit that that went utterly sideways. The target—a twenty-something woman who looked like she could've taught kindergarten—somehow knew the team was coming for her. She knew and she'd changed, so when Josh knocked on her apartment door, well, Little Miss Ferocious came crashing through.

Up until that point, Em had seen her share of blood. She killed people for a living prior to working with Josh, terminating targets either by gun or the occasional stabbing. She preferred guns. They were quick, relatively painless, and not as personal as a knife. Guns provided a definite advantage.

What that monster did to Josh in a split-second clarified a lot of things for Em. One, werewolves *did* exist—they were incredibly fast and best handled from a distance. Two, silver did indeed put a werewolf down. The movies actually got that part right. And three, Em hadn't seen any blood *at all* up to that point. Josh's noggin had flown through the air and, like a hairy basketball, bounced off a wall. One paw swipe and a skull was separated from its body as easy as a glass of water backhanded off a table.

Except a spilled glass of water is a lot easier to clean up.

She'd been the one to kill the target that day, and two months later Barronni contacted her. He was Josh's replacement, and even more serious about the work. And, like Josh, he never answered the one remaining question that bothered her about the job.

Who was ordering hits on werewolves? And how did they know? And who were the guys in the trucks who arrived a little later, before the police, and carried the bodies away?

Seven years in and no answers. That bothered Em. To a point. The money helped her get over it, however. It always did.

A well-kept lawn drifted into sight. Em really did think Claymore Lake had a certain appeal. Not that she would ever move into the country. Not her. She was a city girl. The countryside just wasn't her thing.

The van stopped, and she patted the gun in her pocket. It was loaded with hollow-point silver bullets that expanded on impact, providing greater stopping power and creating a much bigger mess. To her, the bigger the better. House cleaning wasn't her job. Em liked the new and improved ammunition, made her feel every bit as lethal as a werewolf. In this operation, Jude and the others would be the ones making the shot. Em, being the highest-ranking officer on the team, had the honorary distinction of being on point. She didn't mind that in the least. Got a charge out of it.

"You ready?" she asked Jude. He adjusted his black-ops toque and nodded. Em had seen him once without his warm knitted hat. It wasn't pretty. Not at all.

Jude nodded and readied his combat rifle, likewise loaded with silver rounds. Em got out of the van as the vehicle's side door cracked open just a few fingers, enough for Jude to stick the barrel of his gun out. A patio stone walkway led to a cozy cabin with its curtains drawn. No parked car in the driveway. Plastic pink flamingos stood on the lawn. Em wanted to shoot the damn things. She stopped at the path's end and knocked on the door.

No answer.

She knocked again. Still nothing.

All right then. Em glanced around and saw no one in sight. She tried the door knob and discovered it locked. She stepped back and studied the windows, looking for any breach, and saw none. She strolled behind the cabin, sizing up potential entry points as she went. The cabin had a huge deck out back, along with plush furniture and a covered barbecue. The lake was right there, not thirty feet away, at the edge of a well-maintained back lawn. A short pier jutted out into the water. A pair of kayaks was lodged in a crushed stone parking space sheltered by firs.

Em tried the back door and cupped her hands to a window. A clean interior, all empty, waiting for the owners to return on the weekend.

Two down, and a lot more to check.

She returned to the idling van and they drove to the next cabin, repeating the process.

It wasn't until the sixteenth cabin that a broken window next to a front door stopped her cold. She scratched her head, the signal for Jude and company to stay alert, and approached the cabin. No vehicles were in sight, and the dwelling was well-hidden from the road. She stepped up to the door, leaned over the railing, and peered inside. Glass twinkled in the yellow grass below.

Things looked promising.

She circled the two-story dwelling, hunting for clues. She'd learned a long time ago that werewolves always left residual matter when they transformed. Puddles of fleshy detritus. Em and the other team members called them stains, and they were always there. For some damn reason, werewolves seemed unconcerned about cleaning up their own mess. They were like kids in that way.

There. Em stopped and stared at a spot that might've been visited by a gut-shot bear, right between a windowless wall and the nearby treeline. The side of the cabin and the ground was covered in grim maroon. Bloody strands of fur drizzled the edges. Em stared in morbid fascination at the werewolf leftovers. In a way, she was delighted to have found Mr. Kirk's trail, but also disappointed.

Mr. Kirk was clearly one of those monsters who didn't wipe his ass.

Stepping away from the transformation site, Em followed the cabin's wall to the rear, where it faced the water. She clomped over a deck to the patio doors and looked inside.

A note rested on a kitchen table. A discarded pen next to it.

Her senses alive and buzzing, Em glanced around to ensure no one was watching. She slipped her gun out of her coat pocket and held it against her thigh, away from the door. She knocked and waited, knowing full well the chance she was taking. Jude would have a shitfit. Not that she cared. Jude didn't scare her.

No one answered. She peeked once more and saw no

movement. The doors were locked.

Em returned to the front of the cabin. She waved at the van parked in the driveway, indicating she was heading inside. The cabin was empty, the owners long gone. Men emerged from the vehicle's rear and side doors. They were dressed in gray and white winter outerwear highlighted with black tac vests. Automatic weapons were visible.

Em crawled in through the broken window and, a minute later, allowed Jude and company to enter through the front door, MP5 first, laser sights blazing. Two hunters followed him, their submachine guns leveled. Em tailed the three, her own weapon at the ready. The team cleared the first floor like killer ghosts. When Jude signaled they were heading upstairs, Em placed her back to a wall and waited, studying the cabin's interior.

The note on the table caught her attention.

I'M SORRY FOR BREAKING IN BUT IT WAS NECESSARY. THANK YOU FOR THE FOOD, DRINK, AND CLOTHING. I DIDN'T TAKE ANYTHING ELSE.

Em pulled out her phone.

"Yeah, it's me. We picked up his trail…"

*

On the other end of the connection, Enzo Barronni stood in the confines of Morris's cabin and listened. He didn't like the report. He soon hung up, leaving Em's team to their search, and rubbed at the beard hanging off his chin.

He speed-dialed another number and placed the phone to his ear.

"Yes?" spoke a deep voice with the barest trace of eagerness.

"Kirk's on foot and heading west through backwoods country."

The voice waited.

"One team is in pursuit," Barronni continued. "He's got a head start, however, and we don't have the resources to cover everything."

"Do what you can."

Barronni hesitated. "Do you have anyone else in the area?"

"I'll see what I can do."

"The more boots we have on the ground the quicker we can locate him."

That stilled the voice.

"Kirk knows we're after him," Barronni explained. "He might've given up returning to Halifax. He has no phone, no badge, and no money. Em reports that he broke into a cabin and stole some clothing and food. That's all."

Nothing from the other end.

"Not yet," the voice finally said. "Do what you can. Hunt him down. Kill him. Then bring his carcass back to me."

The speaker hung up.

Barronni dropped the phone from his ear, absorbing the instructions.

In the distance, he heard the growing rumble of an engine.

8

Kirk opened his eyes, glimpsing the morning sun through a cobweb of branches. A faint breeze carried the taint of nearby bear shit and piss under his nose. And fur. That got a second, clarifying sniff. The animal hadn't gone far.

Just his luck.

In a dark funk, Kirk removed his feet from the cushion cocoon, inspected them, and saw that his toes were still firmly attached. The boots weren't so good, still damp from yesterday's dip. Maybe he should've sat on the things. Body heat might've warmed them up better. Well, Kirk mulled, at least they hadn't been pissed on by a bear. Not pleased in the least, he worked his feet into the boots' clammy lengths and extracted himself from the truck.

He retrieved the hockey bag.

The fabric looked like shit.

Smelled like shit.

Wonderful, Kirk thought. He rubbed his face to get the blood flowing. It was cold, but, thankfully, he wasn't hungover. He stuffed the bottle of rum back into the bag and drank a third of his remaining water. The urge to take a leak eclipsed all his other needs, so he pulled down his jeans and pajama bottoms and aimed for the front of the truck. The stream hissed as it left him, and his thoughts dissipated into a blank screen.

A growl bulged his eyes.

Kirk glanced over his shoulder and saw the black bear approaching, scuffling along the forest floor as if totally uninterested.

His stream of urine faltered and stopped. The animal appeared much bigger than he remembered.

"Well," he muttered at the six or seven-hundred-pound beast. "Morning, Sunshine."

Sunshine grunted and growled, looking this way and that, and slowed to a stop some fifteen feet away. The bear sniffed and pointed its considerable muzzle at the warden.

"Back for seconds, are you?" Kirk spoke softly as he tucked himself away. "Or just need to use the can again? That *really* pissed me off, y'know."

He faced the bear, unable to remember if that was wise when dealing with them or not. This one wasn't scared of him, and he had no means to drive the animal away. In all his days, he really hadn't dealt with the big omnivores all that much, and when he did, the bears, more often than not, liked to pick fights.

The animal waddled three paces closer.

"Hold on," Kirk said. He scrounged through the hockey bag. Crackers. There was a box or two of crackers in there. He snatched them up, ripped the top off, and tore open the bags. Sunshine stopped and grunted, wondering what Kirk was doing.

A heavy white sprinkle of crackers landed before the beast, prompting the bear to sniff and sample a handful.

Kirk grabbed the hockey bag and backed away from the beast. When the bear was out of sight, he picked up the pace, heading towards the highway and hoping the sound of traffic might ward off the animal. Branches whipped at his head, sometimes hooking into his ski mask. He turned west after a while, and eventually heard the whiz of unseen cars to his left. He glanced over his shoulder to check on old Sunshine's whereabouts.

A breeze carried the bear's smell.

Great, Kirk fumed. Last thing he needed was to get into a fight with a bear. Not at this hour in the morning.

But that's what real *men do*, a voice whispered in his head.

Real *stupid* men, Kirk countered, craning his neck around in search of the bear.

Well, *shit*.

The forest wasn't dense enough to fully conceal the furry wrecking ball scuffling along in pursuit. The animal darted between trees, plodding after him. Little grunts and wails perked Kirk's ear, bear taunts meant to frighten.

Where you going, bitch? Where you going, huh? I didn't say we were finished.

Brush crackled as Kirk increased his pace. He could climb a tree, but the bear could probably climb better than him. He could run for the highway, but he'd never make it. The critter would easily outrun him in a sprint. Changing into his wolf form was an option. Freak the animal out. It would take time to change, but the process alone might scare the bear away.

Decision made, Kirk stopped and dropped the hockey bag. He doffed the bathrobe and clothing underneath as if they were on fire, and summoned the change, willing his werewolf blood to a quick boil. Kirk didn't look forward to feeling his squished guts rearranging themselves somewhere totally unacceptable.

How did Borland do it?

A white, bony spine gleamed in the morning light as Kirk bent over and tore off his boots. Pain lanced up his arms and legs. His guts shifted and twisted as if being wrung free of fluid. The bear approached, not fifteen paces away, a short rush really, sniffing and grunting and not understanding what was happening.

Kirk's musculature shifted with popping bones. Flesh stretched. Muscle expanded.

How did he do it? How did he only become half *a wolf?*

His thoughts screamed like a passing train as the pain and pleasure of morphing switched into high gear. His jaw hinges ached and snapped. Bones shortened and lengthened. His heart was now beating like a freed storm shutter caught in the grip of a tornado. He dropped to his knees and clawed dirt, tearing up grooves.

Sunshine the bear stopped, head shaking, suddenly catching a whiff of something he didn't want any part of.

The morning stretch goodness of the transformation came upon Kirk and he let himself go, riding that final wave, growling at the splitting of skin. He collapsed as his joints ceased crackling. *Warmth*. The cold was shut out and Kirk felt much better.

When he lifted his eyes to Sunshine, he saw the bear had disappeared.

Smart bear.

Chicken shit, but smart.

On four legs, Kirk plodded toward where he saw the animal last. He pressed his snout to the forest floor and sniffed. He grimaced once he caught the bear's powerful odor, and decided he needed to make a point.

He chased after the animal.

It was petty. Uncalled for. And worse, it was stupid. But Kirk wanted to make sure Sunshine got the message: don't shit in another man's hockey bag.

He ran through the bush, blades of light staking the earth, and quickly spotted Sunshine's retreating ass. The animal wasn't running but shuffling away, like a sulking kid beaten at a game, ready to fight anyone smaller just out of spite.

*Were*blood charged Kirk with incredible energy, and his tempter flared. People were trying to kill him. He was penniless, had broken into a home, and was on the run.

Add a bear that shit and pissed in his hockey bag, had eaten his food, and smelled of nasty twig-clinging ass, well, suddenly Kirk wanted a fight.

Not just a fight, but a goddamn broken beer bottle *brawl*.

Sunshine caught wind of Kirk's rapidly approaching hide. The bear stopped and turned to face his charging adversary. The animal growled, perhaps a little unnerved but nowhere ready to flee a glorified dog looking for a fight.

Not in *his* woods.

Kirk slammed into the seven hundred pounds of thick hide. The pair became a snapping, rolling tumbleweed of tooth and claw. Yawning growls cut the air as violent as buzz saws. The beasts struggled with each other's weight on hind legs, pushing each other's jaws away, ducking and weaving and seeking an opening like a pair of hairy wrestlers. Sunshine sought Kirk's throat but got slapped across the nose. Kirk's head was mashed into the ground, taking a drubbing of needles and forest sludge. Sunshine was partially lifted off its feet and raked across the face in a spritz of blood.

Sunshine didn't like the claws.

That awakened the bear inside the bear.

Sunshine roared. The animal slammed into Kirk like an unchained wrecking ball. They crashed together on rear legs, pushing forward, snapping and pawing at each other until Sunshine bowled Kirk over in a flash of claws. The werewolf's left ear was shorn off. The right side of its lips got shredded in a spurt of red. Kirk responded to the pain, acknowledging the licks sustained, his own fury matching that of the raging bear. He shoved the heavier animal back until Sunshine had to twist off-balance.

The animal gave up its back.

Not one to pass up an opportunity, Kirk bit into Sunshine's chunky ass. He bit deep, sinking his oversized canines into fur and flesh and hitting bone.

Sunshine yowled.

And kicked Kirk square in the throat.

It was a reflexive, completely unexpected blow, and the impact unfastened the werewolf's considerable jaws.

Trailing blood, the bear bolted for deep woods, leaving the Halifax warden coughing and growling for breath. Kirk didn't pursue, watching Sunshine disappear amongst the trees until the animal was gone—and gone for good. Or at least long enough for Kirk to get far and away out of the animal's territory.

His throat hurting, Kirk trod back to his discarded clothing. Blood dappled the ground. *Well done, mister bear*, he thought. *Well done.* Sunshine got in a couple of good licks. Kirk enjoyed the old-fashioned tussle and hoped the bear wasn't hurt too badly. He took his time changing back, missing the warmth of his natural coat as soon as it withdrew. His lip strung itself back together and a new baby ear was already blooming. Even his shoulder felt better. Biped once again, Kirk picked up his clothing, thankful that the ground wasn't wet, and got dressed.

The mystery of how Borland had changed into a half-wolf still bothered him. Once the transformation kicked into high gear, Kirk didn't understand how anyone could alter themselves any other way.

He checked his bathrobe for tears and noticed the seams had split in a few places. Nothing too shabby, however, so he pulled it on. Once dressed, Kirk stretched his shoulder, did an internal check, and deemed all was right.

No hangover to speak of, and just kicked a bear's ass.

If his boots were a size or two bigger and just a little drier, he supposed the morning would have been pretty swell.

Except for the little tidbit that he was still being hunted.

Frowning, Kirk hoofed through the woods, keeping the highway somewhere to his left. He realized he stunk and doubted anyone would offer him a lift, so he decided to keep hiking.

The bush opened up to more fields, their surfaces raw and stiffened by the cold, hidden from the highway by thick forest. He followed the edges, stopping once to forage through the hockey bag and pull out his remaining box of crackers. He ate seven of the tasteless squares before his mouth seized up with dryness. A sip of water from his jug greased his throat. Maybe he should've stayed in wolf form and tried hunting down a rabbit. He didn't dwell on that.

Thoughts of where his hunters might be occupied his mind.

And thoughts of Borland.

The final days of autumn had bleached the forest, leaving patchy quilts of red and yellow upon the ground. Crows or ravens flew overhead. Kirk found a small brook, sniffed and sampled the water, and refilled his jug. Then he dipped and scrubbed his hockey bag, sniffing and inspecting it before wringing the thing out. He realized then that he didn't have the ski poles anymore, and decided not look for them. After the wash, he packed what meager provisions he had away and checked on his bathrobe, seeing how the branches had pulled at the seams until they had frayed.

Just wonderful. He was really starting to look and smell the part of a homeless drifter.

Angry at his misfortunes, he bore west, marching hard to burn off the steam building inside. Tall struts of power towers and their humming lines came into view, and by afternoon, Kirk walked in their shadows, following a quad's beaten path.

Jesus, he thought and stopped in the shade of a structure resembling the skeletal frame of an old Japanese castle. He'd never been on the run before. Not like this. All the years holed up in Halifax, he'd become that which his neighbors all saw him as.

A lazy fucking sack of shit.

That burned him, and he cursed Borland for it. Cursed Morris for disappearing, and especially cursed the elders for attempting to kill him. He wondered if he should chance returning to the highway and hitching a ride. At least if he caught a ride, he could get out west faster.

He hitched his hands upon his hips.

And go where out west?

He'd been thinking west all this time yet hadn't really defined exactly where. But, subconsciously, he knew. There was a destination in mind after all, he just hadn't officially announced it.

Carma.

She was in Ontario, though he didn't know where. He did know her phone number. He'd memorized it, had dialed those digits enough times before hanging up to recall it instantly. All he needed was a phone. And a place to call from. And money to make the call.

Kirk's shoulders slumped.

All that led back to civilization.

Knowing he'd regret it, he dragged himself back to the highway.

*

He walked along the divided drag at a mule's pace, ready to run for the forest if he got a weird vibe from the traffic. He stuck his thumb out at the speeding cars and trucks, trying his acting chops by putting on a sad face (not too hard to do) and mentally swearing at each ride as they sped by.

Fifty cars had ignored him by mid-afternoon.

An hour later, it was well over two hundred.

Maybe I'm not getting the hint here, Kirk thought and inspected himself. He truly didn't think he looked all that bad, once you got past the bathrobe. Perhaps a little dusted up from the tussle with Sunshine but nothing too unacceptable. The lingering smell of bear offal didn't help, however, but he only needed a ride to the next town. Maybe a pickup with an open bed. The chance at a phone call wouldn't be so bad, either. Hell, while he was thinking about it, a few coins would be helpful too, and some food.

But that was all. Not so much to ask for.

Kirk refrained from smacking his own skull.

Sometime after the three hundredth car, a fat SUV slowed down as it approached, the first and only vehicle to do so, and Kirk's heart leaped in his chest. *Finally*! Except the SUV was filled with a family, with the mother visibly hissing at her husband.

The machine whizzed by Kirk with his sagging arm.

Two kids in the backseat, their mouths open and aghast, zeroed in upon him. The kids looked to be no more than nine or ten. The undisguised horror on their faces finally convinced him.

Kirk had turned into a dirty vagrant. A good example of what might happen to them if they didn't study hard enough. He watched the SUV shrink in the distance. A few other vehicles flashed by, but he didn't bother lifting his arm. And he stopped counting cars.

No one bothered him.

The long asphalt strip rose in the distance, climbing towards a flat horizon. Daylight waned. The temperature dropped. Headlights switched on, and Kirk grudgingly decided to find a place to sleep for the night.

He veered off the highway, leaving the judging faces behind. The trees took him in, patted him on the head and shoulders, and shielded him from the road. Kirk wandered, knowing he'd waited far too late to return. A hill rose before him, covered in dead brush and graying trees. The slope was much too steep to climb. The sight broke him, and because he was too depressed to go any further, too hungry and too tired, he plopped down on a nearby mossy ledge and leaned on his pissy hockey bag.

His boots had dried out, to a degree. One good thing, at least.

Weary and shivering, Kirk rooted away some of the dead brush. He settled into the hillside, glad that he wasn't flat on the ground, and tried to relax. There was no scent of bears on the wind.

But somewhere out there, the elders wanted him dead.

With that thought in mind, Kirk dozed off.

9

In another part of the world, a phone rang twice in a darkened room.

"Yes?" the elder said.

"We tracked him to the highway but lost him," Barronni whispered. "Possible he might've hitched a ride. He could be anywhere, now."

The elder's face darkened. "I see."

Winds blew hard against a nearby window that refused to budge.

Barronni spoke again. "We're heading towards Truro. We'll hit the town, the motels, and churches. He might've holed up for the night."

"Leave nothing unturned," the elder quietly stressed.

"This has gone large now," Barronni said. "Too large for just us."

The implication wasn't lost on the elder. "I'll muster reinforcements."

He hung up.

The elder stared at the phone, his features partially

hidden in shadow. His hackers had infiltrated certain restricted sites and discovered that the Halifax police force had issued a search and detain order for Douglas Kirk, wanted in connection with four deaths in his city apartment complex. The hackers would monitor the police's progress online and through other various channels. That eye was now open and staring like some mythical monster. The elder doubted the police would ever capture Kirk, however, and even if they did, the elder would make certain the renegade *were* wouldn't live long enough to answer questions. Questions led to identity issues, which led to DNA sampling, which led to more questions and laboratory tests.

Something the elder did not want.

His head rested against his chair as he absorbed the implications of Barronni's update. In the background, the wind slammed against storm-proofed glass. A sigh escaped the elder. He looked to the window, where a vast cityscape lay stamped against an overcast sky.

Barronni was correct. It had gone large. More resources were needed to find and kill Kirk.

It was time to alert the wardens.

And unleash the packs.

*

On the fringes of Montreal, in an apartment lit by a single lamp, a cellphone sang out a pop tune.

A shirtless Ian Bryce, relaxing on a sofa, rolled his eyes and scratched at a meaty bicep. His entire frame rippled as he moved, but not in a defined way, more like a whale swimming just below the ocean surface. Bryce's considerable physique was sheathed in a layer of fat, rendering him bulky in a very intimidating way. He considered the phone and smoothed his thick beard, which he allowed to grow to biker lengths. Wild man lengths.

With a groan, he got up, hitched up the legs of his sweatpants, and hoped the caller didn't expect much of a conversation. Ever since the *were* called Bailey had shoved a barbell down his gullet, Bryce's voice had been screwed up and croaky, producing weird sound bites that might've come from an alien accordion. And it *hurt* to speak, which was another thing. He tried to heal it by transforming in his apartment, but his regenerative nature had surprisingly failed to correct the issue. He wondered how Ezekiel was doing. The New Brunswick warden's entire throat had been ripped out. Bryce wondered if doing that to his own gullet would restore his vocal cords, but he cringed at the thought. Having another *were* do the deed wasn't particularly appealing either.

"Yeah?" he squawked, sounding like his voice was trapped in puberty.

"Ian Bryce?"

His frame stiffened with recognition. "Yes?"

"We have a problem," the elder said.

"I'm listening."

"Do you know Douglas Kirk?"

"Yes."

The elder didn't waste any time. "A year ago we sent Kirk and Moses Morris to Newfoundland. They were tasked with killing a *were* called Borland. Borland was old. Crazy. He'd done things to the local animals, things that risked revealing himself to the human herds, risked exposing us all. Kirk and Morris killed Borland, but both wardens were gravely wounded. They consumed parts of Borland to recover, to deal with the secondary threat of Borland's animals."

The news stunned Bryce. His naked skin tingled. "What?"

"Unknown to either of them, they partook in a meal that is as horrific as it is forbidden. Tell me, when you were in Halifax, you reported that Kirk was acting strangely. Did you notice anything else in particular?"

Bryce remembered. "Only the healing. He healed fast. And he was pretty secretive. Morris, too."

"They knew even then," the elder whispered. "Superlative healing powers. A blessing at first, indeed, but a damning curse. Kirk and Morris have unknowingly doomed themselves. By eating Borland, they've become a very rare breed of cannibal, one not known to common *weres*. A breed with exceptional strength, speed, and healing abilities, with a craving for *were* flesh if they're allowed to survive. Nothing else will satisfy them, and if they cannot feed, they'll become increasingly dangerous. Unstable. Ravenous. Slowly driven insane by their appetites. Until no one is safe. Not even the human herds. They've become monsters. We suspected something amiss from our conversations with them, so we dispatched a pair of teams to kill both. To end them before they could infect other *weres*. One team succeeded in killing Morris. Kirk, however, escaped."

The flood of information overloaded a stunned Bryce, but the revelation about Morris left him speechless.

Moses Morris was dead?

Unaware of Bryce's shock, the elder continued. "Kirk will become increasingly violent over time. He will become insatiable. Gluttonous. The police are already searching for him but they won't find him. They must not. Kirk isn't to be captured by the law. He'll be found and killed by us. Do you understand?"

Bryce realized he was supposed to answer. "Yes."

"Kirk's no longer in contact with us. He's on the run. Without his badge, his telephone, or his wallet. He's managed to evade our teams, but not you or your fellow wardens. Alert the wolves in your pack, Bryce. The Halifax police are circulating a picture of Kirk. One taken from outside the shopping mall where you and the others killed Bailey. We'll forward a copy to you. Distribute them to your pack. Tell them what I've told you: that Kirk's to be killed on sight. Kill him, and when you do, notify us and we'll send a disposal unit."

"All right," Bryce put a hand to his throat, coaxing it to work. "Understood."

"He may be heading west."

"West?"

"Yes. From Nova Scotia, crossing into New Brunswick."

"Where?"

"We don't know."

"West?" Bryce wandered his apartment. He stopped at the closet and glanced at the hilt of his Bowie knife underneath a black toque.

"You've served us well in the past, Ian Bryce," the elder said. "Do so again. Find Kirk, Bryce. Kill him. Bring him to us. Do that and we'll reward you for your effort."

That stopped Bryce in his tracks. "Reward?"

"Reward."

"What kind?"

The elder paused, and Bryce thought he had hung up. Then, "The highest kind."

Whatever *that* was, but Bryce's imagination summoned scenes of becoming an elder, the head of not simply one pack, but *all* packs.

He grasped the sheathed blade by its handle and withdrew the shimmering length of edged silver, both a weapon and symbol of a warden's authority.

"I'll find him," he said, his voice trembling.

The elder hung up.

Bryce tossed his phone onto a nearby counter and studied his knife.

Bright. Eternally sharp.

He sheathed the blade and regarded his phone. He'd alert the others in his domain. Get the word out. They could search wherever, however, they wanted.

Find Kirk and kill him. Not a problem.

Bryce never liked the guy, anyway.

*

In New Brunswick, in a modest apartment on the outskirts of Saint Stephen, Ezekiel Allen answered his cellphone. The short and stocky warden had recovered from his frightening wound, his regenerative powers completely restoring all of the delicate tissue torn out by Bailey. Ezekiel's voice even sounded better these days. Raspier, if that was possible. The ladies loved it, told him he could sing jazz if he tried. He was getting laid left and right because of his once-mangled pipes. Talk about making the most of a bad situation.

Ezekiel listened to the voice on the phone and his face—battered features that might've belonged to a perpetually happy boxer with a career of losing badly—wilted as if doused with pissy toilet water. He sat, the drop damn near wrecking whatever springs remained in his sofa, and held his chin in rapt concern.

Two minutes later, the caller hung up on him.

Ezekiel remained downcast. He placed his phone on a coffee table and sat back, trying to absorb the call.

Moses Morris was dead.

Unbelievable. Put down by command. From the elders themselves.

And it wasn't stopping there.

Ezekiel swallowed, his throat suddenly coated in dust. It wasn't like Morris had been a friend by any means, but in him, Ezekiel did see a kindred spirit. A hard-ass born to break jaws and twist titties. Gone now. The New Brunswick warden put fingers to his temples and rubbed. Not only had he received terrible, terrible news, but orders from the powers above as well. Orders that he didn't like. He very much wanted a drink of the whiskey he kept in the kitchen cupboard. He doubted it would help, but it sure as hell wouldn't hurt.

Moses Morris had already been put down. That would take some getting used to.

And Douglas Kirk must die, the voice had stressed.

Holy shit. Ezekiel sat on the edge of the well-used sofa, his troubled reflection set in the unlit screen of his television. He looked as if he'd just taken a mule-kick to the balls.

In time, he picked up his phone, opened it, and dialed a number, alerting the first *were* in his pack that populated the New Brunswick territory.

*

Rain pelted Toronto's downtown quarter as Carma Jones looked out of a metro bus window. She stood, holding onto an overhead strap, watching a sidewalk teeming with lowered umbrellas. Some were stylish, others cute, and the rest business black.

Her phone rang and she pulled it from an inner coat pocket. "Yes?"

"Carma…" the familiar voice began.

She listened, recognizing the elder, and her face gradually paled.

When she hung up, she took a firmer grip on the overhead strap, oblivious to the passengers crowding her. Her brown eyes, dark enough to be mistaken for black, stared ahead as she replayed the message in her head.

The bus stopped with a lurch, shaking her back to the present. A side door hissed opened and she shoved her way toward the exit, ignoring the complaints and grunts from her fellow passengers. She jumped off the bus and landed with a splash in a wide puddle.

With her own business-black umbrella popped open, Carma walked in a daze, not knowing where exactly to start. She was at least a twenty-minute cab ride from her apartment.

Holy Christ, Douglas, she thought. *What have you done? You've practically executed yourself.*

She remembered their conversation in his truck. What the elder had told her matched what Kirk had said. She suspected there were more detailed versions as well, from both parties. They were holding back information. She could sense it, but she just didn't know what.

She intended to find out.

*

The elder hung up, tapped a finger, and reflected upon the past hour. The wardens had been alerted, and they would mobilize their packs in turn. They would find Kirk. It wouldn't be long. His face had already been shown on a Nova Scotian news program, and if a person spotted the *were* and reported him to the authorities, then the elder would know. The wardens would know. The packs would know. The news feeds would flush Kirk into the open where he would be dealt with decisively. Finally.

A sense of regret struck the elder then.

A part of him wished he was in on the hunt.

10

A bout of violent shivering woke Kirk, just as the sun rose over distant hills. His entire night had gone that way—waking in the grip of a vicious chill before somehow falling back into a doze. He pushed himself up from the hillside slope and wavered for balance. The nearby woods remained empty, as black and forbidding in the morning shadow as the brambles around a graveyard. He was alone. Then the misery set in, a longing to be back in his apartment, in his own pajama bottoms and t-shirt, stretched out on his couch with a book and a dozen beers at his fingertips. He wasn't up for a cross-county hike. Not in fucking November.

His empty stomach turned on his ribs. He flexed his gunshot shoulder and found the arm worked just fine. He studied his hand and wondered, with grim humor, if he could snack on just a couple fingers. Just to get him through the morning, until he could find something with a little more sustenance. A little more meat.

Carma. He had to make contact with her. He could use her advice. Her decisiveness.

But to contact Carma, he needed a phone.

The hockey bag continued to look and smell like shit, and while he only had the empty jug and the bottles stashed inside (he'd finished off the water during the night) it was still a handful, still a weight he no longer liked carrying. Even better, he truly stunk. A sniff here and there informed him that he needed a shower big time. Being on the run for just over a day and sleeping outside for two nights had culminated in an aromatic glove consisting of body odor, dick cheese, bear excrement, and slobber.

Thanks, Sunshine. You prick.

Kirk's stomach growled, letting him know it was there, wanting him to move. He wasn't going to reach a town fast enough on foot. Nor did he have the food to power him through this episode. Kirk looked around, wondering what to do when a pair of hard coat tugs from his stomach caught his attention. Now that his physical pain had diminished, those terrible, terrible cravings would had returned. And doubled.

Kirk didn't want to change, loathed going over to that side, but he stripped off his clothing anyway. Every layer he peeled away only made his shivering worse. He folded the t-shirts, jeans, and pajama bottoms and stowed everything into the untorn end of the hockey bag.

Once finished, he let his *were*blood flow freely. He changed, unhurriedly, and melted in relief at both the rush of power and his thickening fur. Kirk stumbled and rose on four legs. He abandoned the shit-stained hockey bag and dove into a thicket in search of his next meal. The wild was an olfactory delight but he wasn't interested in wild vegetables or grass or shrivelled berries. Kirk wanted meat.

His first victims consisted of a pair of furry voles, which he'd caught in one corner a plowed field. The next bite came a little later, an old rat with its leaf-drizzled nest underneath a discarded beer cooler. Kirk made his third and final meal just before mid-morning, when he found a racoon waddling through the woods. The animal actually provided a good chase before finally diving into a shallow burrow, where it hissed and screamed until dreadful teeth took its life.

Feeling better with a full belly, Kirk retraced his trail back to the hockey bag, wondering what woodland animals might've violated it. To his surprise, the bag was untouched. He considered reverting back to a man but wavered. The thick black fur covering him was warmer than any coat, and he reluctantly admitted he could cover ground faster, more comfortably, as a werewolf.

But the issue was whether or not he wanted to be in the buff when he eventually changed back. He didn't want to break into another cabin. Kirk studied the hockey bag and stuck his snout through one of the shoulder loops. He got his full head through and lifted, hoisting the bag off the ground like an oversized, skanky dog collar. It was awkward, clumsy around his forelegs, but he didn't care. The time saved on four legs would make up for it, and in wolf form, he could readily feed off the land.

Course decided upon, he trotted off, the tattered hockey bag swinging from his neck.

Just before noon, a set of railway tracks greeted him as he

pushed through a particularly dense thicket. Kirk followed the tracks, padding along, grateful for the open space. Clouds drifted and thickened as the landscape shifted back and forth from small forgotten fields to clumps of forest.

Halfway through the afternoon, Kirk heard the train.

The approaching locomotive prompted his curiosity. A minute passed and the bullet-faced snake glided into view, its one eye glaring. Kirk retreated from the tracks and took shelter in a nearby copse of trees. The train rattled past him soon after, silver with a blue stripe along its top, with an observation dome near the back. Heads were in the windows, fleshy blurs that Kirk couldn't rightly distinguish.

The train's thirty-plus cars passed him minutes later.

Once the great machine was out of sight, Kirk stood, struggled with the bag, and followed.

Afternoon darkened into night and a light rain began to fall. Kirk left the rails and stopped underneath a few low boughs. He dropped his sack, pushed it close to the tree trunk, and went hunting. He tracked down a single mouse and nothing else. His nose led him back to the hockey bag and he thought, if he was lucky, perhaps the smell of it would attract something to eat.

Head on his paws, Kirk reflected on the day. He'd covered fair ground on four legs, had eaten, and remained alive and free from the forces looking for him. That thought stayed with him. Rain pattered and hissed beyond the boughs, but he paid it little heed. He was surprisingly comfortable under the tree's broad limbs, lying on the forest floor. His eyes twinkled with memories in the deepening dark. It was difficult to believe that he was sleeping in his own bed just two nights ago.

Rain drops trickled on his snout. Kirk licked them away. He settled in, tucked his nose under his tail, and closed his eyes.

*

Snorts and grunts brought Kirk back to consciousness. He listened, ears perked, and stayed still. Out there in the dark, something drew closer, closing in on him. Branches snapped and crackled, ruining the otherwise peaceful night. Kirk lifted his head but couldn't see anything. The rain shower intensified, and those bestial notes came closer still, shambling from left to right as if drunk. Kirk's ears flickered, tracking the crunch of branches and forest debris. He licked his nose and waited, listening for his approaching visitor.

His arms and legs tensed.

The rain fell harder, crashing down as if a rogue tropical storm had parked right over his head. Branches rocked and stroked his scalp with their fingers, assuring him that the weather would pass. The shower soaked his face.

Out there in the dark, the snorts paused and became quiet.

Kirk waited.

Through that rumbling, blowing squall, the noise returned, but was now tentative.

And then stopped completely, as if the very ground had swallowed it up.

Muscles charged, Kirk focused his attention straight

ahead. His paws pushed off the wet ground and he rose into a crouch. He strained to hear over the crashing deluge, couldn't see anything besides a solid sheet of midnight a nose-length away.

Then the smell crept upon him, a toxic cloud of wet graveyard earth and blood and fresh excrement. The rich scent of rot coated something familiar.... Kirk's nose burned the instant he caught the obscene whiff. The tempest overhead intensified again, the winds bordering on hurricane strength, pressing down upon the trees until their soaked limbs patted his head. He expected a blast of thunder but nothing came.

There, in the dark, Kirk waited.

And growled.

Rain trickled into his eyes and ears but he stayed focused, dying to catch a glimpse of the thing in the dark and wanting to taste clean air again. Every breath tainted his lungs, fouled them to sores. Kirk waited, cringing with every intake, on the verge of barking, but something held him back, a sense that whatever crept closer hadn't quite located him in the storm.

So he held his peace a little longer, sucking back that rotten air.

Trickles turned into streams, blurring Kirk's vison.

A solid mass of fur and bone exploded into him, bowling him over, taking him completely off-guard. Growls filled Kirk's ears.

Sunshine.

The huge animal moved like a charging freight train leaping from the tracks, and it slammed into Kirk, pinning him against the tree trunk, eager to take him down. Sunshine snarled into the warden's face, baring fangs in an evil smile, except Sunshine wasn't a bear anymore. Sunshine had become a weird, bestial mutation of Borland and grizzly, half-cloaked by the night and reeking of hot blood and excrement. Sunshine's muzzle didn't have any lips, and his teeth were as long and frightening as sabers.

Kirk twisted and turned but he could *not* free himself. Sunshine held him down, trapping all four of his limbs as if trained by Greek wrestlers. Kirk struggled and gasped, the overpowering stink leeching his strength.

Sunshine's snout appeared alongside Kirk's left eye.

The animal snorted.

The sabers snapped into Kirk's orbital cavity as if cracking open an exceptionally tough nut.

Kirk bucked and screamed and came awake with a jolt. He burst from the boughs like a malfunctioning rocket, spun and snapped at shadows, clawed at air.

In short time, the rain calmed him, assured him that Sunshine was nothing more than a bad dream. The forest remained empty and dark. Storm clouds growled and the rain hushed his nerves. Sunshine became a memory, fading like cliffs in a fog.

Kirk returned to his place under the boughs.

It took him a lot longer to fall asleep.

Angry clouds shaded the land in a dismal gray, as sheets of rain fell in great shimmering bulbs, crashing into Kirk's exposed side and soaking his fur. He woke in wet misery and missed his Halifax crib even more. He lowered his head and peeked out at that dreamy landscape, thinking he would've appreciated the scenery more if he was inside a cabin window with a fire at his back. Soaked to the bone, he decided on searching for someplace drier to wait out the weather. Perhaps the whole system might blow over.

It took a long time to get moving.

Freezing rain attacked his eyes as he slunk along the tracks, searching for that ideal spot. Breakfast would have to wait, as the local wildlife would be hiding from the storm. Kirk figured he'd be okay, however, and filled his stomach with water from deepening puddles when he passed them.

The cold seeped deeper into him, but he pressed on and soon had traveled perhaps a kilometer in the rain. If there was any wildlife around, it was probably watching him from hidden burrows, wondering what the hell he was doing outside in such shitty weather.

That thought warmed him just a little.

And it was around that time, as Kirk plodded along on crushed stone, when his right forepaw came down on the remains of a tossed beer bottle.

Shards sharper than scissors snipped his big metacarpal pad.

Exquisite pain seized him like an electrical charge and refused to release him. He leaped, yowled, and the embedded sliver went with him. He landed off balance, driving the glass even deeper. Blood blotted the rocks in polka dots. A frantic, pain-fueled Kirk dropped to his belly and licked at his paw. He tasted blood. He rubbed the sliced padding across the train tracks in a frantic attempt to free himself, but the hockey bag, that swinging, shit and piss smelling chunk of badness, got in his way. With a rabid yip he pawed at the bag, his desperation soaring. White energy clamped down on his foreleg, from his shoulder to his claws, where the pain threatened immolation. He yanked his head free of the hangman's loops and immediately went to work on his wound, while ice pellets filled his bloody tracks.

Kirk nipped and licked at the glass, making contact with the edge and feeling it wiggle.

Just a bit.

Whimpering, Kirk nipped harder. Blood lined his teeth and gums. He grazed glass and pushed it away. Another wail escaped him as he licked the thick trickle away and picked at the crystal barb. He crunched glass, whined, and pulled.

The pain paralyzed him.

Kirk snorted, cursed his awkward wolf body, and snapped at the stubborn sliver. The torturous glass shifted just a little more. Changing tactics, he pawed at the steel tracks as if he'd discovered the world's biggest soup bone, each contact producing an off-note piano key of agony that made him work harder. His paws became blurs.

But the glass remained.

Defeated, Kirk stopped and sized up his mutilated paw. He wasn't going to get that awful piece out. Not like this. He was only working that hot, nerve-splicing knife deeper into his flesh.

So he did the only thing he could.

Kirk changed, pulling back his *were* form, forcing himself back into his human body. The bright hurt of the transformation enveloped his impalement. Bones shifted and skin tightened. Fur receded. His bowels let go and he was aware enough to hope he wasn't shitting on his hockey bag.

Then he was a person again, naked and in the middle of nowhere, staggering towards a wall of trees.

He never made it.

Kirk collapsed on yellow grass, holding his badly cut right hand. The sliver jigged between his middle and ring finger, parting skin and tissue and bone like a fire arrow. A shark's tail jutted from his hand, red and slippery and moving as if the very tip sought to burrow all the way to his wrist.

A violent trembling grabbed him, an angry guitar solo of heat, cold, and electricity. He hissed and mewled at the bubbling gash while attempting to get a grip. The glass sliced his fingertips. The effort frustrated him, maddened him, and he clawed at the wound in an ever-deepening frenzy, all the while edging closer to a chasm he knew he had to avoid, a deep hole of unconsciousness that would not remove the glass for him.

Kirk rallied, squealed, and pinched the middle of his palm as hard as he could, as if squeezing a tube of toothpaste.

The bloody tail-tip reversed just a bit.

The glass, possessed by some malefic presence of mind, refused to let go that easily. Kirk could feel its length inside his tattered mitten of meat.

Kirk squeezed again, with all the force of a tightening vice, bringing on a boulder's splash of nausea.

The glass eased out of its bloody sheath with a dribble, enough for him to get a firm pinch. With a single, high-pitched note, Kirk withdrew that ruby lightning bolt from between his abused fingers, and just as the tip emerged from the surreal alien mouth that drooled and suckled after it, the tiniest star went nuclear at the point of contact, right before his eyes.

That soundless blast dropped him in a field of near-frozen grass and he knew no more.

*

The ground was soft. Warm. Kirk opened his eyes and saw old planks shaded a subdued fiery orange. He flexed his hand and found he could do so, realized he was covered in a blanket and lay upon a thin mattress. The smells of earth and body odor lingered on the air, but not so powerful to be offensive, as the pleasant scent of cut firewood permeated throughout. There was also a more familiar smell, but he couldn't quite put his finger on what it was.

Then he heard the plucking of a string.

Kirk rolled over.

"Thought that would get you up," a man spoke with the deepest voice Kirk believed he'd ever encountered. The speaker sat at a square table with a worn guitar in his lap. A fireplace lit up his right profile and lent him a carroty hue. There was a beard, thick, but not unleashed to full potential.

Rain pattered off a roof, harsh in its applause. Fire

crackled and stars floated above the blaze.

"If that didn't work, I was going to wave the pot around your head," the man said.

"Excuse me?"

"Pot. Cooking pot."

The man pointed with the guitar's narrow head, to a steaming pot resting on the table.

Food. Kirk's stomach rumbled. "I can smell it."

The beard hitched into a hidden smile. "I bet. Not often I crack open a can. Very rare I crack open two. One usually does me. People eat too much anyway. But I figure you'd need it."

Another set of string picking, nice and slow, befitting the fireside ambiance. The guy could play.

"Where am I?" Kirk asked.

"My house. Such as it is."

"How'd I get here?"

"Hell if I know. You landed on my front porch and lay there. Buck-naked I might add. You on anything? Crack or blow or…?"

Kirk shook his head.

"Huh," the man said, not wholly convinced. "Well, you just keep that blanket on you. Keep everything civil. Where are your clothes anyway?"

Kirk thought about it. "Out there. Maybe near a railway track."

The guitar twanged off-note. "Up by the tracks? You weren't trying to kill yourself, were you?"

"What? No," Kirk sat up, holding the blanket in place as

he was indeed without a stitch. He placed his back against a wall's rough grain. "I was walking. Maybe a little drunk… and fell."

At the last couple of words, Kirk inspected his damaged hand. The alien mouth had sealed, leaving only a fading pink line. "Maybe clocked my head."

The bearded man grunted. "Maybe. The tracks are a hundred feet or so that way. A long way to walk without any senses. You scared the hell outta me."

As he spoke, he plucked guitar strings for punctuation. "I was debating on what to have for supper when you stopped by. Made me jump. Just my luck you were a fella and not a woman."

"Sorry."

"S'all right. A little company isn't a bad thing."

"So you live along the tracks?"

"Yeah."

"Is there a town around here?"

The guy flattened a hand against the guitar's dark sound hole, hushing it, but the rain filled the silence. "Yeah, there's one upalong. Little place called Drover. I go there sometimes. In the summer. Sell some carvings. Play some music."

Kirk stared, realizing the man's mouth barely moved when he talked, or at least appeared that way. "You wouldn't happen to have a phone, would you?"

"No."

Shit, Kirk's expression said. "Think there would be one in Drover?"

"A phone? Sure. They got lots. At least a hundred people or so living up there. Drover's not a big place. Trains run by it. Roads go through it. Probably won't be a town anymore in the next fifty years or so. Young folks are all heading to the city or someplace else."

"You think they got a payphone?"

"Payphone, payphone." The man thought about it. "Not in town. But there might be one at the bus terminal. Small place. Built onto the service station. If there's one anywhere it might be there. You hungry?"

"Yeah."

"Want some of this?" he said, indicating the pot.

"What is it?"

"Picky, are you?" the beard flexed. "Beans and wieners."

"Yes, please. Thanks."

"All right." He placed the guitar away and looked around the interior, barely the size of Kirk's own living room. Probably smaller. The walls were bare, old, and uninsulated, but the woodworking appeared solid in the firelight. A low barrier divided the space. Kirk realized it was a customer counter, and that he was sitting in a small office building of sorts, with a fireplace in the back. A wiry cot rested against the far wall, tucked close to the fireplace, with a dessert topping of blankets.

"I'm Owen," the bearded man said, pulling a second pot from the stocked shelves. He realized what it was and put it back. "Adams."

"Kirk," he replied without thinking.

Owen got out a pair of scratched plastic bowls and

spoons. He divided up the food, and Kirk thought one bowl received a little more than the other. Owen slap-wiped his hands on his jeans and sat back down at the table. He pointed at the chair on the other side. "You're there, unless you want to eat where you are."

Kirk got up, his frame sheathed in a cotton blanket. "Awkward," he said as he sat at the table.

Owen shrugged. "Be more awkward if you were a woman."

"Sorry."

"Yeah, I don't have great luck in that department."

They ate, noisily, drowning out the rain. Once done, Owen dropped the bowls into an old-fashioned sink. Kirk scanned the walls, eyeing patches of coarse wallpaper that peeled around the upper edges. Old but clean. The mattress he'd woken up on was really a sleeping bag.

"Clean them up in the morning," Owen said of the dishes.

"What is this place?" Kirk asked. "Not a house."

"This? This was supposed to be a station agent's office just up from the town. Small one. Befitting of Drover's stature. But then plans changed and the train company decided they didn't need to stop here. Or Drover. Just go right on through both. This was back in the thirties or forties, y'see, and seein' as the train wasn't going to stop here, well, a lot of people decided not to live here. Some did, of course, don't ask me why. Mostly small scale corn farmers. The soil was decent, I suppose. The land cheap. Clean water nearby. Not a hard decision to make if you like the country.

Anyway, this place just got left here. And the roof is still in fair shape. I found it some thirty-odd years ago. Decided it liveable enough. The price was right so I moved in. Figured if people didn't want me around, they'd kick me out, but no one did."

Owen sat at the table and leaned back. He didn't pick up the guitar. "You need to take a leak, there's an outhouse out back. Twenty paces. Just follow your nose."

"You live here by yourself?" Kirk asked.

"Just me."

Kirk wouldn't ask any more, felt it impolite. "Thanks for taking me in. And feeding me. Not many would do that."

No one would do that, his brain stated.

Owen nodded sagely. "You're welcome. Just passing through, I take it?"

"Yeah. Going west."

"West is nice, they say."

"Yeah, well, we'll see."

"Looking for work or something?"

Kirk smiled. "Or something."

"Gotcha."

"You say you do carvings?"

"And play a little. In the summertime. Carve mostly during the winter months."

"And that gets you by?"

"Until the next tourist season. I don't need much."

Guess not, Kirk figured and glanced around. He saw a shelving unit filled with colorful boxes, all in a row.

"What are those?"

Owen looked. "Puzzles."

"Puzzles?"

"Picture puzzles. Jigsaws."

Kirk smiled, surprised. "You don't read out here?"

"Nah. Not at all. Never did get into reading. Can't read much in the winter time anyway. Gets dark too damn fast. Same with the puzzles, I guess, but I enjoy them better. I collect them when I can. There's a little library in town, could be closing anytime, but they have yard sales and such. I can pick up a five-hundred-piece or a three-thousand-piece puzzle for a buck or two. Those you see over there? They all have their pieces."

"I like puzzles," Kirk said. "Don't hear of too many people doing them anymore."

"Probably too taken up with their phones."

Kirk agreed. "Puzzles."

His life was a puzzle.

One with several missing pieces.

The two men chatted into the night, and Kirk noticed Owen refrained from strumming his old guitar. When he asked him why, the older man stated he hadn't had any guests for a very long time, and didn't think it polite to do so.

"Besides," Owen explained, "conversation's rare for me these days. Can't remember the last time I talked to a person in my home, for what it is. I don't want to be distracted."

A part of Kirk liked that explanation. Another part wondered if Owen was just waiting for him to fall asleep, to ensure that his guest wouldn't try and attack and maybe steal whatever money Owen might've squirreled away.

So they talked.

Until the fire died down, and sleep would not let either of them talk any longer.

*

The next morning Kirk guided Owen back through wet brush and grass, back to the place where he dropped his hockey bag beside the train tracks. The older man had given him an old but serviceable sweater that stretched, and a pair of pants that were about three inches too short in the legs. Still, for walking outside, it was something against the cold. The sky remained grim with gray clouds, and the air swollen with a frigid dampness that suggested more rain in the future. Kirk grimaced as he hiked, eyed the ground for broken glass. He walked barefoot, not knowing where his boots were. Owen had offered him a spare pair of sneakers, but they were too small.

"No one bothers me out here," Owen said as they picked their way along. "Too damn far. Takes me almost half a day to walk to town. Only going to get longer from here on."

"You got a bike?"

"I do, but even that's getting wobbly."

"What'll you do when you get…"

"Older?" Owen asked without offense. "Haven't figured that out yet. There's nothing in town and I really don't exist on paper. Government doesn't know I'm here. I don't get mail. No checks or anything. So I don't know. Maybe I'll just lie down and wait for the end. Maybe I'll walk into town and ask around, maybe I'll get put into an old folks' home or something. That your bag?"

Kirk looked, following Owen's nod, and saw the torn sack discarded amongst some grass, not ten feet from the train tracks. "That's it."

He trod lightly and picked it up.

Owen hunkered down and reached for something in the grass.

"Watch yourself," the old guitar man said. He straightened, holding out a bloody sliver of glass.

"Damn quads" Owen muttered, taking out a handkerchief and wrapping up the fragment. "Always ripping along the tracks and trails. Riders get liquored up and toss their beer bottles all over the place. Someone must've cut themselves."

"Yeah," Kirk said, feeling the heat rush to his face.

"Only hope it was one of them bastards."

Kirk didn't answer. The bag swung at his side and glass tinkled. Owen looked up at the sound.

"Ah," Kirk lay the bag down again and opened it up. He pulled out the rum and whiskey bottles."

Owen's face lit up. "Well, well. Those are good friends to have on the trail."

"You drink?"

"At times."

"They're yours. For last night's sleepover."

"Startin' to like you more and more."

"Here you go, then. For taking my ass in. How'd you get me in the door anyway?"

"Wasn't easy," Owen stated and took the bottle of Uncle Jack. He undid the top and sniffed, a smile spreading across his face. "That's good. Real good. Looks like we got some afternoon entertainment. You got anything else in there?"

"Only wet clothes."

"Them your boots?"

Kirk blinked. They must have spilled free at some point. He retrieved them from the grass. "Your eyes are better than mine."

"Just know the area is all. Those things fit you?"

"Not really. They're too tight."

"That's too bad. One of the worst things in the world, tight boots."

Kirk could think of a few others.

Owen lifted his face to the sky. "Weather's unsettled. Might rain. Might not. I got a clothesline by the house. Let's head on back and hang them clothes up. Maybe get them dry enough for the evening fire."

On the walk back, Kirk smelled the air, the cold possibility of rain, but nothing out of the ordinary. He was somewhere in the countryside and half a day from the nearest town. Unease tingled along his spine. He knew he shouldn't dally with Owen for very long, that he should be on the move as soon as possible. His hunters hadn't given up, that was a fact, and they were behind him, somewhere.

Eyeing his water-logged hockey bag and boots, Kirk considered camping out for another night at least. Of course, he could always leave as a werewolf.

He just might have to.

We'll see, he told himself.

11

They returned to the old station, its entrance partially hidden behind a row of elms. A lake rested not twenty feet below the weather-beaten shack, ruffled by a building wind. Owen approved. He motioned for Kirk to empty the hockey bag, and together the two men hung the wet garments on a clothesline behind the station.

"You think it'll dry?" Kirk asked.

"If the rain holds off."

"In time for me to move on while there's still light?"

"No. Not in time for that. It'll be dark soon."

Kirk frowned.

"Why?" Owen asked. "You in a hurry?"

"Yeah."

"You could leave and walk on with what you're wearing," the old man said.

"Yeah."

"Come inside and let's have a wait. See what happens."

Kirk looked across the water's increasingly angry surface and the surrounding woodland. He shrugged and moped inside.

Once out of the cold, Owen took his time getting a fire going. Kirk studied some of the wood carvings the man had begun. He stood in the far corner of the house, in what would've been the waiting area of the station, and picked a small piece from a shelf. A block of discarded, hand-sawed wood, shaved and picked at by sharpened steel. The craftsmanship surprised him.

"Is this..." he started and held out the carving. "You did this?"

Owen turned from the fireplace, the first few ribbons brightening his profile. "Don't like it?"

"No, it's good. Just never saw a banjo-playing dwarf before."

"That's good, then. Most folks who bought those carvings never saw them before either. That's the novelty."

Kirk studied the shelves' occupants, an odd assortment of fantasy folk in various poses—working in a garden, singing, cooking. "You made all these?"

"Yep. Those are from last year. The ones that didn't sell. Weren't many tourists around town this past summer. Don't know why. Hopefully next year will be better. Sell off the rest. I'll whittle away and see if I can't make another twenty or so. Maybe twenty-five. Takes me about a week to do one. To get it just right."

"The faces are kinda out of focus."

Owen chuckled. "That's my fault. I need glasses for the finer work. Had a magnifying glass but I dropped a load of firewood on the damn thing. I'll buy a new one when I can afford it. Or find one in the landfill."

The old man stood back from the fireplace, pulled up a chair, and, before sitting down, positioned Kirk's boots before the flames. The men sat at the table and Owen placed the bottles of rum and whiskey in front of him. He retrieved two porcelain mugs, one depicting a scenic coastline, the other displaying a white rabbit. The white rabbit went to Kirk.

"One finger or two?" the older man asked, the rum bottle poised.

Kirk slumped. "The whole hand."

So Owen filled it to the brim.

They drank, the crackling fire and claps of mugs punctuating each minute of silence. When the room started to warm, Owen got up and threw cans of soup into a pot. He opened up a closet and waved a hand over his provisions.

"That's a lot of canned food," Kirk said.

"I stock up for the winter."

"Those crackers I see?"

"They are. Unsalted. I get enough of that. If it wasn't for the walking, I think my blood pressure would blow the top of my head off. There are a few farms around. I pick up fresh fruit when they're in season. Blueberries grow around the lake there. I do okay."

They finished off the soup and left the pots and dishes in the sink. The rum went down in warm shivers, but smoothed out as the afternoon went on. After the first mug was finished, it was refilled with whiskey.

"Isn't there a rule about mixing?"

Owen didn't stop pouring. "Not in this house."

So they clacked clay and sipped, the resulting burn equaling the heat from the fireplace.

"This is yours now," Kirk told him, indicating the last of the whiskey. "Shouldn't you be saving this for Christmas or something?"

"I could, but it's better to share a drink with company."

"Suppose so," Kirk muttered, thinking of his paperbacks.

"So what's this you hope to find out west?" Owen asked, around the halfway point of the second salvo of alcohol.

Kirk had just enough of a glow on to answer.

"An old friend."

"Lady friend?"

"Yeah."

"Close lady friend?"

That drew a sigh from Kirk. "Yeah. Sorta. Maybe."

Owen nodded while keeping an eye on the fireplace. "Well, if you want to talk about it, this is it. Chances are I'm not going to remember anything in the morning, anyway."

"Yeah, we were close once."

"You wanted to be closer?"

"Yeah."

"But she didn't?"

Kirk smirked at the bearded man. "You want to tell this story?"

As an answer, Owen hid his smile behind a shot of whiskey. His eyes crinkled around the corners.

"Let's just say…" Kirk thought about it, "that I wanted more from her than maybe she wanted from me. The biggest thing was that I had issues. With myself. And she recognized them. Identified them. Pointed them out. And decided I had to work them out on my own."

Owen nodded. "And did you?"

A knot of wood exploded with a firecracker's bang.

"Still working on it," Kirk quietly reported.

Owen took a drink, wiped his mouth, and turned his attention to the fire. "Y'know, back before I became something of a recluse, I had a few women. One in particular I probably liked a lot more than I should have. Maybe even loved her. I thought she might've felt the same way, and for a few weeks it seemed like… she would have been the one who would've changed my life. I mean, family, nice house, a dog or cat or whatever she'd wanted. But, I was stupid about things. Especially saying dumb things at the worst possible time. In the worst possible place. If I could trace the exact moment where it all started to go bad, it was within a five-minute window. Framed. Just like a picture with a big red X drawn on it, as a warning to others. The things I said made her think I wasn't the one for her."

"You're depressing me now," Kirk mumbled.

"Sorry. I am. But… I'm here, in this place, because I chose to be. There are times when I wish I chose different, but of course, a person can never go back. Still, if she had to appear on my doorstep, say tomorrow morning, and greet me with a smile on her face or even a plain old 'Hello, Owen,' well, I'd leave it all. And try for better."

He slowly waved a hand to complete the spell. "Leave it all in a second."

Kirk nodded. "Yeah. I hear you."

"One last thing on the subject," Owen said. "Like I mentioned. That moment where it all went bad. I don't blame her at all for pushing me away. I'd a done the same thing. Point is, be aware of whatever might have caused that rift, apologize, and never repeat it. Avoid it. Stay away from it like it was bad gas. That's all I have to say about that."

Kirk matched Owen's shot with a respectable one of his own. He sat and thought, and from his drunken radiance, a budding curiosity took hold. One that picked at the back of his mind, unwantedly, because Owen was a decent sort, and Kirk was fortunate to have found him and have his home as a port during a very dangerous storm. For that reason alone, he should not ask the guitar man anything. Not a thing about that special lady in his life, who had left him so long ago.

But he did.

"What did you say to her?" Kirk released, slowly, as if edging his tongue towards a whirling fan.

Owen sighed and shrugged his shoulders.

"Forget I asked," Kirk said.

"No, it's okay. Maybe if I talk about it, it'll get rid of the memory. Paint it over, so to speak.

"Maybe."

Owen fidgeted and straightened, taking his time, causing Kirk to think he wasn't going to say anything more on the subject. But then the guitar man placed a hand on the table and looked into the fire.

"It was our third time together. Third date. Back in the seventies. We went back to my place. She went into the bedroom and switched off the light, but I could still see her, glowing, like silver in moonlight. We both got undressed and, well, went to bed. I pleasured her, then she pleasured me, with not a sound except our breathing. Then we got it on right. It was the sweetest, most wonderful thing I'd ever experienced, I'll tell you that. And half way through that rocking, I slowed down, to catch my breath, and looked into those dark, dark pools that were her eyes, staring back into mine. Still inside her, I ran a hand over her brow, so very smooth, and I asked her. Earnestly. Sincerely. If she'd ever fucked a squirrel."

Kirk blinked. Not quite believing he'd heard correctly. He licked his lips, studied his mug for a moment, and felt the need to scratch at an ear.

"And I mean a red squirrel," Owen clarified. "They can get to be as big as a cat. Sexy animals. Real sexy. The tail does it for me. That S-shaped swirl you just want to grab and hold on to. Real tight. Make them black eyes just pop, you know? That big bushy tail. They wave it at you, y'know, when they're in their trees. Wave it right at you as if to say, 'Come get it. C'mon boy, come get it. You want it. I can tell you want it, and who wouldn't want it? If you catch me, you can have it. You can have it all. The whole thing.' The ears are damn sexy, too. I could fuck one of them ears all day, I think. Fuck it hard. Just pound away until I pass out from dehydration. They talk dirty, too. You listen to a squirrel. They swear but they talk dirty. Mm-hm. All day. Dirty squirrels. Dirty, dirty squirrels. I wrote a song about it. Says it all. Called 'Squirrel Fucking.'"

Kirk smiled, barely able to hold it back.

"Nasty," Owen hissed and took another sip of his drink. He glanced over the rim, saw Kirk squirming, and sprayed whiskey in a bark of laughter.

Kirk joined him.

"You bastard," the Halifax warden finally got out after a solid minute of laughter. He wiped his eyes. "You had me. Right up to the drop."

"I could tell," Owen said. "Had some friends say they couldn't tell when I was being serious or funny at times. Which, sometimes, will make or break the telling."

"That was hilarious." Kirk sighed. "Needed that. Thank you."

In the afterglow of the joke, both men settled down, remembering the moment.

"I asked her to marry me," Owen finally whispered. "That's what I did. Asked her to marry me. On the third date. And I was serious, too. But she... she wasn't. Not at that point. And I don't blame her. Not in the least. Regardless, I said it. And meant it. Meant every word."

Owen shrugged. "The one that got away, right?"

Kirk understood all too well. After a while he said, "Place is getting warm."

"She's an old house," the older man stated and looked over her ceiling. "But she holds the heat. The windows rattle sometimes. The timbers creak. But it's warm in the winter and the rain doesn't get in. She'll do."

Kirk suspected Owen wished for more.

A few minutes later, upon Owen's suggestion, a buzzing Kirk went outside and retrieved his wind-blown clothes. Everything was damp, so the two men hung the t-shirts, jeans and pajama bottoms around the cabin's interior.

"The fire will dry it all," Owen said.

Looking out a window, Kirk noticed neat rows of cut and dried firewood, just behind the station. "You do all that?"

"I did."

"Anyone help you?"

That got him a frown.

"You chopped wood and hauled it here?" Kirk asked doubtfully.

"I chop everything, saw everything, and lug it back here one load at a time. You'll notice the wood isn't that big around. I leave the big ones and just cut the younger ones. Easier to manage. But, sometimes, I'll get angry about something and take an axe to one of them bigger ones."

Owen returned to the table and sized up the remaining whiskey and rum. "How about we finish this all off?"

Kirk thought it was a fine idea.

*

The next morning, Kirk gratefully accepted a jug of water. Owen's fuzzy features looked even more tangled from last night's drinking, and he sounded as if some mischievous imp had salted and fried his vocal chords. It was soup for breakfast, and once they got it down, Kirk felt the residual alcohol drain away. Owen, however, did not.

A little later, with the clouds gone and a bright sun

present, Kirk gathered up his few belongings, pulled on those uncomfortable boots and bathrobe, and left the station house. Owen followed him out the door and stopped on the front step.

"Well, thanks for the company," the guitar man said.

"Thanks for taking me in."

Owen shrugged. "Sorry I can't come into town with you. You head on in. Find the bus station built into the side of Allison's service station. If there's a payphone in town, it'll be there. Here."

The old guitar man held out a fist.

Kirk looked at it. "What's that?"

"Some money."

"I can't take that."

"You want to contact your lady friend, you'll need this."

"You worked hard for that."

"It's not work if you enjoy what you're doing. You take it. If you find that payphone, in Drover or the next town over, it'll need cash. Take it."

Kirk reluctantly did so.

A collection of quarters, loonies, and toonies filled his hand. No paper money.

"You get this out of a can?" Kirk smiled.

"I did, actually. Old coffee can with a bit of cloth at the bottom so the first few coins won't rattle so much. That first bit of change hitting the bottom is a lonely sound. It's not much, but it's a phone call, that's all. No big riches being bestowed here."

And it wasn't. Kirk saw that he had perhaps ten dollars

in his hand, give or take a buck. But knowing how Owen came about getting the money made it worth so much more.

"Thank you, Owen. For everything. Not many would help out a naked guy passed out on their doorstep."

"How did that happen, anyway?"

"I'd rather not say."

Owen nodded, not pressing the issue. "Follow the tracks thataway," he dipped his head northward. "They run right by the town. It's not much, really, but maybe they'll lead you to your phone. And mind yourself around the service station. The owners are flat-out weird. Don't really like them. They give me hard looks, like I'm an escaped convict or something."

"Got it."

"And good luck with your lady friend. You just might be in for a surprise."

"Maybe." Kirk backed away, held up the fistful of coins, and nodded at the old guitar man. "Thank you again."

Owen lifted a hand in goodbye, and retreated into the station house where it was warmer.

Kirk took one last look at the calm lake and the surrounding forest, wondering if he'd ever see the place again. He hoped so. Maybe even repay Owen's neighborly acts of kindness. It suddenly occurred to him that while he was staying with the old man, he never got the urge to kill and eat him. Kirk wondered why that was.

The railroad tracks stretched off into the distance and he walked on their shoulders.

12

By late afternoon, Kirk's tired feet led him to a quaint junction town. A few houses came into view, peeking out from behind thickets of trees that couldn't hide the bright paint jobs or vinyl siding. A collection of old-fashioned Victorians and modest bungalows. Some houses had been built uncomfortably close to each other, but wide swards of undeveloped woodland separated the rest. A single road crossed the railway tracks at one point, a more modern lifeline. Kirk stayed on the tracks, now straddled by two high walls of exposed soil, and garnished by long, unbroken hedges of what might one day grow into raspberry bushes.

Anyone living inside that charming little town would have seen him from the shoulders up.

A chainsaw buzzed in a distant backyard somewhere, but Drover was silent otherwise. Sleepy, not yet aware of its visitor passing through. Kirk remained wary, wondering if the goodwill extended to him by Owen Adams ended with Owen Adams.

Reluctant to leave the tracks, Kirk walked on. The bushes

thinned out and the incline sank. A side road, just beyond a white fence, ran parallel with the railway. He looked for people and saw none. A quiet-looking bungalow came into view, with a heavy-duty quad parked in its backyard and a silver pickup parked five feet from the backdoor. Kirk didn't linger, didn't want to be accused of spying on private property. With the way he looked, he might draw the ire of the property owners, who might very well call in the law.

Kirk wanted to avoid the law.

The white fence disappeared, replaced by a line of towering elms. The trees partially concealed a large, white building with two closed garage bay doors. "Allison's Service Station" appeared in large black lettering, framed in a stretched octagon with a golden trim.

Kirk studied the station. Nothing out of the ordinary, so he left the tracks, hoping the place was open. He passed through the trees and, with all the anxiety of a deer, stepped onto the deserted road. A diamond-shaped sign greeted him as he sped towards the station. The words "BUS STOP" had been altered with red paint, fuzzing out letters until "PUS SIP" remained.

Kirk frowned. There were assholes everywhere.

The service station had two small cars parked in front of an older model he didn't recognize. A few stacked tires filled with dirt lay on their sides next to a low wall of bare rims. The tires got him thinking about chocolate ice cream cones covered in sprinkles for some reason. A shop had been built onto the main garage, to the left, and wide windows allowed a clear view of a small waiting area.

He hurried to the main door.

Behind him, the town remained eerily indifferent.

Bells jingled overhead as he entered, announcing his presence, but no one was there to care. A white counter, covered in metallic napkin dispensers, led to a ticket booth at the far left. A large sign detailing destinations, signs, and prices hung above the window. Shelves of magazines and packaged snacks were behind the counter, well out of reach, along with a soda machine, coffee machine, and racks of sugar-glazed donuts.

A security camera, situated in the corner above a door, watched him with a black eye. Kirk suspected the garage bay was beyond the door. A silver bell perched on the counter dared him to take his best shot. Kirk avoided the urge and instead scouted the building for signs of life. No one waited in the area beyond the empty ticket booth. The parking and bus boarding zones were deserted. He looked to the brown door, the silver bell, and the bus station waiting room.

The countertop gleamed from perhaps an early morning wipe. Shrugging his eyebrows, Kirk rang the bell. That single piercing note hung on the air for seconds. It wasn't silver, but shiny enough to be mistaken for it.

No one appeared.

Kirk rang the bell again and waited.

And waited.

Sighing, he rang the bell a third time and eyed the rows of potato chips, candy bars, and donuts behind the counter. If he stretched over, really stretched, he could grab one. The security camera watched him, however, warning him not to try.

Kirk lifted his hand to ring the bell once again when the garage door flew open.

Thin, mid-height, dressed in a green-black coverall with a camouflage pattern of grease stains and smudges, stood a lady with blue eyes. Dark-blue eyes, frowning. She'd tied her hair back in a girlish ponytail and Kirk caught himself staring. Not because she was the mechanic, but because she was quite attractive.

"You rang?" she asked, mouth twisting unpleasantly.

"I rang."

"Had my head underneath a chassis," she explained and sniffed hard, as if containing a cold. "Couldn't hear a thing."

"It's okay."

"You gotta really hit this thing."

Kirk nodded.

"I mean, *really*."

The very attractive woman, who probably could've graced her own calendar, stepped behind the counter and slapped the bell as if squashing a cockroach.

Repeatedly.

"Like this, see?" she said as she slammed the metal dome with the full force of her arm. Determination colored her cheeks as she pounded out a furious code. "Like this. Gotta hit it like this. Y'see? Like *this*."

She bared teeth as she demonstrated, hitting the bell even harder.

Dingdingding.

Kirk took a step back as the woman wailed on that little bell, seemingly intent on ringing the metal coating off its hide. Any second, he fully expected the chime's blunt top to break the skin of her hand.

The tip of her tongue popped out and her teeth trapped it.

DINGDINGDINGDINGDINGDINGDINGDINGDINGDINGDINGDINGDING.

Then she stopped, and took a deep, meditative breath.

"Like that," she whispered, her energy spike depleted.

A speechless Kirk wasn't entirely certain he'd heard correctly.

The mechanic flexed her hand as if she'd burned it, clenched it into a fist, and dropped it to her side in a way that suggested he had best not bring up the matter.

But he did, anyway. "You okay?"

"I hate that thing," her words slipped out. "I wanted the electronic sign for the garage. One that flashes and changes colors and attracts the eye. A few hundred bucks but the peace and quiet is worth it. No. We got *that*. That one right there. Came with the station, you see. And it works. If all is dead in the garage. It works. If I'm welding or changing tires, or tinkering with a motor's guts, with my face down and ass up, I can't hear a thing. Not a damn thing."

She ran her hands down the front of her coverall, as if wiping them, but her palms lingered just a split second over her breasts, enough for Kirk to notice. A natural enough reaction, but he flinched all the same when his eyes went there, flinched as if scaled by a hot cloud of steam.

The woman watched him. She didn't blink. Didn't speak, either. She looked him in the eye and breathed, as if waiting for him to draw a pistol or something.

Kirk did no such thing. He retreated another step, widening the space between them, and very much considered getting the hell out of there.

Then the brown door swung open a second time. A man, a modern-day, middle-aged ogre, entered the bus station. He was horribly unshaven, his entire chin a prickly rash, and dressed in a tight, form-fitting pinstripe shirt and bowtie. A pair of glasses appeared glued to his face and, for an instant, Kirk thought they were protective goggles. The man pouted at the Halifax warden as if about to bestow the biggest, driest kiss Kirk had ever been on the receiving end of, and then looked to the lady mechanic.

"Did you ring that gosh-darned thing?" He spoke through clenched teeth, as if his jaw had been wired shut. "Hm? Did you?"

The air hitched in Kirk's throat. The overpowering scent of bar soap, the cheap road-stop kind, enveloped the large man like a killer gas. He wondered if the guy had bathed in it or simply just lathered it on, like a self-greasing monkey.

"I rang it," the mechanic answered defiantly, her eyes lingering on Kirk as the tension swelled to near meltdown levels. "I rang the gosh-darn thing. I rang that fudge bar of a half-nut bell. I rang it. Me. And I'll ring its hairless dingleberry top whenever I get the chance. Whenever I want."

She stroked her ponytail. "For fun."

Her tall, portly companion, despite being well-dressed for the position (Kirk assumed he was the bus station attendant—but couldn't get the bowtie), didn't appear to breathe, but he continued to pout with an expression of *I've just sucked the nuts off the biggest lemon you've ever seen*.

"I asked you not to ring the bell, Jenna," the man said. "I've asked you several times. Several times. That bell is for customers only."

"He's a customer."

The big man turned his fashionably framed goggles upon Kirk.

"I only wanted to use the payphone," the warden got out quickly.

"He only wanted to use the payphone, Jenna," the big man rattled off. "He only wanted to use the phone. That was all. Did you tell him?"

Jenna sighed, an expulsion of breath that could've knocked over a house.

"You didn't, did you? You didn't tell him."

"I just got here."

"You were out here for a good minute or so but you spent that time wanging that chicken dinger. No wonder business is terrible. Terrible."

"I got work to do," Jenna said. She marched past the larger man, who recoiled as if she were infected by some unholy disease. Jenna took her time exiting through the garage door and slammed it shut, or at least tried to slam it, but the hydraulic piston set inside prevented that very thing. The door closed with a click.

Kirk decided the attendant had installed that. "You must be…?"

"I'm Alice," the big man stated.

"You."

"Me."

"You're…"

"I'm Alice. I just said I'm Alice. How many times do I have to tell you? You think that's funny or something? For a man to be called a gosh-darned girl's name?"

Kirk didn't answer, was afraid to answer.

"Well it is, darn it," Alice rumbled. "It is funny. Funnier than… funnier than a dog with gum stuck to its gas-tootin' butt. My mom and dad wanted a girl but they got me. Were certain they were getting a girl. They had the name already picked out. Loved the name. But they got me. Can't waste a good gosh-darned name like Alice, so they used it. Dressed me in all the girl's clothes they'd bought for their daughter, too. Just my cheese and rice luck they had a wardrobe already picked out until I turned four."

Kirk held his tongue, strained to keep his face neutral, strained until it hurt.

"Yeppers," Alice continued in that clenched-jaw ramble. "Fun-nee. Sweet pickles. Sweet pickles and juice. Take a guess what toys I had until I was seven? Go on, take a guess. I dare you."

Kirk shook his head, just enough to show he'd heard.

"Well, you should be able to guess," Alice fired off.

"I don't want to guess."

"Guess. Go on. Guess."

"No," Kirk said quietly. "I can't."

"Like the ruck you can't."

"Excuse me?"

"Huh?"

"What did you just say?"

"I said like the ruck."

"The ruck," Kirk repeated dubiously.

"What's the matter, you never heard of that before?"

"I have not."

"Well, you should. Should use it. It's polite. The polite way of saying like the duck, if you get my meaning. Or, what the cluck! That's a good one right there. I'll use that later. Crispy bacon waffles and burnt bums. Maybe not that one. What do you think? You think only church folk don't like to cuss? Hm? Only them fancy duckers? Hm? No sir. Not in a long way. I don't like profanity, but I readily admit to the therapeutic stress release of a good, non-offensive cuss."

"I see," Kirk said, recognizing that someone had missed their medication. "Look, I just came in here for a payphone. I couldn't see one."

Alice straightened and regarded Kirk with that lethal kissy-face pucker, stared at him like a microbiologist dueling with bacteria cultures. "We don't have a payphone."

Well, shit. Kirk thought.

"We took it out," Alice explained. "No one uses a payphone anymore. No one. Everyone's got one of them fancy communicators now. Ever watch Star Trek? That's what the new phones of today are. Modern-day communicators. I don't have one, however. I have one in mind, a design I'm working on. It has a large battery in it. Very large battery. Capable of firing a self-defense charge.

One zap and your attacker's toes will permanently curl. That's my design. I've already initiated the patent process so forget everything I just said."

But Kirk had already zoned out, annoyed that he had endured Alice for this long only to discover there was no phone.

"Thanks," Kirk said and turned to the door.

"We do have a regular phone," Alice said, reeling him back.

Kirk slowly faced the owner. "So you have a phone."

"Never said we didn't have a telephone. Said we don't have a payphone. There's a difference. One takes money. The other doesn't. We have the kind that doesn't take money. A telephone."

Kirk wasn't in the mood to subject himself to the asshole behind the counter. He considered leaving and moving on, maybe even knocking on the door of one of Drover's residents.

"Can I use it?" Kirk finally asked, against his better judgment.

"You can if you're able," came Alice's condescending reply.

Fuck, Kirk fumed. "How much to use your phone?"

Alice considered it. At least, Kirk thought the man was considering it. That tightened button of lips remained in place as if waiting for a drop of moisture to unstick itself.

"Where are you calling?" Alice asked.

"Ontario."

"Toronto?"

"Yeah, Toronto."

"Eight dollars will get you two minutes."

"Two minutes. How long for ten dollars?"

"Five minutes. And not a second over."

Kirk fished out the change and slapped it on the counter, a little louder than intended. Alice considered the money, considered him, and then dipped below the counter as if touching his toes. He placed an old rotary telephone before Kirk, a beige one, with a red-painted finger stop.

"That's your phone?" Kirk deadpanned.

"Of course it's my phone. It was underneath my counter. Who else would keep their telephone underneath my counter?"

Not many, Kirk thought. "Does it work?"

Alice glowered and left the question unanswered.

"Okay to use it?" Kirk asked.

"If you know how."

Kirk understood how Jenna felt. Not a minute in Alice's presence and he was already tempted to throttle him.

Alice nudged the telephone forward, the plastic housing unblemished and glowing.

Kirk picked up the receiver and listened for a tone. Surprisingly there was one.

Alice magically brought forth a little plastic timer as well, and held the device at his shoulder after setting it for five minutes. He aimed the display at Kirk, who kept his mouth shut and stuck his finger in the first number hole.

Alice didn't move.

"This is a private call," Kirk said.

"I understand that," Alice answered, the timer held at his shoulder.

"I'd like to be alone."

"You can't be alone. This is the reception area for the service station. And that's the bus station. I'm the owner of both and I'm also the only person working here. I can't leave either area unattended. Not with customers coming and going all the time. Security, you see."

Customers. Kirk stared at the bottle cap glasses and then, for dramatic effect, looked around the empty reception area before returning to Alice.

The bowtie-wearing freak didn't budge.

"That thing have a long cord?" Kirk asked.

"Only as long as the counter."

Kirk took the phone and slid it to the counter's end. Not impressed, Alice's asshole lips puckered even tighter.

Taking his eyes off the odd character, Kirk dialed Carma's number. The rotary wheel whirred and clicked at the end of every number with old-fashioned charm. He faced the brown door and wondered offhand what Jenna might be working on back there.

One ring.

Two rings.

Three rings.

Kirk frowned and willed Carma to answer. Cemented to his spot, Alice watched with an index finger poised over the timer's start button, five minutes prominently displayed.

The connection went through. "Hello?"

"Carma?"

Beep.

Alice pushed the button and, seemingly uninterested, faced the main window. The timer counted down in his left hand.

"Douglas, is that you?" Carma's distressed voice pulled Kirk back.

"Yeah, it's me."

"Holy shit, Douglas, what the hell's going on? There's a hunt for you, you know that?"

"What?" Kirk stuck a finger in one ear. "What was that?"

"There's a hunt on for you. Initiated and authorized by the elders themselves. They said you were infected with a disease that's turned you into a cannibal. And I mean of *weres*. Wardens are after you. Hell, whole *packs* are after you. I got a telephone call not a day ago and got the word straight from the elder's mouth."

The room faded out and Kirk's knees weakened. His stomach knotted and his skin contracted over his frame like a vacuum seal. "Jesus Christ."

From the other side of the counter, Alice cleared his throat in a high-pitched grunt of disapproval. Kirk ignored him.

"Was this going on when I was in Halifax?" Carma demanded. "Is that the reason you were so damned worried?"

News of the hunt stunned Kirk speechless. There was a hunt on. For him. Wardens were bad enough, but entire packs? Panic rose in his gullet.

"*Douglas?*" Carma yelled, rattling him from his daze.

"Yeah, look, I can't talk right now. I'm on a phone in a guy's service station."

"You're what?"

"I'm in a guy's service station. I…" Kirk remembered Alice was not ten feet away. "I lost everything, Carma. Everything. I only got the clothes on my back here and those aren't even mine. I knew there was something going on so I left the city. On foot."

"Where are you now?"

"Little town called Drover. In Nova Scotia."

"Drover? What're you going to do?"

Kirk tightened his grip on the receiver. "I was going to see you."

She hesitated, and that scared Kirk badly enough for him to forget about the hunt. Then, "I can meet you halfway," she said.

"No," he whispered back. "You stay there. I'll come to you. Safer that way."

"All right. Where?"

"You name the place."

"The Chicken Whistle. That little Irish pub over on Dundas. You remember the place?"

Kirk closed his eyes. "Yeah."

"You have any money?"

"No."

"Douglas!"

He closed his eyes. "Listen, I don't have much time. I'll try to get to Toronto and give you another call when I get in."

"When do you think you'll get here?"

"I don't know, Carma."

"Douglas, it's a big fucking country and you're on foot. It's a two-day *drive* from Ontario to Nova Scotia. It'll take you weeks to walk here."

"Then it'll take weeks. I'll get there. I'll call when I do."

"The Halifax police are circulating a picture of you. It's online."

That stopped him cold. "What?"

"There's a picture of you out there. I've seen it online but it hasn't reached the news channels here. Not yet. Looks like security camera footage taken when you were opening the loading bay doors, at that mall where we fought Bailey."

Kirk would've smiled any other time.

"The picture has most of your face. It's grainy and dark but it's you. So the cops are on your tail. Something about a shootout in an apartment building. *Your* apartment building."

Kirk pinched the bridge of his nose.

"The elders have teams after you, too. People. Private contractors."

"Yeah, I know about those."

"They've already killed—Oh Christ," Carma faltered. "I… I have some… news. Morris is dead."

Kirk stopped breathing.

"I don't know how or when, but he's dead. The elders told me. One of their teams got him. He's gone, Douglas."

"Morris…" Kirk trailed off, shocked to the core.

What was worse, however, was that his stomach suddenly

demanded attention, rattling its cage hard enough that Kirk could've chewed through the telephone cord. His temples pulsed and his tongue curled. The countertop thumped against his hip and he placed a hand down on the flat surface to steady himself. He looked to the ceiling as he pushed the hunger back down, drawing strength from, of all things, the soapy fragrance that clung to Alice's chunky ass.

"Look," Carma said. "Just tell me one thing. Are the elders right? Are you some kind of cannibal now?"

"No," Kirk lied, the word coming out in a lurch. "Not like… Look, I'll see you in the city, okay? Just give me a little time and I'll call you. Say—"

Beep.

The high-pitched note didn't register with Kirk until he realized Carma had become eternally quiet.

"Hello?" he looked from the dead receiver to Alice.

The man had the telephone's cord pulled free of the wall, the end dangling from his hand.

The last few days had pressed down upon Kirk with all the weight of a collapsing ice shelf, and the absolute last thing he needed was some backward, soda-jerking hick fucking around with his telephone call.

"Your time's up," Alice informed him. The station owner made a second mistake in failing to recognize the sudden plummet in room temperature. "I'll take that back."

"Put that back into the wall," Kirk said quietly.

"Your time's up, buddy," Alice reaffirmed, his jaw set, but he noticed the change in his customer's demeanor.

"Put. That fucking wire. Back."

Alice shook his head. "Your time's up and I don't care for your use of—"

Kirk grabbed him.

One instant the warden was at the end of the counter and the next he was clutching at the stiff fabric of Alice's pinstripe shirt.

Alice was a big man, vase-shaped and perhaps well over three hundred pounds.

Kirk pulled him forward, hard and powerful enough that seams ripped in Alice's shirt. Buttons popped like bottle caps as Alice's gut was dragged over the countertop's edge. The bigger man's eyes bulged behind his goggles as Kirk yanked him onto the flat surface.

A frightened Alice panted, on the verge of squealing, and bent his knees underneath his gut. His bowtie twisted like a warped propeller. The telephone dropped to the floor with a clatter.

Kirk got in his rash-splotched face. "Put that cord back into the wall."

Alice wiggled, hissed, and struggled in a frenzied fright. He wheezed as if gripped by asthma. He grabbed Kirk's wrists and pushed back, fighting for leverage, using a notable level of strength.

Kirk rattled him. *Hard.* Shaking the taller man like a can of pop. Alice's shirt came undone, his glasses jiggled, and he squealed, a weird man-pig note filled with surprise and petulant rage.

"*EeeeeemuhhhhEEEEEEE!*"

Kirk shook him again and more shirt fibers gave way. He

clamped a hand around Alice's throat and pulled him closer, prompting the service station owner to screech like a vampire in a tanning salon. Kirk blinked away the red in his vision and relaxed his grip. What the hell had he just done?

The station owner huffed and whimpered and blew snot out his nose. He regarded Kirk with red-faced hatred.

"All right," the Halifax warden said, looking to diffuse the situation. "I'm going to let you go, okay? I'm going to let you go and we'll just go our separate ways and forget—"

A heavy force exploded across the back of Kirk's head.

And the last sensation he was aware of, before he dropped into unconsciousness, was that of falling.

13

At some point during his unexpected nap, Kirk became aware of movement, and of voices, just beyond the black periphery of understanding. Wicked little mewlings that discussed things and seemed to carry on forever. Then he was gone again, his awareness pulled down by the ankles, into a vat of tar-like oblivion, as thick and silencing as cement.

Perhaps he was in cement. Not that Kirk was capable of determining that.

He blinked and realized he'd been asleep in a dreamless sludge, with a screaming headache as a souvenir.

Kirk lifted a hand to the back of his skull and located a fleshy knob the size of a golf ball, as malleable as refrigerated butter. His face and legs were cold, chilled by a copper floor, with his knees jammed into his chest. A glowing square resided above him, perfectly cut out of the dark some six feet above his head. *Window*, he groaned, and the only source of light in the whole cramped space.

With a grimace, Kirk sat up and placed his back against

a wall. He touched the opposite wall with his bare toes, discovering that his bathrobe, offensive t-shirts, and boots had been removed. His jeans and pajama bottoms, however, were still in place. The cell was no bigger than a broom closet. His heel skidded over the edge of a hole, a mouth no bigger than a dinner plate, set into a corner. The sharp tang of bleach irritated his nose. *Toilet*, Kirk realized, wondering what the hell he'd gotten himself into this time.

Curious as to what lay beyond the window, he stood. A brief spin of dizziness caused him to lean against a wall. When his senses steadied, he peeked outside.

A smaller room, painted white, with a handyman's peg board over a table and chair. An electric lamp was perched on the table's surface, its lit cone pointed at the ceiling. A solid door, reinforced with metal straps, was set into the right wall.

Nothing else.

Kirk quickly found the cell's ceiling, low and made of concrete. He slapped the door with an open palm, then slapped it again.

"Hey," he shouted. "*Hey!*"

Nothing moved outside his tiny prison. Freezing needles played with his feet, the cold metal nibbling. His face hurt, specifically his jaw and cheeks. He yawned, winced, and tasted blood.

What the fuck happened?

He slapped the door again. "HEY! You out there, Alice? Huh? Let me out of here. Let me out, goddammit. Let me go and I won't call the cops."

Kirk frowned. "Hey, Alice? C'mon, man. Let me go. And where the fuck are my boots?"

The hell was going on? Kirk wondered, holding his head. He looked out at the table and lamp and waited.

Jenna. Jenna must've clubbed him. Right across the brainpan. He'd been so focused on Alice and his angry squirming that he totally missed the mechanic. And now he was in a concrete box, with only a nightlight outside and a hole in the ground for a shitter. He remembered Carma saying the cops had his picture. Jenna and Alice had probably recognized him, knocked him out, and were now waiting for the cops to arrive.

Caught by some weird dweeb and a freaky mechanic. Capturing a wanted felon was probably the highlight of their existence.

A wanted felon. The thought almost made Kirk smile, but then he remembered the other thing Carma had mentioned.

Morris is dead.

Sweet Jesus.

The elders told me. One of their teams got him.

Morris was gone and Kirk suddenly felt very alone indeed. A knot rose in his throat but he swallowed it back, took a deep breath, and steadied himself. The last person in the world he should be sad over was Moses Morris, but his death hit him hard all the same. True to how miserable Kirk's life had been, Morris was probably the closest thing to a friend he had amongst the *weres*. Not that he ever would have said that to Morris. Morris would not have appreciated being called a friend. Not in the least.

But if Kirk thought about it hard enough, Morris really had only one friend himself, and that was the Halifax warden.

Be seein' ya... partner, Kirk projected, and hoped the message was received.

The door's locks slid open, shattering the silence, and a wedge of light appeared across the table and chair. A second, brighter ceiling light snapped to life in the small room and Kirk's cell.

Alice strolled into the room. The Drover man had changed his pinstriped shirt for a thick sweater decorated with a Christmassy snowman, but Alice's expression above that scene was anything but festive. He walked up to the window and peered inside at his captive.

"You're in big trouble, mister," Alice muttered through that perpetual pout of his.

But then Alice stopped as if shot through the chest. He adjusted his thick glasses, pressed his face closer to the window, and steamed up the glass. He studied Kirk intently. Alice's button mouth opened as his unshaven jaw dropped, revealing a fetching landing pad for flies.

Kirk's anger ebbed away as he stared back. "What?"

But Alice didn't answer. Instead, the big man stared down the length of his nose, placed one finger to his sandpapery chin and flicked it, making the fleshy rolls jiggle.

"Oh... *my*," Alice exhaled with astonishment, his eyes blazing.

Kirk pounded the doorframe but nothing budged.

Alice didn't flinch, unconcerned with the display of force. The man pressed closer to the window, nose almost touching and his breath fogging the glass to an even greater degree.

He rubbed the condensation away with a sleeve.

"Oh my, oh my, oh… my," he repeated in complete fascination, his words distorted by the thick glass.

"*What?*" Kirk demanded.

Alice drew back in a queer mix of horror and something else. He kept flicking his chin rolls, paling as if lunch had just turned on him. He quickly exited the room, switching off the main light and slamming the door as he left.

Kirk dabbed at his face, picked at drying blood, but couldn't understand what Alice had seen.

A short time later the main room's door flew open. Alice returned with Jenna in tow, still dressed in her smudgy uniform. The big man stood to one side and pointed a thick finger in their prisoner's direction.

At a complete loss, Kirk stared back in confusion, pawing at the smooth surface where a knob would normally be.

"Oh wow," Jenna said as she got up close and personal to the window. "Oh… *wow.*"

Alice crowded in, his face looming over her shoulder like an evil caricature. "Is that something or what?" he muttered.

"That's something," Jenna agreed, her features glowing with horrified wonder, as if she'd just partially stomped on a cockroach only to watch the bug pull itself free of the squashed bits.

"Hard to believe, isn't it?"

"It is."

"This changes everything."

Jenna rolled her eyes. "You think?"

"What?" Kirk blasted them. "This changes what? *What?*"

Jenna concealed her smile with a coy hand in a decidedly Japanese way, and exchanged knowing looks with Alice.

That only pissed Kirk off even more.

He hammer-fisted the door, barely rattling it and nothing more.

The outburst of force barely interested Alice and Jenna. They stared at their prisoner with all the concern of staring into an empty fishbowl.

Kirk stopped and regarded them with undisguised loathing.

"What do you think we should do?" Jenna asked. "This is a little beyond me."

"Well," Alice said, seeking to hook his thumbs into suspenders and realizing he wasn't wearing any. The expression alone was enough to get a little smile from Kirk.

"Well, I think we should try something," Alice announced. "Just to make sure the results are the same."

"Like what? They look pretty clear to me."

"All experiments have a test control. We don't have another one of him, so I propose we just repeat the process *with* him."

"You mean hit him again? Now?"

The cold gnawing at Kirk's feet slunk past his shins, past his knees, and spread to his crotch as if tickled by a spider's legs. The chill rose higher, reaching for and clenching his heart. All heat left his face.

Oh shit, he realized.

"Watch this," Alice said, and reached for something out of sight, just beyond the door frame.

Kirk readied himself, hoping that smug asshole was about to open the cell. He clenched and unclenched his hands when perhaps a million volts ripped through him, lighting up and exploding his nervous system like an overloaded bulb, sending fragments of consciousness away.

When Kirk dropped, he dropped hard, and knew no more.

Alice didn't smile when he flicked up the safety guard and gave the dial a hard twist, unleashing a near killer current through the superlative conductor that was the copper floor panel. His prisoner, as Alice thought of the man, jumped perhaps five inches off the plate before flopping back down, out of sight.

Whereupon Alice dialed the current back to zero.

"Just like roasting a chicken," Jenna observed and stepped away from the door.

"I didn't roast him. I electrocuted him. A little."

"That was a simile, you turkey."

"It wasn't a very good one," Alice said and checked on the prisoner. Certain that Kirk was subdued, Alice threw open the six reinforced locks and turned the lever. The fragrant stink of ripe excrement and urine fouled the air.

"Oh my," Alice said, pulling his sweater's neckline up over his nose. "Oh my."

"He soiled himself," Jenna said, screwing up her own face.

"He did that."

"I hate it when they do that."

"Me too."

"It's your turn to clean it up."

Alice's shoulders slumped. Jenna was correct, of course. How he hated it when Jenna was correct. He took a second to inspect a set of shelves next to the cell door, just out of the prisoner's line of sight. Alice believed firmly in not revealing any information to captives, to keep them, literally and figuratively, in the dark. They were somewhat easier to handle that way, or as easy as an abducted person was going to be. He plucked a pair of latex gloves from a box and pulled them on, snapping them about the wrists.

Then he took a box cutter from the shelf.

"Be careful," Jenna warned.

Alice rolled his eyes.

"This one's different," she pointed out to him.

"I *know* he's different."

"I mean *really* different."

Alice ignored her. He sawed through the fabric covering the prisoner, surprised at the lack of underpants. When the clothing was removed, Jenna handed him a garden hose which he aimed at their curious prisoner. In addition to the toilet, the floor had narrow drainage slits cut along its base. Alice set his feet and blasted the corners and their motionless guest.

"There," he declared, and handed the dripping hose back to Jenna. "All done."

There wasn't much time remaining. Alice lugged the

lifeless prisoner into a seated position and propped him against the back wall, grunting all the while. The man was heavy. Alice felt himself sweating and loathed it, loathed it, loathed it.

Really different.

This particular individual was indeed that.

Four hours earlier, after Jenna had clapped a steel wrench across the back of the prisoner's head, Alice had felt a twinge of resentment at being so roughly grabbed, didn't appreciate in the least being hauled over his countertop, in his own gosh darn station. Alice didn't possess the sculpted physique of a health-conscious bodybuilder, but he did exercise. Lifting and flipping tractor tires, deadlifting cement weights. Through the years he'd built up a sizeable amount of physical power in his bulky frame. Sure, he looked like an upright watermelon, but it was a watermelon that could and would seriously mess a person up if the need arose.

But this recent catch, probably a hundred-plus pounds lighter no less, had seized Alice like a teacher seizing a crabby child. That bothered Alice. No, that *infuriated* Alice. To a degree he'd not felt in a very, very long time.

So he struck the senseless man. Just enough to split lips, blacken eyes, and even remove a few teeth. Right there in his station. It wasn't the smartest thing to do upon reflection, not in the waiting area. Jenna let him go, however, and Alice gave his wife credit where it was due. She knew when her man had a thorn lodged in his pee hole, and she knew when it was best to just stand back and let him work the thorn out all by himself.

When Alice had finished, his prisoner's head resembled a weeping, decomposing plum left alone for far too long on a kitchen countertop. The amount of damage he did surprised Alice—the poor bastard would probably be brain damaged. Just a little. But that was okay. That was fine. Money could still be made off brain-damaged goods. Good money. So Alice dragged the bleeding carcass down into the basement, into the special room which was strictly for employees only. Jenna had followed, removing all evidence with a mop and a bucket of bleached water.

Brutalized. That's what Alice had done to his prisoner.

And yet, only hours later when Alice had returned for a quick peek—well!

The split lips had healed. The lacerations were merely pink lines. The swelling had retreated to a nobility's rouge. Instead of looking brutalized, the prisoner appeared to have survived a night of binge drinking and immoral carousing.

Really, really different. Gosh darn it.

Quite the trick. Alice wanted to know if the prisoner could do it again. In fact, he needed to know.

So he righted the man's head and, with the box cutter knife, cut a very deliberate, very deep line across both cheeks, releasing bright rivulets that dropped to his collar bone and upper chest. Alice opened him deep. A long, deep cut that would very much need stitches. *Should* need stitches.

Alice hoped the unconscious man would heal.

If he did, well, Alice really couldn't think about what it meant, but he smelled money. Maybe even another cheese and rice patent.

Over the last nine years or so, Alice and Jenna had built a reputation with individuals associated with the illegal trafficking of human organs on the black market. Secretive people who took shopping lists from privately funded clinics eager to obtain healthy organs and untainted blood for their needy clientele. By any means necessary. While Alice and Jenna took orders every two or three months, there were at times rush jobs that needed to be filled within limited timeframes, usually seventy-two hours. Alice and Jenna weren't always able to secure such orders, and if they didn't, another harvester did.

Seeing his prisoner's regenerative powers firsthand uneased and intrigued Alice.

Mostly intrigued.

He and Jenna just might've hit the sweet pickle motherlode.

14

The morning after confining their newest guest, Alice got up and dressed in his usual attire: beige pants and a fresh pinstriped shirt with matching bowtie. Jenna made pancakes and they ate them with an arterial plug of syrup and butter. After breakfast, Alice cleaned up (as per house rules—if one cooked, the other did the dishes) and walked the short rock path to the rear door of the family business. The morning was quiet, drenched in that sleepy stillness a person could stop and appreciate for hours. It was also overcast and cold, but Alice didn't mind the weather. The short walk only served to wake him up.

And besides. It felt like Christmas morning.

The door opened with a jingle and he flicked on the light switch. He flipped over the OPEN sign, swept the floors, adjusted tourism pamphlets on a rack, and cleaned the countertop. Nothing was really dirty, but Alice dusted and polished as per his morning routine. It got him in a forward-thinking mood.

All the while he worked, he thought about the man in his basement.

Wondered if the cuts on his forehead had healed.

The jingling door interrupted his building excitement. Alice looked up from an order sheet and saw a young lady approach the counter. She wore a far too friendly smile. And too much make-up.

"Good morning," she chirped, high on life.

"Good morning," Alice returned in a wary teeth grind, not recognizing this woman at all.

"How are you?"

"Fine, thank you," Alice said and didn't ask the same of his visitor. He straightened his back a little further, squared his shoulders, and imposed his largeness upon her, projecting the message that he was, in fact, much bigger and would not tolerate any foolishness at such an hour.

"Good, that's good," the lady said. She stopped directly before him, on the other side of the counter. "This the bus stop?"

"Yes, it is."

"You the owner?"

"I am."

"I have a few questions, if you don't mind. Sorry, I just go right into asking questions. That's me. I'm so direct. But it's really important. See, a friend of mine was here yesterday. He used your phone? Wait, I have a picture."

Her smile dimmed as she reached into a pocket and produced a sheet of fax paper, which she unfolded and presented to Alice.

Alice looked at the picture. Recognized the face.

"Was he here yesterday?" the woman asked.

"He was," Alice answered in a dog growl.

"Wonderful!" The woman's face lit up, reminding him of a western geisha not quite right in the head. "I've been trying to track him down for a few days now. He just ups and goes whenever he pleases. We had something of a girlfriend-boyfriend fight. I'm trying to make things right before he does something silly."

Alice didn't comment.

"You didn't happen to notice where he went?" she asked.

"I did," Alice answered. "He jumped on the two-fifteen to Halifax."

"A bus?"

"Yes, that's right, miss. A bus. I remember him. There was no one else buying a ticket that day."

"Little town, huh?" the woman asked. "Not too many people leaving it?"

"Or visiting."

"Amazing it's still on the map," she said, sizing up the station.

"It's quiet."

"But you like it that way," she finished for him, her smile a touch sly.

"We do."

"So, now, this two-fifteen bus," the woman went on. "You sure he got on it?"

"Yes."

"You looked out that window and saw him board the bus?"

"I did," Alice answered without hesitation. "Matter of

fact, I seem to remember him saying something about heading to Toronto, so he'd have to get a connecting bus in Halifax."

"I see," the woman said in a tone that suggested all was not well. She regarded the outdoor boarding zone. "What time would that bus get into Halifax?"

"That bus would've arrived at the station there at three thirty-five," Alice replied. "It's a short milk run, so the driver would be making a few stops along the way. Picking up more passengers and packages. I can check the schedule for buses heading for Toronto."

"No need. You said three thirty-five?"

"That's correct."

"Okay." The woman said this more to herself than to Alice. He studied her face, committing every detail to memory.

"Strange, though," she pondered, placing a finger on her chin. "I actually stopped by that bus station before coming all the way up here. Spent about an afternoon watching people getting off the buses. He didn't get off. I even asked the driver. Showed him the same picture. He said my friend didn't even board the bus. Isn't that strange?"

Alice's brow furrowed. "That is strange."

"What do you think could've happened then?" she asked him directly, cocking her head as if listening to a wall.

"The driver probably forgot," Alice said earnestly, masking his guilt without even a hint of a telltale blush. "Or wasn't looking when your friend got onto the bus. That's my guess. But I saw him board the two-fifteen yesterday."

Alice emphasized his account with a confident nod aimed at the boarding zone.

"That's your guess."

"Yes, miss."

"I see." The woman nodded, unblinking, and stared Alice straight in the eye.

Alice blinked, feigning doubt. "Everything all right, miss?"

She took her time answering.

"Miss?" Alice asked uncertainly and mentally patted himself on the back for his performance.

"Everything's fine," she said in a much too-chipper voice. She topped it off with a giggle probably meant to be girlish but came off as downright creepy. "Certainly is a quiet little town."

"It is," Alice said with a thoughtful pout. "We like it."

"I bet you do," she winked.

That seemed strange, caught him off-guard.

Her business done, the woman stepped back and quickly inspected the station. "Well, I won't keep you any longer. You've been a great help. Thanks for your time."

"You're welcome," Alice said, his expression brightening but without the smile. "I hope you find your friend."

"Oh, I will," the woman said, poised at the front door. "I always do."

She pushed her way through, lifting and dropping her arm as if signaling the start of a race. Alice thought it a bit dramatic, but was glad she was leaving.

A white van rolled into sight and stopped at the gas

pumps. The woman climbed aboard, settling into the passenger seat.

She smiled at Alice as the van turned onto the road.

*

"Well?" Barronni asked as he drove away from the two-in-one service station and bus terminal.

"He says Kirk boarded a bus bound for Halifax yesterday," Em said and sighed. "And that's the only bus that came from this area."

Barronni didn't comment, but his brow furrowed into a knobby maze.

"I don't think he was lying," Em said. "I didn't get that feeling from him. If he was, he's damn good at it. And really, why would he lie? The guy's a knob. You should have been there. Smelled like a rancid soap factory."

Barronni sighed, clearly not impressed with the report.

"Don't worry," Em said. "We'll bag the bastard. Only a matter of time. Like the guy said, the driver probably didn't notice Kirk get on or off the bus. Those guys only count tickets on the milk run and then check the seats afterwards. They don't remember faces."

Em pulled out her phone. "I'll call our guys in Halifax now. Give them the heads up."

"Tell them to keep someone near the bus station at all times. Just in case. And the airport."

"He won't get to the airport," Em said. "Guy's got no cash."

"Just do it."

15

Consciousness returned to Kirk, strengthening like a full moon defying the thickest fog. He moved an arm and felt it flop, as if the bones had been replaced with strings of jelly. So he stayed there, shaking his limbs until blood started to circulate. The smell of shit and piss wrinkled his nose. Moisture coated the copper floor and lingered on the air. His entire frame had been doused. When his limbs were functional again, he ran his fingers along the floor at the wall's base, tracing what felt like gills.

His strength faltered and failed.

Kirk lay there, giving himself a chance to recover, and remembered. Alice had fried him. Fried him and scrambled a few neurons. And then the weird man had entered the cell and stripped Kirk before... what?

He managed to sit up, his legs not fully extended, and lifted his head to the false light framed in the cell window. Not a sound except for his own ragged breathing. He touched his forehead and felt the sealed cut. The line alarmed him. Kirk wondered why the freak had sliced him.

As if sitting on an electric frying pan wasn't bad enough.

He knows, the stark thought cut through Kirk's fog.

He doesn't know, the warden fired back, but a little voice whispered that Alice did. They both did. That's why Alice and Jenna had been staring at him like a dying bug pinned to a cardboard sheet. But, then again, perhaps all sociopaths studied their victims that way.

No, Alice knew Kirk was different. He knew that if he beat Kirk up, his face would repair itself at a miraculous rate. The big man wanted to see if Kirk could do it again.

That sounded right.

The soft light from beyond stamped a faint square on the cell's back wall. Kirk studied it in silence, debating what to do. He needed to get out. He needed to get out now, before that twisted bastard returned.

The room seemed almost too small to fully transform. Borland popped into his head then and he wondered again how the old *were* had done that half-change. He questioned what was so different between them.

Nothing, except age. And experience.

Experience hooked Kirk's attention. Borland hadn't just performed that quick trick on the fly. Borland had practiced.

And, presently, Kirk had plenty of time.

The outside light brightened. A door opened, followed by that heavy step he'd already associated with Alice. Footsteps hurried to the window and a shadowy face appeared in the glass, quickly fogging the surface. Alice's shadowy expression muttered something that sounded like "poppycock," just before his thick forearm wiped the surface clean with a squeak. Then that bright sun in the ceiling flicked to life. Kirk cringed from it, shielding his eyes.

"Ah, excellent," Alice muttered through clenched teeth. "Excellent."

Kirk covered his forehead.

"Too late, mister," Alice spoke, barely moving his mouth. "Too late. I've seen all I need to see. You're a real treat, you are. Simply amazing. I don't usually talk to my prisoners but I'm going to make an exception in your case. I mean, sweet honeysuckle, how do you do it? How do you heal so cheese and rice fast? I cut you to the bone."

That solved one mystery. Now if only Kirk could unravel the others in his life.

"Might as well tell me," Alice warned. "It'll be easier on you. You aren't going anywhere and I can inflict serious pain. *Serious* pain. You won't believe how serious. Just takes a flick of a wrist. A spin of a dial. A real dinger of a shock. The way you are now, sitting there, if I turn on the juice… you'll become a human flapjack."

Alice chuckled, an oddly normal laugh without any malice. "So how about it? You want to tell me everything, or do I have to get mean?"

"You're not mean right now?"

"There's mean and there's evil," Alice clarified. "You've seen the indifferent side of me. You're about to see the mean side. You better hope you never see the evil."

"Buddy, you're a sick fuck."

Alice's features screwed up into a tight knot, his pout more pronounced. He stretched his arm to the right, out of sight, while keeping his eyes on Kirk.

A snap of metal on metal and Kirk flopped about the cell's floor, seized by electrical spasms that scrubbed clean all thought. He vibrated as if God himself were shaking him for spare change. Kirk's teeth clenched. His limbs quaked and the ceiling above shivered. His chest expanded, ribs on the verge of exploding. He couldn't breathe.

The current stopped.

A twisted Kirk collapsed near the toilet, his brain scrambled, limbs twitchy.

"Call me a quick duck again," Alice dared. "Go on. Call me a quick duck one more time. I dare you, mister. I double dare you."

The words cut through the after effects and Kirk saw red. He regarded Alice darkly. "You're... a sick fuck," he panted.

An indignant Alice absorbed that shot. Kirk thought the man was about to kiss the glass.

Then he saw the ogre's shoulder's move.

A bright crackling enveloped the warden, much stronger than before, and it didn't let go. Unlike the movies, there was no sound, only jaw-clamping energy firing through Kirk. He pissed himself. His sphincters clenched. Every artery and vein in his neck bulged and tried to explode at once. His eyes expanded and threatened to pop from his face. He couldn't breathe, couldn't blink. His head rattled against the walls like panicking castanets, and still the electricity did not relent. Kirk bucked and quivered violently. He glimpsed Alice's stern features high above, a split-second snapshot taken from a speeding car.

After what seemed like a week, the electrical current ceased.

A boneless Kirk lay trembling, drooling, and staring.

"That was ten seconds," Alice said, sprinkling the glass with spittle. "Only ten seconds. But I bet it felt a whole lot longer. What do you think would happen if, say, I turned the dial and just walked away? Just walked out of the room? And maybe forgot to return? I think this cell would be filled with people popcorn. Don't you think? I do. A whole lot of popcorn in need of a little butter. You don't want that and I don't want to clean that up. So tell me, how is it you heal so fast?"

One of Kirk's eyes fixed upon that stubbly face, where the glass fogged around the mouth. Kirk tried to blink. The eyelid dragged itself over the cornea and felt like every teardrop had evaporated, and all that remained was dust and fumes.

Kirk had to think about the next part. "Go. Fuck."

Alice scowled like a displeased god.

Yourself. Kirk didn't get the chance to say that, however. For Alice had spun the dial all the way to ten.

*

Thirty seconds. Alice let his prisoner stir-fry for a full thirty seconds, which he counted off as one Mississippi, two Mississippi, and so on. He dared not let Kirk fricassee any longer than that for fear of the man's body exploding into flames.

He couldn't lose his winning lottery ticket. That just

wouldn't do. Besides, Alice had more experiments to conduct.

The prisoner could heal from lacerations and contusions, and probably from shock damage, but what about something more destructive? More painful? More crippling?

That was Alice's mindset as he opened the door, catching the full effect of his prisoner's fried body, along with any remaining fluids and filth. Alice retrieved the hose and blasted the roasted meat that was his captive. He cleaned him up as much as he was willing. Once finished, Alice switched off the hose and stowed it away. He stood, his hands on his hips, and considered the man's bare feet. Then his hands. Alice snapped on a pair of plastic gloves, adjusted them accordingly, and inspected his clean shirt. He pulled on a disposable apron and tied a bow just at the nape of his lower back.

All set, Alice grabbed a set of ankles and pulled the unresponsive man-slab away from the back wall. He propped him against the side, angling the prisoner's left foot and hand towards the door. The fingers were curled like a spider dead of old age. The foot was on its side. Alice stopped, considered the arrangement, and pulled the leg out even further.

He approved of the extra length.

Stage two, Alice thought, taking aim at the exposed foot. He lifted a heavy workman's boot, the soles and toes reinforced with steel.

And stomped with all his might.

*

Breathing heavily, Alice walked away from the secret room beneath his garage. His mind crackled with possibilities, some of them ludicrous. He emerged from below, continued down a short hallway, and exited a side door. It was night, and he followed the path to his cozy two-story house, the lights in the windows soft and warm. Thoughts of the monetary gains he'd receive from his prisoner's fantastic healing ability swirled through his head with cyclonic energy. He entered his home and stopped in his kitchen.

"You feed the dog?" Jenna asked from the living room.

Alice didn't want to raise his voice, so he walked deeper inside the house. The living room lights had been dimmed. Jenna lay upon a sofa, one hand behind her head, one knee cocked. The television broadcasted a science show. Jenna was practically nude, her breasts bared and inviting. A pair of frilly undergarments covered her naughty bits, but if Alice really looked, he could see everything through the sheer material. If he really looked. He didn't. He walked past her and stood beside a vinyl recliner, eyes on the television screen.

"No," he said, answering her question.

Jenna arched her back and regarded him with her dark blue eyes. "How's he doing, then?"

Alice shrugged. "He passed the first experiment with flying colors. That cut? All gone. Just a neat little pink line."

That quieted her.

"What's on?" Alice grumbled.

"SuperScience," she answered, distracted, her head swirling with the same thoughts Alice had been entertaining.

"Nature of Asteroids. Projecting paths of planet killers."

Alice unbuttoned his shirt.

Jenna watched him. "So he passed. Cool. What's next?"

"Stage two."

"What's that?"

"I broke his fingers. And his foot. Toes."

"Ah."

"If all that heals, then I'll make the phone call."

"No stage three?"

Alice draped his shirt over the back of the sofa, minding his wife's knees. He wore a strap undershirt underneath, stretched tightly over his padded frame. Short bristles appeared at his neckline from where he'd neglected to shave. He got to work on his belt.

"I thought about a stage three," he muttered, "but we're not set up for it. I'll leave that for Mr. Gill."

Jenna scissored one leg over the other as one of her fingertips drifted to the bullseye of a full and dark areola. "What is stage three anyway?"

The leather belt hissed as Alice freed it from his pants. "Surgery."

"That sounds messy."

"And neither you nor I want to clean up that mess. I fried him again just now. Never expected a person could hold so much filth."

"I've read an adult human's digestive tract can hold upwards of twenty pounds of hooey."

Alice made a face. "Disgusting."

"Hm."

He opened his pants and they dropped, revealing a pair of white boxers, and meaty legs. A soccer player's legs, wearing black, knee-high socks.

"Maybe we shouldn't feed him?" Jenna asked, watching him.

Alice cocked his head. "I was thinking that. Might be dangerous. He should be in good health upon delivery. I'm not so sure of how far we should push this one. He's…"

The word came to him.

"He's stubborn."

Alice hooked his waistband and let the boxers drop.

"Wouldn't it be something," Jenna said, a smile lighting up her beautiful face, "if he actually could regenerate organs as well? I mean, wouldn't that be freaky? Take out a whole kidney and he'd grow it back. He'd be a farm then. A reusable farm."

"He would." Alice sat his bare ass down in the recliner, the vinyl creaking upon contact. "That would be something. But it's impossible."

He looked to his pubic area and lifted his penis by the head. He stretched it out to about half-way, pulled it to the left and then to the right, inspecting his shorn pubic thicket.

"Not even for a guy who can heal a cut overnight?" Jenna asked, smiling and turning onto her side, burying half her face into the pillow. "Maybe we should go to stage three. It might be in our best interest. I mean, can you imagine the dollar value of such a person?"

Alice released his lad and considered his wife's not so wild idea.

He considered it for a long time.

16

When Kirk awoke from the blast of electricity, his hand and foot screamed at him like only smashed appendages could.

He dared not move, but sitting as he was, he was cramped. He had to move. So he did. He wailed with every jiggle of his broken parts, and nearly passed out when his foot grazed the wall. Actually passed out when he finally faced the door. He wailed and blubbered and cursed. Unconsciousness took him a second time when he saw his hand swollen to baseball glove proportions, the crooked fingers the size of Italian sausages.

Though in eye-watering misery, Kirk wasn't about to let a pair of twisted monsters like Alice and Jenna do him any further harm. He'd figure out a way to kill them both first. They weren't people. They were apex predators in suits of skin.

And in that frame of mind, in that condition of hate and wretchedness, he summoned the change.

It overtook him in seconds. The pain of the transformation swallowed that of his smashed appendages, and just before he opened the valves all the way, he remembered Borland. Remembered that fearsome half-state he'd assumed.

Kirk tried something different. He attempted to control the transformation, just a little, instead of letting matters follow their fluid course. He resisted the natural impulse of relaxing and tried directing instead, struggled to channel the blood. It was difficult, exceptionally difficult, like trying to nip off a mid-flow stream from an exceptionally full bladder.

To his surprise, something physically weakened.

The sensation was so sudden, alien and utterly weird, that Kirk relinquished control an instant later. The transformation process righted itself, like a car drifting back into the proper lane, and continued without missing a beat.

Three minutes later, a werewolf filled the little cell. A werewolf that had to stand on its hind legs.

Well, fuck, Kirk raged, finding himself bunched up in awkward places.

At least his broken bones had repaired themselves.

Growling and grunting, Kirk turned himself around and slapped a paw against the glass window, the resulting *thump* as ominous as a mallet against an ice-breaker's steel hull. He shifted targets, realizing that breaking the glass alone wouldn't free him. It was set too high in the door, which meant even if he did shatter it, he'd need a set of orangutan's arms to reach the outer door knob. He dropped on all fours, but the confined space curled him into a meaty horseshoe. He couldn't muster the full power of his hind legs to smash the door. Frustration mounting, Kirk squirmed and contorted himself in that maddening box. He stood and slapped the entrance with his forepaws, hard felling blows that connected with kettlebell force. Strikes that would shatter skulls and rip off faces.

The door trembled within its frame, but didn't break.

Steel door, Kirk thought, *cement walls. Jesus Christ, who were these people?*

He twisted and turned, attempting to push against the barrier but failing miserably. Panic rose within him, but Kirk swallowed it back, balled it up, and released it upon the door. He pounded that stubborn portal with his forepaws and shoulders. In the end, with his desperation peaking, he relented and wailed on the glass but only succeeded in scratching the surface.

The panic returned.

He had to get out of this box.

You can't cage me, Kirk mentally protested as he struck the door. *You can't cage me. Who do you think I am? You think I'm just a guy? You didn't get just a guy. You got something more this time. You got more than you bargained for. A LOT more.*

A flat paw against the glass punctuated each thought. His terror boiled into anger at being so confined, built up steam and doubled in fury.

You got—you got a fucking muh... His limbs were supercharged. Every impact became a riverboat drumbeat and a paw print of blood.

ONE PISSED OFF—

Monster.

Kirk lost it. And in that one frenzied, all or nothing cannonball discharge of exertion, he split the glass.

A long, icy crinkle appeared in the red-smeared surface.

That one note brought him back. The crack shocked him. He leaned back from the pane, analyzing the sight.

Then he struck the glass again. And again.

And on the seventh try, he punched through with a yelp.

Red dappled the baseball-sized hole. Kirk continued smashing, widening the hole and paying in blood. At one point he thrust his muzzle through and yelped at the slicing glass, but he couldn't do much more. He couldn't break the door by strength alone.

Kirk reluctantly reverted back to his human form.

As a man, he regarded the hole. He'd cleared the glass away right down to sharp nubs that sparkled. Those, he realized, would only be removed by a hammer or pliers or some tool, but not by flesh and bone. But he couldn't give up, not while he was so close.

Not liking the next part, Kirk jammed his left arm through the serrated breach, right up to the shoulder. The door bit him. The door bit him hard. Glass slivers sunk into very tender places, inflicting mind-numbing pain. Kirk took it. He took it all and more. His fingers scrabbled along the door's surface, searching for a knob or latch or anything that might be released. He found nothing. Grunts became moans. Blood spritzed the inside of the door. Maroon beads raced for the floor. Kirk lifted his arm off that terrible maw, the pain bright and blinding, and reached for the edge of the doorframe. Fingertips grazed a hinge and perhaps a sliding bolt lock, but nothing he could open. He groped above his head but the angle was too awkward. Setting his jaw and knowing the next part would hurt, Kirk lowered his arm yet again, searching for that elusive door handle. The glass went back to work. Skin parted. Muscle frayed. Blood stained his ribs in needle-thin lines. His hand swished about and found nothing, the exploration only succeeding in exacerbating his wounds. He barked in frustration, hissed, and reached again. His face lifted and he called on God above for a little help, just a little help, *please*, as strands of connective tissue snipped and parted like threadbare wires.

Have to… he projected over the searing nerve song of his arm.

Then the glass stroked bone. Sawed at joints. The sensation left him weeping, gasping.

All life left his arm.

Defeated, dizzy, and severely weakened, Kirk pulled back three feet of hanging meat, and even that became a challenge. Too weak to lift it clear, he had to use his own mass to pull the tortured limb free. The window disgorged that pale and bloody arm, parting tissue like a wicked flange, drawing grooves along the inside of his flesh and leaving a mark.

Black stars blinded him as he worked his arm free, pulling him to the brink of oblivion. He plopped down with a sick grunt and rested his head against the door. Heartbeats thundered in his temples and ears. Sickness curled his stomach. His arm mewled and cursed, refusing to be coddled, so Kirk let it be and took whatever pain came his way.

Great, he thought sleepily, his tunnel vision narrowing. *Just great.*

His getaway had failed in spectacular fashion.

And the last thought before he passed out—was what that bastard Alice would say when he discovered the broken glass. Part of Kirk didn't care. Part of him hoped it'd scare the living shit out of Alice and his batshit crazy wife or sister or whatever the hell she was.

It would give them something to think about. It would send a warning.

They had a monster trapped under their shop.

And it wanted out.

17

"Sweet fudge stick," Alice whispered, the sight stopping him just past the door's threshold. He steadied himself, horrified and fascinated at the scene. The cell door had been breached, the area awash in blood. He covered his mouth, taking in the destruction.

And the *smell*. It stunk to high heaven.

"Oh my, oh my, oh… my" he rambled. The cell door's numerous locks and bolts had held, but the strength required to break that glass, well, that made Alice weak in the knees. He'd once declared it bulletproof. The salesman had led him to *believe* it was bulletproof, and he in turn had boasted to Jenna it was, in fact, bulletproof.

The glass was *not* bulletproof.

But it was strong. And seeing it smashed made Alice fear. He wondered what in God's name possessed the strength to break the glass. He wavered. The door remained shut but was it truly safe? Alice couldn't remember how many prisoners he'd shut away in that cell. He'd have to get out his very special, very secret ledger and examine the numbers.

Close to a hundred at least, give or take a few heads, but in the fourteen years since he and Jenna had entered the black market trade…

Never had he witnessed *this*.

Alice's trademark pout had slackened into a donut hole of horror. He gathered his wits, reined in his fright, and shut his mouth. The locks on the door appeared secured.

"Well, well, mister," he said with a clenched jaw. "Seems you had quite the… quite the evening."

Alice crept up to the door's blackened void. He stopped a good two feet back, attempting to peek inside. He returned to the main door to switch on the cell's inner light. It flared to life, illuminating stained glass nubs that reminded Alice of hockey players.

Not sure what to expect, Alice stood on his tippy toes and expanded his field of vision, looking over those little vengeful teeth in the window frame.

The top of a head came into view. Alice's breath hitched in his throat. He lifted himself a little higher.

A defiant Kirk looked up, his face pallid. "Heya, you fucking evil cocksucker."

Alice squawked and flung himself back, flattening his considerable bulk against a nearby wall. He fumbled for the electrocution dial and when he couldn't find it he looked and realized he was reaching on the wrong side.

It also occurred to him that his prisoner hadn't tried to attack him.

Ergo, the man wasn't able to, or so Alice's rattled mind reasoned.

That notion lessened his anxiety, but he didn't relax his guard. He circled the door, backing up all the way to the table, before crossing the floor as if circumventing a bottomless pit. His eyes flickered from the broken window to the reassuring dial that would fry the prisoner unconscious.

He gripped the dial and exhaled. Once ready to parley, Alice craned his neck and peered inside a second time, his pudgy, whiskered face creeping into the frame.

"Yeah, that's right," Kirk muttered upon spotting Alice's fearful expression. "I did all that. Hope you fucking shit yourself."

"You did all this?" Alice demanded, his glasses jittery on his cheeks.

"Fuck you."

Alice let that one go. "What in heaven's name are you?"

Kirk didn't answer.

"I'll give you one more chance," Alice warned, his voice gaining strength. "My hand's on the dial. The one that controls the electricity that fried your beans and wieners yesterday. If you don't answer me, I'll turn it to ten, and watch you vibrate until you catch fire. Until your eyes pop from your head and your skin melts from your face. You think about that. You think very hard about that."

Kirk sighed. "You're going to die."

"Not me, mister."

"You don't understand. They'll come looking for me."

Alice's eyes narrowed.

"And they'll follow the trail all the way here. Where I

disappeared. Then they'll ask questions. They'll find you eventually, and you won't be able to hide me from them."

"Who?"

Kirk fell silent. "Government agents."

Alice's mouth twisted as if he'd tasted something bad. "What?"

"You heard me."

"I call bullchips."

Kirk didn't blink. "You call whatever you like. You think someone like me is operating alone? You're in serious trouble. Serious trouble. You went fishing for trout and bagged a whale."

A smacking of lips and Alice's pout returned. "What are you, mister? And spit it out fast."

Kirk waited a heartbeat. "I'm a mutant."

The bad taste returned to Alice's face. "What?"

"You heard me. I'm a mutant. Not that you'll be around to do anything about it. You want to know about my healing? That's one thing I can do. Heal. Super fast. Battlefield regeneration. Practically overnight. Won't need medics then, right? Lose an eye and it grows right back. See this."

Kirk shook out his hand, the one Alice had broken. Kirk flaunted it, making peace and gun signs before flipping Alice the bird. The display shocked the big man and he slunk out of sight, only to return again.

"Yeah," Kirk said. "I'm all better. Wanna see the foot?"

Lips quivered. "Show me."

"Open that door and I'll show you plenty."

Alice didn't. Nor did the saucy remark result in a punishing spin of the dial. "You're a mutant?"

"Government secret project. Developing soldiers for black-ops. You ever hear of search and evade tests?"

"You mean like... for special forces?"

"Yeah, for special forces. Standard search and evade is maybe two days. In my situation, it's a week. I'm two days out. Or one day. Up 'til whenever you knocked me out, anyway."

Alice straightened. Pure and unchecked horror whitened his face.

"They'll find me," Kirk continued. "They always do. It's what they do. So if you have a grain of sense in that skull of yours, you'll let me go before they get here. 'Cause if they find me..."

He paused for dramatic effect. "They find you."

Alice swallowed.

Just before he turned off the cell light and bolted from sight.

God as his witness, Kirk enjoyed that. *Needed* that. It even armored him against the drying smell of fluids expelled during the change. He relaxed in the tiny room and lapped up the good vibes, knowing he probably wouldn't get many more in the time to come.

His smile soured around the edges, darkened and drooped.

He probably shouldn't have said that part about regenerating an eye.

*

'Cause if they find me… they find you.

Like that woman with too much make-up, Alice thought as he steamed into the garage. He stopped, realized his mistake, and flew right back out, ignoring the looks and shouts from Jenna underneath the hood of a small sports coupe. Alice didn't stop until he was in his kitchen, with the telephone on the table.

Government secret project?

Oh cheese and crackers.

There wasn't much Alice feared in life, but he did harbor an unhealthy paranoia for the government. He didn't like them. Didn't like how they operated. Certainly didn't like their pensions well after their public service. The government was composed of people, with all of their faults and insecurities and issues. They were the worst kind of people in Alice's opinion, because they had power, and the higher the position, the greater their power, the greater their influence and the more secrets they knew.

Secret projects. Alice long since suspected the government of hiding such clandestine projects, from anti-gravity flying machines, to AI, to eternal youth. He firmly believed that world leaders didn't die of old age, that their body doubles replaced them while the real person was whisked away to private estates in the South Pacific, where servants granted their every whim.

Super black-ops soldiers. That sounded like the truth to Alice. Gosh darn it, it did. And if it was the truth, that his prisoner was indeed a mutant—which totally worked for him—then Alice had to prepare defenses in case there were more visitors on the horizon.

His hand lingered on the telephone receiver, twitching. He wanted to make the call but something else bothered him. The other thing the prisoner had said about his eye.

Lose an eye and it grows right back.

The receiver was forgotten. Alice straightened and stared off into space, replaying the words. He remembered the fully restored fingers and toes. Those were bones Alice had broken himself, crushed and ground under his own boot, to a degree that they should have been hacked off entirely. But the prisoner had them back and with a smile on his face.

Alice calmed and smiled as well.

Jenna burst into the kitchen. "What is it? Is there a problem? Did you kill him?"

Alice shushed her with a finger.

"Don't shush me," she warned. "Tell me what happened? Do I need the shotgun?"

"No, nothing like that," Alice said. "We've hit pay dirt, babe."

The news disarmed Jenna, that and being called babe. Alice never called her by any cute terms of endearment.

"What do you mean?" she asked, a smile cracking one corner of her grease-smudged mouth.

Alice told her everything.

"Stage three is there," he finished two minutes later. "Right there. Down below. We got it."

Jenna hadn't blinked the entire minute it took for Alice

to tell his story. "Best call Mr. Gill."

"I plan to. I am. Right now."

"What about the special forces?"

"I'll take care of it. Don't you worry."

And surprisingly, Jenna backed away with her smile in full dazzling bloom.

"We're gonna get that house, babe," Alice said, his hand still on the receiver. "We're gonna get that safe room. The indoor shooting range. The big, big movie theater-sized television. All the toys you want and more."

He picked up the receiver and dialed a number he knew by heart. Jenna backed up to a countertop, giddy with excitement, her hands clasped as if making a wish.

"Yeah?" a voice answered, distracting Alice from his lovely oil-changing, piston-checking wife.

"Mr. Gill?"

"Yeah. That you, Al?"

"It's me."

"You got something for me?"

"I do, Mr. Gill. I do indeed. Something very, very good." Alice and Mr. Gill always talked in such a manner, in case the government or any of their spy agencies were listening. They practiced caution, always.

"Yeah?" an interested Mr. Gill asked. "Like what?"

"Remember that conversation we had a long time ago, maybe five, six years back, about 'what if's' and 'if only's'?"

"No."

"I'll refresh your memory. We discussed possibilities. About the best possible case scenario, where if you took something out, the next day a replacement would appear. A real quick-growing farm."

"So?"

"So I think I have a specimen."

A definite pause. "You what?"

"You heard me correctly, Mr. Gill. But it's best that you come here and see for yourself. Before the neighbors find out."

"They know?"

"I think they do."

"That's too bad."

"Maybe not too bad," Alice said. "We'll see. But please hurry."

"I can be there in two days."

"And please bring all your tools."

"All my tools?"

"Yes," Alice said. "I think that would be best. Bring everything."

"I see. All right. I will."

"See you then, Mr. Gill."

Click.

Alice looked at Jenna. "He'll be here in two days."

"Oh my," she said, holding down her excitement. "Would tonight be a night for nachos?"

"Yes," Alice said, his eyes dreamy. "Yes, it would."

18

An opening door roused Kirk from a doze. Cramped in his cell, he looked to the busted window and wondered if Alice would get around to fixing it.

Feet shuffled closer. The cell light came on and a shadow passed the window, dimming Kirk's world for an instant. Alice's wary face crept into view, the thick glasses peeking over the ruined sill.

"You awake in there?" Alice asked.

"I'm awake."

The man appeared ready to run at the slightest twitch. "Brought you dinner."

"I get dinner in here?"

"You want the food or not?"

"Sure."

To Kirk's dismay, Alice stuffed a brown paper lunch bag through the window. On a broom handle.

The bag bobbed just above Kirk's head. He took the bag off the broom handle (found that it was bound by a thick elastic) and dropped it in his lap. Alice's shadow loomed overhead, watching. Reluctantly, Kirk opened the bag.

A plastic-wrapped sandwich and a small carton of two-percent milk, along with a straw. A handful of grapes.

"You eat that," Alice ordered from beyond. "You eat all that and when you're done, toss the bag out here. Don't let me come in there for your garbage. You know what'll happen if I do."

I'll rip your goddamn head from your shoulders, Kirk thought.

"Hey," Alice prompted.

"What?" Kirk groaned.

"You didn't say thank you."

Another rush of wonderment filled Kirk. Alice was a very special kind of evil. "Thanks."

"You're welcome."

Wishing he could get his hands on his captor's neck, Kirk instead settled for the sandwich. He devoured it. Tuna salad. With crunchy lettuce. He finished the food, rolled up the plastic, and deposited it into the bag. The grapes, plucked from the vine and washed, were seedless and fresh, or maybe he was just that hungry. *The change*, he realized. The change to werewolf had kicked his metabolism into hyper-drive, burning whatever energy stores he might've had.

The milk was last. Kirk drank it all and crushed the carton. He dumped the garbage into the bag and handed it to Alice with shaking hands.

Alice snatched the garbage away.

"How was the food?" Alice rumbled.

"Good."

"Jenna made the sandwich. I don't like tuna myself, but she'll buy a caseload when it's on special."

"Got any more?"

"No. Sorry."

Kirk sat down. The feeding awakened another hunger inside of him, one that a simple sandwich wasn't about to satisfy. The hankering for meat had returned, pestering him with little sparkling pangs and quivers in his guts. Those fish tail shivers would grow. Become more demanding. Kirk pressed his back against the wall as if bracing for an earthquake.

"Here," Alice said and poked something through the hole.

Clothing landed on Kirk's ankles. He drew the bundle in and held it up to the light.

A mechanic's green coverall.

"You put that on," Alice instructed through clenched teeth. "Can't have you leave this place looking like a savage."

"Not like the others, right?" Kirk asked.

Alice's head bobbed just beyond the hole like a discolored apple. "Not like the others."

"So what is it? You gonna ship me off to a black market somewhere? I'm a little too old to be adopted."

"You're going to be taken away," Alice allowed.

"That part sounds good," Kirk managed. The food had awakened something in him. His temperature rose. A damp sweat glazed his forehead and skin, and he realized he was leaning towards the window. Towards the brute who stood just outside. Alice suddenly smelled very good to Kirk, very good indeed. Soap and everything else.

Just great, the warden scolded himself, but as a weak afterthought.

"You won't like where you're going."

"Where?" Kirk asked, seeing himself bite Alice's face off and not stopping there.

"I don't know, but you won't be coming back."

The words amplified in Kirk's ears and echoed. He nodded with impatience.

"You're special," Alice declared, oblivious to how enticing his untapped blood was. "Amazing, really. I've been doing this for a long time. You probably guessed that. I've delivered quite a few people over the years. Always someone coming through. Drifters, homeless. Hitch-hikers. The pickings have always been there. It's not hard to separate the good from the bad. And Jenna and I have good eyes. We can pick the healthy ones. But you? You have something I don't understand. You're worth a lot of money. A lot of money, just waiting to be harvested. Not just your body parts and organs, but the clinical applications. The science and research. The possibilities. And because of you, Jenna and I will probably be set for life."

"The people looking for me won't allow that," Kirk whispered, greatly uneased. His sudden craving for meat spiked, heightened by a very real need to do harm to the person outside the cell door. A vein in Kirk's forehead enlarged, pulsed and twitched, exerting painful pressure.

Go away, Kirk projected, visualizing how the next few seconds could become very messy, very messy indeed. *Just get out of here. Now.*

"Them people?" Alice squared his shoulders as if smelling smoke, heedless of the subtle movement just inside the cell. "You know what day it is?"

Good question. Kirk did not. Time had melded together into pain, uncomfortable sleep, and practicing morphing. He didn't know if he'd been a prisoner for two days or twelve. "No."

"If them people were going to find you, I think they would've already. You'll be gone soon. Very soon. And when you go we'll scrub this whole place down. Sanitize it. Make this room disappear. And you're going to disappear with it."

Alice shook his head. "No one's going to find you."

Kirk's fingers jumped on their own volition, a flourish of crab's legs. He jammed them under his butt, trapping them. But the *smell*. Alice's blood, the *blood*. Kirk licked his mouth and swallowed too much saliva. Splinters of pain inserted themselves into his eyeballs. He blinked as if blinded by sunspots.

"And you know something?" Alice blathered on. "Once we get rid of you, we'll probably move to another place. Set up another fly trap. Won't be hard to do with the money we'll get from you. Fact is, we won't have to worry about money ever again."

The howl of an approaching train grew in Kirk's ears. He realized he'd poised himself to leap at the door, keeping Alice's oily profile in sight. The hammering in his temples intensified. Temptation heaped upon temptation. Alice's jaw line moved under that sweet layer of unshaven fat. The big man was close enough. Kirk could grab him, pull him to the window and then *really* eat. Just chow down—

Alice moved away from the door. His footsteps retreated. The lights switched off.

Kirk didn't know if he was disappointed or relieved.

"Hey," he called out weakly. He ignored the phlegmy timber in his voice, willing Alice to return to the window. "How about hosing down the cell now? It's pretty rank in here."

Silence from the other side of the universe.

"You did that." Alice finally answered. "So you can suffer in it."

The door closed. Locks clicked and were secured.

Kirk coughed, shuddered, and tongued his teeth.

He froze.

His incisors had lengthened, not into full fangs, but they had become pointed. Even as he explored and pinched them with his fingers, they retracted and reshaped into regular teeth. Kirk relaxed, his hunger suppressed by curiosity. Had Alice accidently helped him transform into Borland's manwolf?

The urge to feed left him. Kirk drew his legs up to his chest and concentrated on repeating the transformation, but with some effort of control.

Borland had done it. Bailey did, too. He thought there was a connection, but maybe all that connection was, was just the right emotion and a bit of practice?

Kirk was close to solving the secret. He could feel it. He'd figure out the trick. He had to.

His survival depended on it.

19

Five days after Alice imprisoned Kirk, a silver Kia sedan approached Drover's town limits.

The car rolled past the town's battered sign—it wasn't a WELCOME sign, just a generic green label so that the collection of houses beyond that point could be placed on a map. Carma kept both hands on the wheel as she drove through the town, such as it was. There was nothing there. No sign of industry or people. There wasn't even any traffic, just cars parked in driveways. Nothing. Not even a stray dog or cat or any other signs of life. It was just after nine in the morning and cloudy, with a hard crosswind that fought Carma for control of her car.

So small was the town, it didn't take very long to locate the service station.

She spotted the large building to her right and squeezed her brakes just a little harder than expected. Two closed garage bay doors faced the road. An octagon sign with "Allison's Service Station" caught her attention. Though there was no traffic behind her, she signaled a turn and headed for the building.

Five days. Almost a week since she'd talked to Kirk. She lost time debating whether or not she should drive to Nova Scotia instead of waiting for him to arrive in Toronto. The phone call had bugged her. She didn't like the way they'd suddenly disconnected, as if a huge safe had been dropped on him or something. Sure, Douglas might not have his phone but he could have located another and called her, just to explain what had happened. But he didn't. That bothered her enough that she finally packed up and took to the road. If anything, he'd call her while she was driving.

But he didn't. Which only added to her growing concern.

So she drove, enduring yet another long journey. She didn't expect to have to return to the province so soon, not after she and the other wardens had gone to Halifax to put down the *were*-thing known as Bailey.

She never expected she'd be looking for Kirk.

Hunting for Kirk.

Kirk has become a cannibal of weres and must be killed.

The elder's decree had tormented her. She couldn't believe the news, couldn't believe that Kirk had changed into some kind of killer of *weres*. The man could be a wuss. Hell, most of the time he *was* a wuss, but she knew when push came to shove, Douglas Kirk shoved back with the best. But a killer of *weres*? She wasn't convinced.

She knew about his guilt about turning a Newfoundland man into a *were*, and his admission about maybe possessing the same accelerated healing powers that Morris had, but she also sensed something being held back. She wondered if Kirk had confessed the lesser secrets just to throw her off the worst one.

She'd find out.

And if he had turned into some kind of *were* killer, then she would put him down.

The right tire dipped into a pothole, bringing her back to the present. Carma steered the little sedan to the right side of the garage and parked in front of a glass door. She got out, pulled her winter coat tight about herself, and looked around. There wasn't much to the little town of Drover. A set of train tracks, one main road, and a side road, with a scattering of houses built without any forethought to future development. In fact, looking around as she was, she suspected Allison's service station was the only business in town.

Ignoring the rusty metal and rubber debris around the garage, Carman approached the front door which served as the entrance to both the service station and a bus station. She pushed through and frowned at the loud jingling over her skull.

The interior was subdued, reminiscent of the seventies. Scrubbed, sanitized, and preserved, with none of the brand name advertisements lighting up the walls. A silver bell rested in the middle of a long counter, waiting for its morning polish. Carma knew it was waiting, for a man stood behind the counter, poised with a spray can and a washcloth. She called him a man, but in truth he resembled a shaved bear, dressed up in a suit belonging to someone's long deceased uncle. A bowtie decorated his dense neck. Thick glasses studied her and, for an instant, his big lips twitched before the whole package tightened into a pucker.

"May I help you?" the man growled as if suffering from lockjaw.

"Yeah," she said cautiously, smelling the apprehension wafting off the trained gorilla behind the counter—as well as the overpowering smell of soap. "Maybe you can. I'm looking for a friend of mine."

The man didn't blink, showed no reaction at all which, in itself, gave him away.

"A friend," he stated, as if people dropped by all the time searching for missing buddies.

"Yeah," Carma said, studying his face. "He was here about four or five days ago. Made a phone call from a little service station in Drover. You're the only one in town. You're the only *place* in town. Or village. Or… whatever."

The guy grunted, nostrils flaring with disdain.

"He's about your height, maybe a little shorter. Light brown hair. Bearded. Lean—"

"Nope."

Carma stopped, the curt denial slapping her like an open palm. "How about letting me finish, first?"

"No one like that's been around here."

"What do you mean 'no one'? He called me from *here*. Unless there's another town in Nova Scotia called Drover, one that's been formed in the last few days."

The station man's eyes narrowed behind his glasses. He placed the can of polish on the counter and *dinged* the desk bell as if swatting a housefly.

"Well?" Carma frowned.

"I'm thinking."

"Take your time."

The big guy did. He eventually nodded, as if in confession to a previous lie. "Now I remember. Yes. He came in here and he used the telephone. Took me a second. Lotta people come through here."

Carma regarded the station man with a look of *You're joking, right?* "This place? A lot of people come through this place?"

"That's correct, miss."

With overly dramatic pauses, Carma looked right, then left, and even peered out the wide picture window behind her, before concentrating on the man behind the counter.

"So I beat the morning rush, I guess?" she asked.

"It's slow right now," the station man stated with a slight grinding of teeth.

"Yeah, it looks that way. By the way, what's that smell?"

That question struck home. The guy flexed his jaw. "What smell?"

"That smell. Soap? Kitchen cleaner? Or some kinda rust remover? You need to crack a window before something starts to fry."

"I don't smell anything," the man said, his posture stiffening. As an afterthought, he dinged the desk bell again. "But I do remember your friend. Yes, there was someone here a while back."

"Try maybe five days ago."

"All right, five days ago. Yes, I remember. He didn't have any money so I gave him ten dollars and he took a bus into Halifax. And I think he was heading to Toronto."

Carma didn't move, didn't breathe, and didn't like how easy the lie rolled out of the station man's fat mouth. "You gave him ten dollars. For a ticket."

"That's correct."

"I don't think you did that at all."

No reaction from the man.

"I'm not sure what you think you're doing," Carma warned, "but I'm pretty sure my friend didn't go back into Halifax. I would have heard by now. I think you better just 'fess up about what happened, because I'm getting suspicious. You understand that?"

"No need to get suspicious," the station man grumbled.

"Which makes me all the more suspicious."

"I said there's no need to get suspicious."

"Are you disturbed or something?" Carma put to him, the tension ballooning to near explosive levels.

The station man shivered ever so slightly, as if fluffing feathers. "I'm not disturbed. I'm simply stating a fact. There's no need to be suspicious. Or insulting."

"I'm insulting?"

"You are."

He slapped the desk bell.

Dingdingdingdingding!

A nearby door opened and a woman slid through it. She was thin, mid-height, and wearing a dark-green coverall camouflaged with grease. The woman regarded the man with wide, questioning eyes, then the female customer.

Carma kept one eye on the bitch. "I'm calling the cops."

And she pulled out her phone.

"No need, no need for that," the station man blurted. "I… need to know something."

"Okay. What?"

He looked past her, as if reassuring himself she was indeed alone. "Where exactly are you from?"

"What's that got to do with anything?"

"Please. I just need to know."

Carma took her time answering. "Toronto."

The man exchanged looks with the lady mechanic. "One more question… what was he going to do when he arrived in Toronto?"

Carma studied that rash-blotched face. "He was going to call me."

That got a nod and a relieved sigh. "I know where he is."

"Oh, really? That's convenient."

"I'm very sorry, but…" he shrugged his pinstriped shoulders. "You see, he hurt himself."

"He did?" Carma deadpanned.

"Yes. He did."

"Okay."

"Yes," the station man repeated with a sympathetic nod so god-awful exaggerated that Carma almost winced. "I'll show you where he is. I had to be careful, you understand. There are people looking for him."

At least that much was true, Carma thought.

"But he mentioned you might appear in a week or so,

looking for him. I was just being careful."

"Okay," Carma allowed.

"Yes. He had an accident, you see. Swore me to secrecy."

Carma nodded, skeptical. "All right."

"But if you're here now, you can take him away. Just so I don't have to look after him anymore."

"That's a good idea. So you've been looking after him?"

"That's correct, miss."

"And so Chris is okay?"

That question stopped the station man in his momentum. His pout clenched, tightened, like a flower withering under acid.

"He's okay," the big man said, again exchanging looks with the woman.

Hook, line, and sinker. "He never mentioned you," Carma said.

"Chris doesn't speak much. He's in and out of a fever. I can take you to him."

I bet you can. Carma nodded, but the mention of a fever concerned her. Perhaps there was something going on after all? "Lead on. How'd he hurt himself, by the way?"

The man stopped in mid-turn. "Ah… I'll let him explain, if you don't mind."

"Sure."

"There have been others looking for Chris, you see," he explained and moved to a short hallway. "And I've been told to be careful."

Carma was about to follow but stopped just shy of the mechanic. The woman in the green coverall summoned a mannequin's smile and gestured for Carma to follow the station man. Carma met her gaze, stared hard, and didn't buy the routine.

"You can go," Carma said, with no intention of being caught in between the pair.

The woman's smile retracted. She shrugged and went down the hall.

Carma followed.

The mechanic whirled with a speed unexpected.

Carma glimpsed metal just before a fist smashed into her nose.

The connection snapped the warden's head back, stunning her. It was a solid punch, one delivered by a person who knew how to strike. The brass knuckles sealed the deal, however.

Carma collapsed against a wall. Her eyes watered. Fabric ripped as metal clicked somewhere overhead. Someone grabbed her hands and bound them behind her back. Her ankles were pressed together and secured tightly. A shadow made of fog lifted her and placed her high on a flat plane, before taking her through a doorway. The soap smell soaked into her buzzing sinuses. Voices spoke in warped syllables. They descended, roughly, and Carma's chin bounced. Somewhere in that journey, the mechanic appeared and grabbed Carma's cheeks, mashing them together.

More metallic clacking. Then a bright light.

Carma landed on her back, her head bouncing off the floor. A shape loomed over her and Carma realized it was the woman again, her brass-knuckled fist cocked.

"Chris," the station man said, rapping upon a heavily locked door that might've had its window blasted out by a shotgun. "Chris. You have a guest."

Someone spoke beyond the door.

"Not Chris?" the station man asked and looked at Carma. "Well, whatever. Enjoy the company while you can. You'll be leaving here today. Within the hour."

Carma tried to rise and discovered her hands had been duct taped together. So were her feet.

The woman mechanic smiled sweetly.

And punched Carma a second time, squarely in the face.

*

"Chris?" Kirk asked, staring at the hole in the glass. "My name's not Chris."

But Alice had already moved out of sight.

"Hey!"

He struggled to his feet but got dizzy and stopped. He heard the unmistakable sound of a solid punch, then another. There was movement, and then the metallic clang of locks being secured. When the floor stopped heaving, Kirk leaned against the door. Seconds later, he found the energy to pull himself to the window.

His heart shivered. *Not her.*

"Carma."

No response.

"Oh damn…" Kirk trailed. "Carma. Can you hear me?"

She didn't move. Her nose was a mash of flesh and blood.

You'll be leaving here today, Alice had said. *Within the hour.*

Within the hour, maybe even less than that. Which meant that if Kirk was going to escape, it would have to be soon. He looked out at the unconscious warden lying on the cement floor.

"Carma," he said. "Listen. You have to wake up. You have to wake up *now*. We don't have much time."

Just speaking drained him. He wondered just how bad his condition had become. He'd never felt so weak before.

"Carma. Please wake up," he pleaded, focusing on her face. "If you don't, I don't think we're going to get another chance to get out of here…"

20

Under a late morning sun, a black pickup with a crew cab rolled past Drover's town limits. Justin Gill didn't bother with sightseeing. He'd seen it all before and it bored him every time. There was nothing in Drover. The town's only notable feature was the bus station and service garage run by Alice and Jenna. It wasn't quite the honeyed fly trap like some of the other collection stations he frequented throughout the Americas, but Alice and Jenna had established a history of obtaining quality goods and delivering them intact.

In his line of business, Gill appreciated that.

Houses separated by fences, lawns, and trees scrolled past his window. He stared ahead and patted his knees with anticipation, anxious to see what awaited him in Alice's basement. Gill, with his designer pants and winter boots, and his black, double-breasted pea coat, was a creature of finer tastes. His business of procuring rare blood and organs for wealthy clients in critical need of donors, willing or screaming, afforded him a comfortable lifestyle, one that he enjoyed to the fullest every opportunity he had. He didn't wear a toque; he hated covering up his black mane wired with silver so fine that the highlighted strands might very well have been stenciled in. A set of impassive seventies sunglasses hid his blue eyes, startling peepers which had their vision sharpened by lasers not two years earlier. His teeth were routinely whitened to near icecap brightness and he even had a handful of titanium implants that cost him well over forty thousand dollars.

Appearances, Gill knew, were everything, and he was more than willing to travel to maintain his, even if it meant rolling into this particular outback shithole three or four times a year to obtain the precious organic gold his clients paid top dollar for.

He would certainly endure an extra trip for that special breed he and Alice had talked about.

A person who could regenerate himself.

At that thought, Gill's eyebrows arched to their limits, damn-near pole-vaulting to his well-oiled hairline.

A donor who could regrow organs. A living, breathing, human farm. A regenerating meatsicle.

Gill couldn't remember if he was high at the time or just entertaining a character's ramblings (and Alice and Jenna Clay were certainly characters), but that wasn't important. He'd listened to Alice babble about the existence of super humans before, hidden to the populace by the government. A type of conversation that Gill decided to go along with just for shits and giggles, not believing for a second that such a person existed. Not once.

But he'd say one thing for Alice and his eccentric nature—the man delivered. He was, in fact, one of Gill's most reliable and professional harvesters, despite his fantasizing about super humans and pitching plots best reserved for television.

Thus, here Gill was, back in the jungle. He rode with a full outfit no less, because even if Alice was only half-right about the potential donor in his captivity, it still warranted a look. Gill would probably even transfer the subject to a secret laboratory for more tests. At the very worst, Gill figured, the subject would prove to be a waste of time and Gill would have lost a couple of days' work.

But if Alice was right and there *was* evidence of a regenerative ability…

Well.

Gill's selective clientele would be happy indeed. He could very well purchase that island he'd spotted in the Lake Ontario area.

The service station came into view. Behind Gill's personal ride was the unmarked but ambulatory-shaped van that would deliver the donor to Ottawa for processing. Gill's driver, Vatcher, was a lean, rugged man with a mercenary's stare and the air of an English butler. The well-dressed operator had been with Gill for fifteen of the business's seventeen years. Vatcher came from Saskatchewan, and his world view was every bit as cold as that prairie province's winter. He decelerated when the service station came into view, and brought the two-vehicle convoy to a stop outside a garage bay door.

He sounded the horn twice while the van pulled into a turn, positioning itself to reverse into the garage.

Both bay doors opened with a subtle growl. Jenna Clay stood to one side, dressed in her workman's coverall that she somehow made magical, her left hip cocked as if she'd just body-checked some unfortunate bastard. Gill had to admit, Alice had to have done something right to attract his wife. When Vatcher finished parking, Gill got out, straightened out his knee-length pea coat with one slap, and approached her with an affable nod.

"Jenna," he greeted.

"Mr. Gill," she replied, ignoring Vatcher behind him.

The van backed into the garage bay, beeping warnings.

"Where's Alice?" Gill asked.

Upon mentioning the name, Alice stepped out from around a corner, his bulk squeezed into a uniform and matching bowtie better suited for a waiter.

Gill believed that a bowtie went with a tuxedo. Anything less belonged in a circus.

"Alice," he said.

"Mr. Gill," he replied in that characteristic, jaw-clamped-shut reply, as if he'd just chewed his way through a steel pipe.

"I've brought all my tools, as requested," Gill informed him, gesturing to the van and the loose circle of men forming around them, their breath visible on the cold air.

Alice nodded and beckoned with a hand. "I've got good news."

"You do? Besides this miracle of nature you have in your basement?"

"He really is something, Mr. Gill," Alice said. "You'll see. You'll be quite happy. I mean, I broke his bones and the next day they were all perfectly functional."

Gill stopped in his tracks as if catching a whiff of something freshly baked. "Broken bones, you say?"

"That's right."

"Well, that would be something to see."

"I'm telling you, Mr. Gill, we've never come across anyone, anything, quite like this. He truly is special." Alice lifted his chin. "But that's not the surprise."

"It's not?" Mr. Gill asked, his mouth refusing to shut.

*

"Carma," Kirk tried again, pleading with her as he had for the last twenty minutes.

She lay on her side, curled up as if asleep, but the blood covering the floor spoke otherwise. A few strands of her blonde hair soaked in the red.

And, as before, she refused to budge.

"Carma, *please*."

That time, her head twitched.

"Carma! C'mon, wakey, wakey."

She drew her chin in, rubbing her profile in scarlet and leaving streaks upon the concrete. Hair stuck at points, the tips glued to the floor, but she moved with increasing strength.

"That's it," Kirk tried again. "C'mon back."

"Douglas?"

"Yeah."

She attempted to lift her head, groaned softly, and rested for a second.

He smiled. "Yeah, they got you, too."

"They got *you*. I let myself get caught."

"That have something to do with them calling me Chris?"

"Yeah," she said. "Give me a minute."

Kirk nodded, his forehead thumping against the door.

"The bitch hits hard," Carma finally whispered and rolled over like an uneven log. When she hit the wall, she wormed her way into a seated position and regarded Kirk with an exasperated look. Blood caked her mouth and her nose was squished to one side.

"Her name's Jenna," Kirk whispered, cringing at Carma's extreme touch-up. "The other's Alice."

"How'd these goofs catch you?"

"Got clocked upside the head."

"Jesus," Carma said, wincing at him.

"What?"

"Are they starving you?"

"Ah, no," Kirk smiled. He should have realized it. He'd been practicing changing, and every transformation he'd attempted burned more calories. "I'm okay. Just a little weak. Listen, you gotta get free, okay?"

"'Course I gotta get free. Give me a second."

She flexed, focusing her considerable *were*-enhanced strength on the duct tape binding her hands.

And failed.

Her battered features lit up in surprise at the unsuccessful attempt. She tried again, twisted and pulled, bared teeth, and gave up in a huff.

"Holy shit," she panted. "They really make this stuff."

"Can't do it?" Kirk asked.

"I can do it, just give me a minute."

"Do what they do in the movies," Kirk directed. "Scoot your backside through your arms. At least then you'll have your hands in front of you."

"I'm not a contortionist, Douglas. And I happen to have a very muscular ass."

Kirk didn't say anything to that.

Carma tried her bonds again. She struggled for a good ten seconds before giving up with a head shake. "God*damnit*, that's tough. I'm gonna lose some blood on this one."

"You can always change."

That earned him a scowl. "Change with my arms stuck behind my back? Nuh-uh. I don't think so. Just let me catch my breath here."

"We don't have much time."

Carma looked at him. "You going somewhere?"

"I think so."

"What do you mean?"

A weary smile spread over his face. "They know I can heal faster than normal. As far as I know, I'm going to be cut up for my organs and sent to an illegal chop shop for the black market. The kind where desperate people will pay good money for whatever they need."

Carma gawked. "Those things are for real?"

"Guess so. And the people who run it are on their way here."

"Here. To get you."

"And you," Kirk reasoned. "Can't see them leaving you behind."

"They don't know about me."

"They don't have to. You're spare parts. Pretty but…"

Carma frowned. "Great. How much time do we have?"

"I dunno. Not much."

"Like *how* not much?"

"Like any minute."

*

"A woman as well?" Mr. Gill repeated, taking in the news. "You really have been busy. Is she like him?"

Alice shook his head. "I don't think so. I really didn't get a chance to test her. She showed up earlier this morning looking for him. They were supposed to meet in Toronto."

"Figures," Gill smirked. "I just came from that way. Shame we didn't have a means of tracking them down. I could've saved myself a trip."

And several millions, Alice thought but he kept that to himself. "You can have her as well. No sense in leaving scraps on the table."

"No, I suppose not. You remember Mr. Vatcher?"

Mr. Gill indicated the man behind him.

"I do. Mr. Vatcher," Alice greeted. Alice didn't really like Vatcher, and he suspected the feeling was mutual.

The garage doors closed, sealing them all inside the bay.

A pair of men inside the van prepped a gurney with reinforced straps, then joined the others. A third man carried an ominous silver suitcase. Jenna stood by her husband's side and Alice appreciated her reinforcement.

"Well, then, lead on," Mr. Gill smiled, his sunglasses gleaming in the sparse light. "I want to be homeward bound within the hour. Winter driving. Don't know when the snow will hit."

"I understand," Alice muttered and led the way. The men followed him into the service station's front desk area, while Jenna went behind the counter and ran a finger over the silver dome of the bell. Alice continued on down the short corridor, to a door that might've opened to a corner broom closet except for the assortment of locks. He took a moment to fiddle with the security measures. When the door opened, an unpleasant odor of body fluids wrinkled Gill's face and those just behind him.

"You need to air this place out," Gill said, his hand muffling his words.

"I'll do that later," Alice rumbled and flicked a switch. A set of stairs winked into bare incandescent existence.

"Looking forward to this," Gill said, his eyebrows jumping.

Alice often wondered about those well-groomed mouse tails. They arched and frowned so much that Gill could communicate without uttering a word, and when he did speak, his constantly shifting eyebrows lent an air of condescension.

"I know you are," Alice rumbled as he descended. "Me too."

"Have you done anything else to him since you called me?" Gill asked.

"No. Nothing. I'm not outfitted for that stuff. Only the little things, like I mentioned. Bruised him. Cut him. Broke some bones." Alice spoke as if checking off items on a grocery list. "Nothing any bigger. Not after stomping on his hand and foot. I knew I had something special by that point."

"And he fully healed?"

Alice turned around with a pout firmly in place. "Everything. Within a day. I could've set up a camera to record the whole thing but I don't have one. I was convinced enough to call you, and you know *I* know you intend to conduct your own tests. I wouldn't have called you otherwise."

Gill's eyebrows went up again like two needles on a bullshit detector. Alice suspected the man had one well-exercised set of frontalis muscles. Probably corrugators, as well.

They descended to a landing, turned to a second set of stairs, and descended again. The third and final set brought them to a small open space where a second, solid-looking door waited. Locks and bolts covered the right side and Alice got to work on them. He paused at the last and half-turned.

"Just a warning," Alice whispered to the men at his back and standing on the stairs, "I didn't mention this part over the phone. He says he's a mutant."

"Excuse me?" Gill asked, eyebrows damn-near merging with his hairline.

"That's what he says. Said he was with a secret government project dealing with increasing a whole bunch of abilities. Healing was one of them. Strength was another."

"Strength?"

"Yeah, ah… he's very strong. He busted the window in the cell door and that was pretty thick glass. Not quite tempered but layered."

"He broke… your window," an impressed Mr. Gill whispered.

"He did. Just keep that in mind. Said that some folks were looking for him and there was one about a week ago, but I sent her away and she never came back. There was no one else after that. Except for today. The woman, now, she's a friend. I remember him talking to her on the phone. So just be careful about government agents."

"Won't be a concern," Gill stated dismissively. He removed his sunglasses and added, "Let's take a look."

Vatcher stood just by his boss's side, his face impassive.

Alice faced the door and gripped the last lock.

*

Gonna lose some skin on this one, Carma thought as she pulled and twisted on her bonds, feeling the tape give just a fraction.

"Try doing it while changing," Kirk called from his cell.

"It's gonna hurt if I do that with my arms behind my back."

"It's gonna hurt more if you don't."

Carma sighed. The man was right. She had nothing to lose.

She summoned the change, allowing her *were*-blood to flow freely through her veins. Her body responded like a mothballed turbine coming to life. Power crackled and surged into her torso and limbs. Her spine straightened with a spasm and her jaws stretched. Her eyes, bloodshot and protruding, near popped from her skull while her head whipped from side to side. She flexed her supercharged arms, snapping the tape like a flimsy rubber band. She curled in upon herself, gritting her teeth, taking the swelling waves of pain and pleasure. Her growing frame split the seams of her clothing. Claws and teeth extended and flexed. Her nose corrected itself and elongated into a muzzle. Ears lengthened and all of her senses came online as the change completed itself.

Seconds later, the rattling of the outer door's locks caught her attention. She squared up, yellow eyes focused, tawny fur sleek and rippling with powerful musculature. All sound had stopped beyond the barrier, and she wondered if the person outside had heard her.

But then one final *click* broke the silence.

She held her breath.

Alice opened the door. He wasn't alone. A small gathering of men stood behind him, filling the narrow corridor. The well-dressed man beside Alice tensed, visibly stricken by the unexpected sight before them. Cries of warning went up and men reached for concealed weapons.

Carma charged.

Alice's bespectacled eyes flashed wide as if magnified a hundred times. One paw ripped his face off in an explosion of blood, backing his head up on his shoulders. The blow bounced his raggedy body off the nearby wall, a single drum beat amongst a high-pitched wailing of pipes. Alice's corpse slumped to the floor, smearing the wall with color.

Carma plunged into the others. She crushed the skull of the well-dressed man and chomped the hand off a man beside him. She pushed forward, catapulting herself amongst the others. There was no finesse in the slaughter, just undiluted rage. Screams filled the stairwell, the peals high enough to turn bone marrow to ice. She caught a head in her jaws and crushed it in a crack of bone, then rushed toward the man highest on the steps, raking his back from shoulders to buttocks in a grisly spray of flesh and cloth. Carma trampled two other men and shredded them in great gouts of scarlet. She twisted and turned in the narrow space, snapping and clawing at anything that moved.

A gunshot and her shoulder instantly burned. She whirled and saw, at the bottom of the stairs, the man with the missing hand, his wrist bubbling. His other hand, surprisingly steady, held a gun. Their eyes met. Carma lunged. The steady gunman fired twice more before she slammed into him. She squished him against the wall, bit into his side with a gnashing of carnassials, and tasted metallic kidney. Securing her bite, she whipped him back and forth. Limbs flapped at her face and back.

Carma dropped her dead chew toy and bounded up the stairs. She turned on a landing and spotted one final survivor pounding up the steps. She leaped and caught a foot halfway to the top, twisting it in a crinkle of bone. The man squealed and sought to shoot her, just before she stomped on his ribs like a flimsy shoe box. All fight left him.

A smell caught Carma's attention, one of perfume.

She looked to the top of the stairs.

And there, framed in the open doorway, stood the mechanic. The one Kirk had called Jenna. The one who had hit her. Repeatedly.

Carma jumped off the bloody mat beneath her and charged the closing door.

*

The noise caught Jenna's attention. She walked to the open door leading to the basement and paused, eyes narrowing at the violent caterwauling. A loud crash shook the staircase as one of Mr. Gill's people now lay flat, bloodied, on a lower step. Jenna watched in horror as a giant dog dragged him down and proceeded to stomp him to a pulp. The beast put a paw through the dead man's chest, breaking ribs like dry kindling.

The animal spotted her.

Jenna slammed the door and secured the first bolt just as the monster hit the barrier head on. Fright seized Jenna but she worked on as the door shook. Her fingers couldn't quite secure the remaining locks. Unlike the doors in the basement, this one was made of thick wood. She got a grip on a bolt just as the wolf slammed the door again, the thick surface shivering. The pounding increased, the door bucked. Jenna struggled with the locks but failed to secure them under the constant barrage.

The wood finally cracked.

Jenna shrieked.

Fibers split. Splinters fell. Claws pulled at shards squealing under the frenzied assault. An enormous, toothy snout poked through with a roar. The muzzle withdrew and pushed forth again. A spike of wood lanced the monster's black lip, drawing a spurting line along the bottom jaws. The wolf recoiled and shoved its head entirely through, heedless of its wound, snapping and twisting and widening the breach.

Yellow eyes locked on Jenna and she stumbled back. Unlike her man, she watched all manner of television shows, the ones with the paranormal investigators being her favorite. And in those shows, she always swore at the idiots who disbelieved the obvious supernatural clues that damned near left her screaming vanilla profanities (Alice didn't like the hard stuff) at their stupidity. Jenna vowed if she ever found herself tracking a suspected undead creature or some other animated terror of the night, she would not ignore the obvious. She would believe that shit and damn well fight.

And as God was her witness, the thing bursting through her doorway was a goddamn *werewolf*.

It was all clear to her now.

The meat in the basement wasn't a mutant at all, as Alice had told her. The meat in the basement was a ravenous monster of the night, when full moons rose over the land. She didn't know what magical abilities a werewolf had, but she knew one weakness.

She ran back to the counter, the door exploding behind her.

But that was okay.

That was just fine.

Because just before Mr. Gill and his men arrived to check out Alice's miracle prisoner, Jenna had discovered something. Something that just put the beast down. She'd been rummaging through the car parked right outside—the one belonging to that bitch they'd clocked in the face and dragged into the basement.

It hadn't taken Jenna long to find the leather sheath in the glove box. Inside was a dagger with a highly reflective blade, like the silverware she and Alice had swiped from their last victim—an annoying salesman selling kitchen cutlery.

Strange for a little bitch to be carrying such an expensive and exotic weapon. She'd brought it back into the station and placed it on the countertop, just when Mr. Gill and his travelling body snatchers drove up to the station.

Now it made sense. To a point, anyway.

Those things downstairs weren't *mutants*. They were monsters. Jenna had an honest-to-God werewolf in her basement, and for some reason unknown, the good Lord had also supplied the means to protect herself. Funny, considering all the vile shit she and Alice had done.

Jenna snatched up the gleaming weapon. In her small but strong hands, the blade was the size of a short sword.

She spun around, already a cool one-liner forming in her head.

The enormity of the monster emerging from the corridor took Jenna's breath away. The thing crept towards her, its shoulders waist-high, and wide. She couldn't see how long the beast was, but it was long. The werewolf didn't make a sound when it stopped at the far end of the counter. Its golden eyes beheld her, a low growl rumbling through the interior like a motorcycle parked in front of a microphone. Blood spattered the floor; the clock above counted off the last seconds Jenna might have upon the planet.

"C'mon then," she said, defying the fear wreaking her heart. Jenna held the knife in a high guard, its twinkling point aimed at the floor. "C'mon and see—"

What you get was what she meant to say.

The wolf lunged, slamming into Jenna's mid-section and buckling her in two.

*

The smell of cooling blood wafted through the hole in the window, tormenting Kirk. He listened, dying to hear anything and getting nothing. There was a distant crash, then a scream—a woman's scream—curt and piercing. Then nothing.

Kirk waited, looking into the room, the massacre in plain view. A rosy dark tide seeped across the floor, and the smell of it wrenched a moan from his throat. The gloomy deluge oozed along, unhurried, splitting into two currents.

Kirk licked his lips.

The divided flows forked towards his door.

Oh shit, he thought as the blood seeped closer. A wind rose, confined to his ears only. His pulse exceeded recommended rpms. He tracked the blood, counting off the seconds as it reached for the door's base, until he could no longer see it from his angle.

Kirk dropped to his knees, his cheek pressed to the door. Sweat beaded his forehead. He flattened his palms on the cement floor and lowered himself as if in prayer. His nose touched the door's seam. That rich, unrestricted flow of goodness was only inches away. Kirk licked his lips. Maybe some would leak through.

He pressed his tongue deep into the scant line between metal and concrete, waiting for contact. All he needed was a *taste*, goddammit. Just *one* taste.

"Douglas?"

Carma's ragged voice startled him. He withdrew from the door.

"Douglas?"

"Yeah," he got to his feet.

Carma's face appeared in the broken window. She was naked, pale, and bleeding along a gash in her right shoulder.

The wound paralyzed Kirk.

"You still alive in there?" she asked, rubbing at a reformed nose.

"Yeah."

She smiled weakly and fumbled with the locks. Kirk watched her head bob up and down, but his attention wandered to her wound.

Her *tantalizing* wound.

Carma paused at the last bolt. "Got them all," she muttered, exhausted. "That last one was... was a real bitch. You know what... she did?"

Kirk didn't know. Didn't really care. He had bigger

problems. Blood streaked Carma's white back, as bright and sweet as candied apples.

"She stabbed me," Carma said as she wrestled free the last lock. "Bitch... actually stabbed me. I thought I was faster. But she must've... must've gotten one last blast of adrenaline. She made it count."

Carma stumbled back from the door and landed, of all places, in the bloody pool issuing from the human wreckage she'd left in the hall. Kirk pushed the door open, his confinement finished. He gathered Carma into his arms and she rested her head against his chest. Her blood soaked into Kirk's coverall, the same coverall Alice had thrown at him. That metallic aroma swamped his senses. Lord above, she smelled... *good*.

"You better... deal with this," she whispered.

Kirk wavered, nostrils flaring, transfixed by the raw ruby fissure that continued to bleed. His lips drew back and his jaws ached. The room swayed and warped. *Silver*. Jenna had stabbed her with silver. That evil taint got him thinking straight. He needed fire to scorch and seal the wound.

Then he remembered a second way to save her. The same way he'd saved Ross Kelly. He could bite her, sink his teeth into that gruesome puncture wound. Bite deep and let his deviant strain of lycanthropy flow into her.

He'd be doing her a favor.

Carma's wound would seal up completely. She'd be faster, *stronger*...

"Kirk," she whispered, and the word echoed in his head. The wound continued to weep, covering her shoulder. The underground prison faded in color. Everything except the blood. That shade deepened, twinkled in the growing monochromic splendor.

"Kirk?" Carma asked from somewhere outside the room.

Kirk recoiled in horror, realizing he'd been lifting her to his mouth. He regained his senses, shook his head clear of vicious thoughts, and stood. He carried Carma across the floor, leaving footprints in the blood. Outside, he recognized the unmoving lump of Alice to the right of the doorway, his pinstriped shirt dyed a frightening shade, his bowtie hanging askew. Kirk ignored the missing face and the mass of material covering the floor like a dishcloth saturated in oil. Bodies littered the stairs, the smell intoxicating.

He focused on the first landing and carefully ascended.

Hands and limbs of dead men sought to trip him. Blood slicked the stairs and oozed between his toes. The last thing he needed was to fall facedown into that stew of death and shredded parts. If he did, he knew he would start chewing, and if that happened, he wasn't sure he could stop.

But that wasn't what really frightened him.

If he started feeding on the men, he knew, eventually, he'd take big sopping bites out of Carma.

That made him smile.

"Are you laughing?" Carma asked, her cheek against his chest.

"No."

"You are," she accused. "You're fucking laughing. I'm dying here… and you're chuckling… your ass off. You're something else, Douglas Kirk."

"That's right," he whispered into her hair. "I'm laughing. You got stabbed by a bitch."

"With my own badge," Carma muttered in self-loathing.

"Don't you worry about that." Kirk climbed clear of the dead, turned on the landing, and stomped up the next round of steps.

"Where'd she get it?" he asked. Carma's voice distracted him from other thoughts.

"From my... car."

Kirk reached another landing, turned a corner, and saw the destroyed door at the top of the stairs. His calves burned. His senses swam. His stomach tightened and whined, wondering why he hadn't eaten yet...

He lumbered through the doorway, cracking Carma's ankles against the frame. She acknowledged the blow with a rubbery bob of her head.

"Take it easy," she moaned, as if half-asleep.

That got Kirk moving even faster.

He stopped at the front desk, turning left and right, wondering where to go. Bloody footprints marked their trail from the basement, converging with another path to that point. The spatters led to Jenna's torn body behind the counter. A jagged 'U' of meat and bone was missing from her left shoulder and neckline.

"Cold," Carma hissed, barely saying the word.

"We're practically outside," Kirk said.

She didn't answer.

That scared him. Urgency gripped Kirk as he considered the entrance and the car parked beyond before focusing on the garage bay door. He pulled the brown door open, seeing the parked pickup and the open doors of a van.

The van resembled an ambulance; IVs dangled over a menacing gurney, the tubing connected to clear sacks filled with mysterious fluids. With a grunt Kirk deposited Carma's limp form on the floor. He climbed aboard, mindful of the woman curling up at his feet, and searched a cabinet. He clawed through an assortment of bandages, scissors, and surgical tape, but nothing of the preventative measure Kirk needed.

He jumped out of the back and zeroed in on a door inside the garage, to the left of a tall pegboard. In seconds he was outside, running over a pathway of white patio stones, towards a two-story house not twenty strides away. Alice and Jenna's house of horrors, he assumed. Kirk let himself in. He stood in the kitchen and sighted the yellow drawers. *Junk drawer*, he thought. There had to be a junk drawer.

He found it, next to the fridge. He jerked it open and quickly located a lighter. Then he yanked the tablecloth free with a clatter of plastic flowers and glass vases. Surprisingly, a bulky telephone set stayed in place.

He bolted back to the garage.

Blood trickled to the concrete floor as Carma lay on her wounded side, curled into a loose knot of hurt. The sight of all that white flesh alarmed Kirk, and when he dangled the tablecloth over the lighter, he flicked the wheel hard enough to drop the device entirely. He snatched up the lighter and tried again.

The flame leaped, quickly igniting the cloth.

Stooping beside Carma with a flaming ribbon, Kirk pushed her onto her back.

She screamed at the fire's touch.

21

"Douglas?"

Kirk turned and regarded Carma lying on Alice and Jenna's sofa. He hunched down and gently stroked her hair.

"Hi," he whispered.

"Hi."

He nodded at the response, happy to hear her speak.

"Was it bad?" she asked.

"It was close."

"You burned me."

"Yeah."

"You know…" Carma said weakly. "When I was out, I could smell meat cooking. Strange, huh?"

"Not to me."

Her eyes slid to one side, to study the ceiling. "Where are we?"

"Alice and Jenna's house."

"Where?"

"Alice—"

"I heard you the first time," Carma interrupted and

studied his face. "You still look like shit."

Kirk smiled and rested his head on the sofa's arm.

"I see you got a blanket for me," Carma observed.

"Much as I hated to do it. A figure like yours."

She smirked, then whispered, "We can't stay here, Douglas."

"I know."

"We should be moving soon."

"You got your keys? Or should we take one of the other cars?"

Carma sighed. "My jeans. They're in my jeans. My phone, too. I think. If they didn't take it."

"That means I'll have to go into the station again. The house is just behind it. Nice place, actually, considering who lived in it."

"Someone'll come here," Carma said.

Kirk smiled. "Way ahead of you. After I sealed that stab wound and you passed out, I locked all the front doors to the station and flipped over the 'OPEN' sign. There's only a sedan out front—"

"That's mine."

"Okay. Otherwise, the place looks closed. We should be good for the night. Drover's not a big place. I don't think this station has a lot of business. I'll move your car. Get it out of sight so as not to arouse the neighbors."

"Did you eat anything?"

Kirk studied her for a few seconds. "Not yet. I was waiting for you."

"Bring me something."

Having his orders, Kirk brought her leftover spaghetti with meat sauce. There was half a pot of the stuff in the fridge, along with an assortment of other cold meats.

"This isn't what I want," Carma said, disappointed.

"It's what you're getting."

She tucked the blanket around her naked self, sat up with some pain, and slowly ate. Kirk joined her.

*

While they dined in relative silence, Carma's cellphone buzzed and spun in place beneath the countertop in the bus station.

It rang six times before it went silent.

*

After they'd finished the spaghetti, Carma ordered Kirk to bring over every other edible remaining in the fridge. She ate everything, including foul slabs of sliced ham that should have been chucked days earlier.

"That shit looks evil," Kirk said.

"Went down okay."

"It won't come out okay."

"I'll worry about that tomorrow. Anything else over there?" Carma asked.

"There's a freezer with pizza, meat patties, sausages, a few roasts…"

Carma relaxed. "So get cooking. You know how this goes."

"Yeah. Before I get to that, I've been wanting to ask you. Why'd you come here?"

"Why do you think?" she asked weakly. "Needed to find out what was happening to you. Good thing I did. I think I mentioned you look like shit."

Kirk smiled. She'd never change. "I'm not what the elders say I am, Carma."

She didn't answer right away. "Listen. Talk about that later, okay? Maybe after I'm feeling better. Then, we'll figure things out."

He searched her face for untruths and saw none. "All right. Just to be clear, we should be gone from here in the morning. I'll feel better once we're on the road."

"Find my badge," Carma said. "And my phone. Car keys, too. There are spare clothes in my car."

"I'll get the phone and keys."

"And the clothes."

"You look good to me."

"I bet."

"I'll get everything," Kirk said. "Don't you worry."

"Wake me if you need me," Carma said and frowned.

I will, Kirk projected and went to work.

*

Not ten minutes later, he found Carma's silver blade in a sticky blood spatter behind the garage's counter, next to one very dead Jenna. Kirk tried hard not to look too closely at the corpse, but his peripheral caught plenty. Underneath the counter lay the weapon's leather sheath, as well as a cellphone, a woman's wallet, and a set of car keys. Kirk felt a pang of relief upon finding the items so easily. He needed a break.

His attention shifted to the gory footprints covering the floor, and before he did anything else, he located a janitor's room in the bus station. With the coverall he wore, he thought he'd be able to pass himself off as a janitor for a short time. *A barefoot janitor*, he winced. That ruse wouldn't last for long, so he got to work. He filled a bucket with hot water, grabbed a mop, and started scrubbing all the smears and prints. He worked quietly, steadily, wringing out his mop with bare hands when necessary, erasing all signs of blood right back to the wrecked basement door. The stink wafting from the slaughter below stopped him for a few moments. So much rotting meat lay at the bottom of the stairs, but he wasn't about to touch any of it. Neither was Carma. He composed himself and kicked the wooden splinters cluttering the floor into the stairwell.

Then he gripped the mop one last time, meaning to wring out every last drop.

He stopped in mid-twist.

The sound of an approaching engine narrowed his eyes. *Well, shit.*

The sound grew louder—a big diesel engine, probably a big rig or a bus. He snatched up his bucket and mop and hurried to the entryway. He inspected the wet, gleaming floor, and deemed it clean. The bucket rattled as he shoved it behind the counter.

The engine drew closer.

Kirk wavered, not sure of where to hide his bloody hobo self, before ducking behind the countertop. There he waited on hands and knees, eyes on the verge of popping from his face.

A bus pulled into the service station and stopped with a squeal and huff of hydraulic brakes. There it stayed, thrumming like some great metallic hound sniffing injustice on the air.

Kirk held his head in his hands and feared the worst.

The machine rumbled, questioning the closed sign in the doorway. In the sleepy silence of Drover, Kirk suddenly appreciated just how loud the long-distance passenger vehicles could be. A hiss of a swinging door caused him to cringe. Visions filled his head, of dozens of faceless visitors standing outside the station's glass door, reading the CLOSED sign, and wondering just what they could do in a shithole like Drover.

Not much, Kirk mentally informed them. *So just get back on that bus and leave.*

Someone knocked on the front door's glass, and Kirk flinched as though it were a quick burst of machine gun fire.

His head sunk between his shoulders.

"Hello?" a woman asked in a wondering tone.

He cringed.

Just go. Just go away.

"Hello?" she repeated to no avail.

He pictured her with a hand cupped against the glass. A faceless driver who knew Alice well enough to know his daily schedule, and never in all her years of visiting the town had the man ever flipped the station's sign to CLOSED. Not this time of the day. Alice wasn't the type who wouldn't miss a day's work for any reason, and certainly wouldn't excuse his absence with a mere sign stuck in the window. That just wouldn't do.

Kirk gripped his hair.

A metallic whine marked the passing of a minute. It wasn't the engine, which was still running, so Kirk remained still for a few seconds more.

Something thumped against the station's glass door, followed by another moment of waiting. Perhaps she was studying the station's inner depths, scanning for Alice's pinstriped torso and his angry dork face.

The engine droned on, now a soundtrack to the developing predicament.

A bus door slammed, ending Kirk's suspense. He exhaled and waited. The engine revved. Gears shifted and wheels crackled over asphalt. The bus rolled away from the station, paused in another squeal of brakes, and then picked up speed. The machine hurried away, the sound lessening with every thankful second.

A few heartbeats later, it tapered off into nothing.

Kirk remained motionless, even though his elbows bothered him.

A good five minutes later he stuck his head out and saw a cardboard box nudged against the door. A white label was affixed to the top of the package. There were no people hanging about the station's front.

The coast was clear. Except for the parcel.

You can stay there, buddy, Kirk thought. He snatched up Carma's silver blade and swished it around in the bucket. Once it was clean, he shook it dry and jammed the weapon into its sheath. The knife, cellphone, wallet, and keys went into his pockets. He went outside and discovered the car door unlocked and an overnight bag stuffed with spare clothes. He grabbed the bag, locked the station's main entrance, and left the parcel where it was dropped. Seeing no one around, he plodded toward the house.

The sofa was empty. Carma was gone.

The sight paralyzed him for a moment. "Carma?"

No answer.

He moved to the dining room, and eventually went upstairs. Soft snores led him to a tastefully decorated bedroom that might've been time-warped in from the fifties. White walls as pure as snow surrounded a single double-sized bed covered with thick brown blankets. An unlit lamp in the shape of a lantern stood on guard next to Carma's sleeping head. She had managed to walk upstairs and slip beneath the blankets, which meant good things. The place was empty of clothing and Kirk deduced the room was for guests, even though it was difficult to conceive that Alice and Jenna had friends.

The overnight bag thumped softly on the floor. Kirk studied Carma's form, the top blanket pulled tight to her nose. She slept on her side, her right shoulder bare. A wide bandage had been applied to the wound, the center of the pad blotted with a dime-sized spot of darkness. He considered pulling the blanket up over the wound, but decided not to disturb her. She looked comfortable.

And, frankly, he liked watching her sleep. Liked seeing how her face relaxed and the rhythmic rise and fall of her frame.

Kirk chewed on the inside of his lip and wondered who he was kidding.

He loved watching her sleep. Always had. Probably always would.

Even if it did only happen in captured replays of the mind.

He committed the scene to memory and backed out of the room, not wanting to wake her.

Kirk missed Carma cracking open a sleepy eye.

The steps were carpeted, muffling his descent. He wandered into the kitchen, barely registering how dark the room had become. The sheathed blade, cellphone, and wallet all went onto the table. The car keys went into his chest pocket. With the evening settling in, Kirk wandered into the living room and plopped down on the sofa. He stared out of wide windows, at the black husk of the garage and bus station. The building hid the residence from the road, which was probably Alice and Jenna's intentions.

The house was quiet.

The sofa was comfortable, despite him knowing the previous owners.

Kirk closed his eyes and drifted, allowing himself just a few minutes of peace.

He lifted his head with a start, blinked, and scratched at his growing beard. His stomach rumbled, and he remembered Morris.

Dead and gone.

You poor bastard.

Ross Kelly popped into Kirk's mind then. Seconds later,

he was dialing Ross's number on Alice's telephone set on the kitchen table. A clock informed him that it was just after six o'clock in the evening. That surprised him. He thought he'd only dozed for a few minutes.

The call went through, ringing as if summoning monsters from a void. Kirk scanned the kitchen, hoping that Ross Kelly would answer the call.

But he didn't.

An automated voice cut in. "Your call could not be completed. Please check your listing and try again."

Oh Jesus, Kirk thought. He hung up and wondered what had happened. Then he remembered one of Ross's neighbors—his number was only two digits different from Ross's. Kirk immediately dialed, getting the number correct after the third attempt.

The call went through. The phone wavered as he suspected the worst, but no automated voice cut in.

On perhaps the eighth ring, he pulled the phone away just as a distant voice said, "Hello?"

Kirk jammed the phone back into his ear. "Alvin? That you?"

Alvin Peters, Ross's friend with the breathing problems.

The voice paused. "Yes, my son, 'tis me. That you, Dougie?"

"Alvin, where's Ross?" Kirk demanded.

Another pause, more awkward than the last. "This is Dougie, right?"

Kirk pinched the bridge of his nose. Lord, he hated being called that. "Yeah, it's Doug, yeah."

"Jaysus *Christ* Dougie! I didn't recognize the number at all. We gets all sorts of fuckin' tele-morons callin' from Gawd knows where, askin' Gawd knows what. All Jesus sorts. There was even a fuckin' scam where the smart bloodsabitches had somehow fuckin' cloned the cops' numbers. The *cops*, now! How ye like that?"

"Alvin," Kirk persisted, forcing a calmness into his voice that deserved a medal. "Where's Ross?"

"Ah," Alvin faltered. "He's dead, Dougie. Gone. The cops think he was shot, but nothing's been confirmed yet. Just a bunch of tracks around his house. Whoever did it burned him up in his own home. Burned old Ross's shack to the ground. It… it was terrible. Horrible. I mean…"

The gush of words stabbed Kirk to his core. "What happened?"

"No one knows," Alvin explained. "The cops don't know. They're investigatin' but they can't figure anything out. All they found was…"

At this, Alvin's voice cracked. "All they found was Ross's teeth. And bones. Sacred heart of Mary. Some were sayin' it was a mob hit, but that ain't true. I mean, that man was pretty much the only family I had around here and I'll take the stand that he had nothin' to do with that crowd. He was cleaner than fresh tighty whiteys. D'fuck could it be, Dougie? By the Lord God—"

"Ross is gone," Kirk whispered into the receiver.

Alvin slowed down, sensing the other's shock. "Yeah. He's gone. We're gonna bury his remains when the police is all finished. Little town cemetery. Up on the hill. Out back of his place. Right next to his mudder and fadder."

All breath had leaked out of the Halifax warden. He gazed off into space, eyes stricken and moist, his throat constricting.

Ross Kelly, too. Kirk remembered how he thought he was saving the man's life by changing him. In the end, however, he'd killed him after all.

"Y'still there?" Alvin asked.

Guilt flooded Kirk's system, stalling him. Beyond the living room windows, at that instant, a shadow passed in front of the glass. A spiderlike wraith, hunched and soundless, darting from left to right. The unexpected appearance of the phantom took but a second to process.

"Dougie? Jesus, Dougie don't leave me hangin' here," Alvin yakked. "Bad enough to almost miss ya—y'know I was trying to find your number, but Rossy never had it written down anywhere and I never bothered to ask. I mean—"

A figure loomed up before the clear living room pane. The ghostly outline moved like someone attempting to free themselves from a black sack.

"I have to go," Kirk whispered.

"Wha?"

"Call me later at this number."

He whispered Carma's cellphone number, knowing it by heart. "Got it?"

"Yeah, but—"

Kirk broke the connection, slipping the receiver back into its cradle. He sank below the kitchen table as quietly as possible. No other sound disturbed the house. Kirk crouched, kept his eyes on the shape in the window, and pressed his back against a cupboard. He kept his head low and waited, scanning the kitchen window directly across from him.

It took him a moment to realize that the shape had vanished.

Someone knocked at the door.

Kirk tensed, wondering who would visit after sundown. Maybe Alice had a private auction planned and these were the late arrivals.

"Alice, you in there?" a voice called.

Alice is not in here, Kirk projected, *so go away*. His attention centered on the kitchen window, knowing he was exposed. Anyone could see him pressed up against the cupboards if they walked to that window and peered inside. He dropped to his stomach and slipped back into the living room.

The knocking didn't repeat.

Kirk slid over a rug and stopped behind the sofa. There he stayed, listening, hearing nothing but his own breathing.

Five minutes. Ten. Perhaps fifteen.

Time dragged, torturing Kirk until he stuck his head for a peek. As far as he could tell, the visitor had departed. He wondered if it really was a neighbor or someone Alice and Jenna thought of as a friend. In any case, the episode rattled his nerves. Staying in the house was a mistake. He and Carma needed to get away from this place and quickly, because he suspected something was coming for them.

The stairs creaked as he climbed them two at a time.

When he stopped at the bed, he was breathing hard.

"Carma," he said, running a hand over her head.

"I'm awake."

"You are?"

"Yeah, heard someone knocking at the door," she said in a low tone. "Who was it?"

"Don't know. Maybe a friend."

"These fuck-ups have friends?"

"Looks that way. I think we should move."

"Yeah," she said.

Kirk left her for the master bedroom, stopping in a hallway to peek through a window. Night masked the cold grounds below, but he couldn't detect a soul down there. He hurried into the bedroom, found a closet, and yanked out a pair of backpacks. Into these he stuffed stockings, sweaters, and t-shirts. He still had on the coverall that Alice had given him and it was fine for now, but Kirk needed decent footwear. There was a set of formal dress shoes but they were three sizes too big, so he left them.

A glint of metal caught his attention.

A strongbox with a dial was tucked into the closet's lower corner. Kirk regarded the thing, picked the box up and shook it. The contents rattled. He tugged on the box's handle.

Locked.

He stuffed the strongbox inside the backpack, then grabbed a set of women's sneakers, an extra sweater and t-shirt, and a pair of stretchy pants. With these he returned to Carma.

"Anything?" she asked, holding the blanket around her shoulders.

"Yeah. Here."

He dropped the packs on the bed and held out the selected clothing. Carma looked at her bag, then the t-shirt and sweater, and finally him. "What are those?"

"Extra," he informed her. "A little bigger. Maybe more comfortable."

"Sold," Carma said. "I could start bleeding again anytime. Rather do it in her clothes."

Kirk supposes so.

"You're gonna have to help me." Carma told him.

"What?"

"I can't lift my shoulder," she explained. "Matter of fact, this is gonna hurt like a bitch. Help me get dressed. I'll put on the clothes you brought me."

She shrugged off the blanket.

Perhaps it was the lack of light, or her husky whisper, but the picture of Carma's bare upper body caught him off-guard.

"Quit staring," she scolded.

"I wasn't staring."

"My face is up here."

Kirk cleared his throat. "What do you want me to do?"

"Just hold up that t-shirt for a minute."

He did and Carma, with considerable pain, struggled to get into the clothing. The sweater was worse, the sleeves torturous. In the end, she gave up, sweat coating her face.

"Get a towel," she told him. "Make a sling. I'll wear the sweater over the arm."

Kirk went into the washroom. The towels there were a little too plush. A hallway closet had a stash of summer sheets. He grabbed two and returned to Carma.

"Find anything?" she asked.

Kirk held up the sheet.

"Nice," Carma said.

He smiled and produced her knife. A minute later, a rough sling hung around Carma's neck. She hissed as he fitted her limp arm into the loop.

"All right," she panted and eyed the sweater. "Let's try that again. Just one arm this time."

That time it worked. Kirk pulled the sweater down over her crippled arm, her face a rictus of discomfort the whole time. But she got the sweater on.

"Okay," she gasped. "All downhill from here. Help me with those yoga pants and let's get out of here."

About fifteen minutes later, Kirk and Carma walked from the house like a couple who'd downed far too many tequila shots. They leaned heavily on each other as they threaded their way around the lightless hulk of the station. Once they reached the vehicle, Kirk held the passenger door open and he eased her inside.

"Oh man," she said, her head thudding against the seat rest. "This really sucks. I'm in agony here."

"Want some aspirin?" Kirk asked, and got a glare for an answer.

"Just wondering."

Kirk looked around the property. Lights glowed in the night, marking the nearby houses of Drover. He walked around the car, wincing at the pebbles biting at his bare feet, and glanced around one last time. He settled on the front counter, barely visible in the dark. The glimmer of the bell caught his attention, perhaps waiting for Jenna to appear and slap its shiny dome.

Kirk got the impulse to torch the place. *Wasting time*, he knew, and that sense of approaching doom flared within him once again. He got in the car and started up the engine.

"You in?" he asked Carma.

"Yeah. Get my seatbelt on."

"You sure?"

"Yeah. It'll hurt, but," she smiled, "you're a shitty driver."

"You should've seen me a week ago," he said and leaned across her. "I was wheelin'."

He paused, finding his face quite close to hers. He refocused, pulled the seatbelt down, and buckled her in.

"How you doing?" he asked, settling back.

"Not good," she whispered. "Not good. But… at least it's not bleeding. I don't think it is."

"No, it's not." Kirk swallowed.

He knew. He would've smelled it.

Without another word, he put the car into drive and they left Drover for good.

22

Two hours later, Kirk pulled into a gas station that had closed for the night. Low lights illuminated the gas pumps. A few derelict cars littered the back of the building. He parked the rig and switched off the engine. A sleeping Carma had angled herself towards the window, her breath fogging the glass.

She opened her eyes a second later. "We there?"

"No."

"Where are we going, anyway?"

"Good question," Kirk replied, staring ahead. "We need to talk first."

Carma adjusted herself in the seatbelt and grimaced. "Okay."

"I'm not a cannibal," Kirk said flatly.

"I figured that part."

"You did?"

"The length of time I've been out? Yeah. You could've made a sandwich out of me. So, yeah, pretty sure."

"There's more…"

Carma watched him. "Don't like the sound of that."

"And I don't blame you. Just don't freak out. Truth is, I did… eat… *were*-flesh. Once. In Newfoundland. Only once."

Surprisingly, Carma didn't say a word.

Kirk pressed on. He recounted the war he and Morris had fought with Borland and the *were*-breeds on the island. Told her how he had to eat the nearest source of meat in order to survive and to ensure that the dogs didn't inflict their warped infection on any of the locals in the nearby town. He told her how the side-effects of such a grisly meal quickly became apparent, how both he and Morris could heal much faster, even recovering from silver-inflicted wounds. They were physically faster and stronger as well.

"But there's something else," Kirk said, stopping just short of the big reveal.

She waited with a neutral expression.

"I, ah, we…" he licked his lips. "We also started getting… urges. For *were*-meat. Hankerings. Cravings. Really bad ones. Not so bad in the beginning, but they got worse. Now it's always there, but talking or doing something takes my mind off it. I can ignore it. There are still times when it really comes on, like really, really hard. Then it takes everything to fight it down."

"What do you do?" Carma asked quietly. "When the cravings get bad?"

"Pig out on anything that's handy. Not people or *weres* or anything like that. Not whatever the elders told you. But everything else. That helps. Sorta."

"You don't sound so sure of that."

"Yeah," Kirk stated and drummed his fingers on the steering wheel. "But, just know that I'm not a cannibal. I mean, it was only once, Carma. Only that one time. And it was life or death. If I hadn't, God knows what those dogs would've done. What they would've done to those people. I made the right choice at the time."

"And now the elders want you dead," Carma said.

"I told them everything," Kirk explained softly. "I mean… they're the elders. That's what we're supposed to do. Right? Morris did as well. Now he's gone and so is Ross Kelly."

"He's the one—"

"—On the island who I saved by biting," Kirk finished. "He's gone, too. I called his buddy while you were sleeping. He told me everything. Ross got burned up in his own house."

He allowed Carma time to take it all in. She stared ahead at the gas pumps, wincing, and mulling things over.

"So you do have some kind of disease," she said. "Of a sort."

That wasn't what Kirk expected. "Yeah. I suppose."

"Why were you heading to Toronto?"

Kirk smiled weakly, exhaustion catching up to him. "To see you. Get your guidance on things. You're smarter than me. More decisive. I'm just a soldier."

Carma frowned. "You're a soldier. I'll give you that. You follow orders, but there's a reluctance there. Always has been."

The pain grabbed her and she cringed, head lilting towards her shoulder. "You were coming to Toronto to see me, you said?"

"Well, yeah, to see you. See what you thought of the next step."

"Which is?"

Kirk didn't answer right away. "Go to the elders. See what they could do for me. Maybe explain things. Get a truce. Get them to lift the hunt."

Carma faced him. "Listen. The elders made up their minds about you. That much is clear. They already put down Morris and your other buddy Ross. You go to the elders and there's only one thing they're going to do. One thing. I was ordered to hunt you down. They don't issue hunts for shits and giggles. They want you dead. And I can understand why. What happens if you—if what you have gets to another *were*? What happens if it gets to a *were* who doesn't have your self-control? Or if you bite a human?"

"I don't know," Kirk whispered.

"The elders might try and do something for you, but that might mean they stick you in a cell like the one you've just escaped. Put you in a box and watch you. See what happens. See if you go crazy or sprout a second head or something. I'm just saying," Carma saw his horrified look. "Look, I don't know a damn thing about what's going on with you but I know the elders. They don't like complications. Especially not with us. They're all about control."

A sullen Kirk nodded. "So what do I do?"

Carma shifted in her seat, her lips a tight line. "The way

I see it, you can try and disappear off the face of the planet, but that isn't going to work. The elders are tapped into everything. Every camera, satellite system, and grid. And if they aren't tapped into it, it's because they don't know about it yet. So they will find you. Eventually."

That revelation made Kirk squirm, and a hot tide of anger rose up in his chest. He had become a werewolf while doing the elders' dirty work. Both he and Morris. And Ross never did a damn thing. The thought made him angrier.

"What if I find them first?" he said.

That silenced Carma. "What do you mean?"

"I mean find them," Kirk wavered, "and kill them."

Carma's mouth dropped open. "Whoa. What? My oh my. Where'd *that* come from?"

"You said it. Those bastards have made their position pretty clear. They killed Morris and Ross without so much as a fucking word. And if I go into hiding, they'll find me and do me the same way. Or the packs will just tear me apart. But… there's something more going on here, Carma. I just don't know what it is. I know one thing. I'm not going to just disappear. I'm going to find them first. Maybe give them the chance to explain themselves. And if they don't, then we'll go to war."

That last word was met with total silence.

"Wow," Carma breathed. "Douglas Kirk gets nasty. Who would've guessed. Hope I'm around to see it."

"You're here now."

"Which brings me to my next question," Carma countered. "What about me?"

"What about you?"

"Well, you've just admitted you're going against the only law we know. The ruling body of us all. The highest of the high. As an appointed warden of that law and order, I think I'm obligated to put you down. I mean, we never took a formal oath or anything like that, but I'm pretty sure you're talking about—oh, what's the word?—sedition? Treason? Betrayal? One of them. Overthrowing our rulers, so to speak."

That's a good point, Kirk thought. "They did it to me first. I wouldn't have gone to the island if they hadn't sent me. Neither would have Morris. I might've screwed up by changing Ross, but neither one of them deserved what they got. There was no conversation. No warning."

"Probably just easier to do it the way they did it," Carma suggested. "Surprise you. Quick and dirty. Don't get me wrong. I'm not saying they did right…"

"So," Kirk looked at her. "You won't come with me?"

They stared at each other then, the dashboard lights bright.

"I don't know what to say," Carma admitted.

"You can get out now. Walk away."

"That would be the smart thing to do. Tell you what. Let me think on it. For a little while, okay?"

"Think on it," Kirk repeated, sounding doubtful even to himself. "You aren't going to turn on me?"

Carma rolled her eyes. "You got my knife?"

"In one of the backpacks."

"You hold on to it for a while. Just in case you think I might stab you with it."

Kirk dropped his head. "Carma—"

"No, really," she cut him off. "You hold on to it for a while. My phone, too. It'll make you feel better. At least until I make up my mind. For the record, I think you're in the right. I think the elders fucked-up. Morris was a bastard, but he was loyal and they killed him without a trial. Your buddy Ross probably never knew what hit him. And you? You haven't tried eating me yet, and that's enough for me."

"That didn't sound the least bit pervy."

"Good," Carma said. "I didn't mean it to be. You turkey. Anyway, I'm leaning in your favor. Maybe we should visit the head office. Have a meet-and-greet with the executive types. Discuss our grievances. Now, next question. All this talk of meeting the elders. You know where they are?"

That was a good question. Kirk couldn't answer it.

"Neither do I," Carma said. "Come to think of it, I've never been in their presence. Not once. If they talk to you, it's always by phone. Never in person. Funny, huh?"

"Yeah," Kirk agreed pensively. "That might be a problem."

"With phone tech these days, they could be anywhere on the planet, but they sound like they're just next door. So how do we find them?"

Weariness sunk into Kirk. He looked around the empty parking lot. Highway traffic was next to nothing. "We'll come up with something."

"Sure," Carma said, distracted with her own thoughts.

Kirk reached down and adjusted his seat, lowering himself almost to a flat plane.

"That's a good idea," she said.

"You want help lowering your seat?"

She considered it, then, "Yeah. Please."

Kirk got out of the car, taking a hit of the cold night air. He sucked down a lungful and held it for a few seconds. He glanced around, detecting a trace of fumes from the day's activity, a blend of gas, leaking fluids, and window wash. He walked over to the passenger side and opened the door.

Carma looked up. "You know, life is going to suck from here on in."

"You mean your shoulder?"

"Yeah."

"Can't move it at all?" Kirk asked, even though he knew the answer. Silver was the *were's* natural bane. The earth's poison. Its bite was like acid and negated all their miraculous regenerative powers.

Except his.

"It's just hanging there," Carma explained. "The bitch fucking apple-cored me. Gonna be interesting when I change over."

Kirk hunkered down and gently adjusted her seat back, lining it up with his own.

"Thanks," she said.

"You'll get used to it."

Carma smiled cynically. "There are dogs walking around with three legs. I'll manage. Might not have to worry about that, anyway. Not if I go along with you."

Kirk didn't comment right away. "Let's just sleep on this. Gas this thing up in the morning. Maybe we'll think of something then. You have any money?"

"All in my wallet."

"I thought women called it a purse?"

Carma glared, daring him to say more.

That got a smile out of him. He closed her door, rounded the car, and climbed in beside her. Sleeping in a car seat wasn't his preferred way of crashing, but his strength was fading fast. Thankfully, the dull, carnivorous vibe buzzing inside him had lessened to practically nothing, granting him some measure of peace.

Kirk was asleep in a minute.

And somewhere in his dreams, Carma whispered, *I'm in.*

*

Kirk flinched upon waking.

He stared at the window and grimaced. The glass had fogged up. He wiped a hand across the surface, revealing a pre-dawn overcast sky. Across the parking lot, a man walked away from his white pickup, towards the convenience store of the gas station. His clean-shaven face regarded the little sedan parked on the far side of the lot, then he concentrated on a set of keys.

Kirk watched him unlock the main door and walk inside.

The hunger overtook the Halifax warden then, a pushy thing that originated in his guts and reached for his mouth, urging him to feed, to gorge himself on anything.

He got out of the car, careful not to wake Carma. Paced around the vehicle while frosted pebbles stabbed at his bare feet.

The pain wasn't enough.

Kirk stretched, unlocking his spine and neck with audible pops. He considered the gas station. Lights appeared within the building. The guy who'd entered shuffled around behind the counter. Kirk looked away before thinking evil thoughts. He saw the highway running east-west, and a wall of smudged forest on either side. The forest interested him. He could lose himself in there. Change. Stay a wolf forever.

Kirk paced around the car, the cold working on his feet. He'd gotten soft over the years. He knew it. Maybe the elders knew it, too. If he was truly going to kill them, he would need to be merciless. Ruthless. At the top of his game. Trouble was, Kirk didn't *have* any game.

He faced the car. Carma's head drooped to the left. She'd saved his ass back in Drover. She saved his ass big time and he hoped she'd go to war with him. He wondered if he should trust her if she did. Carma hadn't wanted anything to do with him in years. Made it a point to avoid him. Yet, here she was. Ruined shoulder and all.

That all meant something, Kirk decided. He realized that, in mulling over her presence, the hunger had retreated.

He had to do something before that wave struck again.

"We there yet?" Carma asked sleepily when he opened a rear door.

"Not yet," he said. "How much money you got?"

"About seven hundred dollars."

"You're well off."

"I had a good year," she said weakly.

Kirk didn't like how she sounded. "How you doing?"

"Hungry. Shoulder's aching."

Goddamn silver. He knew its poison all too well. Almost bled to death in the aftermath of killing Borland. Or at least bled until he didn't have a drop left in him, as he wasn't rightly sure if *weres* could bleed to death. Not that he wanted to find out, but he understood her pain.

"The station's open," he said. "I'll get you breakfast."

"They have a restaurant in there?" Carma asked with a note of hope.

Kirk looked. "Yeah, looks that way. You want eggs?"

"I want the trucker's special. I'll have three."

That put a smile on Kirk's face. He found her wallet in one of the backpacks and pulled out two brown hundred-dollar bills. Then, as an afterthought, he pulled out two more. Seven hundred dollars. Enough for a day or two, but not for what he needed to do.

"Trucker's special sounds good," he lied. "How about I take you out to breakfast. Right here?"

"It's my money."

"Okay, how about you loan me some cash so I can take you to breakfast?"

Carma sighed. "You're pushin' your luck, Douglas Kirk."

Two other cars shot along the highway. A third slowed and turned into the station's parking lot. Two people were aboard.

"This place is coming to life," Kirk said.

Carma looked over herself. "I look like shit."

"*I* look like shit," he stressed.

"We'll need clothes."

The strongbox in the back seat captured Kirk's attention. "The place is only just opening. Hold on a second, okay?"

"Okay."

He walked over to the station's main entrance, accepting the freezing misery, and pulled open the door. A bell jingled overhead. It was too soon for bells. Kirk forced himself not to rip the goddamn dinger off the doorframe.

"You're letting the heat out," a guy said from behind a counter. The pickup driver had donned a bright orange vest with the name "Donnie" stitched over his left pocket. Donnie looked to be in his fifties, a few pounds overweight, and smelling of black coffee and sugar.

"Buddy?" Donnie repeated with a questioning stare.

"Sorry," Kirk replied and stepped inside. The door closed.

"We're about ten minutes out from opening," Donnie informed him.

Kirk nodded and glanced around. Under bright fluorescent lights, the interior gleamed a near-sterilized level of cleanliness. Drink coolers were set against the left wall. Aisles of road munchies and even canned food dominated the middle of the floor. Someone had stacked a neck-high tower of soda pop on sale. A bank of coffee machines and sandwich racks were on the right, along with a wide archway that led to a long, white countertop. A collection of empty booths and tables lay beyond the counter.

"Uh, what time does the restaurant open?"

"Seven-thirty," Donnie answered, studying Kirk's coverall and coming to a stop at his feet. The pause at the end was wary. "You forget something, buddy?"

Kirk regarded his lack of footwear. "No, no, just coming from a party and someone walked away with my... clothes. And shoes."

"Got shafted, eh?"

"Yeah," Kirk answered sheepishly. "I got shafted. Big time. What time is it now?"

"Seven twenty-one."

Great. Kirk remembered the strongbox. "You got a screwdriver or something I can use to get into my car trunk? The lock's busted."

"Someone shaft your car, too?"

Kirk suspected Donnie was roaring with laughter on the inside.

"Yeah, they got my car too."

"Y'know, in my day," Donnie started, "that level of shaft would get a person into a world of pain. Once, at university, we knifed our way into a guy's dorm room while he was away for the weekend. Stripped out the furniture and left it on other floors. Watered down his underwear and stuck it all into the lounge's freezer. And after all that, we put hay down on the floor of his room and stuck a goat in there. We rented it from a local farmer for thirty bucks."

"Wow," Kirk muttered, impressed.

Donnie nodded proudly. "That part backfired. The guy was gone for the whole weekend, right? We had the goat in there on Friday night. Damn thing cried during the day and night and you could hear it anywhere on the building's floor. Stunk the place out, too."

"That's evil."

"We helped clean it all up, 'course," Donnie assured him. "After the guy got back Sunday afternoon. We didn't hate the guy. It was all in fun. Good times."

Then, remembering the original request, Donnie reached under the front counter and pulled out a heavy screwdriver and a wooden mallet. "This do?"

"Thanks."

"Gonna ruin your lock though," Donnie said, handing over the tools.

"Yeah, well, if you hear the alarm go off, it's just me."

Donnie smiled and resumed puttering about his cash register. Dismissed, Kirk returned to the car, thinking about that confined goat. All penned up and nowhere to go, bleating.

"What are you going to do with that?" Carma asked as he opened the rear door.

"Break this thing open," he informed her, holding up the strongbox. He took it around the back of the car, out of sight. One quick look told him that Donnie wasn't particularly interested in what he was doing, but Kirk still hunkered down, placed the screwdriver's tip to the dial, and readied the mallet.

The fuck was Donnie doing with a mallet under the counter, anyway? Kirk asked himself. The screwdriver he could understand.

He smashed the lock with one blow, stabbing the flat head deep inside. Kirk worked the tool around, and couldn't quite open it on the first try. The strength of the box surprised him and stubbornly refused to open, even with his enhanced strength. Alice and Jenna might've been a lot of things, but they didn't skimp on strongboxes.

Growing frustrated, he hammered at the dial.

"You building a railroad back there?" Carma called out.

"Just working some things out."

"Can you work it out quieter?"

Kirk could. He threw his weight and strength onto the screwdriver. The strongbox popped apart like a baby spitting up milk.

Two rings landed on the pavement.

But that wasn't the only thing that caught his attention.

Gold rings, bracelets, and earrings. Even a couple of gold chains. A broth of wealth. And partially hidden within that rich stew were five neat bundles of cash, bound by rubber bands. Kirk saw them, smiled briefly, until he got thinking about the jewelry. All that glitter and bling disturbed him. Several rings were wedding bands. Some contained valuable stones which might have been diamonds. Kirk frowned, his mood sinking, realizing where the jewelry had come from, and wondered how many lives Alice and Jenna had taken before Carma put an end to them.

Kirk stuck a finger in and shifted through the metal. *You sick fucks.* There had to be several thousand dollars' worth of jewelry in the box. He hadn't even counted the cash. He picked up one brick of cash, hefted it, and pulled the band off with a snap.

Cash flipped across his palm. Hundreds and fifties.

When he finished counting, he planted himself on the

cold asphalt, placed his back to the bumper, and let his breath out in a hiss. *Holy shit*. He had five thousand, three hundred and fifty dollars in his hands. And that was just the one roll. He tossed the cash onto the jewelry and fished out the other wads. The money sprang free of their elastic bonds and purred as he filed through them with a thumb. Chestnut brown and salmon pink. Hundreds and fifties once again, the bills twinkling with infused anti-counterfeiting measures.

All told, Kirk figured there was well over twenty-five thousand in the box. Maybe even thirty. Untraceable, ready to use hard currency.

"Everything okay back there?" Carma asked.

"Yeah," Kirk smiled, happy with the sudden spike in their finances. Cash problem resolved. His smile faded at what he might've missed in Alice and Jenna's house. This was just one cash trove, readily accessible and easily found. He wondered how many other, much harder-to-find stashes they might've squirreled away. Jewelry too valuable to toss and illegal money from sales of flesh, paid in full.

Blood money. Meat money. Kirk put the cash back and closed the wrecked box. Seconds later, he placed everything on the backseat's floor and covered it with the backpacks.

"What's wrong?" Carma asked when he stopped at her window.

"I got the box open."

"And?"

"You don't wanna know."

"Course I wanna know."

Kirk told her.

"Those sick fucks," Carma declared softly.

"You got them both," Kirk pointed out.

"After all those years, what were they doing back there?" Carma sighed. "They died too quickly."

Kirk needed to eat. "Still hungry?"

"Yeah."

"Think you can make it across the parking lot? Big, strong woman like you?"

"If I can't, you can carry me."

Kirk opened her door.

*

They feasted.

Carma devoured three mighty trucker specials while Kirk raised her by one. Sausages, eggs, bacon, beans in tomato sauce, hash browns, and a smoke stack of toast. They drank coffee and juice and didn't bother with conversation, so keen on refilling their tanks. Once the food was gone, they leaned back and sighed.

"We just pigged out in front of these people," Carma said, indicating the waitresses and a handful of folks who had wandered in during their meal.

"Don't care," Kirk said. "I'd do it again if I could."

"We better get moving."

"On the road to nowhere." Kirk waved over one of the waitresses, a white-haired lady named Rosalind. "Could we have our bill, please?"

"You're leaving?" she smiled, flashing shiny, perfect teeth.

"Yeah, if we can stand."

"I'm eating for two," Carma confessed and patted her belly. "Two months along."

"For two?" Rosalind brightened. "Honey, you were eating for at least quintuplets. And you," she directed at Kirk, "I expect will explode any second, leaving this poor woman all alone."

Kirk smiled and took the bill. He paid in full at the till and left a generous tip. He walked Carma out to her car as more travelers stopped at the station. Surprisingly, not too many people noticed what the pair of wardens wore.

"We really need to blend in," Kirk said.

"Definitely." Carma checked out the sneakers that once belonged to Jenna. "That bitch had fucking big feet, man."

"That's why you're scuffing along?"

"That's exactly why. We need to do some shopping. *You* need to do some shopping. We look like a couple of trailer park rejects."

"Not a very nice thing to say," Kirk said as he opened her car door.

"I could've done that," Carma remarked and held up her left hand. "This one works."

"You can't close it."

"You can close it for me."

Carma eased herself into the car, struggling at points. Pain contorted her face, but to her credit she didn't cry out.

"All in?" Kirk asked.

"Yeah."

He fastened her seatbelt, trying hard to ignore how close

they were to each other. Once finished, he closed the door and got in on the other side.

Carma was upright in her seat, unconscious, with her chin flat against her collarbone.

"Carma," Kirk blurted, gripping her knee. "Carma!"

She stirred. "I'm okay."

"You passed out."

"Just… tired."

"Holy shit you scared me."

"It's okay. We're good. But Kirk?"

"Yeah?"

"Maybe… we should. Rent a room. Somewhere."

23

The divided highway crossed a land readying itself for winter. Carma slept restlessly as Kirk drove, his worry welling up like fluid filling a drowning person's lungs. The sun hit him at an angle, bright and uncomfortable, and every time he glanced over she seemed a little worse. Her pale skin glistened like a corpse enduring a summer's drizzle. Her chest barely moved at all, and twice he placed a hand in front of her face to feel a weak puff of breath.

The traffic wasn't so heavy, so Kirk put his foot down, speeding northwest on the 104. They passed into Cumberland County, surged past gaping rock pits, and somewhere along a curvy strip of highway Kirk almost lost it.

The divided highway consisted of two lanes. The fat, white ass of a long-distance trucker straddled one of them just ahead of Kirk. And on the trucker's left, seemingly content to hang off the big rig's bumper like an unwanted parasite, was a jacked-up pickup. Whether the trucker was unwilling to allow his smaller cousin to pass him, or the pickup driver was in Sunday mode, content to overtake the greater machine at leisure, Kirk didn't know.

But it was pissing him off.

After ten seconds of driving in their wake, he honked the horn. To no effect.

"You bastards," Kirk muttered, believing that the pickup driver was deliberately blocking the way, oblivious to the little sedan trying to get by. He glanced at Carma and his temper rose.

A long, gradual incline slowed both vehicles ahead, and neither driver seemed too concerned with Kirk's honking.

"You *bastards*," he whispered with venom. The shoulders were a narrow gamble, barely wide enough to allow a car to pull over if needed, and he knew he wasn't a good enough driver to race along that highwire without a good chance of skidding off the embankment.

So he stayed on the trucks' tails, hating them with every passing second. He flicked on his emergency lights and even switched from the right lane to the left.

The pair of drivers ignored him.

"Oh, you *fucking* bastards," he swore.

"Kirk."

He tore his eyes away from the vehicles.

Carma, head tilted back and panting.

"You okay?" Kirk asked.

"Stop switching lanes."

"Sorry," he said, nodding that he would.

"Seriously."

"Okay."

"I'm going to barf… if you don't."

The highway dipped, allowing a glimpse of what lay ahead. Traffic. A long, glimmering string of speed-conscious metal. A linear meteor belt that promised to make his and Carma's lives miserable. Kirk glanced in his rearview mirror and saw other motorists gaining on him.

Traffic. Everywhere, like blood platelets closing in on a fresh cut.

"Pull over," Carma lurched, her face the color of bedroom dust.

Her hand flew to her mouth.

Kirk flicked his indicator and decelerated, pulling the wheel to the right. Carma leaned into her door, fingers scrabbling at the latch. She cracked it open and fresh air flooded the interior. The sedan's tires crackled on the gravel shoulder as Carma stuck her head out and violently unloaded three mighty trucker specials. Kirk cringed. In between retches and gasps for air, she somehow found time to moan as the tightening shoulder belt added to her misery.

Kirk stopped the car, nearly had his own door ripped off by a speeding minivan, and checked the coast before getting out. He raced to Carma's side, crushed stone stabbing his bare feet. He pushed her door open wider, trying hard to ignore what covered the rocky ground.

"Oh," she moaned and hitched again, releasing another impressive tide of gastric chowder. The seatbelt held her rump in place. Strands of hair dangled, hiding her profile. Kirk hesitated, leaned in, and pulled her locks back.

"That's okay," he whispered as traffic whipped by. "Get it out of you."

"Oh shit."

Another fragrant torrent, one that speckled Kirk's bare feet. He flinched as if scalded.

"You need that seatbelt undone?" he asked.

"No," she said miserably. She wiped her mouth and hung out, taking shallow breaths.

Carma stayed face-down for a long time, long enough for him to wonder if she was okay.

"Man," she whispered. "I ate a lot."

"It's the silver," he said.

"Yeah."

"I mean, seriously, how often do any of us actually get cut or shot by silver?"

"Not often."

"That's right."

"But I ate," Carma pleaded weakly, turning her head just a bit. "All *that*. I should be… getting better."

Kirk eased back the neckline of her sweater, uncovering her wound. The bandage held firm, but the seepage blotting the fabric looked bigger. *No*, he corrected, it didn't look bigger, it *was* bigger. From a dime to a quarter. Horror caressed the nape of his neck.

Carma heaved again and Kirk couldn't react fast enough to get clear.

"Oh, god," she whispered upon finishing.

"Take your time," he said. "Just take your time. Deep breaths."

Carma turned a single, red eye upon him. "That's what made me... barf... just now."

"All right, all right, then just..." Kirk struggled to help somehow, "...take it easy."

"Came on all of a sudden," Carma whispered. "My shoulder's hot. But I thought... I thought..."

"Can you ride in the car?" Kirk asked.

"Maybe I should change over."

"On the side of the highway?" he muttered.

"Just. Kidding."

"We'll find a motel," Kirk promised. "Get you off the road."

"Yeah."

"You're okay to ride?"

"Yeah. I think."

Kirk reached in and lowered the window. Stains spattered the bottom part of the door. Carma eased herself back and he pulled the seatbelt away from her, to spare her some pain. When she was tucked away, he closed the door.

"How about now?" he asked when he settled into the driver's seat.

"You're going to drive me nuts if you keep doing that," Carma warned him.

"Just worried, is all."

Carma stared at the traffic rushing by. "Yeah. I know. I'm not good."

"Not good?"

"Okay. I'm shitty."

"Okay," he said and realized the car was still running.

He'd only stopped and slapped it into park. "Okay, we'll get you somewhere."

"Stay in one lane," she ordered.

Kirk lowered his own window and checked over his shoulder.

"Okay," he said, and pulled back onto the highway.

The County Roadside Motel was the place they needed. The rest stop was one of those single-story strip motels one might see in a horror movie. The building consisted of about fifteen or so units, located just off the highway, behind a wide shoal of yellow grass that separated private business asphalt from the provincially maintained. Kirk knew the individual behind the front desk could smell the residue of Carma's sickness off him, could tell by the way the man struggled to not examine Kirk's appearance, but the warden didn't give a shit. Kirk signed off on the room in record time, fidgeting like he had to take the world's biggest dump. The front desk guy even pointed out the nearby washroom if Kirk needed to go that badly.

At ten-twenty in the morning, he opened the door to a beige motel room and carried Carma over the threshold. Her head, glistening with sweat, was stuck to his chest. She didn't speak, didn't so much as move. The unit's bed was a double, covered in tasteful beige comforters with a pleasant floral design. Kirk lowered Carma onto its softness.

"We there?" she asked, barely opening her eyes.

"Yeah," he said and closed the door.

"Where are we?"

"Some place, I don't know." He pulled a chair away from a desk and sat at her side. "How you doing?"

"Still shitty. But… maybe it's easing off."

Kirk wasn't sure if he believed her. She rolled onto her side and lay there, facing him, her hair fallen across her eyes. After a second's indecision, he cleared it away, prompting Carma to squint.

"Just making you presentable," he explained softly.

"Hm."

"You'll pull through. We're not on the road anymore," Kirk reasoned with a little smile. "Never thought you were one to get car sick."

"Sure did. Came out like gunshit."

"You mean gunshot?"

Carma paused. "No. I mean gunshit. Think about it."

"I don't wanna."

"Don't blame you. Oh man. This is better," she said and nuzzled the pillow. "Much better."

Kirk located a waste bucket and positioned it bedside. He was especially glad to see a white garbage bag lining the receptacle.

"Smart," Carma said, sounding near death.

"Not so dumbass now, am I?"

They shared a smile.

Then the smell got to him. "Listen," he started. "You think you're well enough to get cleaned up?"

Carma considered it for a second. She nodded and Kirk helped her sit. "Get this off me," she said, indicating the sweater. He removed it as gently as possible and tossed the clothing towards the open door of the bathroom. Her t-shirt underneath was untouched.

"That's the worst of it," he said.

"Yeah," Carma agreed. "The sweater took the brunt."

Then she giggled, and pitched forward into his shoulder. The action surprised Kirk, and he didn't move, as solid as a wall.

"This remind you… of anything?"

"No."

"When you changed? Your… first time?"

Kirk's nose grazed the outer rim of her left ear and he closed his eyes. "Yeah. I remember."

"You… you puked," she sighed, amused. "All that shit you ate… and when you, you changed back…"

Blah, she whispered into his shoulder.

"That was a long time ago," Kirk said, rubbing her back.

"Okay, listen, how's this sound?" he said, trying to change the subject. "I'll leave you here to rest up and go unload the car, and then I'll get us something to eat. Something not so greasy."

"That was good grease going down."

"And almost killed you coming back up. Which reminds me. Stay still."

He stretched out her t-shirt's neckline. An oil spot stained the bandage underneath. "Let me check this."

"Okay."

He slid his fingernails under the adhesive's hem and ripped.

And stared.

Carma turned her head with a sick frown.

The wide slit had closed, but one section bubbled and frothed, like a mouth bordering on overcapacity. The skin around the wound went from scorched-earth black to angry red. Neither color comforted Kirk.

"Whoa," he whispered, not knowing where to start.

Carma hung her head, unable to speak.

"I'll get to a store," he said. "Load up on everything. Food. Clothes. Anything you need. I'll put fire to that again when I get back. Maybe a second dousing will do the trick."

Carma didn't reply.

He rubbed her back again, his hand grazing a bony spine, hoping to get her mind off the cut. "I need your size. Shoe size, too."

"I got my clothes."

"In case you need more."

She told him.

He jotted down the numbers on a notepad fetched from the desk.

"Nothing pink," she said. "If any… of those. Clothes. Are pink."

Kirk smiled.

"Quit smiling… when I say that," she muttered. "Takes all the fun out."

He nodded. He'd try better in the future.

Carma lay back and focused on the ceiling. "You better get going."

"Yeah."

"Go on. I'm going to sleep. For a bit. You know what you're doing. So go. Do it."

Kirk left.

Carma lay in bed, alone, wallowing in that sharp ache that didn't lessen in the least. It felt as if someone was attempting to pry her flesh from her bones with a chisel and hammer.

She touched her shoulder and pressed the damp cloth down, grimacing at the resulting fire. She pressed more, taking the bright burn, until something popped underneath her fingertips. Rivulets dribbled over her skin.

Just great, Carma fumed and lifted the cloth. Blood and dark matter stained the fabric, as if she'd just soaked up a dribble of spilled coffee. Not much, but enough to disappoint her. *Just wonderful.*

She was definitely going to need another fire treatment.

Her arm refused to budge, the entire limb feeling like an unresponsive, throbbing lump of meat.

She stabbed me, Carma thought. *Deep. Straight down.* And the early burn Kirk had applied only fused the surface. The interior was still smoking, still festering.

"This sucks," she murmured, "donkey cocks."

Not five seconds later, her phone buzzed.

She already hated whoever the caller was and the ferocious, mind-numbing clutch of pain when she moved. Carma didn't give up, however. She reached for her bag and retrieved the phone.

Sweat covered her face when she lay back, and her stomach threatened to purge yet again.

The phone stopped ringing.

"Oh, you prick," she whispered and rested the device on her chest, riding out waves of nausea. When she recovered enough, she opened the phone and checked the number.

The elders.

Even more interesting, they'd called a couple of times. Checking up on her.

Carma stared at the phone's interface for a long time, the pain in her shoulder receding.

Her thumb lingered on the receiver button.

*

The nearest supermarket was located in the small town of Southchester Station. A large white sign over the main doors said *Hennigan's* in large print, with the afterthought of *The freshest food around.*

For some reason, the place got Kirk thinking of chickens.

He'd already stopped at a small clothing store and snatched up a selection of men's and women's clothing, underwear, and sneakers. His appearance and his purchases earned him a forced façade of courtesy from the lady on cash. Upon paying for his items, he asked to use the public washroom, where he quickly changed, and applied generous amounts of deodorant to the places needing it most. His feet loved his new socks and hikers. *New sneakers.* Had to love 'em. The torture had ended.

So when he walked into the supermarket, he did so with a spring in his stride and relatively free of pain.

Chicken. For some damn reason, he wanted a roasted

chicken. He grabbed a shopping cart and charged through the aisles, urged on by Carma's deteriorating condition. The right front wheel possessed a funky wiggle, but after the last few days of imprisonment, he sort of appreciated that little touch of normality. In his new clothing free of price tags (which he plucked before wearing) he grabbed provisions. For the road, mostly. Bottled water, bread, canned vegetables, and a bag of chocolate chip cookies. He passed a pair of shoppers in the baking section, on his way to the rear of the supermarket.

To the meat section.

Salmon steaks greeted him first. Then cod fillets, haddock, and shrimp, followed by breaded shrimp, pork products, and chicken. But what stopped Kirk in his tracks was the selection of beef. Pictures of smiling cows graced the wall overhead, their bodies artfully divided by dotted lines, each delectable cut identified.

A window allowed a peek inside the cutting room. Three sexless butchers in white sanitary uniforms fed meat chunks through band saws. Cuts were prepped for market.

Kirk could have watched them all day.

Carma was waiting, however, so he walked on, passed all that glorious meat, wishing for a barbecue the size of a vengeful Krakatoa.

Chicken.

The little cluckers were at the end. Kirk slowed and drifted along the open displays as if caught in a lazy stream. He made it to the roasted section and extracted a pair of saucy-looking birds. He deposited them in the cart, paused, and plucked a third, thinking that any leftovers would keep in the motel room. Or he could store it in the car. The temperatures fell low enough at night that the only fear would be the meat freezing.

Kirk wheeled the cart around, looking for the check-out, when the hunger grabbed him.

He stopped, eyes narrowed, and realized he was damn-near high off the smell permeating from the nearby cuts of beef. The meat demanded to be recognized, hooking his complete attention. His stomach contracted as if someone had grabbed a fistful of guts and squeezed. An inner whining rose in his gullet, insisting that he do something about the situation. His mouth spritzed and he swallowed, running a hand over his bearded face, with nothing between him and all that freshly cut red sustenance.

He held onto the cart for support, squaring off against a sizeable roast.

The huge slab of moist muscle tempted him, its glorious texture radiant under his gaze. It dared him to make a move.

So Kirk did.

The roast went into the top basket, partially squishing the loaf of bread already sitting there. Kirk didn't care. He turned and forced his way through the snack aisle, snatching up essentials as his cart shook and shivered. He cut around curious shoppers alerted by his cart's wiggling wheel. A pillar of soda pop cases, the twenty-four can size, flashed by. He halted at the only visible cashier and there he waited, fidgeted, and probably appeared on the verge of a seizure.

The cashier was a tall, middle-aged woman with glasses,

and her customer was a hockey mom. Between them flowed a full week's groceries, underneath a fixed scanner that chirped dutifully, while they discussed last night's episode of *A Game of Thrones*.

Kirk scratched at parts and shifted from one foot to the other.

The hockey mom smelled of cats and only added to his discomfort. When the sprawl of household goods shifted forward enough for him to start unloading his cart, Kirk forced himself to reach as casually as possible for the plastic divider and placed it down, careful not to attract attention, not wanting to make a scene. It wasn't the airport or a crowded city street, but his increasing hankering to feed compelled him to dig in right there.

Kirk did nothing of the sort. Instead, he counted down seconds while the two women chuckled. The hockey mom talked with her hands, nodding, gesticulating as if directing drunken traffic. The cashier nodded, smiled, agreeing with every word, and even paused at times, long enough to make Kirk want to shriek.

Then something very disturbing happened.

The conversation between cashier and hockey mom, as it played out before him, became a drone of warped piano keys. The speakers slowed, as if submerged in clear gel. Kirk froze, looked ahead, and became conscious of a growing thumping, in tandem. The rhythm created an eerie echo that made his chest ache. Then his eyes bulged.

Oh shit.

He blinked as if experiencing a headache. The *thumping*,

dear God, he recognized the sound, knew exactly what he was hearing.

Heartbeats.

Cold horror sucked the color from his face. He licked his lips. His pulse quickened. The women continued talking, blissfully unaware who was next to them. The hockey mom fed a credit card into a machine, her profile elongating into a frightful caricature where Kirk saw teeth.

Then his attention went to their throats.

In particular, the detailed outline of their arterial system, surfacing in black traceries that pulsated with deep currents. Any second Kirk expected dotted divider lines to appear, pointing out the tastiest cuts. He felt himself sinking, losing touch with control. The women's heartbeats slowed as if chilled by glacial waters, while the light around them intensified in blazing halos.

Kirk tore his gaze away. Fixed on a tower of packaged beef jerky. Decals showed a toothy cartoon face, chomping into full-bodied strips with gusto.

Another label displayed cartoon kids eagerly feasting on sandwiches, but their wide eyes belonged to sharks.

Yet another display had a group of beer buddies sitting around a table, gorging themselves on white pasta and red meat sauce. The forks and spoons twinkled.

Kirk covered his eyes, shutting out the images.

Oh Jesus Christ.

He knew then that he was going to murder every last person within reach, and then anyone in the parking lot.

But somehow, through sheer force of will, he didn't. He

pushed it all back, shoved all thoughts of gluttonous mayhem from his mind. It wasn't easy, and the cravings didn't exactly leave, but he caged his urges, covered them in a mental blanket, and shoved it under a bed.

When the cashier scanned Kirk's items, the Halifax warden stood with a lowered head and a fistful of readied cash.

He knew the cashier sensed something wrong, but God bless her, she didn't ask. Didn't speak to him in the least.

He almost forgot the change, had to about-face and return for it for fear of the cashier following him into the parking lot. Kirk didn't want that. If she did, bad things would happen. He was that close.

The sun burned his eyes as he emerged from the supermarket's hell. The hockey mom slammed the rear door of her SUV and went around to the driver's side. Kirk walked briskly, shoving his wobbling cart towards Carma's car, hearing little voices mewling at the back of his mind, like the mouths of worms chewing away at the white pudding of his brain. He threw the food into the backseat, swayed as if he'd just shotgunned a dozen beers, and clawed at one environmentally friendly bag. Paper towels. He rooted through another bag or two before locating the one containing the roast. Not the cooked chicken, but the raw beef, so full of goodness that the very sinews shimmered as if sprinkled with ruby dust.

Kirk had parked the farthest away from the supermarket's entrance, facing a wall of elms and underbrush. No one else was around. The hockey mom had already driven away, completely under his radar. He got into the car and opened the bag. The roast came out and he stripped it of the plastic coating. He unrolled a highway of paper towels and draped it over his new jeans and shirt. A second look around confirmed that he was still alone. Kirk leaned over the sedan's gear stick and lowered his head.

He picked up the roast with both hands.

And ate.

Three other cars had secured safe harbor at the motel when Kirk got back. He parked in front of the rented unit, got out, and went to the door.

Three knocks later, she answered. "Yeah?"

"It's me."

"Key's under the mat."

Kirk smiled and opened the door. He unloaded the car, dumping the food on the room's table. Carma remained on the bed, in stretchy pants and a t-shirt, resting on her back with her arm in a sling. She watched him work.

"Get anything good?" she asked in a frayed voice.

"All sorts."

"Like what?"

Kirk presented the roasted chicken. "Barbecue."

Carma brightened. "That does look good."

"You talking about me or the chicken?"

"The chicken, you turkey. The chicken."

"Because if you haven't noticed…"

"I saw," Carma looked to the ceiling. "Nice. New

clothes. You wash them somewhere along the way?"

"Ah, no."

"You know how many people might've already tried those same clothes on?"

Kirk studied himself as if he'd been splashed by mud. "Nope."

"Then don't. Personally, I don't wear anything unless I wash it first."

He didn't like where the conversation was going. "I did buy you clothes."

She cocked an eyebrow.

"Got you some sneakers and some thick socks. Jeans and t-shirts. Ah, underwear—" he said, covering his mouth and muffling the word.

"Underwear," Carma stated stoically.

"Yeah."

'You bought me underwear."

"Yeah."

"I never told you my sizes."

"I, ah, guessed." In truth, he remembered. "Just in case you needed them. Ah, extra, I mean."

"All right," she granted. "Let's see them."

He went back out to the car and returned bearing gifts in designer paper bags. He dumped everything onto the bed. Carma didn't move, not impressed in the least with his enthusiasm.

"You been snacking?" she asked.

"Yeah." He quickly rubbed his mouth again, even though he'd scrubbed it before the car's rearview mirror. "A little something."

"I smell cow."

"You are… correct. I did. I ate a cow. On the way over here. Wasn't easy."

"You're gonna piss off the farmers."

Kirk smiled. "I had an episode at the supermarket. Really bad one. Kept it together until I got back to the car. And yeah, I ate a roast. There. Way back of the parking lot. No one saw me, though. I made sure."

Carma shook her head. "Yep. That's what I smell."

"How you doing?" he asked and sat at the table.

"Okay."

"Okay? That's good."

"Better than before. Someone called. It was a 709 number."

Kirk raised his head. "That's Newfoundland."

Alvin. Kirk never did get back to him. He gripped his forehead and squeezed for juice. "I know him. Alvin. Ross Kelly's buddy. Yeah. I gave him your number. I'll have to call him back."

"The elders called as well."

That bomb stopped all thought. "The elders."

"Yep."

Kirk waited for more but Carma didn't offer it.

"What did they want?" he finally asked.

"I didn't answer it."

"You didn't?"

"No."

Kirk leaned back and studied her. "Why?"

"Because I'm fucked-up here, Douglas," she said with all

the angst of someone not well, despite what they might have said. "I'm fucked-up and not too happy about talking with the bosses. Knowing them, they might even have the phone line tapped or something."

That was something Kirk hadn't considered. "Could they?"

Carma met his eyes. "Tap the lines?"

"Yeah?"

"I'm sure they could. They have techs."

Kirk's nerves buzzed with anxiety. "Maybe we should ditch the phone."

"Maybe you should just relax a little."

"You're cranky," he noted softly.

Instead of commenting, Carma lifted her head and, with her good arm, rooted through the bags of clothing. Her expression softened at the footwear, hardened at the undergarments.

"You're going to have to wash all of this," she informed him. "The motel has a laundromat."

"You want all this washed?" he repeated.

She held up the undergarments. "Especially these. Chop, chop. You might as well do something."

Kirk allowed a smile.

"The hell you so happy about?" she asked.

"You're giving orders. That's a good sign."

Carma smirked. "For one of us."

Kirk gathered up her new clothes. "All washed. You're the boss."

"I am. Cranky, too. Probably why I'm not dead, yet."

"Try and eat something while I'm gone."

"I might wait until you're back," she said. "We can have dinner together."

"You mean supper."

"I mean dinner."

"Supper's the last meal of the day."

"And dinner's the main meal," Carma pointed out.

Kirk chuckled as he moved to the door. "Wow. That brings back memories."

She didn't comment, content to watch him from the bed.

"I'll be back," he said.

"I know."

24

The laundromat consisted of three washers, three dryers, and an abused vending machine that might've taken one or two boots upside the head. Static control sheets littered the corners like discarded gobs of webbing. Yellow walls were noticeably chipped and gouged in places, as if a drunken cyclone had grabbed a chair and whipped it around. There were, in fact, a pair of lawn chairs near the back. One chair had a scorch mark on its arm.

Kirk was glad the beigeness of the place hadn't spread to the room. He got some detergent from a vending machine, loaded up a washer, and dropped into an unmarked chair.

The elders called, Carma had said. *I didn't answer it.*

He chewed on that while the washer chugged through its cycles.

Then old Borland's voice entered the fray. *De lies*, he hissed from beyond. *De liiiiies.*

The memory startled Kirk, and he wondered where it had come from. He bent over, knees to elbows, and stared at the floor.

Borland's voice didn't stop. *She's wit them. Even now, she's on de phone to dem, lettin' dem bloodsabitches know where ye are. And where are ye? In a little room, wit yer back to a wall, wit a wide window lookin' in. Might as well paint a big fat fuckin' bullseye on yer forehead. She's sent ye off to distance herself from ye, so dey can take ye down. Easily. Guaranteed.*

Kirk chased Borland's cryptic words from his head, dismissing the notion. There were lies, but he knew Carma wasn't one of them. Not by a long shot.

She couldn't be. Not her.

Kirk looked through the wide picture window onto the parking lot. The evening descended, drawing the day to a close.

He sat and stared. Waited.

Thought.

Just after five-thirty, Kirk returned to his room and paused at the door. Outside of unit eleven was a young girl of maybe five or six, all bundled in winter clothing. She hung off the overhang's support post with both hands, swinging back and forth, while her mother, just out of sight inside the room, spoke to her through a window.

Kirk smiled faintly and opened the door.

"Hey," Carma greeted.

"Hey."

"Finish your chores?" she asked and pulled herself into a sitting position.

"Yeah."

"Great. Let's see them."

Kirk dropped the bag onto the bed, shaking the clothes free.

Carma reached over and sifted through them. "Nice. Just like warm bread."

"Cooled off on the way over here."

"What's it like out there?" she asked.

"Cold," Kirk replied and sat at the table. "Temperature's dropping. Feels like snow. How you feeling now?"

Carma nibbled on one corner of her mouth. "You can stop asking me that. I feel the same as before. Like I've been stabbed by silver."

"Sorry."

"No need to be sorry," she said. "Wasn't you who stabbed me."

"You wouldn't be here if it wasn't for me."

"That's true."

"So why did you come here?" The words came out so naturally that Kirk surprised himself.

Carma regarded him, considering the question. "To see for myself. What was going on."

"That's all?"

Another lengthy pause, which she ended with a shake of her head. "Let's eat."

So they did.

Once finished, Carma leaned back from the table and the empty trays that once contained barbecued chickens. She guzzled water from a bottle and turned her attention to her disabled shoulder. Kirk watched her the whole time.

"Anything for dessert?" Carma finally asked with a touch

of despondency, not pleased with what she saw.

"Yeah," he said. "Just a second."

He reached for one last grocery bag and opened it up. He produced two family-sized bags of potato chips. One Ketchup-flavored and one All Dressed.

"That's not really dessert."

An indignant Kirk held up a finger, requesting patience, and pulled out four huge chocolate bars. Coffee Crisp, Wunderbar, and a pair of Crunchies.

Carma's eyebrows damn near jumped off her face.

"Did I do good?" Kirk asked.

"You did good. Even better if you have a tub of maple ice cream in there."

"Sorry," he said through a frown. "No ice cream."

"This'll do. This'll do."

"The Wunderbar's mine, though."

She picked up the Coffee Crisp and tore the wrapper clear. After the first bite, she sighed and studied the ingredients. "Needed this."

"Yeah," Kirk muttered through his own mouth load.

"So bad. Yet so good."

"So good," he repeated.

They each took another bite, and while they munched, their eyes met.

And didn't stray.

An hour later, Carma was on the bed, staring at the ceiling. A soft glow came from a night table lamp, the only one in the room. Kirk sat in a chair beside her, his butt balanced on the edge, his feet stretched out as if being warmed by a fire.

"What are we doing, Douglas?" Carma asked, shifting and grimacing at the pull of her dead arm. "I mean, really. What are we doing?"

"We're going to see the wizards," he said simply.

"I'm having second thoughts."

"I know what I'm doing," Kirk said. "You can still get out."

Carma sighed. She was about to speak when her phone buzzed, polishing the night table's surface with a spastic whirl. They shared a look of sleepy curiosity. The phone insisted to be answered a second time. Carma picked it up, cringing as she did, and studied the number.

"It's them," she whispered, fully awake.

The elders. The knowledge petrified Kirk. "What do you want to do?"

"Answer it."

"They might have it tapped," he said.

"They might. Still want to talk to them?"

Kirk fidgeted. "Go for it."

"I'll put it on speakerphone."

Not a bad idea, he thought.

"Yes," Carma finally answered, holding the phone out so that he could hear.

"Carma."

The sound of that familiar, whispery voice caused Kirk to tense as if the very phone itself might do him harm.

"Yes?" Carma said. "What do you want?"

"Where are you?"

She looked Kirk in the eyes. "I'm in Halifax."

The voice didn't respond.

"Decided to get a little more active in my search for Kirk," she explained. "See what I could find."

"And did you find him?"

Carma didn't answer right away. "I did."

"And is he there? With you?"

Again she didn't answer right away and Kirk loved her for it. She met his eyes and he nodded.

"He is," she said.

"Hello, Kirk," the elder greeted.

The mere mention of his name sent chills through him. His breathing quickened and he cleared his throat.

"Hello," Kirk said, nearly croaking the word.

"Carma," the elder went on. "You're very much aware of what Kirk has done. Why haven't you killed him?"

"I don't see a need to," she answered.

"You're disobeying an order?"

A corner of the room held Carma's attention, her profile darkening. "I had to see Kirk's condition for myself. Judge for myself. I don't think he's a threat to anyone."

"Is that why you haven't answered your phone?"

"Elder," Kirk broke in, wanting to take the line of questioning off her. "I want to talk. Look. There's something going on with me, that's a given, but maybe it's not all bad. I mean, the rate of healing alone should be looked at. And silver? The immunity to silver? Maybe there's something good that can come from all this?"

The voice didn't answer.

"Hello?" Kirk asked, unsure if the creature on the other end was still listening.

"There's only one thing left to be done, Douglas Kirk," the voice declared gently. "And that's your death. Neither of you know what's coursing through your veins, Kirk. You don't know because there's never been a need for you to know. We do, however. By willingly ingesting *were* flesh, you've tainted the magic that makes you what you are. You've corrupted yourself. Are you experiencing the hunger yet? Of course you are. It will consume you, eventually. Horribly. Leaving you as a mindless, rabid dog every bit as destructive as Bailey would have been if you hadn't put him down. We cannot have that, for obvious reasons. Not in today's world. Carma, has he bitten you?"

Kirk and Carma exchanged looks.

"No," she answered.

"Are you in danger?"

"No."

"Then I'll make this offer to you," the voice said. "You still have your knife?"

Carma didn't answer.

"I've already explained Kirk's threat. To us and to the human herds. He's with you, now. Take your weapon and kill him."

Kirk's heart hammered against his ribs.

Carma visibly paled and shook her head. "I will not," she whispered.

The words stung the elder, and it withdrew from the

conversation for eerie moments. Then, "You've made your choice?"

She met Kirk's steady but nervous expression. "I guess I have."

Silence from the telephone.

"Elder?" Kirk eventually asked.

No response.

"Elder?"

Carma examined the phone before lifting it to her ear. "He's gone."

Kirk rose, pushing the chair back. The room's thick curtains were closed, hiding the parking lot from view. He suddenly didn't feel safe.

He pulled the curtain back a finger's width and peered outside.

"Anything wrong?" Carma asked, tossing the phone onto the bed.

"I don't see anything," Kirk said.

"I feel sick."

Kirk wasn't sure if she was talking about her wound or about her blatant defiance of the elders. Despite all his previous tough talk, he was about to shit himself now that the battle lines had been formally drawn. And the elder's words, that he would become something akin to Bailey, that scared Kirk. Badly.

He swallowed, feeling the dry click. "You should've—"

"What? Killed you?" Carma snapped. "Jesus Christ, get over it already. If I wanted you dead I would've done it a long time ago."

"I was going to say 'you should've left.' You heard what he said."

"About you? Yeah, I heard. Thing is, I have a brain."

"What do you mean by that?"

"You said it yourself. Something's not right here. If you wanted me dead you would've done it already. You haven't. Just the opposite. Unless you're saving me for a snack or something."

Kirk supposed that was true. "I think we better get out of here."

"Now?"

"Yeah, get your gear on. I don't like this place anymore."

And he meant it. Waves of danger lapped against his instincts, urging him to get to the car and leave. Wicked vibes that grew stronger by the second.

Carma slowly reached for her new sneakers. Kirk moved to help her.

The phone buzzed a second time, freezing them both. They looked at the device pulsating like a triggered tripwire. Neither warden moved to answer it.

Kirk's attention went to the door.

Outside was the softest shuffle of footsteps.

His eyes widened, sirens went off in his head.

Then the world exploded.

25

One hour earlier.

The first van pulled into the motel parking lot just after nightfall. It rumbled towards the head office and parked just out of sight of the guest units. The vehicle's engine switched off, and the side door slid open with a metallic shudder. Em got out from the back, her designer boots sparkly in the deepening dark and swirls of exhaust. She pulled her winter coat around herself, shivered dramatically, and approached the head office door.

Heat slammed into her upon entering, stopping her dead in her tracks.

"Wooo," she said, fanning her face with a mitten. "Holy hot flashes. This a motel or a Turkish steam bath?"

The two people behind the desk, the dayshift handing over the duties to the night, paused in their evening transition. They stared at her. One man, wearing a sleek gray blazer over a white shirt, appeared particularly alarmed at the newcomer. He glanced at his female co-worker, who was similarly dressed except for a red carnation over her right chest pocket. She also rocked a black dip of a ponytail.

"Well?" Em asked again.

"It is warm in here," the female employee commented.

"That's my fault," he said. "Sorry. I keep the heat on in the lobby. I have bad circulation."

"You must," Em declared, taking in the room's details as she walked to the front desk. She drummed her fingers along the hardwood edge. An office doorway was just behind the guy and she glanced that way with a thoughtful overbite. "Listen. I hate to do this to you, but I'm looking for my sister. She was traveling this way and I can't get in contact with her. Dirty little blonde, not a lick of fat on her. Pretty if she tried, but kinda bitchy. Actually, *really* bitchy. Anyone like that come in here?"

The receptionists exchanged uncertain looks.

"Miss that's confidential infor—"

"I know," Em interrupted, "but I'm talking about my sister here. She's a druggie on the run. Actually ran when we staged an intervention for her. You know about the upsurge in fentanyl usage?"

That got their attention.

"Yeah, that's her," Em whispered, inwardly delighted at the heart strings she'd plucked. "I lived that for a year. Barely got out alive. My sister hasn't just yet. But by the grace of God, she will.

"Was her arm in a cast or something?" the man finally asked.

Em put on a concerned face. "Not when she left the city

a day ago. Her man with her?"

"There was a man," the man said, worry clouding his features. "He rented a room for the night but... I only saw her from the window. She went into the unit with him."

"Sounds like her," Carma said. "So he rented a room."

"He did, but..."

The receptionists glanced at each other again. It was fucking annoying to Em the way they were attempting to read each other's minds. She dipped her head to one side, thinking murderous thoughts, her eyes widening with an unspoken *but...*

"But it's still motel policy not to give out that information," the man explained.

"Ahhhh," Em said. "I see. Well. I understand that. I think I've found my sister though. Which room would that be?"

The two motel staff stared once again, unaccustomed to being so pumped for information. Em was beginning to dislike them very much.

"That's confidential as well," the motel woman said, supporting her counterpart.

"I see." Em regarded one then the other. "Well, can you tell me about the units? There's only one way in, right? Through the front door?"

"That's correct, the front door," the woman answered.

"Okay, now let me ask you this. Of the two of you, who would you say reacts best under extreme stress?"

"Excuse me?" the woman asked.

"Who works best under pressure? Say the motel was on

fire and you had to evacuate or something. Like that."

The female looked to her male counterpart, who shrugged.

"I'd say she is," he stated.

"Excellent," Em said and brought up her gun from below the counter. She revealed the suppressed weapon so smoothly that neither staff member had the time to process what was happening. She shot the man in the chest, the wall behind him exploding in red. A spent casing bounced off the floor as he staggered, completely surprised, and collapsed.

The motel woman with the ponytail backed up against the bloody wall.

"What room are they in?" Em asked.

"Fourteen. Unit fourteen."

"How many units are in this shithole?"

"Fifteen."

"How many are full?"

The woman shook her head in defiance, true to whatever code of ethics the motel existed by. Em shot her twice in the heart. When she fell, Em proceeded around the desk, fired two more shots into her victims, and placed her feet wide while she planted her gun alongside a keyboard. She shouldn't have wasted silver rounds on regular folks. She only had so many of those magical bullets remaining.

She focused on the monitor. The keyboard chattered as she typed.

"Le grunt," Em growled, coming up with nothing.

She'd shot the bitch too soon and now she had to figure out the system all by her lonesome. That fouled her otherwise chipper mood. A moment later, she had the names of the motel occupants on a small sheet of paper. She glanced under the terminal and saw a switch. She flicked it and green lettering spelling NO VACANCY came to life behind the window's open blinds.

"Convenient," Em muttered. She studied the little nooks and crannies of the desk area. Numbered key fobs hung from a rack fixed to the rear wall. Most of the keys had duplicates, but four units only had singles.

"Slow night," she observed and took the four sets of keys, including number fourteen. She opened the cash drawer, thankful for the relative low tech, and pulled out all the bills, leaving the change. She stuffed her gun inside her coat, found another piece of paper, scrawled CLOSED TIL FURTHER NOTICE on it, and stuck the note to the inside window of the main entrance.

She stepped outside, the night air invigorating. A few snowflakes fluttered past the motel's light fixtures, hinting at a developing flurry. Em strolled along the motel's carpeted walkway, past unoccupied unit doors, until she stopped at number five. A blue minivan was parked in front of the door.

Em smoothed out her coat and knocked.

A man answered. "Yes?" he asked through the door.

"Hi," she said, warmly enough to turn her own stomach. "I'm Martha Blausset. I own the County Roadside. How are you doing tonight?"

The door opened. "Okay, thanks," a middle-aged man answered, sticking his face into the night.

"Room comfortable?"

"Oh yes, thanks," he nodded, but Em could tell he suspected something was on the wind.

"Mr. Battis?"

"Yes."

Em frowned with theatrical disappointment. "Mr. Battis, I'm sorry to inform you that we're experiencing something of an emergency here tonight. There's been a major gas leak and we've been advised by the provincial SSOT and Transport Canada to evacuate all our guests this very instant. For your safety. We're very sorry for this major inconvenience."

"You're kidding," a befuddled Battis said weakly, mouth hanging open.

"What is it, Buster?" an unseen woman asked.

Buster Battis? Em suppressed her snark.

"There's a gas leak at the motel," Buster reported. "They want us to leave."

"What, *now?*"

A woman close to Buster Battis's age peeked over his shoulder. *The missus*, Em presumed, and both of them severely beaten by an ugly-stick.

"We're truly, very sorry for this inconvenience." Em spread it on thicker than butter. "Look, here's your money for the night, as well as an additional two hundred dollars towards your next stay. There's a Four Seasons just up the TCH, about an hour's drive away, and they have additional rooms, which I've already booked on your behalf. Just leave the keys on your room's table."

"Oh," said Buster Battis, suddenly placated by the money

and the alternative accommodations. Em handed him the cash. As for the Four Season's room, by the time Buster Battis and his wife found out there was no such reservation, the business at the County Roadside would be long over with and the dead removed.

"Well, that's not a bad thing," he said, cash in hand. "Is it really dangerous?"

"Yes it is," Em said. "So get your asses outta here."

She left Buster Battis standing in the doorway with that slack-jawed expression of shock and wonder she oh so loved. Em returned to the main office, went behind the front desk, and made a show of attending to very important business.

A clock displayed 6:42 in glowing red numerals.

At 6:47, the minivan drove by the main office, brake lights flaring. Em waved at the vehicle. The Battis's vehicle headed toward the highway and joined the rest of the night traffic.

"That's one," Em said to the dead people at her feet. She realized she was standing in blood. Not the smartest thing to do, but she'd clean them later.

Humming Christmas tunes, Em went to unit nine and eleven and informed the people therein—a single man in one and a mother and her brat in the other—to likewise vacate the premises. Like the Battis couple, they were surprised but calmed down at the mention of the refund, the reserved room at the competitor hotel, and the extra two hundred dollars to cover the expense. Em walked back to the main office, killing time, really, and again waved at the departing car and a pickup truck with the decals "Marty's

Engine Parts!" boldly displayed on the side.

Two and three, Em thought. This good neighbor act was the shit. She could play the role all night.

The clock read quarter after seven. No mad rush, just a one-by-one exit.

Until only one guest remained.

Em stepped outside, considered the lazy cotton puffs of snow made even prettier by the few lamplights situated around the parking lot. In a few minutes, the whole area would be covered in pre-Christmas white. There was no breeze. Highway traffic zoomed by the motel, passing like missiles. She looked down the wide, sheltered walkway, untouched by the falling snow, in the direction of unit fourteen. Very soon now, she would earn a sizeable amount of bank.

Thinking about hot tubs, Em returned to the white van. She noticed that two more vans had arrived, pulled up alongside their identical cousin. She stopped and rapped on the metallic shell.

The side door opened.

"All clear," Em reported to a glowering Barronni. "Playground's all ours."

Five men in full battle dress occupied the interior. Black automatic MP5s shone in their hands. Multiple magazines were taped together and fixed underneath the submachine guns. Kevlar vests and helmets covered their chests and heads. Balaclavas hid their faces. The men, combined with a few cabinets near the front of the vehicle, made quarters very tight indeed. Em found herself pressed against Barronni's arm and was very much aware of the heat emanating off him.

"Are they in the room?" Barronni asked, his own mask rolled up to his forehead.

"I guess so. There's a car parked in front of the door. Must be theirs."

"I'll take care of the car," Jude remarked. They all knew Kirk had escaped the first attempt on his life in his pickup. They would not make that mistake again.

"Any rear doors?" another hunter asked.

"None."

"You get all the workers?" someone asked.

Em answered with a scowl.

"How many?" Barronni asked.

"Only two," she said, taking an offered Balaclava and pulling it over her head. "Dayshift handing over duties to the night. Might be more on the way but I doubt it. The place isn't that big."

"How'd you get rid of the other guests?" that same someone asked.

"Easy. Just told them I'd heard from the SSOT and Transport Canada that we had a very dangerous gas leak."

"SSOT?"

"Same shit, only thicker."

A masked face shook his head in amusement.

Barronni didn't so much as blink, however. He took out his cellphone and glanced at its glowing screen. "The call's going through now. Power up."

The group switched on holographic weapons systems mounted on their MP5s and adjusted their sights for near-dark conditions.

"Everyone out," Barronni ordered.

The side door slid open, a little too noisy for Em. They exited the van and lined up along the motel's wall, soft soled boots barely making a sound. Additional armored hunters got out of the other vans. They formed another line next to the first, resembling a combat-ready Emergency Response Team. There were no markings on their gear, however. No lettering, and the equipment and weapons all scrubbed clear of serial numbers, brands, and unit logos.

Em stood near the middle of the assembled line, her own gun held by her ear. There would be no knocking on motel doors. This time, they would go in hot, guns blazing.

Barronni stopped at Em's side. He resembled a tall, sleepy reaper looking to finish his busy shift. He held his MP5 at port with one hand while studying his phone with the other. Heads turned in the line, waiting on the signal to commit.

They didn't wait very long.

"We're green," Barronni whispered. He put the phone away and pulled down his facemask. He went to the front of the line and curled himself around the corner.

And like a monstrous black serpent emerging from a vat of pitch, the hunters followed, hunched low, weapons at the ready.

Em was amongst them.

They slunk along the walkway as the snow continued falling in white feathers. Motel unit five went by, then ten, and Em's back started to ache from being bent over. They arrived at unit fourteen and stopped not seven feet from the door.

Barronni scooted underneath the room's only window, moved past the door, and straightened on the opposite side. He pointed to the top and bottom hinges, as well as the door knob and points where unseen bolt locks might be placed. The nearest hunter stopped at the entrance and jammed malleable wads of C-4 to every designated spot. Once done, he joined Barronni and hugged the wall. Jude went to the car and crawled under it, working his magic to ensure the vehicle would not be going anywhere. Once done, he slipped out and scooted to the other side of the room entrance, getting into position with a thumbs up.

Standing in front of Barronni, the demolition man produced a wireless detonator.

Halfway along the line of poised attackers, Em cringed at the approaching boom.

Barronni raised a fist, held it for a second, and chopped at the air.

26

The door flew off its hinges with a stunning thunderclap, actually surfing off Kirk's spine, and flapped off the wall as the blast pitched him forward. Fire flashed around the doorway. He hauled Carma off the bed as he went over the other side. She didn't cry out as they landed and rolled, but then he couldn't hear much beyond a flatline ringing in his ears.

A second explosion then, and Kirk squinted at an opaque screen, as if someone had poured white paint directly into his eyes.

Carma went rigid in Kirk's arms, grimacing and clamping a single hand to her ear. Kirk recovered faster than she did, still had presence of mind. They were lying at the far end of the bed. From underneath the mattress, two sets of boots stamped inside the room, framed against a glowing backdrop of night, snow and orange smoldering wood. He twisted, on his back, as boots thumped across carpet.

Gunfire *brapped*.

The bed jumped and trembled. Springs twanged. Spits

of fabric and metal punched through the underbelly of the bed, marking the gunfire's advance with dusty sputters. Kirk's jaws ached.

Silver. They had silver rounds.

Carma opened her mouth to scream.

They were going to die here, the true purpose behind the elder's curt conversation suddenly clear. The voice had kept them talking long enough just to get their team into position, long enough to get Carma's answer, and once the elder hung up, the real show began in a supercharged burst of violence.

Kirk knew they were both dead, unless… a miracle happened. A miracle only he could access.

So he summoned the change, releasing the *were*blood and pumping it through his limbs, trying to achieve that frightening state that Walt Borland had reached, that half-man beast that had surprised and nearly killed both Kirk and Morris on one snowy day in Newfoundland.

Kirk pushed his effort into overdrive, the thought of Carma's death fueling his desperation.

Something shattered inside of him.

Something that, in that split fragment of time, he knew he'd never mend again.

Fangs sprouted. Knife-like claws burst from his fingertips. His musculature stretched to the point of snapping free of his bones while his skin tightened. The walls of his entire arterial system threatened to burst from the rocket spike in blood pressure. Through bloodshot eyes, he saw boots round the corner of the bed. Figures stood poised on the mattress above him.

Kirk saw their widening eyes.

With supernatural strength the warden flipped the bed, heaving the mass and the men standing upon it at the door. Cries of surprise and alarm reached a fever pitch. One soldier at the foot of the bed trained his gun at the *were*. Kirk kicked the weapon away. He rolled to his feet, grabbed the man by his tactical vest, and whipped him into a second shooter, crashing both into a wall.

A figure wormed free of the blocked doorway. Gunfire ripped the air, tracers flashed.

But Kirk was already moving.

The motel unit's broad window exploded as he plunged through it. Glass showered the backs of soldier types crouched along the wall. Kirk landed, spun around, and charged just as one fired. Burning light opened the warden's cheek to the bone.

Then he was amongst them.

Kirk shredded a masked face in a flash of claws and gore.

He slammed a head into a wall.

He grabbed one gun barrel just as the soldier fired, the blast disintegrating the face of another masked man. Kirk punched the shooter, mashing bone deep into a sinus cavity.

Men screamed as the wolf-thing surged amongst them, raking claws across faces, torqueing heads left and right, or simply shoving them against walls. Kirk pushed one man into a wooden post that crumpled like candy. The overhang sagged. He grabbed a soldier and threw him through another window. Someone fired and bullets peppered the slumping roof. Splinters rained across Kirk's back. He launched one man twenty feet into the parking lot, skimming him across asphalt like a flat rock on a calm lake. With unearthly speed, Kirk grabbed a nearby soldier and whirled as three attackers fired multiple bursts. Bullets slammed into the warden's epileptic meat shield. Kirk crouched, holding onto the soldier's flak-protected torso, enduring the bullet storm until a round slashed through the man's neck in a burst of blood.

Kirk powered forward. He barreled through a collection of legs before flinging his captive's dead weight at the gunmen.

The men dodged the flailing corpse and then Kirk was amongst them.

He slapped one shell-head hard enough to break a neck.

Another had his gun arm snapped at the elbow. Red bone speared through the fabric. Kirk uppercut with a flash of claws that finished the man and threw him far and away.

The remaining soldiers moved in slow motion as the supercharged *were* tore through the confused mass, wreaking terrible damage. Kirk caught a throat and ripped, spraying the walkway in black. He climbed over a man desperately trying to reload, and twisted the head around in a gift-paper crinkle of vertebrae. Kirk screamed, wide-eyed and fangs flashing.

A bullet slammed into his right shoulder and his arm jumped in pain.

A second round cut through his hip in a puff of gore, twirling him in a rushed pirouette.

A woman.

Her balaclava was pushed up, uncovering a smile resplendent. She stood in a duelist's pose in the parking lot, her right arm outstretched and ending in a sidearm. The weapon's barrel as big as a cannon and pointed right at Kirk's skull.

A burst of automatic gunfire cut across the woman's midsection, buckling her, driving her back.

Carma appeared in the doorway of their room, firing an MP5 from her left hip.

Kirk fell as Carma leaned heavily against the frame. She twisted left and right to a rabid drum machine. Light shredded two more soldiers in inky clouds, dropping them where they stood.

A soldier rushed his return fire and blew out a section of the doorframe. Carma sagged and blazed back, stitching a line up his body armor until one round popped his collarbone in a grisly halo, blasting him off his feet.

Then on some unseen note, Carma turned to her right, facing one final gunman who had propped himself into a sitting position against the motel wall.

He held his MP5 with one arm, already aimed.

Kirk shrieked as the two fired at each other.

Carma squawked as multiple rounds pitched into her right side, plastering her against the doorframe. Her burst frazzled the drooping overhang, shredding wooden slats and drizzling the air with slivers.

Kirk vaulted off the ground, howling. He sprinted ten feet to the last gunman, grabbed a helmeted head and twisted, shutting off the gunfire with a bony crackle.

Carma lay on her back, atop a heap of dead. Blood saturated her t-shirt.

"I can't..." she whispered, her teeth traced in red. She'd released the weapon and her fingers twitched. "I can't..."

Kirk winced, his fangs alien in his mouth. "*Stay still,*" he commanded in a reverberating voice.

He lifted her shirt.

The sight mortified him to a whimper.

Carma's right side, from just above her hip to her lower ribs, resembled a snowman's smile. Blood seeped from that gory grin, the skin very pale indeed.

"Wait," Kirk growled.

"Douglas—"

"*WAIT!*" he barked and Carma shivered. He knew it wasn't from fear.

Instinct turned his head. In the lazy snowfall, two figures moved and attempted to collect themselves.

One was the woman, sitting in the parking lot, her balaclava pulled back to better suck air into a diaphragm just unlocking itself.

Another was a soldier moving amongst a heap of dead men.

Kirk knew they weren't soldiers. They were trained killers—hunters sent to put them both down.

Fury took the Halifax warden.

He snatched up a nearby MP5—it felt awkward in his left hand—and limped toward a man fumbling to extract himself from his dead companions. Kirk placed the gun to the hunter's cheek and fired. Meat and bone boomeranged into the night. The hunter dropped on the spot.

Kirk regarded the woman through the falling snow. She had managed to get to her knees, far from finished. She saw him, smiled, and straightened as if completing a prayer.

Wincing and trailing blood, Kirk shuffled towards her.

Em saw the werewolf coming for her, distantly wondering how the monster had retained a biped form. Concrete pumped through her arms and legs, weighing them down. The werewolf—Douglas Kirk—was pissed. She could plainly see that. His horrid, shadowy complexion unnerved her, as did his fanged maw. The blood dripping in his wake did nothing to slow him down. He was far from dead.

Just her luck.

Kirk's female companion was motionless in the doorway, and that lifted Em's spirits. At least they'd tagged one target.

Em smiled as Douglas Kirk approached.

"I'll talk," she whined in a wretched tone, though mad glee filled her eyes. "I—I'll tell you—"

He shot her in the face.

She fell back, arms splayed, legs bending at graceless angles. Kirk stood over her and fired a second blast, erasing her features in a violent, stuttering flash.

Once finished, he staggered to the main office. Along the way, his bestial features retracted, his surging strength receded. His heartrate slowed into an erratic thumping. Then the pain reached him, seizing his chest in a near paralyzing vice. Snow continued to fall. He spotted the vans and changed direction with a moan. An idea was forming.

The keys were in the first van's ignition. His right arm hanging, Kirk got in on the passenger side. He groped for the keys and spattered the steering column in blood. He started the engine, took a deep breath, and fired up the dash lighter. Bright stars orbited Kirk's vision as he sat in the driver's seat. His heart hammered like a free-swinging pendulum, and he dreaded each titanic beat. After what seemed like years, he yanked the lighter free.

The coiled end glowed red-hot evil.

Kirk jammed the superheated metal into his hip wound. He screamed, bucked in the seat, but kept the lighter in place despite the wrath overwhelming his system. When he could take no more, he pulled the lighter out, licked his lips, and inspected the bullet hole fried shut. His throat clenched with a girlish squeal, bobbed in a swallow, and he stuck the car lighter into his right shoulder wound, damn-near dropping the searing metallic knob.

Flesh sizzled. Blood cooked.

Kirk skittered along the precipice of passing out, his consciousness spinning like a fragment of a detonated bomb. Somehow, he held on and finished roasting himself. Once done, he wasted no time and stuck the lighter back into its dashboard socket.

Fluid sputtered and snapped, but Kirk recharged the lighter, and when he was done, he slid from the vehicle like a half-squashed slug.

He shuffled back to unit fourteen, step by bone-grinding step, towards Carma.

She had pulled herself out of the doorway and into the

motel unit, leaving a glossy streak that frightened Kirk badly. Her throaty wheezes broke his heart.

"Carma," he panted.

Her eyes flickered, sunk deep into bloodied cheeks, painfully aware that she was in a dire condition.

Kirk ripped the comforter from the bed and applied its thickness to her ruined side. The pressure he exerted caused Carma's head to roll. He eased off and pulled the blanket away.

The bullet holes continued to ooze. Kirk pressed cloth to that morbid smile, very much aware of how little time he had. Carma writhed weakly under his hands.

"Hold on," he told her. "Don't be a bitch here. Don't be a bitch. You know you hate that saying, so don't live it."

She grunted a yes.

Kirk pulled the comforter away and applied the lighter's glowing eye without warning. Carma arched her back, the act almost pulling the lighter from his fingers. He held on, pushing that awful branding iron deeper. Wisps rose from the contact, but the blood didn't stop.

Not enough, Kirk realized and considered the night table. *Motel note pad.*

Aware that he was moaning, Kirk ripped a sheet from the pad and stuck the paper's edge to the dimmed lighter. The paper ignited. He dropped the little torch onto the bed. The cottony sheets caught and when the flames grew, he grabbed the comforter and fed that to the blaze.

The blanket became a droopy lick of fire. Kirk dropped to his knees. Carma watched him, her eyes sleepy.

"Sorry," he whispered, very much meaning it.

He applied the flame to her wounds.

Carma screeched. Bucked. Struggled to escape. Kirk threw himself across her thighs and trapped her left arm, keeping her in place. She emptied her lungs on one piercing note and her head thumped against the carpet. Jaw clenched, Kirk held her, even when the flames started licking his side. He buried his head into the floor, taking the burn, forcing himself to stay.

Then he became aware of the smoke.

The bed.

Kirk looked up to see it on fire.

Just before the room's sprinkler system doused the entire room.

27

Smoke streamers escaped the open doorway as the fire quickly died underneath the sprinkler's downpour. A drenched Kirk emerged into the night, awkwardly carrying an unconscious Carma. Her flesh had been badly burned, and her wounds still drooled blood. His strength waned and failed. The transformation back to human was bad enough, but his own silver-induced wounds drained him fast.

He needed to get Carma to a safe place.

That safe place was unit eleven, the door left open by its recently departed guests.

Kirk staggered inside and dumped Carma on the double bed. He touched her cheek. She shied away from his fingers, but that was good enough for him. At least she was still alive.

His ears twitched then—creeping footsteps from behind, barely detectable over the sprinklers next door.

Kirk spun and saw a figure standing in the doorway. One of the hunters, his helmet and balaclava ripped off for comfort, sweaty hair spiked. A thick splash of gore coated the right side of his neck, all the way up to his cheek and ear.

Blood saturated the man's goatee and dripped from his chin.

But that wasn't what really got Kirk's attention.

The man had been shot. Critically. His upper right arm and collarbone gleamed through shredded clothing, spewing fluid. That part of his body looked like a freshly dug hole in the middle of a grassy meadow, one that had erupted in oil.

And as the sight of all that ruined meat stunned the Halifax warden to inaction, the hunter awkwardly, determinedly, lifted a submachine gun.

Kirk stormed forward as the hunter fired. Spears of light cut through the room. Kirk tackled the man's mid-section and carried him into the night. He slammed the killer into the pavement, the impact sending the weapon skittering.

The hunter swung at a Kirk's head.

Surprised by the crosscut, the warden blocked the punch and slapped the man twice, heavy blows that cranked the attacker's head and left him giddy. But Kirk suspected the hunter wasn't a man. The shattered arm and collarbone should have killed an ordinary person. All that raw meat… the sight captivated Kirk, the smell tantalizing. He resisted for seconds, gasping at times, before finally tearing himself away with a whimper.

Kirk picked up the fallen MP5, stood, and held the weapon at his side. The elders had forbidden all use of firearms, deeming them unclean. Kirk had used a shotgun back in Newfoundland, when he needed an equalizer to put down Borland's ravenous breeds. He didn't have a problem then, not with those monsters, but with a true *were*, he hesitated. The feeling that overcame him was one of guilt.

Then he thought of Carma.

He glanced over his shoulder. She remained on the bed, unmoving. Her face covered in stuffing from a shredded pillow. *Jesus Christ*, he thought. Panic encapsulated him and his heart double-timed. *That one last burst...*

"You..." Kirk directed at the hunter but couldn't finish the sentence. He staggered back to the room and collapsed on the bed beside her. He cleared the soft foam away from Carma's head, seeing how the rip of bullets had missed her skull by inches.

Kirk let his relief go in a single, long-winded expulsion of breath. "You lucky bitch," he whispered.

Though her eyes remained closed, her mouth turned upward in the barest twinge of a smile.

Knee-weakening gratitude flooded his system and he didn't move for seconds. When he did, he looked to the parking lot.

The hunter was gone.

Kirk stumbled outside at his fastest speed, keeping the MP5 pointed into the frosted night. The pain in his arm was bearable. His eyes watered from the exertion.

There. Halfway up the lot and leaving ink spots in the snow. The hunter staggered towards the parked vans.

Kirk took his time drawing a bead on his target. When he squeezed the trigger, the recoil almost drove him to his knees.

The short blast cut across his target's legs. The hunter collapsed, landing on his chest. There he stayed, one arm reaching in the vans' direction.

Though his shoulder pained him, Kirk kept his gun trained on his target as he approached. When the warden stopped beside the wounded *were*, as he was certain this was no mere mortal, he inserted a foot underneath the shapechanger's chest and flipped the creature over.

"You're a *were*," Kirk accused, cheek pressed to metal.

The *were* didn't reply. His eyes rolled, looking for a way out, before settling on Kirk.

"Didn't think you were supposed to use guns on hunts," the Halifax warden said. "Or even at all."

That got a weak smile from the *were* at his feet. "Plenty… you don't know."

The lies. Borland whispered in Kirk's mind.

"Where are the elders?" Kirk demanded and leaned in, gouging the *were's* cheek with the MP5's hot barrel.

The creature looked away. A cough rattled his entire frame.

"Where are they?" Kirk pressed the muzzle deeper.

"They'll find… you."

"Tell me."

The *were* ignored him.

Kirk eased off on the weapon. "What's your name?"

"Barronni," whispered the dying creature. Blood oozed from the ugly gash around the neck. Falling snow dappled the wound briefly, dissolving in its heat.

A wind rose in Kirk's ears and he licked his lips. He released the MP5 and it clattered on the pavement. The smell unlocked his knees and pulled him to the ground. This time, he didn't resist.

Barronni watched, his grimace verging on a wet smile.

"Don't," he whispered. The *were's* eyes twinkled under the parking lot's meager lights while the sprinkler system hissed in the background.

The blood drew Kirk closer. The pounding in his temples increased. His heartbeat slowed as if chemically sedated. His fangs emerged and he realized he'd somehow crossed over into Borland's state of half-change once again.

"Don't," Barronni murmured, much weaker this time, turning his head. The magical black fluid seeping from the *were's* neck flowed with a little more energy. The color deepened and shimmered under the streetlights, pulling Kirk closer.

The warden stretched his jaws open wide, looked away, and zeroed in on that rich flow. His mouth watered. And the *smell…*

Kirk's willpower waned. Wavered.

Fangs snapped in the wintry light. *So good.* It smelled so good.

His control faltered. All became calm.

Kirk chomped into the throat. He gorged himself, feeling the creature's life ebb away with each gluttonous bite, avoiding the places tainted by silver.

Barronni offered no resistance.

Minutes later, a dazed Kirk pushed himself away from the lifeless husk. He took a moment to gather himself, like a person who'd eaten at a Thanksgiving dinner well past capacity. He realized with horror that he'd been licking bone splinters, lapping away at marrow.

Don't, Barronni had said. Well, the warden did. And much more than just a quick bite. Much more. Kirk thought he might've been able to make Barronni talk about the elder's whereabouts. Might've. If Kirk could have mustered a little more self-control.

But God help him, he felt better already.

Kirk cleaned his mouth and wiped his hand on the dead *were's* sleeve. His stomach knotted and contracted, though not unpleasantly. He didn't dwell on Barronni's dead features, or the ravenous work he'd done on the creature's neck, collar, and shoulders. Kirk stood on shaky legs. Corpses littered the parking lot.

He looked to unit eleven.

Saw Carma on the bed, staring right back at him.

He went to her side, believing his pain was just a touch less intense. Carma studied him with drooping eyes, her consciousness failing.

"I'm. In hard shape," she whispered, half way to blacking out.

Kirk felt her forehead, grimly aware that his appetite no longer bothered him. "You'll be fine."

"Yeah," she smiled as if in a dream.

"We gotta move," Kirk said.

"You get them?"

"All of them."

"Badass."

Kirk cracked a smile. "Desperate."

"Carry me."

"Wait," he said and went back outside.

The car wouldn't be big enough to carry a stretched out Carma, and Kirk wanted to make her as comfortable as possible while he figured things out. He hobbled towards the dead carcass of Barronni, knelt beside the ravaged corpse, and eyed the bleeding destruction he'd wrought. Barronni's eyes were thankfully closed, his mouth gone slack, but his upper body appeared to have been flayed and scooped out by chainsaws.

I did that, Kirk mentally moaned. *I did that.*

I'm not a monster.

But the once protective mantra did nothing for him this time. Kirk got a hold of himself and rooted through Barronni's pockets. He located a set of keys and looked to the vans parked on the far side of the motel. Seconds later, he climbed aboard and started up one of the vehicles. He backed up to unit eleven, hoping to slip a mattress into the rear.

When he opened the van's double doors, a series of cabinets caught his attention, and he took a moment to open them.

"Whoa," Kirk whispered.

An arsenal lay before him. A short row of handguns and automatic weapons filled the cabinet while extra magazines lay stacked on the floor. A spare Kevlar vest had also been tucked away. Kirk marveled over the small weapons cache, wondering where these people had obtained such an ordinance and who even financed them.

The elders, of course.

Guns. That puzzled Kirk. Wardens were supposed to be

responsible for taking down rogue *weres* with silver knives, jaws, or even fire if necessary. He couldn't fathom why the elders had a team of humans and *weres* armed to the teeth with weapons they weren't supposed to use on a sanctioned hunt. Weapons loaded with silver bullets, no less. The very notion went against everything he'd been told. Using firearms on a hunt was... *dirty*, for lack of a better word. Deplorable. Dishonorable, even.

Puzzlement faded to anger. He got moving.

Unit ten's door had been locked so Kirk put his shoulder to it, almost falling over from the effort. Once in, he wasted no time stealing a mattress and shoving it and a duvet into the van's rear.

Kirk then went for Carma.

"Come on," he said. When he lifted her off the bed, her mewling once again tore at his heart.

Carma held up her phone, the normally bright display dimmed with blood.

"Maybe tracking us," she hissed, "with this."

"Okay."

He lowered her onto the van's mattress and, after making sure she was tucked away, took the phone from her hand. *Maybe tracking us*. After the full-on attack seconds after the elder had hung up, Kirk suspected it was a certainty. His own phone was back at his Halifax apartment, which was no doubt one reason why the hunters hadn't been able to catch up with him.

Kirk hefted the phone and regarded the night.

He hurled the device over the motel.

"Track that," he snarled and trudged back to unit fourteen. The fire hadn't touched the leftover food or their bags, so he grabbed everything, including the strongbox left aboard Carma's car. Kirk loaded everything into the back and climbed aboard the van. He started up the engine as Carma stirred behind him.

Kirk put the vehicle in drive and drove off into the night.

28

Some three hours later, Kirk pulled off the highway, stopping on a white frosted clearing meant for drivers to get out and stretch their legs. He had no such intention. Carma stirred on the mattress. He got out of the driver's seat and knelt at her side, smoothing the hair from her forehead. Her skin burned.

"We there yet?" she asked.

Kirk smiled. "No."

"We stopped?"

He traced the curve of her cheek. "Yeah. Side of the highway."

She stared at the wall. "Middle of nowhere."

"You got it."

"Shit," Carma whispered, and her forehead wrinkled. "You're lost, aren't you?"

"No. No, I'm not lost." He turned to the bags of untouched food. "You better eat something."

He grabbed a bag, rattling the plastic, and rooted through the contents.

"Douglas," she said, pain wrapped around the word.

"Yeah?"

"I can't eat."

"You have to."

She took her time answering, the dashboard light just barely reaching her hair, leaving the rest of her face in shadow. "I'm all shot up," she whispered.

"You'll be fine."

She didn't say anything to that and Kirk's throat tightened. His eyes watered. He dropped the bag of food and leaned over her. His forehead stopped not an inch from her profile. He caressed her face and she didn't flinch. A bad sign.

She turned, her brow making contact with his. Her brown eyes glimmered, one feature that had never ceased to mesmerize him. Kirk realized that was a lie. Everything about her mesmerized him. Dazzled him, from the day he first met her, to the day she left, and every day in between until she returned to his life.

"Listen," he croaked. "I have… I have an idea."

"Yeah?"

He steadied himself, not believing he was even going to suggest it, but he couldn't live with the alternative. "I could bite you."

The words hung on the air. Carma didn't pull back, but she narrowed her eyes, frowning at the notion.

"Listen," Kirk stressed. "Whatever's in me, I can pass on to you. One bite. Okay?"

"That's… unauthorized."

Kirk looked away for a second, marveling sadly at a protest that was all Carma. "Those guys back there, Carma? One was a *were*. I didn't check the others but there was at least one… And they all used guns with, with silver rounds, okay? *That's* unauthorized."

"Yeah," she agreed, weakly.

"And, frankly," he continued, very close to her face, "I can't imagine what things would be like without you. I mean, who would boss me around?"

Carma scowled, and Kirk couldn't contain his unhappy smile. "You hear me?"

"Yeah."

"So what do you say?"

She took her time, as much as she could afford, and closed her eyes as if meditating upon the question. As the seconds passed, he wondered if she was still even conscious.

"Sure," she finally whispered, sounding defeated. The word came out so softly, Kirk wasn't entirely certain if she was agreeing with him or shushing him.

In the end, he didn't care.

He pulled off his clothing and tossed it aside. Kirk intended to fully change over to the werewolf for this bite, just to make sure the transfer occurred. His blood was already pumping when he triggered the transformation, bringing it on with barely a hitch. He kept an eye on Carma while his body contorted and underwent the supernatural changes, hearing the barest breathing in a chest that didn't appear to move.

Faster, he pushed, fully aware of the dangers, but not

caring in the least if his liver parked itself in the same space as his balls. Not this time.

His spine crackled like bubble wrap. His snout pushed itself out from his face, the stress on his sinus cavity causing his eyes and nose to gush. And in that sudden popping and stretching of fleshy matter, an alarm went off in Kirk's head.

Carma had ceased breathing.

Oh no! Kirk pushed, shoving the change through with every fiber of his being. His fingers erupted into talons. His ribs expanded and popped and his guts shifted and cramped. Fully transformed, he loped around in the van, feeling one massive paw graze her leg. He sniffed at Carma's right cheek and recoiled at her toxic stench.

Dying.

But not quite dead, not yet.

Kirk turned around, walked over her as if chasing his tail. The van rocked on its chassis. A miserable yowl left him as he zeroed in on the bullet wound smirk. His lips pulled back from his rack of teeth and he hunkered down, the space confining, awkward.

He bit deep into her side. Blood rushed down his throat.

Carma didn't make a sound.

*

The sun peeked through the van's windshield, rustling Kirk from where he'd fallen asleep. He propped himself up from the mattress, careful not to disturb Carma. Little snores sprinkled the air and Kirk paid attention to a minute's worth before settling back down, his naked side pressed against her clothed one.

He'd rushed his change last night and the physical discomfort was nothing compared to waiting for Carma to respond to his bite. After biting her, Kirk lay beside her as a wolf, suffering through each minute until they became an hour.

Until suddenly, thankfully, she had taken one deep, refueling gulp of air.

He'd kissed her face in relief.

He'd changed back minutes afterwards, taking a more natural speed so that important parts slid back in their proper places. When he'd completed the transformation, he stayed by her and flipped the duvet to hide the bloody stains.

And there they'd slept, with the blanket pulled to their chins.

Kirk stretched and stared at the ceiling. He shifted with a groan, seeing his breath on the air and feeling the nip of a wintry morning. His wounds didn't bother him so much; actually, they had healed rather nicely. The silver barely ached. Whatever was tainting his blood was miraculous. He only hoped he had passed it along to Carma.

She had turned onto her good side, away from him, during the night. A knot of duvet covered the lower part of her face, as she'd hogged a good portion of the blanket during the early morning hours. Kirk didn't mind. There was plenty of blanket for them both. He got an arm underneath, lifted, and discovered she had tucked her toes in as well.

Christ, Carma, he swore, but the smile on his face said otherwise. A deep cold penetrated the van's walls, so Kirk snuggled in close, basking in her radiant heat. He sniffed and was surprised to detect the retreating silver poison in her system. Trace amounts of the hated metal lingered about the entry and exit points of her wounds, but the bite marks and bullet holes had already sealed.

Kirk liked what he saw. She was alive.

If he had to, he'd feed her his right arm to keep her heart beating.

Not that it bothered him. The limb would grow back. He was pretty sure it would.

After a time he sat up and examined the duvet. The bloody spots were near his feet and, thankfully, they hadn't seeped through. At least they had spare clothing. Kirk looked for the clothes he'd stripped off before becoming a werewolf.

"Kirk," Carma whispered.

That stopped him. "Yeah?"

"Shit or get off the pot."

That furrowed his brow.

"Get down here and cover up," she complained in a whisper. "It's fucking cold, man."

Oh.

Kirk did as he was told, pulling the duvet over himself and sealing all the breaches. Carma snuggled into him, until they were practically spooning. He decided what the hell, and draped an arm over her.

"Not the side," she said immediately.

"Sorry."

"Still tender."

"Right." He withdrew his arm, brushing her hip. He

stayed there, aware of his situation as if he'd awoken in a mine field. He tried to relax and, to his surprise, she pushed into him further, her hair burying his nose.

"Oh my," he said.

"Just because it's warm," Carma said. "That's all."

"'Course."

"And don't pop a chubby. Don't you dare. Don't even think about popping one. Hear me?"

"Right. No chubby. Got it."

"All I need is a hard-on in my lower back."

"Right," Kirk said, but he tingled when she said *hard-on*. "Carma?"

"Yeah?"

"You feeling better?"

"Yeah. I am. You bit me, didn't you?"

Kirk sighed into her hair. "Yeah. Sorry. I thought… I thought you were dead. Or almost dead."

"And you brought me back."

"Yeah."

"Reminds me of… when I first bit you. And took you into the fold."

Kirk remembered. All too well. "You never forget your first," he murmured.

"That was authorized, of course," she pointed out.

"Of course."

"How long ago was that?"

"A long time. Years."

"Seems like only weeks, doesn't it?"

Kirk grunted a half-hearted agreement.

"So what should I expect?" she asked.

"You know... you already sound stronger."

"Thanks. So?"

Kirk thought about it. "Well, you should heal completely from the silver. I think silver will still kill us, but it might take a lot more. Still not sure on that so don't test it."

"Gotcha."

"No scars, and you might very well be able to use your arm again. You just need to eat. Like always."

He paused, wondering how much he should tell her.

Carma picked up on it right away. "And?"

"You'll be faster. Stronger. And..."

"I'll get a hankering for eating *weres*?"

No fooling her. "Good guess."

Carma didn't comment.

"Yeah," he said. "You'll get... hankerings. Subtle in the beginning, especially in the first few weeks and months. Then they'll get stronger. Sometimes really strong. But they seem to be less when you're in full-on wolf form."

"Why is that?"

"I don't know," he admitted softly. "Just is. But we can't be wolves forever."

"You were getting these cravings while we were hunting Bailey, weren't you?"

"Yeah."

"And you didn't say a word to me."

"No."

"Thanks a lot."

That time, Kirk kept his mouth shut.

"What…" Carma began, "what do you do when the cravings get too strong?"

"I eat. Raw roasts. Stuff my face with anything, really."

"And that helps?"

Kirk's forehead touched the back of her skull. "Not really. I thought the kills I made as a wolf were helping, but like I said, just being a werewolf might be a better explanation. Maybe both. You know me. I don't usually change over, so maybe more testing's needed."

"Wow."

"Now you know," he whispered. "I didn't want to do this to you but…" Kirk hesitated, and decided to go for it. "I hated losing you more."

When the last few words left him, hope and dread double-teamed him. Her silence told him he'd gone too damn far, that he shouldn't have said that last part. Owen Adams entered his mind then, and he remembered the old wood carver's story about how he'd asked his girlfriend of only three dates to marry him.

For several excruciating seconds Carma didn't say a word. So long in fact, Kirk wondered if she'd heard him at all. Perhaps she'd passed out or fallen asleep.

But then she spoke. "Thank you. For saving my life."

No resentment. No frustration. No tensing in her muscles or even a damning pulling away from him. He waited for the worst, expecting a blast or even a scalding lecture. You never really lived until Carma told you off at least once.

Except none of that happened.

"You good?" he asked carefully, the dread rising in his gullet, but needing to make sure.

"Just thinking is all."

Oh sweet Jesus, thank you. He'd just dodged a bullet.

But the dread remained in the pit of his stomach. And a feeling of guilt. "It's a curse, Carma. A curse. That's why the elders want me dead."

"Yeah. We'll see about that." She shifted. Sighed. Her rump pushed against his pelvis and the movement startled him. He decided to remain perfectly still. It was all he needed. Especially after her warning about chubbies. Women-folk. It was like a test every day.

"This is good," she said, changing subjects entirely, and relaxed. Despite their mutual predicament, Kirk agreed with her.

They stayed that way for a long time, appreciating the shared warmth. And the quiet.

"We're on the highway?" she finally asked.

"Yeah. Somewhere."

"We should get moving."

Wise. Very wise. "In a few minutes."

Carma didn't argue.

Twenty minutes later, after a breakfast of cold chicken and canned vegetables, Kirk was behind the wheel and driving them west, through New Brunswick, along the TCH 2. Carma rattled on the mattress, half-smothered by the duvet and snoring comfortably. Kirk kept the radio off just to listen to her. Yesterday had been too close for him. More than he would ever admit.

Traffic thickened but he kept with the flow, grateful not to have a pair of idiots ahead of him as before. He pulled into a service station twice, for drinks, sandwiches, bathroom breaks, and gas. Carma didn't budge from the mattress or speak much. Kirk didn't mind. He was too glad to have her back. For a little while at least.

Memories of the motel haunted him. Carma had declared her intentions to the elders and minutes later the assault team had stormed the room. The elders had passed judgement. If Carma was with him, she'd die with him.

All the more reason to strike west and kill the miserable fucks.

He decided he wanted to hear a little music, and discovered the van had satellite radio. After a quick scan, he found a station playing a nice mix of seventies music. When ABBA came on, playing *Mamma Mia*, Kirk resisted the temptation of playing it loud. He didn't want to disturb Carma. ABBA was, in his opinion, the cat's ass.

"Is that ABBA?" she asked from behind.

Kirk kept his eyes on the road. "Uh, yeah."

"You listen to ABBA."

"When I can."

"So you like them?"

"Yes. Yes, I do."

Silence for a while. "I like ABBA," she said softly.

"Everyone likes ABBA," he said. "They just don't admit it."

"I like the Carpenters, too. And Alice Cooper."

That put a smile on his face. "Did I wake you?"

"No."

"Sorry if I did."

"I was awake a while. Just lying here. Thinking."

"How's your shoulder? And your side?"

"Much better," Carma said with a trace of amazement. "The pain is almost all gone. I can't believe it. I thought I was dead."

"It's magic."

"It's something," she agreed. "How you doing?"

"Me? I'm fine."

"Tired?"

"Getting there."

"Where are we?"

Kirk thought about it. "About two hundred klicks away from Fredericton."

"Not bad. For a person who doesn't know where he's going."

"Not a clue," he muttered. "You get a chance, you should check out the cabinets back there."

"Yeah? Why?"

"Oh, I think you'll be surprised."

Carma quieted. "They'll be looking for us. Everywhere."

"Yeah," Kirk said, suddenly solemn.

"What did you do with my phone?"

"Threw it away."

"Good. We have to expect them catching up with us eventually."

"Yeah." Kirk knew she was right.

Carma grew quiet, and before long, her snoring accompanied whatever music the radio played.

29

The morning sun glared into Ian Bryce's vision as he drove east, amplifying the ferocity etched into his eyes. The cellphone buzzed in the cup holder, distracting him from the road. Just his luck to be on the move when *they* called. He hated talking while driving, hated people who did, but he fumbled for the phone anyway. The unit was ungainly in his right hand, the combination made awkward by steering with his left, but Bryce managed. He put the phone to his ear and focused on the highway.

"Yeah?" he said, hating the crow squawk produced by his mangled vocal chords.

"Where are you?" asked the all-too familiar voice.

"New Brunswick. Just west of Moncton."

"Are you alone?"

A yellow sports coupe raced by Bryce's pickup, distracting him for a moment. "Yeah."

"We have a situation. Kirk is near you."

That surprised Bryce. "How do you know?"

The voice ignored the question. "And Carma is with him."

"Carma?"

"She's with Kirk."

"You mean like a hostage?" Bryce exclaimed.

"No, I mean she's with him. Joined him."

That put a block of ice to Bryce's spine.

"She's against us now," the voice continued. "Kill her as well."

Bryce's mouth hung open, utterly speechless.

"Do you hear me?"

"Yeah," the warden mumbled, overcoming his shock. "Yeah, kill Carma. I hear you, but, I mean, how do you know?"

"We know."

Which wasn't really an answer, but Bryce took it all the same.

"All right," he said, not that he had any qualms about putting her down as well. "Kill Carma, too. No problem. I'll do it."

"No, you won't."

I won't? That really piqued Bryce's curiosity, and pissed him off as well.

"Where's your pack?" the elder asked.

"Spread out. Between here and Quebec."

"Call in your most trusted members. The most capable. The most violent. Call them immediately after I hang up. Tell them to meet you at this address."

"Just a minute," Bryce said and indicated that he was getting off the highway. He pulled onto the shoulder, parked, and pulled up the GPS. "All right. Where?"

The voice told him.

"Got it," Bryce said, finding the area on the map.

"Gather your dogs there. Someone will meet you and you'll get further instructions."

"Okay, when?"

But the elder had already broken the connection.

"Well, shit." Bryce smoothed down his considerable beard. He checked the map again. It was off the main drag and in the middle of nowhere. A two-hour drive off the beaten road, back the way he'd already traveled.

The pack he'd brought with him from Quebec was spread out across the territory, sniffing away for a trace of Kirk's whereabouts, haunting transportation hubs. They weren't any more than an hour or three away from his position. Bryce wasn't exactly sure why the elders didn't directly contact the *weres* themselves. They relied on the wardens to do this for some reason, acting as the middle men in the hierarchy, performing multiple roles of law enforcer, judge, jury, and executioner, and sometimes even messenger. It was how their system worked, at least how they wanted the system to work, but the recent hunt for Bailey and the resulting deaths amongst the wardens' ranks—wardens yet to be replaced—created gaps in the chains of communication. Once Kirk and Carma were removed, who would the elders get to fill those gaps?

Bryce reminded himself why he was out there, what waited for him if he completed the elders' commands. Carma had been his pack leader once, and he knew a little about her, knew her to be very efficient and a definite candidate for advancement. To hear that she'd been targeted for death was a surprise. A big surprise, but also a great opportunity for him to focus on his own advancement.

Call in your most trusted weres. The most capable. The most violent.

Bryce had alerted all eight werewolves in his pack. He considered each of them, knowing who to choose. The ones he had in mind fit the elder's orders perfectly. Bryce imagined there would be *beaucoup* brownie points for them as well.

The cellphone's interface glowed against his eyes.

Bryce punched in the first number.

*

Later that night, standing in a field where the hay grew to the hip, Bryce cringed just a little as the first vehicle approached. Headlights flashed and bounced as the car dipped into deep potholes, chugging along an old road that might've been bombed at one time. The strip was that shitty and that was no stretch of a lie. Bryce feared he'd lost a tire while traveling up that same bit of backwoods hell, which was about as smooth as a length of corrugated iron. No doubt he'd hear it from the driver of the nearing car.

Violent and capable was what the brass wanted. Well, they got it. Hard-asses and ball breakers extraordinaire, each one. Bryce didn't think there was anyone on the East Coast who was as dangerous, especially now that Moses Morris was out of the way. They'd definitely skirted *were* law, killed out of season, but he couldn't prove it. A part of him didn't want to call *any* of these individuals, but he had to admit, the ones he summoned had no reservations about getting dirty if requested.

These werewolves were, in the truest sense of the word, monsters.

Bryce could handle them, but a part of him wasn't happy about it.

Cones of light continued to rise and fall as the car bucked and rattled over the terrible road. Bryce wandered in from the hayfield, over to the shadows of a timeworn barn perhaps abandoned for years. When he first drove to this place and parked, he could hear the rats in the barn's depths, keeping to the dark, their claws skittering on old wood. The structure stood in a hayfield no longer maintained. A forest surrounded the entire clearing, their uneven spires black underneath the clear night sky.

Two other cars appeared at the field's edge, the lights flashing over uncut hay crimpled and buckled by frost. Bryce pulled his coat tighter and rolled his shoulders. The lead vehicle—a pickup—pulled up to his left. The engine died along with the lights. Doors opened. Two figures emerged, sliding out into view like golems that had been slumbering for centuries. They closed the doors and walked towards Bryce.

"That you, Bryce?" Arnold Kingsley grunted.

"'Course it's me, y'dumb fuck."

Arnold tensed, but Bryce didn't give a shit squirt. Arnold was older than the warden but passed over for promotion several times. Bryce didn't know what the *were* had done in the past to anger the elders, but he suspected it was something to do with going on a killing rampage and decimating a farmer's herd of cattle in a little town along the Quebec-Ontario border. The only reason Arnold was still around was because no one could prove it was him who'd done the killing. Hard, thick-necked and with an alarming capacity for violence, he fit the elders' bill like a bull-sized dick in a cat's ass.

Arnold's companion was another ball breaker called Colin Lawson. Lawson was a shit disturber of the highest caliber. He'd been changed into a *were* by accident rather than choice, and allowed to live for some reason or another. Lawson possessed a particularly square-shaped head as if he'd been cultivated like one of those ultra-expensive Japanese melons. Of average height, he appeared best suited for playing hockey with a chainsaw instead of a stick, preferring to stop pucks with his face.

Bryce could handle them both.

And he'd break them if they got out of line.

"Well," Arnold said, spreading his arms. "We're here."

"Be patient," Bryce told them, his beard concealing his mouth. "And be quiet."

"That sure was a shitty road," Lawson commented. "I mean *that* was a shitty road."

"Sure was," Arnold agreed. "Pure shit."

"*Knobby* shit."

"The knobbiest."

Bryce scowled. "What part of 'be quiet' did you skid marks not fucking understand?"

The werewolves regarded each other with a guilty silence. The second approaching car rumbled and bounced towards the late-night meeting, the chassis taking a pounding. The vehicle bucked and jumped like a kid cutting loose in a mattress factory. The driver had a lead foot and obviously didn't give a shit about his car.

A Ford mustang—one of the newer models—pulled in to the far right of the barn, stirring up dust and dirt in its headlights. The car vibrated on the spot for seconds before dying with a metallic choke. The door opened and another large individual emerged into the night.

The *were's* name was Martin Cuffaro, from the northern part of Montreal, one of the older dogs in the pack. Draped in shadow, the thick mane and beard covering the guy's face made his head look misshapen. Cuffaro was a soldier, which was exactly why Bryce had called him. He was also something of a cleaner for a few of the more notorious families in the city. Bryce didn't really care that Cuffaro made criminals disappear. The line of work fit the guy, really, and in all fairness, the people Cuffaro killed weren't ones to be missed anyway. Bryce gave him a pass because of his civic duty to the city. It wasn't like the *were* was chowing down on civilians. And if there was anyone trustworthy enough to follow through on a killing, it was Cuffaro.

Arnold and Lawson regarded Cuffaro like an unleashed bully on the playground. At least they were keeping their mouths shut. For a little while.

A third vehicle drove up the road, materializing from the dark recesses of the forest.

"You really are having a fuckin' party here, ain'tcha Bryce?" Lawson said with a smile.

"How many are coming, anyway?" Arnold asked.

"Just us four," Bryce informed him. "And a someone."

"A someone?" Lawson repeated. "And who the hell is that?"

"The elder said a someone, so don't ask any more questions, got it?"

Lawson and Arnold lowered their heads in submission. Bryce ignored them, watching the car's approach.

The car became a van, a shiny black one under the moonlight.

The gathered werewolves waited as the vehicle rolled up and stopped amongst the other rides. The driver killed the headlights and shut off the engine. The door swung open.

A man wearing a Russian fur cap got out and looked around.

"You Bryce?" the newcomer asked Cuffaro. Cuffaro pointed in the right direction.

"I'm him," Bryce said, walking closer. "Where'd you come from?"

"Over there," the guy rumbled without indicating any direction. He was in his mid-thirties and spoke in a strained voice. Bryce also noticed that the man was practically eye to eye with him, and carrying considerably more girth, like a fridge with legs and a sweater.

"What's wrong with your voice?" Arnold asked. "Get your throat jacked up like Bryce here?"

The Fridge ignored the question. "Come around back."

The bulky newcomer led all four to the van's rear and pulled the door open. Inside were three large cabinets. He hauled himself aboard with a grunt and pawed at the first one, opening it. Metal clicked on metal as the Fridge extracted a weapon.

"The fuck is that?" Bryce asked.

"It's an HK UMP-9."

"All right," Bryce said with more patience than he actually had. "So it's a gun."

"It's not just a gun."

"Does it shoot bullets?"

"Look," the Fridge said, evading the question. "This is a high-tech submachine gun. "Very popular in Europe with special forces units."

"I don't care. Why are you handing it to me?"

"You're going after Douglas Kirk, right?"

"Yeah. So?"

"Then you'll need these."

The Fridge started handing out the weapons. The *weres'* faces drooped with distaste.

"Once we're done here," the Fridge explained, "you get into your cars. Go someplace central." To Bryce he said, "Keep your phone on. The elders will be in touch when you're on the move. You might need to get to an address fast."

Lawson sniffed at the weapon's curved magazine. "I smell silver."

A peeved Arnold ran the gun under his nose and drew back as if he'd inhaled fresh shit. "There's silver in this thing."

The Fridge hunkered down on the van's tail light, quite nimble for such a big man, and cocked his head. "So?"

Arnold and Lawson exchanged troubled looks before turning to Bryce.

The warden stared. "We don't use guns."

"It's against our nature," Cuffaro added, holding his own weapon like a dead cat.

"And aren't wardens the only ones able to carry silver?" Lawson asked Bryce.

"That's right," Bryce answered. "We are."

The Fridge smiled, unwavering on the balls of his feet. "You're good boys. But let me tell you something. Not everything you know is quite true, and there are rules in place for a very good reason, rules you might get to learn one day. So, for now, work with me here. This particular hunt, you'll need a little extra. And listen to this next part, okay? I'm not asking you to use them."

The smile on the Fridge's face vanished. "I'm fucking telling you. Use the guns. That means all of you."

Lawson regarded Bryce.

"Don't look at him," the Fridge remarked in a quiet tone. "You listen to me. Bryce might be pack leader once I leave here, but I speak for the elders. You take these guns and you fucking use them when you see your targets. Mow them down and empty the mags into them. I'm talking head shots and heart shots. Got it?"

Bryce nodded. The others squirmed, however..

"Wait there," the Fridge said. He turned in the van and opened another cabinet with a clatter. He pulled out several black matte vests and helmets. He tossed a set to each *were*, who either caught the pieces or didn't. A helmet bounced off Lawson's gut, and the werewolf bared teeth at the connection.

"What're these?" Arnold asked.

"They're fucking muffins," the Fridge said.

"They're bulletproof vests, you moron," Cuffaro said quietly.

Arnold scowled poison at the retorts.

"They're vests," the Fridge said. "Kevlar. You wear them. There's a good chance that Kirk has weapons like you. Might've taken them from the last kill team that didn't finish the job. Don't screw up your face, because if he has them, you gotta assume he's willing to use them. Got it?"

Another round of reluctant nods. Except for Bryce.

"Kirk doesn't seem the type," the warden muttered.

"I bet he doesn't seem the type to chow down on *weres* either, right?" the Fridge countered.

Bryce didn't answer.

Lawson inspected his UMP-9, inadvertently pointing it at Cuffaro. The mafia killer pushed the weapon barrel away from his face.

"You never fired one of these before?" the Fridge asked Lawson.

"'Course not."

"Any of you ever fire a weapon like this?"

The *weres* didn't answer. The silent admission didn't surprise the Fridge. He opened another cabinet. The van trembled as he moved around, and when he turned back, he slammed a crate on the edge of the van's floor.

The crate contained a load of curved magazines, filled right to the top.

The Fridge hopped out.

"All right," he said, brandishing his own submachine gun. He took a moment to screw a sound suppressor onto the weapon's muzzle. "Watch me."

30

Kirk parked in a half-filled lot behind a grocery store and switched off the engine. An old street lamp lit up the edges of the night. The dashboard clock said it was just after seven o'clock, and his ass felt vulcanized from the long drive. He gripped the steering wheel, arched his back, and glanced around.

"Where are we?" Carma asked sleepily.

"Fredericton. Back of some grocery store."

She looked up at him from the mattress. "What's the plan?"

"I need a real bed," Kirk said. "Just for the night. How you feeling?"

"Not bad."

"Think you can walk a block or so?"

"A block," she repeated. "Maybe. Why didn't you just park there?"

"Didn't want to risk drawing attention to the van. Just in case. Someone might come looking and I don't want to be ambushed in another motel."

Carma thought about it. "We could drive out of the city. Find a road somewhere and park the van, change, and spend the night in the bush."

Kirk cocked an eyebrow. "You up for that?"

As an answer, Carma sat up, bracing herself with her left arm. At some point in time, she'd pulled her sweater on. Her right arm came up, the makeshift sling dangling from her hand. She stretched her arm out, clenching and unclenching her fist.

"My God, Douglas," she said in amazement and met his surprised stare. "What have you done to me?"

"I don't know," he confessed. "And I shouldn't be surprised. But I am."

"I couldn't move this thing a day ago."

"It's something else."

"Everything else you said is true, too?"

Kirk nodded. "Yeah. Sorry. You don't feel anything?"

"I feel hungry but... nothing like you described." She checked her gunshot wounds, feeling her front and back, and shook her head. "All sealed up. You see anything?"

Carma lifted her sweater. Scars and dead skin marked the healed wounds, resembling nothing more than like a bad burn.

"Well?" she asked.

"Looks good," Kirk said. "Nothing more than a mild case of Psoriasis now."

"Holy shit." Carma lowered the sweater and turned herself around, upsetting the duvet. "This is incredible. I mean, I feel better than fine. And to think I was fucking crippled this time yesterday. I'm speechless."

She stood cautiously. "This is more than incredible. I mean, I couldn't do anything before. I was practically dead. And if by some miracle I survived, I couldn't think of what life would be like. This changes everything. I'm *whole* again."

Her fist flashed out, completing two quick jabs.

"We gotta tell the others about this, Douglas," she said. "They have to know. Who knows how many *weres* have been shot up or burned over the years and had to live in misery? This is a new *life*, for God's sake."

"Yeah."

Kirk's downcast expression dampened her enthusiasm. "What?"

"It's going to get worse, Carma."

"Yeah, you mentioned that."

"I mean it. It's like experiencing withdrawal, if you've ever been addicted to anything. I've never felt anything like it before, especially when it comes on hard. I mean, I was eating raw meat in parking lots to get myself under control."

"And that worked, right?"

"Yeah. That worked, to a point. It kept me from killing someone."

"But you said changing over did the trick?"

"Yeah," Kirk admitted with a half-shrug. "A little. Seemed that way."

"Well, it's not winter yet," Carma said.

"What do you mean?"

"Let's skip the hotel," Carma continued, looking out the

rear window, "and hit the hills."

"You mean change over?"

"I've got to. I feel energized like I've never been before. Gotta see what it's like on the other side. Burn off some of this jet fuel."

Kirk studied her for a few solemn seconds. "All right. I'll go."

"'Course you're going," she frowned in an expression of *duh*.

And he loved it.

Kirk locked up the vehicle and looked around, spying the nearest lamp and the smattering of cars nearby.

Carma pulled him towards a dark treeline. "C'mon. No one's going to take the van. Leave it."

"How long you want to go for?" he asked, not entirely up for the change.

"As long as it takes."

Great, he thought.

They crossed the parking lot, leaving the white glow of the supermarket behind. The night was cold, the temperature dropping quickly, and windless. Kirk followed Carma into the trees, taking in the wonderful scent. He slowed and searched the sky for a moon.

Carma reached back and pulled him along. "Nothing up there, tonight. Hurry up."

"How far do you want to go?"

"Far as I have to," she answered.

They made their way away from civilization, into gullies and out, over crunchy bogs and moss. Kirk glanced over his shoulder and lost all sight of the supermarket, but the town's radiance hung in the sky as if the land beneath it writhed in nuclear fire.

Several minutes later, in a glade hemmed by tall trees, Carma stopped.

"I was wondering when you'd pick a spot," Kirk muttered and looked back. "Jesus, Carma. We must be back in Nova Scotia."

Her answering smile lit up the dark. "Right now I feel like I can run back to Nova Scotia. Holy shit, Douglas. This stuff has to be bottled. I feel better than great. Don't know if it's because I don't have the bum shoulder anymore or because I'm happy to be alive or what, but I'm fucking charged to capacity."

Kirk stood a little more than arm's length away from her, his hands stuffed into his pockets. He watched her arch her back and take in the night sky.

"Here is good," she said, and pulled off her sweater.

Kirk sighed. "Here," he said, unsure of where exactly they were. "There could be houses just over the next hill."

Carma was already stripping off her yoga-pants and kicking off her sneakers. "There's no one. Can't you smell it?"

Kirk could, detecting nothing that would suggest a human presence. They were alone in the wild. "I've changed my mind. It's too cold for this."

Carma straightened from where she'd gathered up her clothing and neatly placed everything on top of her sneakers, making a little cairn. She was already naked, and the sight of her took Kirk's breath away.

"Don't think you can catch me?" she asked.

The question left him blinking.

Carma smiled and started her change.

Not a moment later, Kirk started pulling at his clothing, letting his garments drop where they may. He had no shame.

Three minutes later he rose from the grass on four legs, sniffed the air, and immediately found Carma's trail. She'd gone on without him. That was fine. He didn't mean to simply chase her—he meant to catch her, as they'd once done a lifetime ago, in a memory Kirk had clung to ever since.

He bounded out of the glade, taking after her scent. His legs pumped tirelessly, and every fiber of his being felt better than in a long time. Best of all, the cravings usually simmering at the edge of his consciousness were non-existent. Kirk didn't know if it was because of his recent feeding of *were* flesh or just running with Carma. Running *after* Carma, he corrected himself.

The night transformed the forest into a maze. He leaped over and scooted under fallen trees, paused atop frosted boulders and smelled the rushing waters of nearby streams. He listened, very much aware that the forest had gone quiet as he passed through it, suppressing the night as she'd done before him. Keeping on her trail, he sped around thick trunks and disturbed underbrush, until he detected the bent and broken foliage from Carma's wake.

This was a dream, he suspected. He was asleep somewhere, back in the van. Had to be a dream. He prayed to God above that it wasn't, however. Prayed for the Big Guy not to be so cruel.

And somewhere in the night, Carma howled.

Kirk ran harder.

He charged through the underbrush. Rough boughs scraped his head and sides as he pounded over a mat of woodland debris. The dark woods didn't slow him as he tracked her, closing the distance.

To the base of a tree. Marked by urine.

Well, *shit*.

Kirk sniffed around the area and located her trail once more. He'd lost time with the trick, but he'd make up for it. Power ripped through his frame, driving him forward, deeper into the forest halls.

She evaded him, however, charged by a frightful energy that enabled her to stay ahead of him.

Sometime around midnight, he stalked her to an open field, where the very earth seemed to fall away at the edges, and all that remained was a platter. A single tree, its mushroom dome a dusky gray, dominated the middle of the snow-white clearing. The smell of healthy tilled earth hung on the air, pleasing to breathe. Kirk plodded out of the forest, stopped, and stared.

There, bouncing around the tree's base and utterly intoxicated with life, was Carma.

She yowled and pranced, bolted at times before slowing and sniffing at the ground. The soft patter of her paws in snow and earth rang out across the field. Kirk watched her play about the mighty trunk, just taking in the sight and committing it to memory. She was high on life and totally heedless of his presence. He could have joined her at the tree, nipping at her haunches or her tail, and might have finally reached his dream's conclusion by catching her, but even as she danced, Kirk knew he would do no such thing.

For fear she might run away.

And rather than risk that disappointment, he backed himself up to the treeline and lay upon a mat of orange needles underneath an overhang of boughs. There he stayed, watching her rave, until he grew weary and lowered his head onto his forelegs. Even then he kept on watching. The hunger didn't bother him, nor did the cold.

And somewhere on the way to morning, he fell asleep.

He woke up, feeling Carma pressed into his side. Kirk lifted his head, running his chin over her back where she'd taken rest, curled up beside him like a Christmas wreath. Her fur rose and fell, her breathing deep. Kirk didn't move, didn't want to disturb her. Mostly though, he didn't want the moment to end.

His eyes narrowed, and he took longer breaths. He couldn't remember the last time… he was so happy.

He might not have caught her, but he'd somehow done just that all the same.

Morning frost stiffened the vegetation surrounding the sleeping werewolves, their coats pressed firmly against each other for warmth. Carma rose and shook herself free of the twigs and leaves clinging to her fur, then nudged Kirk with her wet nose. When he didn't respond, she licked him. Repeatedly.

That woke him.

Before he could respond with anything more, she ran off into the bush.

Kirk watched her dart away. He wasn't so fast to rise after that morning kiss and took a few seconds to let the wet warmth of her tongue sink in.

The woman knew how to wake a guy up.

He rose and stretched his back. Shook himself and yawned. Then he remembered Carma would be changing back after finding their pile of clothes, and that she'd be quite naked.

That got him moving.

She was midway through her change when he joined her. He stood guard while she completed the crossover, and when she'd finished, he took a shameless second to appreciate the woman before him. Until Carma met his eyes and frowned.

Kirk initiated his own supernatural makeover, and when he was finished, she stood, fully dressed.

"Hurry up," she said.

"See something?" he asked, reaching for his stack of clothes while very much aware of the temperature.

"No, but I'm freezing. Must've dropped ten degrees overnight. You notice those streams we splashed through? The grass was frozen."

Kirk got dressed.

Carma caught him sneaking peeks in her direction and was none too pleased. "It was a morning kiss, all right? Get your mind out of the gutter."

"Can't help it," he said, pulling on his footwear. "I feel pretty good this morning."

"Running around in the great outdoors will do that."

"Yeah," Kirk said.

Carma caught the uncertainty on his face. A coy smile flickered across her features before she walked away.

Kirk saw the look and his good feelings returned. He caught up with her and they walked side by side.

"Got any of those cravings?" she eventually asked.

"No. None. Not yet, anyway. Like I said, I feel pretty good. Great, to be honest."

"Me too."

They circled the parking lot of the van twice before Kirk reached for the driver's side door handle. Deeming the coast clear, he climbed aboard and drove to the treeline where Carma waited. She got in and they headed for the nearest Tim Horton's. They stopped at the drive-through, where they ordered breakfast wraps and sandwiches. Kirk paid the server, took the bag, and passed it to Carma.

Once settled in, he drove through town.

"So what's the plan?" Carma asked.

Kirk shrugged. "Same as before. No idea."

"We can't keep driving west. We'll run out of road

eventually. One of us better have an idea soon." Carma opened the paper bag and peered inside. "You want yours now or later then?"

Kirk took his breakfast wrap and dug in.

Two hours later, on the Trans-Canada Highway, a yawning Kirk pulled into a service station.

"How about I drive for a while?" Carma asked.

"Good idea." He said and rolled to a stop alongside one set of self-serve pumps. "Yeah. Take the next shift. I'll crash on the mattress for a while."

"You know something," Carma said, "I've got one of those things."

"What things?"

"An idea."

"Yeah?"

"Pull in over there." Carma pointed to an empty parking lot. "This'll take some time. You can gas up later. I might know how to find the elders. But we'll need someone with a phone, and a person willing to make the call."

Kirk steered the van between an SUV and a pickup. He parked and straightened in his seat. "Okay, let's hear it."

"We kill a *were*."

That stopped him cold. "What?"

"Let me start again," Carma said. "We don't have to actually kill a *were*, all we need to do is call in the disposal unit. The same crew that we'd call when a *were* is killed."

"They know where the elders are?"

"Well, that's the iffy part. They might. I mean, someone has to sign their checks, right? They aren't disposing of dead carcasses for nothing. So they must know something. I mean, they either work for the elders directly or indirectly, so if the disposal unit doesn't know, then maybe they know someone who does."

Kirk warmed up to the idea. "I don't know the number to call them."

"That's what I was stuck on," Carma said. "We usually called the elders directly and they ordered the clean-up crew."

"And we pretty much torched that bridge, I think."

She held up a finger, not so quick to agree. "Allow me to explain further."

"I'm listening."

"Ezekiel."

"What?" Kirk deadpanned.

"Ezekiel Allen. We get him to make the call."

The dull roar of passing traffic filled the lull in the conversation.

"You want to contact a warden?" Kirk asked. "One who's probably out looking for us right now?"

"It's possible he is looking for us. There's a good chance of it."

"So why even suggest it?"

"Because I don't think he is," Carma said, meeting his puzzled gaze.

31

Ezekiel Allen sat and stewed in his hole-in-the-wall living room. The apartment building he lived in wasn't a big place, nor was it especially convenient, not with the nearest supermarket on the other side of town and the liquor store another ten-minute drive to the right of that. If he had to draw lines from his place to the supermarket, the booze shop, and then back again, he'd have an isosceles triangle, where an untold number of days and nights had gone unaccounted for. He'd gotten lost in that mystic zone many a moon, some nights passed out flat on his ass in a drunken stupor, only to wake up to the not-so-gentle prodding of the local authorities. Ezekiel didn't mind. The town cops knew him enough to let him off with a warning. He wasn't an angry drunk. Far from it. In fact, the more he drank, the more his spirits lifted. Only two things did that for him. Drinking, and running through the wild as a werewolf. And fucking.

Okay, three things. But that was it.

The drinking wasn't helping him that late afternoon,

which was, in fact, just an extension of last night. He'd passed out on his sofa, behind a wall of liquor bottles that resembled the glossy minarets of a mythical Arabian city. Ezekiel pulled himself to a seated position on the couch and listened to the dirge of hard rock crashing through his speakers—not too loud, mind you, as the walls in the place were thinner than the pinched taint of a mouse. His wasted gaze settled upon the wall just above his television. The time glared back at him from below the display, urging him to get his ass motivated. Get up, get washed (or at least deodorized) and get moving. To the pop shop, his affectionate name for the liquor store, to refuel again. This time… with vodka.

He'd woken up with a hankering for Moscow Mules.

Ezekiel knew he wasn't fit for driving, not even if he'd had a license or a car. His dearly departed friend, Baxter—whose death was one of two reasons behind Ezekiel's current drunken spree—had a car but that was still in a parking lot in Halifax (and was something else on the warden's to-do list). He did have the number of a favorite cab driver. An older lady by the name of Lucy who didn't mind picking up his carcass and driving him where he wanted to go. Ezekiel made her laugh, or so she said, and while she was in her sixties, he knew how she looked back in the day. He remembered when she'd been a kid of seven, two years before he was cycled out of the area and into another part of the New Brunswick territory. Ezekiel didn't have as many scars back then, but he recalled the fearless little girl selling cookies at his door, knocking away even when her fellow guide members wouldn't go near his place. He appreciated balls like that. Even bought four boxes off her.

Christ, he wondered, listing toward the armrest and wondering if he had any munchies in the cupboard. He wondered if he had any food in the place at all. The supermarket was just a jaunt away, but he didn't really want to deviate too far from the pop shop. Not in his condition. And he didn't expect his condition to improve with the dying day. Truth be known, he fully intended to become even more shitfaced, as he'd been ever since he'd gotten that damn call from the elders, the second reason behind his alcoholic *tour de force*. They didn't call him often. In fact, they hardly called him at all, but last week's jingle was enough for him to shun the phone entirely. A week was a long time to binge, much like the one presently being embarked upon, but fuck it. Ezekiel had things to sort out. Important things. And important things took *time*.

He just hoped matters would take care of themselves by the time he sobered up. He dearly hoped so. There was no way he was partaking in—

A knocking at his door hooked his attention, and he paused with a not-so-happy smile.

"Better be some goddamn cookies," Ezekiel slurred. "S'all I can say. Better be some goddamn cookies. Or chips. All Dressed. Ketchup would be all right, too."

As would Smoky Bacon, but he kept that to himself. He lumbered to the door, took a deep breath, switched off the light in the adjacent bathroom, and didn't bother checking the peephole.

"Or pizza," he muttered as an afterthought, but he knew

that wasn't going to happen anytime soon. He didn't order a pizza. At least he *thought* he didn't order a pizza.

He turned the knob.

His eyes popped wide. There, on his doorstep, stood Carma Jones and a very much alive Douglas Kirk, surprising the living shit out of him.

"Holy—"

Kirk grabbed Ezekiel by the shoulder and pulled him back into the apartment. He tripped, and landed on top of Ezekiel, blasting the wind out of the New Brunswick warden.

"*Chrrruuu*—" the hungover *were* grunted.

Kirk got to his knees, two hands firmly on Ezekiel's chest. Carma slammed the door behind them.

"Whar'd you do to him?" she asked.

"Knocked the wind out of him."

Ezekiel rolled onto his side and drew his legs up as if Kirk had rung his balls with a silver golf club. The New Brunswick warden tried to breathe, sounding like a straw sucking at those last few drops in a large cup of ice.

He eventually got his wind back, just as Kirk shoved a gun barrel into his cheek.

Ezekiel had the presence of mind to cease all movement and eyeball the very stern face behind the weapon. A weapon that reeked of silver.

"Breathe, now," Kirk instructed, holding the *were* by the shoulder while attempting to drill for a tooth with the MP5's mouthy end. "But stay still. And don't move. Not a fuckin' twitch. This thing has a light trigger."

"Light?" Ezekiel exclaimed in his death-metal frayed vocal chords. "The fuck's *that* supposed to mean?"

"It means it could go off with the slightest pressure."

That settled Ezekiel down. He eyed the two wardens as if trying to refocus. His breathing eventually evened out, and he looked from Kirk to Carma.

"Hello, Carma," he said, the words squished by the gun. "Kirk."

"We thought we'd stop by," Carma explained, stepping around the pair and venturing deeper into the apartment. "See how you were doing."

Ezekiel didn't answer, his attention squarely upon the Halifax warden.

"Thinking of making a call?" Kirk asked.

The surprise on Ezekiel's face was genuine. "What? No. No."

"Ezekiel," Carma paused. "Where's your phone?"

Kirk eased off on the gun just a little.

"Thanks," Ezekiel said gruffly. "Ah, Christ. I think I shit myself. You surprised me."

"Your phone?"

"Wait," Carma said and looked to the living room's coffee table. "That it there? On the coffee table?"

"Yeah."

She went for the device, picked it up and inspected the face.

"Good to see you," Ezekiel managed while she scrolled through the phone's list of most recent calls.

Kirk loomed over the flattened warden, who smiled weakly.

"See you haven't been answering your calls lately," Carma noted.

"Huh? Wha'?" Ezekiel asked. Kirk reapplied pressure with the gun.

"I see the elders have been calling."

"Yeah," Ezekiel grimaced.

"What about?"

"Ah, him."

"Douglas?" Carma asked.

"Yeah," Ezekiel answered.

"Not me?"

"No."

"You sure?"

Ezekiel's eyes narrowed. "Yeah, why?"

Kirk smacked the warden's head with the gun before shoving the barrel back into his cheek.

"No, nothing about you," Ezekiel grumbled. "Been a week and a bit, anyway."

"What did they say about Douglas?" Carma asked.

"They want him dead. Said he was crazy. That he needed to be killed."

"They say anything else?" Carma asked, taking the phone into the small kitchen.

"No. Yes. Said Kirk was eating *weres*."

"And you alerted your pack?"

"Yeah."

"How many?"

"Seven."

Carma pressed her butt against a countertop. "So there

are seven werewolves out there looking for Kirk."

"Yeah."

"So why did you stay back?"

Ezekiel didn't answer right away. "You know why."

"Say it," Carma ordered.

"Huh?"

That made Kirk lean over. "Try again."

Ezekiel grimaced.

"Douglas needs to hear you say it," Carma added.

Kirk sensed something not entirely right.

Ezekiel sighed in defeat. "I didn't want to hunt him. Wouldn't have been right."

The admission surprised Kirk. He drew back, lessening the pressure on the gun. Ezekiel didn't react.

"You asked me earlier, Douglas," Carma began, "why I thought Ezekiel wasn't looking for you. For us. You see, not ten minutes after the elders contacted me about you, Ezekiel called. He got the same message. We talked, didn't we Ezekiel?"

"Yeah."

Kirk looked from one warden to the other. "And?"

"I wasn't sure if he was serious or not," Carma explained. "Ezekiel isn't as predictable as the others. But at the time he told me he had a real problem with the order."

"A real problem?" Kirk repeated.

"Yeah," Carma said. "Seems you saved his life. Back in Halifax. When he, Baxter, and Morris first went into that medical examiner's building looking for Bailey. Or that thing that used to be Bailey."

A frown creased Kirk's weary features. "I just pulled him back to the truck."

"You got him out of there," Carma explained. "Ezekiel said as much. If you weren't there, the cops would've been on the scene, or worse—Bailey might've returned. Neither happened, of course, but Ezekiel didn't know that at the time. You got all three of them out and Ezekiel remembered it. Isn't that right?"

Kirk studied the trapped warden's lumpy features.

"Yeah," Ezekiel whispered dejectedly.

"And," Carma continued, "despite being a hard ass and getting orders from the top, Ezekiel felt he owed you one. Making him a little troubled over what he was going to do."

Kirk removed the weapon from the *were's* face.

"Thanks," the New Brunswick warden said. "But I did alert the pack. That was it, though. I wasn't going to partake. Wasn't going to go after you. That way, I figured we were even. Sort of."

A thump came from outside the front door, attracting Carma. She looked out the peephole. "Your neighbors are noisy."

"Barney and Elizabeth," Ezekiel said. "One level down."

Kirk ignored him. "So you alerted your pack and decided to forgo the hunt?"

"Pretty much."

"And now?"

"Now... what?" Ezekiel asked.

"Well, I'm here."

The hungover warden sighed again. "You got a gun to

my head. 'Course I'm not going to do anything."

"You could've told me this earlier," Kirk said to Carma.

"Didn't want to get your hopes up. I had a hunch was all. And truthfully, we still don't know if he'll help us."

Ezekiel frowned in puzzlement.

"Well," Kirk said, staring down at his captive. "Thanks. For not coming after me."

"I did send the pack."

"Did you answer any of those calls?" Carma turned away from the door. "From the elders?"

Ezekiel shook his head.

"You'll have to call sometime," she pointed out.

"I know."

"They'll be wondering what happened to you."

"I know."

"And they'll be more than a little pissed off."

A miserable Ezekiel rolled his eyes. "I know. That's why I've been drinking."

Empty bottles cluttered the coffee table. The apartment reeked of sweat, body odor, and spilled alcohol.

"Hoping, maybe," Ezekiel went on, "maybe one of my pack would call. Or I'd get a text saying Kirk was taken down. Then I could call the elders. Make up any story I wanted. Maybe say I was following a hunch. Searching another area."

"Lying to the elders, Ezekiel?" Carma *tsked*.

"Yeah." Half of the New Brunswick warden's face hitched up unpleasantly, as if he'd just awoken from a miserable sleep. "What about you, then?"

"Me?" Carma asked.

"Yeah, you. Last I heard, you didn't know what you were doing."

"I made up my mind. Went looking for trouble and found it big time. Now, I'm wanted dead. Just like Douglas here."

The statement blew through Ezekiel's boozy fog. He regarded her in astonishment. "What?"

Carma and Kirk exchanged looks.

"You comfortable?" she eventually asked Ezekiel. "Then I'll tell you what's been going on in the last week or so and what we want you to do."

32

Headlights on low beam, a car crept along the road as if searching for a lost animal. A pickup hung off the car's rear bumper not ten feet behind it. The sun departed the sky and streetlights flickered to life. Bryce was at the wheel of the lead vehicle, wearing the colors and gear of a security officer. It wasn't exactly police issue, but the Fridge—as Bryce still thought of him—had said it wouldn't matter as long as it looked official.

The four werewolves had gone someplace central, as instructed by the Fridge, and waited for twenty-one hours, sitting in their cars in a little unnamed town. Bryce got a phone call not two hours before, telling them to get over to Ezekiel Allen's address at best speed without attracting the attention of the law.

That had been a trick.

Bryce's HK UMP-9 rested down by his leg. Cuffaro was in the back seat, also decked out for battle. Neither of the *weres* liked being weighed down with the modern warfare gear, feeling dirty to the core. The Fridge told him that they'd been conditioned to think that way, and to get over it for the next couple of days. That had been midway through the unexpected lesson in firing automatic weapons.

"That's it," Cuffaro announced from the back seat. He leaned forward and pointed at the end of a cluttered cul-de-sac. The area was a good half-kilometer from the nearest house, situated in an undeveloped forest located at the absolute edge of town. It looked quiet. Felt quiet.

All in all, it was an excellent choice for a warden to live.

"I see it," Bryce said.

Streetlights cast long-necked shadows across mini lawns. Stone walkways divided the grass and led to the apartment building. The structure was three levels high, with a single open-air stairwell ascending the middle, dividing the individual units. The place reminded Bryce of a city slum, surgically cut away from a diseased hole and transported to the middle of nowhere. He suspected all manner of spray-painted artwork decorated the walls.

Before the building was an assortment of vehicles parked in a semi-circle, gleaming as if fresh off an assembly line. A hockey net had been hauled up on a low rise, next to a collection of town garbage units and recycling bins. There was no other indicator of children. No bikes, no strewn toys, no nothing. It was suppertime, and no one was outside. The car thermostat declared zero degrees. Lights were on in four of six apartment windows.

Four out of six, Bryce thought. That was fine. Ezekiel Allen lived on the top floor. Unit Six. His lights were on. The neighbors across the way weren't home, or so it appeared, but three other units below Six were. On the second level, the door on the left opened and closed, briefly revealing the landing. The stairwell was otherwise without lighting, projecting a prison vibe.

Bryce stopped the car. The pickup with Arnold and Lawson halted right behind him in a shrill squeak of brakes. Bryce reached for his phone and made the call, as instructed, when he located Ezekiel Allen's home.

"Yes?" the elder answered at the first ring.

"We're here," Bryce reported.

"Good. And?"

"He's home."

"Is there a parking lot?"

"Not really. Just cars parked around a cul-de-sac."

"Can you see a white van?"

He could. "Yeah."

The elder paused. "That's them. That's Kirk and Carma. You have your weapons?"

"Yeah."

"Then go kill them. Save the New Brunswick warden if you can."

Something bothered Bryce. "How did you know they'd be here?"

The voice ignored the question. "If Mr. Allen has been wounded by them, then kill him as well."

The order surprised Bryce. "Kill Ezekiel?"

"If necessary."

A bewildered Bryce took a moment to process the command.

"Are there others living in that apartment building?" the elder asked.

"Yeah. Looks like it."

"How many?"

Bryce sized up the building again. "Hard to say. Three other apartments have their lights on. Can't tell how many are inside."

"Kill them all."

"What?" Bryce stopped moving.

"Kill them all," the elder continued. "And burn the building. Burn everything. Then drive away. Do you understand?"

"You—" Bryce was appalled. "You want us to off everyone there? The people and the wardens?"

The question turned Cuffaro's head.

"Kill them all," the elder repeated, testy. "Kill everything. Leave nothing alive. Retrieve the bodies of Kirk and Carma, however. Even Ezekiel, if you have to kill him. Don't let them burn. Contact me after you're done. I'll provide further instructions."

The connection died.

Bryce lowered his phone and stared at the apartments, a warm picture withstanding the deepening cold. The scene could have been framed and hung on a wall.

"You hear that?" Bryce asked Cuffaro's hairy head.

"I did. We have to kill everyone in that place?"

"That's what he wants."

"Everyone."

"Everyone. No prisoners," Bryce said, his sense of duty

as a warden, to protect the human herds from werewolves, now warped. He was hard-assed, but the command left him conflicted.

Cuffaro, however, nodded in approval and lowered himself between the two seats, to better see the apartment building. "Almost feels like Christmas."

Almost feels like Christmas. A rap on Bryce's window startled him. Arnold stood there, along with Lawson. Both wore their security uniforms. There was something sinister in disguising the pair as law enforcement agents.

Bryce lowered the window.

"So what are we doing?" Arnold asked.

Bryce motioned them closer and relayed the news.

"Kill them all?" Lawson whispered, visibly intrigued.

"Can we eat 'em?" Arnold asked.

The question appalled the warden. "Christ, no you can't fucking eat them. We have to burn the place afterwards, anyway. No witness. No evidence."

That quieted the lot. Arnold and Lawson gazed upon the structure with mischievous smirks, eager to get to work. Bryce sighed inwardly. The elders wanted the most violent, they got them. It wasn't even a Harvest Moon.

"We doing this or what?" Cuffaro asked.

"Yeah, we're doing this," Bryce said.

"Pitter patter," Arnold grinned, anxious to get moving.

"Shut the fuck up," Bryce muttered, opening his door and bumping the *were* across the thighs. "And get out of my way."

Bryce got out, his thoughts wandering back to how the

elders had known Kirk and Carma were at Ezekiel's home.

He never did get an answer.

*

Ezekiel's face, with his crooked-tooth smile twisted into a disbelieving grimace, widened his eyes as if he'd heard far too much. Kirk had let him sit up while Carma told him everything that had happened to her, right from the time she'd liberated Kirk from Alice and Jenna.

"Whoa," Ezekiel whispered. "That's fucked-up."

The silence grew as he processed the information. "So, you were crippled?"

"I was practically dead," Carma said, sitting in the nearby sofa chair. "Whatever's in us is damn potent."

"Except it makes you want to go cannibal," Ezekiel noted. "That ain't exactly a good thing."

"No. No it's not."

Ezekiel regarded Kirk, standing in front of the television. "You can put that away now. I'm not going to do anything."

"She hasn't gotten to the best part," Kirk said, keeping the gun ready.

"The best part?"

"Not yet," Carma said and took a breath.

"Wait," Ezekiel held up his hands. "I got a question. That okay?"

"Shoot," Carma said.

*

A series of lamp fixtures adorned the stairwell's upper corners, but they failed to work for some reason. The four *weres* stopped at the ground-level apartment and huddled within the shadows. A brass knocker hung on the door. Tacky, but it served its purpose. Arnold took up position at one side and looked back at the others. Bryce nodded.

The *were* knocked twice, sharp metallic whacks that made the warden shudder. They waited. Bryce leaned back a bit, gazing up at the second level.

The scrabbling at the inner lock brought his attention back.

"Yeah?" a young bald man asked from between a chained gap.

Arnold held up a badge and fake identification. "We're looking for an Ezekiel Allen. This his building?"

The guy swallowed and looked from the offered ID to the armed man at his door. He then realized there was a whole team just behind the lead officer. That really made him fidget. He swallowed again. "What's this about?"

"Keep your voice down, sir," Arnold said in a hush. "Also, you and anyone else you might have inside your apartment have one minute to vacate the premises. We have to get you to a safe zone. Immediately."

The guy's eyes bulged. "What?"

Arnold waved the others by, who proceeded to the next landing.

"What's going on?" the young guy got out, on the verge of panicking.

"Sir, we don't really have time. Is that your wife?"

The young man glanced over his shoulder. A plain but attractive woman in her mid-thirties stood at his back.

"My girlfriend."

That elicited a scowl from the woman.

"Common law wife," the guy blurted and withered under a deepening glare.

"You best gather your things and get ready to leave. I'll wait here," Arnold said and hefted his automatic firearm. The sight of the fearsome weapon caused the young guy to step back and yank the door shut. A scuffle of activity came from inside the apartment and Arnold looked impatiently to the cluttered cul-de-sac.

Locks were undone. The door opened.

"Plan's changed," Arnold said and shouldered his way inside, backing the couple farther into their apartment.

"What's the problem?" the woman asked as Arnold kicked the door closed.

"Got a signal from the other operators," he answered. "Looks like we're stuck here."

He smiled at the woman and fired, the UMP-9 bucking in his hands, the sound no louder than a slick zipper. He ripped a jagged line across the couple, lifting them both off their feet. The woman flipped over the back of a nearby sofa, her pajama-clad legs forming a V before she slid out of sight. The man flopped over a dinner table, overturning the piece and spattering a brainy knot of spaghetti against a wall.

In the ensuing peace, Arnold considered his smoking submachine gun. Regarded the two people he'd just shot.

The young guy squeaked, the air leaking from his lips, as if he'd just stubbed his toe in a dream.

Arnold stepped in close. He set the weapon against his

shoulder and took aim at a lolling head speckled in scarlet.

The *were* squeezed the trigger.

*

"So how did they find you?" Ezekiel asked, still on the floor. "At the motel, I mean?"

"Figured they tracked us," Kirk answered. "Something in the cellphones."

"The cellphones?"

"The elders are linked into everything," Carma added. "Doesn't surprise me that they had the phones tapped. Wired. Whatever the term. Probably could listen in on conversations anywhere in the country, which is why we decided to drop in on you."

Ezekiel's own phone rested on the coffee table and he studied the device with growing unease. "What?"

"No word of a lie, Ezekiel," Carma said. "Not a minute after I hung up on those bastards, a goddamn SWAT team came through the motel door, guns blazing. Just like that. Once they knew I was with Kirk, they wanted me dead. I'd gone over to the dark side."

Ezekiel's mouth hung open. "That's fucked-up."

"We got rid of the phone," Carma went on. "So here we are. Face to face. See where you stand."

The New Brunswick warden held his head as if it were full and ready to burst.

"Take a minute," Kirk advised.

"So what's meeting with the elders going to do?" Ezekiel eventually asked.

"We get them to call off the hunt," Carma said. "And get some answers. If they don't want to do either, we kill them."

"Kill…" Ezekiel couldn't finish the sentence.

"Them," Carma finished and swished a finger across her throat.

Ezekiel stared at the woman. "That's fucking insane. The packs won't… they'll come after you."

"Then we'll kill them, too," Kirk said, meaning every syllable.

Ezekiel gawked at him.

"After some answers," Kirk said, "I've been wondering why Morris and I were really sent to Newfoundland. Why we were ordered to kill Borland. Why some wardens died in putting Bailey down. Why we only use silver knives instead of guns. Why I'm like the way I am after eating a *were*. Why I am able to completely heal from silver and why that doesn't interest the elders in the least. *Especially* that one. I mean, it's silver, Ezekiel. *Silver*. There has to be an elder or two wanting to know that one, but they want us dead instead. Why? Only now am I starting to wonder, to question things. I want answers and they have them. And if that's not good enough for you, Zeke, then how about this—I'm going to put the elders down for Morris. And for a man I turned named Ross Kelly."

"Revenge," Ezekiel whispered.

"Revenge," Kirk agreed. He cocked an ear toward the door.

*

On the second level, Cuffaro knocked on one of the two opposing doors while Lawson rapped on the other. Bryce hung back, waiting for Arnold to rejoin the group. Anxiety flowed through Bryce, as he realized he'd just allowed a *were* to shoot and kill a civilian. With a weapon loaded with silver rounds. That shit just didn't work for him. As much as he wanted to rise in the ranks of the elders, the killing bothered Bryce.

The first door opened. Cuffaro talked to the woman peeking through the chained gap, selling her the same story that Arnold had used. The second door opened and things took a dramatic shift. Lawson forced his way into the apartment, firing his suppressed UMP-9 as he went. That scuffle alerted the woman Cuffaro spoke to, so he shot the woman point blank, blowing her back and out of sight. The *were* then destroyed the chain with a second burst and invaded the unit. A man cried out in surprise, before the UMP-9 permanently silenced him.

It was loud. Sloppy.

Bryce cringed and looked to the landing above him.

Arnold plodded up the stairs from below, holding his weapon across his chest like a commando. He nodded at Bryce, who didn't comment on the guilty grease smears coating the *were's* lower face.

Cuffaro emerged from his apartment. Two second later, Lawson appeared.

Bryce shook his head, not impressed. "He knows we're coming."

"Good," Arnold declared.

But Bryce wasn't as keen. Everything felt wrong and was only getting worse. Once upon a time he'd thought of Kirk as a weak-willed slacker who merely followed orders. Even back in Halifax, when Kirk was half the duo responsible for killing Bailey, Bryce wasn't impressed.

On the verge of finally killing a fellow warden, however, questions were forming in his brain. And they weren't just about Kirk, but Carma as well. Especially her. Carma had been a pack leader and had carried a considerable amount of weight in their secret world.

"Something wrong?"

The question brought Bryce back to the present. Arnold had asked it.

"Nothing," Bryce answered and looked to a poised Cuffaro and Lawson. "Get going."

Then, directly overhead, they heard it.

A door opened with the softest violin-string creak. A regular person might not have heard the single off-note, but the four *weres* did. The sound froze them and Bryce realized with a sinking feeling that they'd just lost their advantage of surprise.

Cuffaro, Lawson, and Arnold all looked up, listening, waiting for a reaction.

Nothing happened.

The sound didn't repeat and no one descended from the third floor. Arnold hefted his UMP-9 to his shoulder, staring through the sights on a target that didn't appear. A cautious Cuffaro leaned forward, trying to spot movement on the landing directly overhead, and withdrew with a head shake.

Bryce, however, knew someone was up there. Someone who knew they were coming. He even thought, and he strained to clarify, that he had heard breathing up there, or caught the tail end of a deep, fuel-injecting breath, like a diver before leaping off a platform. There was no sound after that, however, and that made Bryce all the more cautious.

Cuffaro met the pack leader's eyes, and that one glance conveyed the same message. He'd been on enough manhunts to know the game was afoot. Lawson trained his weapon at the final set of stairs while Arnold implored Bryce to give the word.

Bryce waved his three minions onwards and followed. They crept up the stairs, Cuffaro angling his weapon upwards, looking for a target.

He froze.

As did Lawson and Arnold.

Bryce looked up.

At the top of the stairs was a dark outline of a man, standing against a canvas of night. His face swathed in shadow. Empty hands hung at his sides. His head was slightly lowered toward the ascending kill squad, like a headmaster rightly displeased at what his students had been conspiring to do.

Bryce knew it was Kirk. Unarmed and waiting.

"Shoot—" he ordered, bringing up his weapon.

Kirk leaped, arms wide in a supernatural display of agility. Cuffaro fired, the burst cutting underneath the airborne warden, missing him entirely. Tracers screamed bright in the stairwell, biting off low-hanging sections of the roof.

For a split second, amidst the flash and bang of gunfire, Kirk seemed to hang in the air, motionless.

And in that instant, elongated teeth seemed as sharp as sickles.

Then the speed kicked in, as if the renegade warden had guzzled an entire tank of nitrous oxide. Kirk landed between Cuffaro and Lawson and kicked Lawson in the chest, knocking him down the stairs into Arnold. Cuffaro whirled around, attempting to aim, but Kirk slapped the weapon away a split-second before hammering the *were's* head into a wall.

Arnold shoved Lawson out of his way, sending him deeper down the stairwell. Arnold whooped and fired, missing Kirk entirely, the bullets chewing out the wall. Fragments of cinderblock and concrete choked the air. Ricochets blew out a dead lamp from a corner. Kirk ducked under the burst and rushed forward. He seized Arnold by the throat, nipping off the war-cry. The Halifax warden slammed Arnold face-down onto the stairwell's iron railing with a reverberating *gong*. The *were* shivered and went limp.

Bryce evaded Lawson's fall while trying to aim at Kirk. But Kirk wasn't a fully changed werewolf. He still wore his man-suit, except he wasn't a man.

Not a man, Bryce's mind shrieked.

The frightening sight cost him.

In one instant Kirk was perhaps ten feet away from Bryce, but in that single heartbeat of hesitation, Kirk appeared before him and yanked the UMP-9 from his grasp. He slapped Bryce's face, raking a cheek and nose free in an explosion of pain and shock.

Bryce bounced off a wall, stunned by the powerful blow. He felt as if he'd just been body-slammed by a two-legged battleship. Blood blinded him. Somehow, he held onto his consciousness, not quite clued into the fact that his right eye had been sliced through, and that a sizeable section of his scalp hung over the oozing orbital cavity. He watched through the misty vision afforded by his other eye as Kirk attacked Lawson, twisting his helmeted head around.

Bone snapped. Lawson didn't cry out.

Cuffaro crouched on the stairs just above, aiming his UMP-9 one-handed as Kirk attempted to free Lawson's skull from his torso. Arnold's dying grunts perked the air.

Cuffaro steadied his sights.

A woman appeared at the top of the landing, her arm extended.

She had a gun.

Carma blasted Cuffaro from behind, nailing him to the concrete with the first salvo and turning him halfway around with the next. Cuffaro flinched, bucked, and fell. Most bullets struck Kevlar, but some found flesh, jerking the *were* about until one round snapped his head back in a spray of fleshy matter and tar.

Kirk flattened himself when Carma fired. When she stopped, he looked to her, then lumbered through the wreckage of the *were* hit squad, grabbing Arnold's shivering form in a scene reminiscent of something sinister caught on film…

Except it was right in front of Bryce.

And he wasn't about to wait.

His legs powered up underneath him. His heart revved, and his body sprang forward into full-flight mode.

While Kirk busied himself with dispatching Arnold, Bryce rushed to the iron railing of the second landing and leaped into the night.

33

A scuffling boot patter caught Kirk's attention. He looked up from his victim to glimpse a huge figure jumping over the second-floor railing and dropping out of sight.

"Kirk!" Carma shouted. She turned and rushed to the third floor's railing. She aimed and fired, machine gun blazing after the fleeing target.

"I'll get him." Kirk flung aside the unmoving *were* in his hands and charged the second-floor landing. He vaulted the wrought iron hurdle of the railing, clearing it easily, and was airborne.

Out of the corner of his eye, the escaping figure turned to the right of the building, running towards the gothic dark of the nearby forest.

Kirk's frame shook as he landed in a full squat. His feet buzzed from the impact, the pain ignored by his system overloaded on *were*blood and adrenaline. He blasted from his starting position, arms pumping at his sides, heedless of the dark specks flying from his hands and forearms. Kirk focused on the escaping *were*. The would-be killer fled into the woods and the warden followed, bounding over ground that crunched and crackled.

Tree trunks flashed by as he ducked and weaved through a wild growing maze redolent of chilled soil and timberland spice. Ahead of him, the shadowy figure bolted through the trees, almost as fast as the pursuing warden. Where his prey zigged and zagged, as if fearing a blast of gunfire, Kirk kept as straight a line as possible.

Deeper they ran into the wilderness, their breathing and footfalls the only sounds in the forest. The trees grew taller, thicker, the vegetation increasingly dense. Kirk saw well enough with his enhanced sight, and dodged and ducked limbs when they materialized out of the dark. The gap between him and the *were* killer gradually closed, until he could see the shadowy figure's shoulders. The *were* bled as well, the blood dappled the forest floor in dewy blotches.

The fleeing shadow jumped across a wide gulley and landed with a grunt. He didn't pause, bursting through a curtain of underbrush.

Kirk followed not four seconds behind, flying over the empty space and landing a good five feet beyond the mossy edge. He barely lost his stride and pounded forward, crashing through the same bushy veil as his prey.

The *were* raced up an incline and disappeared from sight. Kirk pursued, clawing his way up a slope thick with creepers and undergrowth, heaving fistfuls of earthy matter into the air in his wake. Branches clawed for his eyes, scratched his cheeks, but Kirk never felt better, never felt more alive. He felt damn-near invincible.

He reached the top and looked around with a huff, taking a second to spot his prey.

There. In the distance, a phantom darted amongst the trees. Not far at all.

Kirk took after him.

A root caught the warden's foot and yanked him to the ground. A collection of rocks stabbed his jaw, drawing blood. Something pointed grazed his forehead and opened the skin to the bone. He landed on his chest, the wind escaping him in a rush. His diaphragm seized up and it took precious seconds for Kirk to unlock it, gasping and squeaking for every unwilling ounce of breath. He dabbed at his face, wiping his hands on the firm ground.

Then he was on the move again.

*

A low limb almost took Bryce's head off as he passed it, but he ducked at the last moment.

He didn't miss the branch, however.

Like a bony nail, the tip reached out and hooked the ragged skin flapping from the right side of his face. It stretched it to the brink of ripping it free of his scalp entirely. Bryce stopped with an agonized grunt. He twisted, off-balance by the sudden halt and the thing fastened to his face. He snapped off the offending branch and jerked the sliver free. The branch just missed his right eye.

His eye, Bryce snarled, suddenly aware of his wound, blinking his left and seeing absolutely nothing from the right. He'd grow it back in time if he got the chance, but he wasn't sure he would. Not unless he escaped Kirk.

Or unless he turned and dealt with him.

That thought burned through his pain, made him think.

He was running. The realization bothered him immensely, even more so than killing humans with silver-loaded weapons. Ian Bryce *never* ran from a fight. The cold night air lapped at his bleeding face as he turned around and regarded his frantic path. Indignation flared. For nearly sixty years he was the ruling badass of his northern territory. He wrestled grizzlies under spring moons and tossed axes at summer lumberjacks. He lived off the land and had seen sights that would make mortals and *weres* alike shiver in their skins. And he'd taken this job with the hope of elevating himself to upper management in the very near future.

Bryce hissed through stained teeth and stinging cheek slits. He drew himself up to his full six-three height and wrung out his considerable beard with one hand, freeing the blood collected there like grapes on the vine. It ran down the front of his body armor, for all the good the Kevlar did him. He'd lost his UMP-9 back at the apartment building, but that didn't really concern him. The Fridge had told Bryce he was conditioned to despise the weapon, but having it explained to him wasn't like switching on a light. He still hated using the automatic popgun.

Footsteps approached, far off but closing fast. It was Kirk, transformed into that hideously fucked-up wolf-man thing he'd become. Bryce couldn't wait to tell the elders about that, couldn't wait to bring them Kirk's carcass.

Because that's what he was expected to do.

What he was *told* to do.

And God damn it, Bryce meant to deliver.

He slicked back the piece of hanging scalp to his head, but the chunk slipped back over his cheek. Bryce let it hang, because it was frightening, shocking, and it would gain him a few seconds in his coming fight.

The footsteps were closer now, more urgent.

Bryce reached down and extracted his knife from a boot. Ten inches of silver, honed to a scalpel's edge. In his hand, the weapon looked like a short sword. In that deep matte dark of the forest, where there was no moon to be seen, Bryce took his blade in an underhand grip and crouched over, scouring the pitch for his prey.

"C'mon you little shit," he said, and to his surprise, that squawky tenor had smoothed out substantially. The sound surprised him.

"C'mon," Bryce growled to the night, his juices coming to a boil.

That little wolf-man rat bastard had gotten lucky back at the apartment. Took the four of them off-guard. Bryce was ready now. He'd conquered whatever fear he might've had for the Halifax warden, and smiled with savage chagrin at ever feeling such an emotion. Not for the likes of chickenshit Kirk. Slack-ass Kirk. Morris did all the work killing Bailey, and Kirk was there only to suck in the Pictou warden's thunder.

Well, Bryce didn't have any thunder, but he held a lightning bolt in his hand, and he fully intended to gut Kirk with it.

At the absolute edge of his singular vision, Bryce saw a shadow pass through the trees and stop. It turned towards him, perhaps twenty feet away.

"Right here," Bryce called out, slapping his shoulder and bellowing a grizzly's challenge. "Right here you nimble little fuck! Get your ass over here, Kirk, 'cause I'm out of patience but got plenty of fuckin' fury. *C'mon.*"

"Bryce?" Kirk asked, his voice oddly warped, like he was speaking through a mouthful of industrial sludge.

"Yeah," Bryce shouted back. "You know it's me, don't you? Don't you, you sick little bastard."

The murky outline that was Kirk came closer. "Bryce, the elders sent you."

"'Course they sent me, you fucking idiot, but just to let you know, I would've done this for fun, anyway."

That stopped Kirk in his tracks. "I'm not what they say I am."

A harsh smile spread across Byrce's face. "That so? They said you were a monster, Kirk. A monster that's gone full-blown cannibal. And from what I've seen back there, I'd say they're right."

"They're only half right."

Bryce laughed. "Yeah, what part? 'Cause it all sounds fucked-up to me."

"They're lying to you," Kirk said, taking another step closer, sounding as if four or five people were speaking from the one body. "It's all a lie. Everything. I'll explain—"

But the big warden couldn't be bothered. Kirk was only delaying the inevitable. "You know what I think of you, Kirk?

From the very first time I met you, I knew you weren't one of us. I knew. Could fucking *smell* it. Anyone could. Morris sure as fuck could. We even talked about you once. The one thing we agreed on was that you were a fucking slouch with no direction and no life to speak of. A fucking waste of skin. A little dogshit who'd been pistol-whipped and taken orders all his life and got lucky with becoming a *were*. I don't know who turned you or why, but they fucked-up. You're not one of us. Not then and sure as hell not now. You're meat, but as it turns out, you're also my ticket to upper management."

Kirk's eyes and teeth twinkled in the dark.

"Didn't like that, did you, you little prick," Bryce smiled and brandished his knife. He assumed a combative stance, his single eye narrowed by hate, his strength spiked with rage. "Right here. I'll show you what I do to grizzlies. Then I got a phone call to make."

"You're wrong," Kirk said softly, his hands lowered to his side.

"Yeah, what part?"

"Everything."

The forest floor crackled as Kirk resumed his approach. He took two steps before exploding into an incredible burst of speed, crossing the distance between the pair in a frightening blink. So fast, in fact, Bryce swung his knife a split-second after Kirk blasted into his mid-section and bounced him off a nearby elm, the impact like two boulders colliding.

Bryce landed on his back.

Kirk was on top—and tore out the warden's throat by the fistful.

34

Carma leaned out over the railing and peered in the direction Kirk had gone. She considered going after him, but her guts warned her not to. The dead *weres* in the stairwell convinced her of that. Besides, there was unfinished business to attend to. Carma frowned as she regarded the three killers sprayed over the walls and concrete steps. They were dead, of course. Had to be dead.

The smell hit her then, a thick, rich broth of blood and gut matter, drawing her away from the railing. Carma rallied against the aroma and placed the wrist of her gun hand underneath her nose. It didn't help.

She could smell them.

Weres.

They were weres.

And they were rich and fizzy and oh so good, begging to be sampled. Her ears performed odd sound checks she was only faintly aware of, her attention glued to all those bodies and limbs stewing an increasingly tempting sauce that covered everything. One of the *weres* stirred, as if sensing danger, and that broke the spell. Carma watched as he lifted his head and pulled himself away from the others, crawling blindly towards a wall. The concrete halted his crawl. That soft bump dropped him. He rolled onto his back with a wheezy gasp, revealing a face.

Carma's breath hitched in her throat.

The dying *were* was a shredded punching bag, with stuffing hanging from seams split wide apart.

"Jesus," Ezekiel muttered behind her. He'd emerged from his apartment like a survivor from a nuclear blast.

"Get back," Carma said.

But the warden didn't listen. He gazed upon the dripping pit of concrete and steel and visibly balked at the carnage.

Yeah, Carma thought. *It's like that.*

"They're *weres*," he said.

She nodded. She knew what had to be done. A task she didn't really want to do, but she had to. Carma handed Ezekiel her machine gun. She extracted her knife. Composing herself, she took the first tentative step down, knowing she'd had to clean her sneakers afterwards, and that blood was a bitch to wash out of fabric. She crept down to the three corpses, and singled out the one on his back.

The silver shone in the scant light.

The first *were*, the one staring at the ceiling, gurgled when she stabbed him through the throat. She drew back at the resulting mess, waited for a second, and finished the job so that the creature would not rise again. The smell damn-near overpowered her senses, made her lightheaded for reasons she dreaded. Carma longed for a breath of fresh air, untainted air, but she continued with her work regardless. She finished off the other two, who didn't even flinch under the cutting knife.

When it was done, she rejoined a silent Ezekiel and leaned out over the railing.

The air was a little sweeter there, and every breath sobered her. Her senses returned.

"Jesus Christ," Ezekiel muttered nearby. "I got neighbors, Carma."

Not anymore, she thought, but what she said was, "Go check on them."

Ezekiel looked at her. She didn't have time to debate. "Go on. Make it fast."

"Christ almighty," Ezekiel whispered again, which was no help at all. The stubby warden glanced over his shoulder, towards the cul-de-sac below, as if a swarm of police cruisers would be flooding the area at any moment.

"Hurry, Zeke," Carma said, forcing some semblance of calm into her voice even though she was far from that state herself.

The warden moved past her. He descended a few steps before faltering. "Fucking stairs is covered in shit, Carma."

"Grab a mop and some bleach on your way back up, then," she said, holding her forehead.

Ezekiel didn't reply. He stomped to the lower floors.

He wasn't gone long.

"Carma," he said, coming back up the stairs.

"Yeah?"

"They're dead." He stuck his head out over the second-floor landing. "All dead."

"Figures. Still think the cops are coming?"

Ezekiel didn't answer right away. "They killed people. Humans. Shot them dead."

"Get up here then," she said, looking back the way Kirk had gone. "We'll figure this shit out."

In seconds, Ezekiel was beside her, peering in the same direction, but also watching the road leading to the apartment building.

"What if he don't come back?" he asked.

Carma sighed. "He'll come back."

"Yeah but… what if he don't?"

"Zeke?"

"Yeah?"

"He'll come back."

So they waited. And watched.

And no more than thirty minutes later, Kirk appeared.

Ezekiel pointed but Carma had already spotted the Halifax warden. He appeared around the building's corner, black against the white siding, and walked like a specter drifting across a foggy English moor at midnight. Carma wanted to call out but she was uneased by the sight of him. Kirk walked as if he'd been killed and magically reanimated, creeping along the lower apartment.

An uncertain Ezekiel drew back from the rail.

Kirk turned the corner without looking up and climbed the stairwell, disappearing from sight. Heavy footfalls echoed, shuffling along the landing, before ascending again.

Carma faced the steps behind her. Kirk's faint shadow eventually appeared on the wall below.

And stopped.

The head and upper torso were motionless, as if transfixed. Carma dreaded to think what it was.

"Douglas?" she asked.

He didn't answer, didn't speak at all.

"Douglas?"

She hesitated before asking again, sizing up the corpses littering the stairs as the eerie silence swelled. Movement on the wall caught her attention, and Kirk's shadow seemed to sink into the floor. Wet matter splattered, and the stairwell amplified the sound. Carma peered around the corner, into the stairwell, angling herself to see the next set of steps.

Her breath hitched in her throat.

Kirk was there. On his knees, hunched over a *were's* body where it had collapsed. His upper body shook as he did things to the corpse.

"Douglas?" she asked again.

More wet sounds. A bone snapped as if someone were opening a can of pop.

"Holy shit," Ezekiel whispered, leaning in to see.

"Douglas," Carma said, louder that time.

Whether it was his name or her voice that reached him, she didn't know, but Kirk drew back and gasped as if completing an extreme deep-sea dive. His hand slapped the wall to steady himself. He wiped a palm over his face. Dark matter dripped from his beard, the spatter echoing in the stairwell.

Kirk inspected his hand and Carma expected him to wipe it clean.

To her horror, he did the exact opposite.

He licked it.

"*Douglas?*"

He tensed as if caught in a naughty act and looked up, zeroing in on her voice.

"You..." *okay?* Carma was about to ask but stopped herself. Kirk was obviously *not* okay. Kirk was as close to okay as she was to the celestial rings of Saturn.

And if fear was in the air, then it originated from Ezekiel, who witnessed the entire scene just as she did.

"You finished?" Carma finally managed.

Kirk didn't answer. He hunched over, a shape in the dark.

Carma tightened her grip on her submachine gun, having taken it back from Ezekiel. She wasn't a hundred percent sure if Kirk recognized her. She was, however, aware of being sized up as a potential next course in a very sloppy banquet.

"What do we do?" Ezekiel asked close to her ear.

"Just take it easy," she told him.

A soft crunch distracted her.

Holy shit.

Kirk was once again chowing down on the fallen *weres*.

Horror turned into annoyance and Carma remembered the gun. She aimed above Kirk's head and fired, the blast ripping into the wall in a sprinkle of dust.

The micro-explosion startled Kirk, and he crouched, poised to leap.

Carma trained her sights on him and didn't waver.

"Douglas. Back. The fuck. Off."

Perhaps it was the weapon. Perhaps it was the 'no-fuckery will be tolerated' tone she injected into her words. Whatever the reason, Kirk seemed to relax just a fraction, enough for her to recognize he hadn't completely gone over the edge. He studied his handiwork, reflected upon the gruesome designs, and wavered around the edges. With cautious grace he stood and staggered, as if at the end of some drug-induced delirium.

Carma knew better.

It wasn't a dream or a hallucination. It was the euphoria of a goddamn feeding frenzy.

And in the ensuing peace, where the only sound was that of Ezekiel swallowing, Carma suspected no police force would be responding to this massacre, because no one had called them.

"Douglas," Carma said. "You back with us?"

"Yeah," he answered right away, as if awakening from a daydream.

"You think you're okay to get to work?"

The question lingered, long enough for Carma to fear some dark undertow had yanked Kirk's consciousness back down into a vat of savagery.

He surprised her. "Yeah. 'Course."

"You've gone and done it this time," she said and lowered the machine gun.

"Yeah," he answered quietly, in a very Douglas tone of voice. One she identified as mortified guilt.

"You sure you're okay?"

"Yeah," Kirk answered and placed a hand to his mouth again. He pulled it away in horror. "I need a towel."

"You need a fucking firehose," Carma noted.

Kirk nodded and leaned against a wall, refusing to look at the lumps of flesh at his feet.

But he eventually did. "I got him, Carma."

"Good."

"It was Bryce."

That got her attention.

"Holy shit," Ezekiel muttered, shifting his weight.

"Ian Bryce," Carma repeated. "Who are the others?"

"No one I know, but they're all *weres*," Kirk stated in a placated voice, and again inspected the mess covering him.

"I think you're with us now, Ezekiel," Carma directed at the warden. "They somehow knew we were here. That's why Bryce brought along a few friends. To take care of business."

"How'd they know you were here?" Ezekiel asked in a strained voice. "You said you tossed your phone."

Carma met Kirk's questioning stare as unease ballooned inside of her.

"How could they track us?" she put to Kirk.

"I don't know," he answered. "They didn't really start coming after us until you found me. And we figured it was the phone so we ditched that. So what's left?"

"Your clothes?" Ezekiel asked.

"Oh Jesus Christ," Carma whispered, attracting the others' attention. "No fucking way."

She rushed through Ezekiel's open apartment door, flicked on a light, and walked straight to the kitchen.

Ezekiel and a blood-soaked Kirk arrived as she placed her gun on the countertop.

She'd already pulled out her Bowie knife.

The weapon—bestowed only to wardens—shimmered as she turned it over, careful not to handle the silver. Leather twine covered the hilt and handle, offering a secure grip.

"Give me a knife," Carma said, holding out a hand.

Ezekiel filled it with his own edged symbol of warden authority.

She bent over the weapon and worked at the leather strips, sawing and picking until freeing a short strand. She pulled the piece free, unraveling the molded material wrapped around the pommel.

"Maybe not around there," Ezekiel said, pointing with a stubby finger. "Go higher, near the cross. The guard."

"Why there?"

"Right now, you're picking at the knife's butt. If someone had to, they'd be hammering with that part."

Made sense. Carma pricked at the leather near the guard. She soon exposed a bone handle molded around a silver spike.

A white grain of rice fell to the countertop, the metallic *tick* freezing the three wardens.

"The hell is that?" Kirk asked.

Carma blotted the item with a fingertip and turned it over in the light. One end of the device was shaded red while the other was milky, like a minuscule capsule. Utterly alien to the original function of the knife.

"Looks like a bloody pill," Ezekiel muttered.

"It does," Carma said, holding the device aloft.

"What is it?" Kirk asked her.

"Oh, it's a bug."

"Maybe an RFID chip," Ezekiel stated and got a pair of puzzled looks. "What?" he said defensively. "I read."

"So what are they?" Kirk asked.

"Identification, tell a person where something is, where someone is," Ezekiel shrugged. "Small, though."

"What's the range on one of these?" Carma asked.

Ezekiel made a face. "Don't know. This tech's been around for a while now. Meant to replace bar codes, I think. I first read about it like ten or eleven years ago. God knows how much it's developed."

"How'd they get it into the knife?" Kirk demanded.

"Check mine," Ezekiel said.

Minutes later, a second chip rested beside the first, and the room became that much more solemn.

"Holy shit," Carma breathed, horrified.

"How did they get it into the knife?" Kirk asked a second time. "I always had mine on me. Always."

"Did you?" Carma asked. "I mean, I know I didn't. I carried it when I had to but otherwise it was back in my apartment. A locked apartment. Hidden, too, but who knows. Maybe they got in, got to the knife. We can all feel silver once we're close to it. Like walking, talking divining rods. Easy enough to find the blade and bug it."

That got the others thinking.

"Holy shit," Carma repeated, taking a step back. "We're bugged. Been bugged. The whole time."

"Up until a few years back, anyway," Ezekiel muttered.

"How could they have tracked us before then?" Kirk put forth.

"Who knows? Maybe they didn't."

"Question is," Carma interrupted, "why track us at all? We're *wardens* for Christ's sake."

Neither of the men had an answer.

"They track us," Kirk said, "and we keep track of the packs. Phone numbers. Addresses."

"That part I understand," Carma stressed, "but why tracking chips?"

Another unsettling bout of silence. Kirk abruptly moved to the apartment's picture window looking out over the cul-de-sac and closed the curtains. He peeked out from one corner before returning to the kitchen and addressing Ezekiel. "Get your phone. I want you to make a call."

"To who?"

"The elders. And this is what you're going to say…"

When Kirk told Ezekiel the rest, the New Brunswick warden looked ready to fall over.

35

"Yes?" the elder's voice asked.

"This is Ezekiel."

A pause on the other end. "Yes?"

"There's been a fight here. At my place."

"Refresh my memory. Where is your place?"

Ezekiel told him.

"What kind of fight?" the elder asked.

"A *fight*," the warden stressed, the nervous energy genuine. "A goddamn cutthroat ball wringer of a fistfight. Only it wasn't only fists, there was—there was fucking guns involved. I think Bryce is below. Him and a few others. They're all shot up. Fuckin' *perforated*. Douglas Kirk is here too, along with Carma Jones."

"What?" Genuine surprise.

"I know, right? The fuck is going on? Carma and Kirk knocked on my door not two hours ago and barged in here, looking for my cellphone. They were going to call you."

Silence, so Ezekiel carried on. "They held me at gunpoint. A pair of wardens held me at gunpoint, threatened to shoot me full of silver. Then before I knew what was happening, Bryce and his pack were coming up the stairwell. I don't know how Carma and Kirk knew, but they knew they were coming up the stairs, so Kirk went outside. That's when the shooting started."

"They're dead?"

"Everyone's dead."

"Everyone?" the elder repeated.

"I…" Ezekiel hesitated, a hand at his throat. "I killed Carma. Stabbed her through the back when she wasn't looking."

A damn-near incredulous moment of wonder from the elder. "You stabbed her."

"Through the back."

"She's dead?"

"Oh yeah. Left my fucking knife in her."

"Where are the others?" the elder asked impatiently.

"All over the place," Ezekiel gushed. "The stairwell looks like someone popped a big fucking blood blister out there. My fucking neighbors are dead, too. My fuckin' neighbors! The cops will be here any minute. I need a disposal crew lickety-split."

"Of course."

"I gotta get out of here."

"That would be wise. Wait there for the crew. I happen to have one nearby."

Nearby. Ezekiel checked his surprise at that one. "Okay. Send them over. Fast. Send three or four if you got them."

"Wait there."

The elder broke the connection.

A drained Ezekiel placed the cellphone on the counter.

"Well?" Kirk asked.

"He's sending over a crew now."

"Just happened to have one in the area," Carma added. "Convenient."

"He was surprised." Ezekiel looked from one warden to the other. "I could tell. He wasn't expecting me to be alive. Didn't even ask that many questions. When he found out you two were dead, that was it. Send in the cleaners."

"So they're on the way," Carma said and put her back against the fridge. "Excellent."

"Yeah."

"I think you should meet them, alone," Kirk suggested. "We'll hang back. With the guns."

Ezekiel's brunch scrunched up in puzzlement. "Why?"

"Just in case they try to kill you."

"The fuck they wanna kill me for? I'm a warden."

"You're a warden who's with us," Kirk explained, watching him under a lowered brow. "Who's been exposed to us."

"Worse," Carma said. "You're a loose end. Easier to just kill you and forget about you."

That revelation horrified Ezekiel.

They quieted then, hearing nothing but the wind from the open doorway.

"Someone might call the neighbors," Ezekiel said quietly, somewhat recovered from the shock. "Maybe friends. Or maybe someone might drop by."

"Best turn off all the lights in those apartments," Carma advised. "Leave yours on."

"Fucking massacre in the stairwell," Ezekiel grumped on the way out the door. "If someone stops by…"

"We don't have much time," Kirk said and followed.

"Where you going?" Carma asked.

"To get Bryce's body. Can't leave him in the woods."

"No, we can't," she agreed. "I'll help. It'll be faster. That crew probably isn't that far away."

*

The crew wasn't.

The wardens heard the engine before they spotted the vehicle, a low grumble none too happy about creeping along the street at night. A long white morgue on wheels emerged from the dark. It was a tall truck, one of those mover jobs. Headlights glared, scouring the night, not particular in the least about who it spied, just as long as it took someone. The trailer was huge, capable of holding a small army.

The rig stopped in the middle of the cul-de-sac in a flare of brakes and hissing hydraulics. A low-browed grill smiled under the headlights' cold brilliance. The mechanical beast idled, as if deciding on what to eat first.

The three wardens peeked out from behind the apartment's curtains. Kirk couldn't see who was driving, as he was mesmerized by the vehicle's evil chrome face.

"Christ," Ezekiel muttered. "Fucking thing could take away half the town."

"Maybe they move furniture in their spare time," Carma

said on Kirk's left. "Definitely could park a small bus inside that thing."

"Like an eighteen-wheeled great white shark," Ezekiel observed.

"Definitely them," Kirk whispered. "Here to clean up in minutes."

The others didn't comment. They rarely called in such aid, and on the rare occurrence when they did, it was usually a van. The sheer size of the vehicle in the cul-de-sac made them a little nervous, especially about what lurked inside the machine.

With a motorized chuff, the rig backed up while it chirped warnings. The truck reversed a ponderous ninety-degree turn, its considerable bulk missing a pair of parked cars by a narrow foot. The machine stopped in a plume of red exhaust, right at the head of the apartment's walkway. The driver straightened the vehicle and aimed it back towards the main road, ready for a quick getaway if needed.

The rear doors swung open and figures dressed in ball caps and baggy white coveralls hopped onto the walkway. Some carried what looked like sports equipment bags.

Eight of them gathered, standing in the back of the truck, their faces hidden in shadow. A much bigger crew than anyone had expected. The force studied the apartment building while a ninth man emerged from the opened doors of the truck. For seconds the small army stood in the windless dark and stared, unmoving, as if listening to a private soundtrack.

Then, on some unseen signal, they marched towards the stairwell.

"They're coming," Carma said.

"Yeah." Kirk drew back and faced her. The plan was to leave the apartment through the picture window's balcony, climb onto the roof, and come up behind the disposal crew. Oddly enough, Kirk wasn't nervous about the ambush. If anything, his reluctance had been replaced by excitement.

"Be careful," Carma ordered in a low voice. "I'll stomp your ass if you aren't."

Kirk studied her, smiled, and disappeared through the curtains.

In the after-flutter of hanging fabric, Ezekiel regarded her with a decidedly dirty smirk.

"Fuck off, Zeke," she warned.

Seconds later, the sound of boots on the stairs reached the apartment. Carma retreated to the entry and disappeared into the darkened bathroom. Ezekiel released the curtain and went to the door. The footfalls grew louder until they stopped directly outside the apartment.

A soft rap broke the tension.

"We're up," Carma murmured.

Ezekiel nodded and winked. He leaned into the peephole. "Yeah?"

"Mr. Allen?"

"Yeah."

"We're here for the cleaning, Mr. Allen," the voice asked through the door, "but we haven't located Carma Jones or Douglas Kirk. Are they with you?"

"They are," Ezekiel said. "Hold on."

The stumpy warden steeled himself. It was show time. Ezekiel unlocked and opened the door. A tall man waited, clean shaven, with eyebrows thick enough to sustain wildlife. There were two others behind him, just as tall, with oddly similar facial features. The lack of light in the stairwell no doubt contributed to that effect, but Ezekiel still thought he was looking at three clones, spawned from the same freakish petri dish.

"Where's the rest of the crew?" the warden asked. "I was watching you from the window."

"They're below," the lead clone reported. "Transporting the bodies to the truck. May we come in?"

Ezekiel held up his hands and backed away.

"Where are the bodies?" the lead clone asked as all three entered the apartment.

"Bathroom. In the tub," Ezekiel gestured over his shoulder with a thumb. "Letting them bleed out. Glad you got here when you did. They were starting to stink."

"Excellent."

At that word, the clones flanking the leader raised guns—not just any guns, but the small, futuristic submachine variety.

And even after Carma and Kirk had explained things to him, a part of Ezekiel still thought there had to have been a mistake somehow. That none of this was truly happening.

The display of weapons wasn't really expected. Ezekiel's fright was genuine.

Automatic gunfire blazed from the darkened adjacent

bathroom, cutting into the armed visitors. The burst riddled the two gunslinger clones, flinging them into the kitchen alcove. The leader whirled at the shots. Ezekiel grabbed him, turned, and whipped him ten feet, bouncing the man off the living room wall and denting gyprock. The clone disappeared behind the couch. Ezekiel went after him as if hunting a cockroach.

Carma booted the front door closed and checked on her kills in the kitchen.

"This thing really kicks," she called out.

Adrenaline firing through his system, Ezekiel searched for the killer behind his sofa. He pulled the furniture out, exposing the clone looking up in stunned reflex. The warden grabbed him by the collar and yanked him clear. The clone grimaced, got to his feet, and actually pawed at the warden's face.

Ezekiel didn't appreciate that.

He slapped his prisoner twice, hard enough to rattle teeth and bone, and dropped the would-be killer on his ass.

"You awake?" he asked the senseless man.

The clone turned his head and cracked open an eye, that side of his face already inflating. He licked at blood streaming from his nose.

Ezekiel clamped a hand around the man's throat.

"Where are the elders?" the warden demanded in a whisper.

"What?"

Ezekiel squeezed his prisoner's neck like a stubborn tension ball. The man's eyes bulged.

"Elders," he repeated. "Where are they?"

Carma appeared, studying the dazed clone.

"I don't know…"

Ezekiel gripped and released a second time. "Next time something breaks. Got it?"

"Yeah," the clone replied weakly. "But… I don't know."

"Where were you taking the bodies?" Carma asked, changing the question.

"Winnipeg," he managed. "Winnipeg."

The wardens traded befuddled looks.

"Manitoba?" Carma asked dubiously.

"Yeah," the man replied.

"You guys intended on driving all night or something?" Ezekiel asked and got the barest nod.

"Makes sense," Carma mused. "There's enough of them to drive in shifts. But why the urgency?"

"Yeah," Ezekiel released the throat and grabbed a chin. "Why the fucking urgency?"

"Always did it that way," the clone squawked in pain and terror, the words mangled by squished lips.

"You always did it…" Carma trailed off. "How many of these jaunts do you do?"

The lead clone didn't answer.

"How many?" Ezekiel repeated, tightening his grip.

"I don't know," the man squeaked.

"I think you do," Carma accused. "I think you know the exact number. You look a little too organized not to know. I bet if I have to root around in that truck you drove up in, I'd find a tablet or a clipboard with the exact number. Some proof of record."

Ezekiel's face darkened with the logic.

"Five," the clone wheezed.

The number silenced the two wardens.

"This year?" Carma asked.

The clone squirmed. "Every year."

"You fuckheads are called in five times a year?" a bewildered Ezekiel asked.

The clone nodded. "Sometimes more."

"The hell is going on, Carma?" Ezekiel put to her.

"I don't know. But I intend to find out."

The main door closed and Kirk hurried into the living room. "You got one."

"Just one," Carma reported. "All we need. What about the others?"

"All dead," Kirk said. "All human."

The other wardens didn't ask how he'd determined the disposal team was not made up of werewolves. Kirk hadn't completely cleaned his face or his hands.

'How was your climb?" she asked him, changing the subject.

"Slick," he told her. "Pigeon shit everywhere. You find out anything?"

"Yeah," she said as Ezekiel exerted pressure on the lead clone's face, producing an uncomfortable note of pain.

"Looks like we're going to Winnipeg," Carma said.

"Winnipeg?" Kirk repeated.

"You're organized," Carma directed at the clone. "You have to report when Ezekiel's dead and the place is all cleared?"

Even though Ezekiel's hand covered the clone's chin, they still saw him swallow. He nodded in defeat, too scared for anything else.

"Got your phone?" Carma asked.

Another nod.

"Then make the call," she said. "On speaker. Tell them whatever you would've told them if you'd killed Zeke. And be convincing. I don't think I have to say much more than that, right?"

"Right," the clone whispered.

A glowering Ezekiel released him and the clone once again enjoyed unrestricted movement. He looked from face to face, knowing full well he was meat if he tried anything. Once composed, the clone reached into a pocket and retrieved a cellphone.

The wardens loomed over him as he speed-dialed a number.

"This is Hale," he reported, his teeth combing his upper lip. "It's all done. Allen's dead. We're packing everyone up now."

No one answered.

No one answered for the longest time. The wardens tensed, wondering if the presence on the other end had detected the deception.

They waited, willing the voice to respond.

"Good," came that unmistakable timber belonging to the elder. "Did Allen say anything?"

"No," Hale said, eying the named warden. "He died in his socks."

"Finish up, then. And get on the road."

"I hear you," Hale replied and, with a little nod, ended the conversation. He offered the phone.

Carma took it and confirmed the elder was gone.

"What's 'finish up' mean?" Kirk asked.

Hale shifted uncomfortably, debating if he should answer. "We're supposed to burn the place. To the ground. No evidence."

That quieted the wardens.

Carma slapped Ezekiel across the shoulder. "We can do that," she said.

36

The disposal truck pulled away from the building as the first flickers of firelight brightened the apartment's darkened windows. Ezekiel hung out in the back of the rig with Hale trussed up with duct tape in the middle of the floor. The New Brunswick warden wasn't in the best of moods. Kirk had gone through every apartment and even the stairwell, setting up gasoline bombs taken from the sports equipment bags of the dead disposal team. Hale had provided instructions on how to set the timers and Kirk had worked alone, relieving Ezekiel from the chore of blowing up his own home.

The New Brunswick warden sat and brooded, shaking his head at the growing conflagration framed in the truck's rear windows.

"Was only there a few more years, anyway," Ezekiel muttered as they drove away.

Kirk knew what the man was going through. Twenty years or twenty days didn't make a difference. Home was still home, and it was always difficult to leave.

The truck took a turn, and the apartment building disappeared from sight. Ezekiel sat on a padded bench lining the left wall and lowered his head. Kirk watched him, decided to keep his mouth shut, and looked to the freezer unit. That had been one of the big surprises in the crew's truck. The unit resembled an oblong pizza box welded to a gurney, except it was big enough to stick two people inside if they were stacked. Not a huge issue considering the occupants would be dead.

"Keeps the smell in," Hale had said before having his mouth taped shut.

Kirk noted the man had remained quite docile under Ezekiel's menacing eye. Hale was smart. Kirk hoped he wasn't too smart.

"Winnipeg," he said after a time, sitting in the passenger seat and looking to the open road. Street lights flashed overhead.

"Gonna be a long drive," Carma stated from behind the steering wheel.

"We can do it," Kirk said. "Drive in shifts. Like they did."

He glanced back into the truck's rear, renovated into something part trailer, part bus, and part refrigerator. Two rows of extra seating, a bench, cabinets, and the freezer. More automatic weapons and silver-tipped ammunition. The large amount of ammunition had surprised the wardens. Enough bullets for an extended shoot-out and more than enough for the disposal crew's purposes. Obviously the elders thought otherwise. Kirk was glad to see the extra ammo. He no longer had any reservations about using firearms. Silver-loaded or otherwise.

"You okay?" Carma asked quietly as she drove through an intersection.

"I'm fine," Kirk answered, distracted. "Mind the traffic."

That earned him a scowl. "What traffic?" she asked. "I think I passed one car going in the other direction in the last ten minutes."

"There might be bikers."

"There are no bikers this hour."

"Deer, then."

Carma shook her head.

"Sinkholes," Kirk suggested.

She checked her side mirror. After a time, she said, "You took care of that team pretty much."

A shard of streetlight ran over Kirk's features. "Yeah."

"I mean… you ripped them apart. Gotta admit, I wasn't expecting that mess in the stairwell. Barely heard you doing it, in fact. Not exactly the Douglas I know."

Kirk kept his mouth shut.

There hadn't been any noise from the disposal team because he'd completely surprised them. He'd shifted into wolf-man with nary a problem, the change much easier than before. The remainder of the team had been in the stairwell, two levels down, and no one had any weapons drawn. Kirk had scythed through them all, wrecking faces and breaking bones with barely an effort, feeling as if he were stuck in fast-forward of an exceptionally violent movie. And worse, he didn't feel a twinge of remorse for killing them. Not one drop of regret. That knowledge disturbed him more than the act itself.

Upon leaving his apartment, Ezekiel didn't bat an eye at the carnage but Carma, she'd been surprised. To her credit, she didn't make a thing of it until just then, well after setting up the apartment building for a fiery eruption. Not even a word while they were transferring their few possessions from the white van to the larger truck.

Kirk appreciated that.

"Got caught up in the moment," he finally said, the words somewhat obscured by the engine's drone.

Taking her attention off the road, Carma glanced his way. That one wary look spoke volumes.

*

"You doing okay back there?" Kirk asked around two o' clock in the morning. He'd switched with Carma at midnight, allowing her some shut eye. She slept on the passenger side, the seat lowered to a flat plane. Her face was turned to the door, partially hidden.

Kirk had glanced that way every now and again.

Until he remembered Ezekiel Allen in the back, guarding Hale. Kirk didn't know much about the New Brunswick warden, thought him to be a country goon with far too much time on his hands. At the moment, however, the bulldoggish Ezekiel worried Kirk. The *were* had been drinking when they met him, but he'd had more than enough time to sober up and realize he was displaced. Not only was he removed from his home, to which there would be no returning, he'd learned that the elders, the only ruling authority he'd ever answered to, had ordered his death.

Kirk wondered if Zeke would blame that sentencing on Carma and him.

"Ezekiel?"

Nothing.

Then, "Yeah?"

Kirk chanced a quick look, saw him near the truck's rear, leaning forward with his elbows on his knees. Brooding. Simmering. A quarterback of destruction cognizant that his ass was parked squarely on a reddening burner.

His unblinking eyes trained squarely on the prisoner.

"You okay?" Kirk asked again.

Another pause. "No."

"Wanna talk about it?"

That got the warden's attention. He leaned back and studied Kirk. Ezekiel was far from pretty, and in the dim light, he was downright scary. Extreme buzz cut, off-kilter eyes, and crooked teeth, the *were* looked like a member of a bomb disposal unit who diffused explosives by swallowing them whole. Kirk remembered Halifax, when Ezekiel had first entered his apartment. He'd thought the *were* was perhaps two shades away from crazy, and one look away from a fight. Or murder.

Kirk barely knew the warden, wasn't exactly sure what he might do to the prisoner at his feet.

"If you do what you're thinking," Kirk said, trending softly, "y'know…"

He couldn't finish the sentence, didn't know what to say.

"Just drive, warden," Ezekiel said in his smoker's voice.

The headlights lit up a stop sign. Kirk absorbed the words and, instead of driving on like he might've done a couple of months ago, he braked and pulled over to the shoulder. The moon was a bright sickle overhead as Kirk got out of the truck and closed his door. He walked to the rear door and opened it, meeting Ezekiel's gaze.

"You got something to say, say it now," Kirk said.

Ezekiel scowled. He slid off the bench and hopped to the ground with a crunch of gravel. The broad warden squared off against Kirk, dark eyes gleaming. "Got nothing to say."

"You sure?" Kirk said. "Because if you do, this is where we part. I'm not driving halfway across the country looking over my shoulder and wondering if you're going to turn on us. If you're thinking about that, let me remind you. Hale called the elders. It was pretty clear that they wanted you dead."

"Because you came to me," Ezekiel countered. "If you hadn't, I'd still be pleasantly shitfaced at my place."

"Probably, but then you'd be living out your days not knowing the truth. Not knowing why some good wardens died in Halifax. Not knowing why Bailey wanted us dead or why Morris really died. Not knowing about what's happening to me and Carma. Or why some wardens are using silver bullets against their own kind."

"I could live without all that shit."

"Listen," Kirk raised a finger. "You come back from the dead with our heads and the elders might cut you some slack. They just might. But I doubt it. In case I haven't been clear,

I don't trust those bastards. And after they tried killing you, neither should you."

Ezekiel stared, his eyes suddenly tired, like a dog chained to a post. "You don't have to worry about me. I want to see the elders, too. See what they have to say."

"I don't think they'll have much to say."

"No?"

"No," Kirk said. "So we'll have to make them talk."

That put a little smile on Ezekiel's face.

*

Later that morning, as the dark faded to reveal heavy clouds, the truck pulled into a service station. The vehicle rounded the highway pit stop, chuffing as it circled three parked transports. A smattering of morning drivers headed inside for their predestined coffee hits. Other patrons gathered around a coffee machine in the convenience store section while a few others sat at a counter in the adjoining restaurant.

"We need gas," Kirk groaned and stretched his back. "Have a good sleep?"

"Not really," Carma replied. "Hard to sleep in a truck."

Kirk heard that. He was the same way. "You awake back there?" he called to Ezekiel, not bothering to look over his shoulder.

"Yeah," Ezekiel grunted. "Need to take a leak."

"Me too."

"We all do," Carma said. "Even him."

The wardens considered their captive on the floor, very much awake and aware of the attention he was getting.

Carma hunkered down and studied Hale. A second later, she ripped the tape from his mouth.

"*Oww*," Hale winced. "*Christ*, lady."

"Shut up," Ezekiel said. "Big baby."

"That *hurt*," Hale protested.

"I'll tape those bushy eyebrows of yours next," Ezekiel warned.

Carma silenced the blocky warden with a glare, then looked back to Hale. She felt the man's breast pocket and pulled out what looked like a security card. The words *Atticus Y Corporation* embossed the plastic in black and red. She fanned the air with the card and then unzipped the front of the man's coverall. She searched inside for a wallet and located it three seconds later in his jeans' back pocket.

"Forgot to leave this in a locker?" she asked, presenting the leather.

Hale frowned.

Ezekiel planted a boot in the man's shoulder.

"I always have it," Hale muttered. "We don't show up for a fight, only after."

"That so?" Carma asked and joined Ezekiel on the bench. "Looks like you were ready for one."

"Just precautionary," Hale sighed, his head drooped to the floor. "That's all. Never had a run-in yet. At least not while I've been with the company."

"The company?"

"Atticus Y. 'Y' for Yor."

"This company?" Carma held up the security card. "Atticus Y. Yor?"

"No, it's just Atticus Yor, but we call it Atticus Y. Sometimes AYC. C for 'corporation'."

"You get paid for this?"

"Yeah."

"Well?"

"Yeah. Really well."

"Benefits?"

"Oh yeah."

Ezekiel kicked him. Hard. The impact bucked Hale in two.

"That's for hauling away dead-ass *weres*," the hardened warden growled.

Hale took a minute to compose himself. "Half of us don't know what you are and the other half don't care," he eventually said, his words strained. "Seriously. The money we make on a run? Just for cleaning up a mess and delivering a corpse or two? Huge. Besides, silver bullets will kill anyone. Man or monster. Some of the guys figured that Atticus Y was a front for something else. Secret service or some shit. No one asks questions. Before you're hired, you go through a psyche check, to gauge your mental fortitude. Then you sign contracts and confidentiality agreements. But, like I said, the money's so good you don't ask questions. You're just glad to have the job."

"And you?" Carma asked. "You believed?"

Hale put a tongue to his teeth. "I believed. Every word."

"Do you care?"

He didn't answer, but glanced at Ezekiel.

A reflective Carma thumbed through the wallet. "Driver's

license. You're Jesse, I see. Organ donor card. Very giving of you. Credit card. Air Miles. Blood type card. No family pics?"

Hale tensed.

Ezekiel wandered behind Hale. The company man didn't like the move. He squirmed. Kirk remained between the seats, watching the show.

"Best answer the question," Carma said to Hale, "because I'm not stopping him."

"Yes," Hale hissed. "Yes, I do. Yes."

"You want to see them again?"

Hale glared.

"Look," Carma explained. "It's like this. We're not interested in you. We only need you to get to Winnipeg and find the elders."

"I don't know any elders." Hale's head thudded on the floor. "I don't know anyone."

"Who was that you reported to on the phone?"

"Rose, I think. Christopher Rose."

"He's the head of Atticus Y?"

"Maybe."

Ezekiel prodded Hale's spine with a boot.

"He's the owner," the man released, "but I think the company's run by a board or something. We never see any of that, anyway. Too low on the pay scale."

"You always report directly to Rose?"

Hale closed his eyes.

Ezekiel prodded harder.

"No," Hale gasped. "Not always. A lady named Tracy Wellford."

"All right then," Carma said. "Does Ms. Wellford get updates on where you are?"

"Sometimes, yeah. Or Mr. Rose will call if we're late," Hale hesitated. "We're hardly ever late."

"Do they track you?" Kirk asked from between the seats.

Hale didn't look so sure. "I don't know. I don't think so."

"Doesn't matter," Carma said. "We're going to Winnipeg anyway. What's there?"

"Corporate headquarters," Hale said. "We unload the bodies there. Ms. Wellford takes whatever we bring. We don't see anything else after that."

"Why do you take the bodies there?" she asked.

He looked her in the eye. "I don't know."

"Does Rose get rid of them? Burn them, maybe?"

Hale shook his head, not knowing the answer. "We just transport. That's all."

The truck's idling sounded like a monster after feeding, impatient to get moving. Carma studied the security card's front and back before popping it in her own pocket.

"What's the address?" she asked.

Hale visibly trembled around the edges, vacillating on whether to say anything or not. In the end, he told her. "The Exchange District. Downtown."

Carma relaxed, satisfied with the information. "Ezekiel, take him inside. Let him use a toilet. Freshen up a bit. We got a long drive ahead of us. And Hale? Ezekiel is going to be watching you the whole time. You try to run and you'll die. Not only will you die, your family will too. I have your information right here. Understand me?"

Looking as if he'd just swallowed poison, Hale slowly nodded. Ezekiel pulled out his newly debugged dagger and cut away the man's bonds. Once done, he allowed Hale to stand. Ezekiel opened the rear, flooding the interior with air so cold that Kirk's eyes dried out. The New Brunswick warden pushed Hale outside and closed the door.

"What do you think?" Kirk asked.

"About what?" Carma asked back.

"What he said."

"All sounds good to me," Carma answered. "I don't think he's lying. Only thing is we're walking straight into the lion's den. Or wolf's den."

"Good."

Carma met his gaze. "What're you thinking about doing?"

"I think we see Mr. Rose," Kirk said. "He's got to be an elder. Maybe we can get some answers out of him."

"And then?"

Kirk didn't hesitate. "Force him to call off the hunt. Then kill him."

"How we going to see him?" Carma asked. "He'll have security."

"Already figured that part out."

"Yeah? Want to share?"

Kirk smiled. "Why did you kiss me the other morning? In the woods, when we changed."

"Best way to wake you up," she said, not shying away from his gaze.

"Was that all?"

Carma studied his face, his eyes, and even his mouth, but returned to his eyes. She didn't speak and, for a heartbeat, Kirk thought he detected a softening in her face and posture. Interpreting it as a positive signal, he joined her on the bench.

After a second, he turned to face her.

"Douglas," she said, matching him.

"Yeah?"

But then she frowned, and the anticipation dissipated like air squealing free of a tire.

"We got work to do," she said and patted his cheek. She scanned the area around the truck. "You brought along the cash? I'll pick up whatever food I can in there. Hope the sandwiches and breakfast wraps are fresh. You get the gas."

She gathered up a coat Ezekiel had given her, pulled it on, and climbed out of the truck.

37

Three hours later Kirk spotted a narrow dirt road. It was a crack of a detour heading northeast, leaving the highway and splitting otherwise thick woods. Needing a break from driving, he decelerated and indicated his attention to get off the road. The action caused Carma to jerk awake from her doze.

"What's going on?" she asked.

"Gonna get off the road," Kirk said. "Stretch my legs."

Carma checked her side mirror. "Anyone on our tail?"

Kirk shook his head.

She continued to look into her mirror.

"Relax," he said. "I'd let you know if something was up."

But Carma didn't relax.

The truck bounced when it left the pavement. There was a frightening dip, sharp enough for the incline to nudge the undercarriage, but then the road leveled out. A set of ruts with a tuft of grass straight up the middle ran into the forest. Kirk steered the truck around some of the deeper potholes and slowed for the shallow ones. The afternoon light dulled under thick tree tops, and the road ahead narrowed until boughs grazed the truck's side.

"Where you going again?" Carma asked.

"Might as well see where it goes," Kirk said as Ezekiel appeared between them. "Road's too narrow to back out."

"This is a quad trail," Ezekiel muttered. "And this truck's got a fat ass."

"We're committed now," Kirk said. "Maybe it'll open up somewhere ahead."

And the forest did open up, into a wide clearing where parallel towers of steel scaffolding and the cables connecting them cast shadows across upturned ground. The line of erected powerlines stretched east-west, disappearing over hills and around corners of thick woods. The road crossed under the cables, heading even deeper into unknown territory. Kirk figured they were well away from the main highway. The land was rough and rocky, but he had no trouble completing a ninety-degree turn.

"Okay," he announced as he parked the truck.

Kirk studied the rugged terrain before opening his door. Fresh air flooded the interior.

"Just a few minutes," he said and got out. "Zeke, open up that back door, would you?"

Ezekiel went to do just that.

"You getting out?" Kirk asked Carma. "Maybe have something to eat?"

"A picnic, maybe?"

Kirk shook his head. "Y'know, I can't tell when you're being serious or sarcastic."

With a mysterious smirk, Carma got out of the truck.

The rear doors opened, and Hale looked up at the afternoon sky like a miner trapped underground for too long. The company man considered the broad expanse to his left and right, then regarded his secured ankles. Ezekiel slapped the back of the captive's head, getting a muffled *Ow* from the duct-taped mouth.

Carma appeared around the truck's corner and stretched her back. "What do you have back there, Zeke?"

The warden walked out of the interior's gloom, holding four plastic bags. "We got some breakfast wraps. Some sandwiches, more sandwiches. Some donuts that's got all its shit squeezed out of them. Chips and bars. Beef jerky."

"There should be some apples in there," Kirk said, knowing he bought them at the last pit stop.

Ezekiel opened another bag. "Yeah, right here. And drinks. Water and pop."

"You really went to town," Carma said to Kirk, who held out his hands for one of the bags.

In answer, Ezekiel ripped the duct tape from Hale's face, leaving the company man with a toothy grimace.

They ate in relative peace, their thoughts private. Hale sat just behind Ezekiel, eating his food noisily enough for Carma and Kirk to exchange looks.

Once finished with his meal, Ezekiel balled up the garbage and shoved it into a plastic bag. He stayed there, glowering for a bit, and cleared his throat.

"Just wanted you guys to know," Ezekiel said, eyeing Kirk first and then Carma. "I appreciate… you bringing me along."

"Yeah?" Carma asked. "Even though by meeting up with you, we kinda sorta brought all this shit down on your head."

Ezekiel's eyes flicked between the pair. "Yeah. Even so. Like you said, they were going to kill me anyway. So fuck 'em."

Carma and Kirk exchanged looks. Hale's head drooped.

"You okay back there?" Kirk asked.

His wrists bound, a pensive Hale managed a thumbs-up.

"I've been thinking," Carma said. "Zeke, can you fire one of those guns?"

The question hung on the air before dropping on the warden. He shifted uneasily. "No."

"No?" she repeated.

Ezekiel shook his head.

"Wanna learn?" she asked.

He drew an uneasy breath and tongued the inside of his lower lip. "Not really."

"Well," Carma declared, "sorry, Ezekiel Allen. This time around, 'not really' doesn't flush shit down a toilet."

"It's a gun, Carma," Ezekiel pleaded. "You know how it is."

"I know how it is to get shot at and not be able to shoot back," she countered. "Believe me, you get over your firearm problem pretty damn quick."

"She has a point," Kirk added and got a frown from the New Brunswick warden.

"You go in there," Carma directed Ezekiel to the truck's interior, "and you pick out one of those weapons. And get a few spare magazines. We'll go through the basics."

Ezekiel leaned back with a groan. "I don't know, Carma,"

"I *do* know, now do what I say."

He fidgeted, clearly not pleased in the least.

"Zeke, get over it before I kick you right in the peanuts. Got it?"

With an even louder groan, Ezekiel got up and wandered off towards one of the gun cabinets. Metal clicked and clattered.

Kirk regarded Carma. "How'd you get over handling guns?"

"Let's just say I never really understood the elders' position on them. What about you? You didn't seem too bothered, either."

That brought back memories of fighting *were* breeds in Newfoundland. Kirk remembered the shotgun. "I got over it."

"I'll say you did. Big time. I thought you handled one pretty well."

"You see enough movies, you get a general idea."

"Uh-huh."

A miserable Ezekiel dragged himself back with an MP5 and a handful of extra magazines. Kirk felt a sudden surge of empathy for the warden.

Carma considered the weapon and looked around the pole line. "All right. Step one's complete, though I swear, Zeke, a two-year-old with a shitty diaper moves faster. See over there? That big fir with the broad trunk. See it?"

Ezekiel grunted.

"Then get over here and take a few practice shots at it, okay?"

Not happy in the least, he did as told. "What about the traffic?"

"We're far enough away," she said.

"They're gonna hear, Carma."

"There are silencers," Kirk suggested.

She thought about it. "Get one."

A concerned Hale pulled his legs back as Kirk clambered into the back of the truck. Seconds later, he returned with a silencer. He took the MP5 from Ezekiel, studied the weapon, and fixed it to the barrel in short time.

"Here," Kirk said and handed the weapon back. "All yours."

The warden grunted thanks.

"Now shoot that tree."

Ezekiel squinted in the target's direction.

"Quit dragging your ass," Carma warned and looked to Kirk. "Did you twist something pink of his while I wasn't looking?"

"Did no such thing," he answered. It was a half-truth, anyway.

"Then get shooting, Zeke," Carma instructed. "Can't head into the city with an unproven soldier."

That got a glare. "What you'd just say?" Ezekiel growled.

"With a gun, I meant, with a gun," Carma assured him. When Ezekiel settled down and looked to the tree, she gave a cautious glance of *Don't go there* to Kirk.

With pure loathing, Ezekiel studied the weapon in his hands and, with great reluctance, eventually placed the stock's butt to his shoulder. He stared down the firearm's sights, shifted his hairy profile against the metal, and squinted once again. Then he backed off and lowered the weapon, took greater measure of the target, and brought the gun back to his shoulder again. He grimaced as if deadlifting a ton of lead, and after a few seconds stooped at the knee, as if frozen in mid-stride. He held that pose for long seconds before straightening again.

"Christ almighty," Carma seethed. "You're sorely testing my patience here."

"I'm trying to get comfortable."

"You're pissing me off."

Ezekiel regarded the tree and assumed a firing stance once again, no doubt emulating what he'd seen in the movies.

He took a breath and squeezed the trigger.

Nothing happened.

He squeezed the trigger a second time, then a third before studying the weapon with a puzzled expression.

"There's a switch—" Kirk started.

"Got it," Ezekiel cut him off and fingered the weapon's side.

"And the bolt on top there," Kirk offered again.

"The what?"

"On the top, you pull the bolt back." Kirk mimed the motion, which Ezekiel put into practice a heartbeat later.

He sighted the tree once again and pulled the trigger.

Pop.

The recoil surprised Ezekiel, and when the ejected spent casing landed on the ground, he leaned over and studied it with grim interest.

Carma and Kirk stared at the untouched bark.

"Try again," she ordered

Pop.

A tree limb twitched, once perhaps a foot away from the desired target.

Pop.

"Goddamn piece of shit," Ezekiel swore and studied the MP5's selection of fire modes. He muttered murderous thoughts while picking his rate of fire. Once done, he snuggled the gun stock tight to his shoulder.

The weapon fired with that unmistakable, hyper-charged sewing machine chatter, the suppressor hiding the flash. He pulled off-target but Ezekiel muscled it back towards the tree. Needles flew. Severed branches jumped and dropped to the ground. Ezekiel grunted repeatedly, loudly, over the extended blast, an odd sound of anger and satisfaction.

Until the gun abruptly went dry with a click.

Ezekiel cleared the air with a wave of his hand and studied the weapon again.

"Reload it," Carma said.

But after fiddling with the gun for a few seconds, it became clear Ezekiel didn't know how.

"Here," she said and walked over to him. She took the MP5 and the fresh magazine and demonstrated. "Stick in here, listen for the click, pull the bolt here, and…"

Carma aimed at the tree. She missed with the first burst, but hit with the following.

She handed the weapon back to him.

Ezekiel grudgingly took it.

He took aim, fired, and missed.

On full auto.

The magazine emptied with another click just as he swerved the continuous burst towards the target, splintering the outer edge of the trunk.

"How long we got?" Ezekiel asked.

"Not long," Carma answered. She looked back to Kirk who indicated that time was almost up.

"Five more minutes," she said.

Fifteen minutes later, the truck rolled back onto the main highway.

An uncomfortable silence pervaded the interior. Ezekiel sat in the rear and stewed in a funk of personal defeat, still not happy with having to use a gun and realizing that he was a terrible shot. Kirk suspected the knowledge might demoralize the warden, so he sought to change the conversation.

"Don't worry about it," he soothed, taking the glare from Carma. She wasn't happy either with the warden's skill at arms.

"Don't worry," Kirk repeated. "You just carry it. Loaded, of course. We'll take care of the rest."

"Hate the thing," Ezekiel muttered over the engine's drone.

"Look," Kirk said. "Maybe if we have time, we'll try for another shooting session."

"I don't think we have the time for that," Carma said. "Or the ammo."

Cars streaked by the truck. The highway had slimmed into only two lanes, presenting a touch of congestion.

"Never handled anything like that, I keep telling you," Ezekiel said. "I'm a warden for Christ's sakes. I don't use *guns*."

"Times have changed," Carma said, turning in her passenger seat to meet him eye-to-eye. "For the worse. Like Douglas said, take one of those guns and maybe, with a little luck, you won't have to use it."

"Yeah."

Hale sat on the floor across from Ezekiel and wisely kept his untaped mouth shut. The warden glanced at the prisoner every now and again as if expecting a smart-assed comment, but the company man didn't say a word.

"I mean, people take courses on how to use those things," Ezekiel rumbled on. "Not as easy as it looks on TV. And the silver rounds only make it worse. I was feeling it in my teeth the whole time."

"Is that bad?" Hale asked, surprising them all.

"Like chewing on aluminum foil," Ezekiel answered. "Except worse."

"Oh, I wouldn't like that either," Hale finished.

The company man's voice prompted Kirk to glance into his side mirror.

His heart skipped across what felt like a mile-long chasm before starting up again.

Edging into view, just enough to make out the car's model, was a police cruiser.

"If anything," Carma said, oblivious to the approaching law enforcement officials. "Just stand next to me while you're trying to shoot. At least then…"

She trailed off as she noticed Kirk's distraction. She looked over her shoulder, paled, and then checked her own side mirror.

The great white shape of the police cruiser wavered left and right ever so slightly, hanging just behind the disposal crew truck, pulling closer with every passing second.

Kirk's heartbeat increased. He sat up straight as if proper posture might somehow help.

"You seein' this?" Carma asked, her question stopping all conversation in the back of the truck.

"Yeah," Kirk answered, taking his foot off the gas and coasting until he hit a hundred kilometers an hour on the nose.

"Just drive then," Carma said.

Kirk checked on the cruiser again.

"What's wrong?" Ezekiel asked.

"Cops are behind us."

And, like anyone hearing that particular tidbit of information, Ezekiel stuck his head up for a quick peek, just to confirm that the police were indeed following them.

"Sit *down*," Carma barked.

Ezekiel sat.

Hale's head whipped from him to her to the rear windows.

"Zeke," Carma said, "if Hale tries anything, especially if he looks out that window, you can kill him."

The company man wilted. Ezekiel suddenly lost all interest in the police not two car-lengths back from their tail and glared at the prisoner.

But Kirk couldn't worry about any of that. He gripped the wheel, willing the police to pass them by and drive on, to keep on patrolling the highway. He didn't think they knew him or his companions. But if they pulled the truck over, they would probably just discover that the driver very much resembled a man wanted for questioning about a few dead bodies in a Halifax apartment complex. If that happened, calls might be made, internet might be accessed, and who knew just *how* connected the elders might be.

Kirk did not want to find out.

"Just keep driving," Carma said.

"Yeah."

"And don't slow down too much, that might set them off too."

"Already doing the limit," Kirk reported and checked his side mirror again.

The cruiser drifted mere inches to the left before correcting itself. It wavered in that way for several seconds, not gaining ground or losing. Kirk felt like he was being followed by a shark. Unease became nervousness. The cruiser didn't drop back. Nor did it try to pass them. The car ahead of Kirk sped into the distance, well above the limit, blissfully unaware of the law lurking behind them.

"Uh-oh," Carma said.

"What?" Kirk lurched, seeing the cruiser's hood and grill in his mirror.

"We might have trouble."

"What do you mean?"

"That car that just took off?"

"Yeah?"

"They're letting them go," she said. "That means they're checking us out."

Shit, Kirk realized, and leaned back in his seat even further.

"Just stay cool," Carma said in a calming tone. "No false moves. Let them check out the plate. Your stickers are all up to date, aren't they, Hale?"

Ezekiel kicked the man's feet, getting his attention.

"I don't know," the company man blurted. "I just take the keys and drive."

Great, Kirk sighed and swallowed. "Guess we'll find out in a few seconds then."

They entered a long curve, perhaps the longest of Kirk's life, and he almost smiled at how well-behaved the rest of the fucking traffic had become. Not a speedster or drag racer amongst the lot, but there were plenty before the cops showed up. Funny how that happened.

Thus, in the absence of wrongdoers and not encouraged in the least to do otherwise, the cruiser stayed right behind the moving truck, ghosting him.

Ghosting. Kirk clenched his jaw. No truer word could describe how the white machine just hung back there. Reading his license plates, running whatever checks the police might do in such a situation, or just getting off on playing with a poor motorist's nerves.

Cars in the opposing lane seemed fewer to Kirk, and he continually checked his mirrors.

"You're doing good," Carma said at length, pushed back into her own seat and observing her mirror. Her right hand gripped her seatbelt at the shoulder.

"They're still back there," Kirk said.

"I can see them."

Kirk could see them as well. "I'm going to be sick here."

"Just keep driving, they'll pass us eventually."

The curve straightened into a long strip, the true distance hidden by a well-placed hill.

Then it hit Kirk. "You can see them?"

"Yeah," Carma said.

He checked his side mirror. The cruiser was still wavering back and forth, but holding on. Trouble was, he knew how big the truck was.

"Even now?" he asked.

"Yeah, they're right there."

Kirk shifted in his seat.

And almost shit himself right there.

A *second* cruiser had joined the leisurely chase, a controlled car-length right behind the first.

"Oh no," he whispered.

"There's another car?" Carma asked as she strained to see.

"Yeah, right behind the first one."

"Well, shit. Where'd he come from?"

"He just got there." Kirk strangled the steering wheel,

expecting the police to switch on those swirling lights and sirens any second.

But they didn't, which was damn-near *worse*.

In the back, Ezekiel kept his attention on Hale, who looked like a beleaguered passenger just informed that his ship was about to sink.

The two police cruisers continued to follow Kirk up and over the hill. There was no other traffic behind the police cars.

"I could pull over," he said.

That got Carma's attention.

"Maybe Ezekiel could go out the back," he continued. "Hit them hard. There's three of us. We could do it."

"Are you hearing yourself?" Carma asked.

"Yeah."

"I'm not killing any police."

"You said they work for the elders."

"I might've said the elders are hooked into the police. By which I meant communications. I don't think they actually control them. Influence maybe, but not control."

"I'm getting worried here, Carma."

"Then don't look ahead."

Kirk did so, anyway.

A kilometer away and closing fast in the opposing lane was a third police cruiser, like a loner rejoining the pack. There was no mistaking the rack of lights on the roof.

"Well shit," Kirk said, his guts going cold. But for some reason, his foot didn't leave the accelerator. His speed didn't drop below the current hundred klicks an hour. His heart, however, revved dangerously in his chest.

"If they hit the sirens," Carma said, "then we'll go with your plan. But just subdue them. Okay?"

Kirk nodded, eyes riveted to the converging cop car.

The approaching cruiser switched on its indicator and, seconds later, pulled across Kirk's lane and onto a dirt road.

Kirk drove past the vehicle.

The cruisers behind him braked and indicated right turns. They slowed and, one after the other, followed the third car down that forested throat into parts unknown.

The way ahead was clear, devoid of all traffic.

"Oh shit," Kirk whispered as relief flooded through him.

Carma exhaled mightily and studied her side mirror.

The cruisers did not return.

"You want me to drive for a bit?" she asked.

38

A day and a half later, at approximately three thirty-one in the afternoon, the disposal truck entered Winnipeg's city limits and motored along the downtown drag of Main Street. They'd arrived, surprisingly, without any further incidents with police cruisers.

The three wardens had shared driving duties, stopped only to refuel, to gather food for the road, and to take toilet breaks. They slept in the back of the truck when necessary, and kept Hale under watch the whole time. The company man lived in the city's suburbs and seemed somewhat disheartened at not being able to return home. He sat up and eyed familiar landmarks through the truck's rear window. From the bench, Kirk watched his every move. Hale had been an accommodating prisoner for the entirety of the trip, despite having his hands and feet regularly duct-taped. Memories of Alice and Jenna passed through his mind, and he understood better than anyone what it felt like to be held captive.

Kirk would hate to have to kill the man, so close to his home.

But he would if he had to.

"Don't worry," a weary Kirk said. "You'll be seeing them soon enough."

A despondent and equally tired Hale looked away from the snow-spattered window. The man stared at Kirk, attempting to determine a lie, before returning back to scrolling the cityscape outside.

"What's it look like up there?" Kirk called out to the cab, not taking his eyes off the prisoner.

"Looks like a city," Carma said. "Still snowing."

The snow had started just after dawn and fell in those great big fluffs that reminded Kirk of exploding pillows. They weren't too worried about driving conditions. Hale had informed them that the truck had all-seasonals. For early winter, all-seasonals would do.

Kirk scooted to the end of the bench and wiped away the condensation obscuring the other rear window. Huge structures of stone, steel, and concrete appeared in various shades of gray and winter white. Bonnets of snow covered the trees lining the roadsides. City dwellers left tracks on white sidewalks. Street signs passed by, but Kirk couldn't read them. He peered ahead and saw the behemoth granite bases of tall buildings. One monster in particular captured his attention. The windshield limited the view to only about five or six stories up, but what Kirk saw was enough to chill his innards with dread and excitement. Rows of trees sculpted into the shape of bulbs and covered with tarps dotted the front of the building. Uniformed security guards stood where the snow did not reach, underneath a wide concrete overhang. The name 'Atticus Yor' and its accompanying corporate logo blazed above the revolving doors in regal gold and green.

"That's it," Hale said in a quiet voice.

The building scrolled out of view as the truck continued along the busy boulevard. Carma turned around in her seat. "Where do we go from here?"

"There's an underground parking lot," Hale said. "Just drive around back."

"How do we get there?"

Hale gave directions. Ezekiel drove the truck through a whitening intersection laced with black lines.

"You do anything before you get there?" Carma asked Hale.

The man hesitated. "I call."

Carma tossed Kirk the phone. He got the number from Hale, punched it in, and held the receiver out to the man's profile.

"Yeah," Hale muttered into the device. "We're here."

A voice spoke.

"Nah," Hale answered, "just tired. Long night."

He indicated the conversation was over and Kirk tossed the phone onto the bench.

"You did good," Kirk said.

Hale didn't answer.

"Now, you can drive this thing?" Carma asked.

"Yeah," the man said.

"Good," Carma said. "Douglas is going to cut you free and Ezekiel is going to pull over. You're going to take the wheel. I'll be sitting right behind you with a gun aimed at your lower back. You do whatever you have to do to enter the parking lot. Take us where you'd take any other body. Got that?"

"Yeah."

"Do all that and you'll live. Simple."

Hale didn't respond.

Ezekiel pulled over to the curb and Hale took over at the wheel. As promised, Carma sat behind him and jammed an UMP-9's barrel into Hale's lower back.

"Here we go," Carma said and slapped him on the shoulder.

The truck rolled towards a squat concrete building erected in front of a closed gate. The Atticus Y logo shone upon the structure's brow. Hale halted the truck, lowered his window, and handed his card to a security officer. No words were exchanged. Kirk waited, holding his breath, and when the silence stretched just a little too long, he shot a concerned look at Carma.

Just as Hale got his security card back.

"All good?" Carma asked.

"Yeah, all good."

"You guys normally don't talk much?"

"No," Hale replied, staring ahead at the sealed gate. "It's a different guy on today. And this is sorta… routine. AY gets deliveries all the time."

Just ahead, under the falling snow, the gate crackled to life. It lifted slowly, revealing a sloping concrete cavern. Fat tubes of fluorescent lighting lined the ceiling. Yellow reflective paint covered the pavement in broken, glowing dashes. Daylight receded.

"Drive on," Carma instructed.

The truck dipped as it rolled down the incline, the engine roaring in the confined space. The interior darkened around them as the truck descended. Two levels, three. Cars gleamed wetly beyond brightly lit security checkpoints. Men and women stood inside small security offices, their postures as stiff as faceless mannequins. Hale ignored them. He carefully completed a turn, bringing another ramp into view. He drove down that, turned, and proceeded down a fifth.

"Whoa," Ezekiel said. "This thing's deep."

"Six levels down," Hale said in a low voice, concentrating on his driving. "Underneath a building with a base the size of a football field. First five levels are all parking spots for regular employees."

"How many workers?" Carma asked.

"I don't know. Six, seven hundred. Maybe a thousand."

"What's this Rose guy into again?"

"Everything."

The truck took a final curve and the ceiling lights brightened to cosmic levels, the glare flashing across the windshield. A loading platform came into view. Three figures stood on it. A huge black wall rose at their backs and disappeared in the lights. One of the men strode casually to the platform's edge, a disk-thin notepad in his hand.

"Stop the truck," Carma ordered.

Hale did.

"Three guys are waiting for us," Carma said. "This normal?"

"They take the package up the freight elevator," Hale said. "That's the elevator's right behind them. That black wall."

"All three?"

Hale thought about it. "Only two. One usually stays back."

"You're not lying to me?"

The fright was genuine. "No! No—that's all true."

Carma studied him. "Where does it go?"

"Don't know. That's beyond me. My job ends when I sign the touchpad."

That made sense.

"Where's this Tracy Wellford?"

"I don't know. She's not always there. Like today."

Given that Hale looked like he was about to shit himself, Carma decided to trust him.

"Drive on," she said, then, "Ezekiel."

The New Brunswick warden climbed out of the passenger seat and went to the rear of the truck. Kirk pulled out a second MP5 from the cabinet. He offered it to Ezekiel.

Who turned his nose up at the weapon.

"You might need it," Kirk cautioned.

"Can't bring myself to use it."

"Take it anyway. Drop it if you have to."

Ezekiel vacillated but took the weapon, clearly unimpressed.

Three men waited upon the platform, standing amongst the near-blinding halos of light. Hale brought the truck around ninety degrees, preparing to put it in reverse. Carma and Kirk exchanged looks, the shade darkened her features.

"Come here," she said.

Kirk obediently went to her side. She indicated him to take a seat, which he did.

"You be careful," she warned him.

"Yeah," he said.

"Hey."

The truck shifted into reverse and, to Kirk's surprise, Carma leaned forward and kissed him, the contact soft and lasting, the effect electric. She held it, longer than she should have, while the truck's backup alarm chirped in their ears. When she finally broke away, Kirk inhaled as if starved for breath.

"Now get going," she ordered, leaning back and adjusting her grip on her UMP-9, the weapon still jammed into the lower back of the driver's seat. "Dumbass."

It took him a second, but Kirk did as he was told. Ezekiel was waiting for him at the back door, a crooked grin distorting his face.

The truck stopped with a shudder, the bumper tapping the platform's edge.

The lead man circled around to the rear, his bald head scrunching into a frown at the lack of people in the truck. Kirk watched him, saw the other two men walk up behind him. All three wore the white coveralls and ball caps of warehouse workers. None of them carried weapons.

No one was expecting the wardens—*living* wardens.

The truck door opened.

Ezekiel aimed his MP5 at the three men, freezing them in place.

"No one moves," Kirk warned them. "Don't even lift a hand."

The warehouse workers appeared ready to shit themselves.

"Get in here," Kirk ordered. "All nice and natural. If one of you shouts or moves, he shoots all three. Move."

At first Kirk thought they weren't going to listen, but then the front man stepped into the interior. That unlocked the other two workers and they got aboard. Kirk closed the door behind them, hiding them from any nearby security cameras.

"Out of those coveralls," Kirk ordered.

The men hesitated before complying, mindful of Ezekiel and his fearsome firearm.

"Back here," Carma said, keeping her own weapon trained on Hale as she directed him out of the driver's seat.

"Don't shoot me," Hale pleaded, his eyes suddenly watering.

"Face the wall," she ordered, placing her back against a cabinet. Quarters grew tight with the additional men.

Hale complied and she planted a foot into the back of his knee. He collapsed, hands splayed against the wall.

"Stay still," Carma commanded, jamming the UMP-9's barrel into his spine.

The workers removed their coveralls. Kirk motioned for them to get on their knees with their hands behind their backs. The duct tape came out, and the wardens mummified the four men.

"Done," Kirk said, tossing away the empty roll. He

pushed a distressed Hale over, who squealed and fell against a rear seat. While Ezekiel held a gun on the men, Kirk pulled out three Kevlar vests from the cabinet, two of which he'd snatched from the dead *weres* in Bryce's pack. They were heavy, but not terribly so, and the wardens helped each other buckling them on.

Carma sniffed at her armor as she donned it. "You clean this thing when I asked you to?"

"I did," Ezekiel said.

"I can still smell blood on it."

Ezekiel shrugged. "There's only so much I can do with disinfectant wipes."

Carma didn't comment on that. She hurried into one of the three sets of coveralls, pulling them on over her vest and regular clothes. The extra layers added an illusionary fifty pounds. She topped off the look with a ball cap.

"Heavy?" Kirk asked.

Carma gave him a hard look.

"Weren't expecting us at all," Ezekiel said, completing his own disguise. "These are just drones."

"You heard him," Carma said, looking to Kirk. "Management's only expecting two to go upstairs. You're in the coffin."

"Doesn't bother me," Kirk said.

He hopped inside the freezer unit, lay back, and relaxed his muscles. The interior fit him easily enough; it was capable of holding perhaps two bodies stacked atop each other. Carma handed him a pair of submachine guns and extra magazines.

"All set?" she asked once done.

Kirk nodded.

She closed the freezer's lid.

They left the bound men in the truck and rolled Kirk to the freight elevator. Ball caps lowered, Ezekiel pushed while Carma walked alongside, hiding her UMP-9 between the freezer unit and her leg. When they reached the huge doors, she pushed a button.

The outer panels slid up and out of sight with a whisper. Ceiling lamps illuminated the inside of the elevator car and revealed a second set of doors at the back. Brown paneling covered the walls. Carma stepped into the spacious cavity, well aware that an unknown number of her kind had been brought to this place, feeling as if she were walking inside a giant's coffin. She checked for security cameras, lifting her head slowly, until she spotted one in the back corner. She turned smoothly, keeping her gun hidden. Ezekiel pushed the freezer in, keeping his head lowered as if laboring with the unit.

There were only two buttons on the elevator's control panel. Carma pushed 'UP'. The doors closed with a hiss and the elevator rose.

The two wardens kept their heads down, but Carma rested one hand on the freezer's lid, softly patting the surface as if to reassure its occupant. In truth, she was nervous. Hale might've been bluffing after all. Any number of little details, wrong moves, or flinches might give them away. But she hoped that, despite the security measures, time might have dulled their watchfulness, blunted the elder's alertness.

Despite that thought, her gun hand was slick with sweat. She looked up, searching for an indicator as to what floor they were passing. There was nothing of the sort.

Ten seconds.

Twenty.

Thirty.

Holy shit. Carma wondered how tall the building was.

Forty seconds.

Fifty.

The elevator slowed to a stop.

"This is it," she whispered out of the corner of her mouth.

"'Bout fuckin' time," Ezekiel growled back.

"Think anyone noticed I'm a girl?"

"Or that I'm a short bastard?"

The doors pulled apart, opening into a well-lit room with marble flooring. High ferns hid the corners. Two security guards, visible from the shoulders up, sat behind a wide desk as if on guard in a bunker. A third man looked upon Ezekiel and Carma with a question forming on his face. The fourth person, however, standing at the far end of the desk and wearing a well-cut black and red suit, was a woman.

The puzzled guard raised a hand. "You're not—"

Carma brought up the UMP-9 and fired. The burst cut the guard in two and flung him away. Without pause she turned and sprayed the two guards behind the desk, riddling heads and shoulders. Paper flew as if caught in a wind storm. Coffee cups danced. A dish of candy exploded.

The woman screamed and ran, but Ezekiel caught her shoulder before she rounded a corner.

With a yell, she took his offending hand, twisted it, and launched the warden ass over tits into a nearby wall. Ezekiel crumpled to the base.

"Freeze!" Carma barked and fired just to prove a point. Expensive wood paneling and plaster blew apart in dazzling explosion of chips and powder.

The woman stopped and raised her hands with a frightened grimace.

"Against the wall," Carma barked. The woman obeyed, backing up just as a chagrined Ezekiel regained his feet.

"You killed them," the woman said, horrified.

"You Tracy Wellford?" Carma asked and slapped a hand on the freezer. The lid popped open and Kirk sat up, bringing up one of the MP5s.

The woman's shock grew when she saw who it was, and Carma knew she had her woman. It took a moment but Wellford eventually nodded.

"Where's Rose?" Kirk demanded.

Wellford wasn't a striking woman, with her hair cut far too short and her round face touched up with a minimal amount of make-up, but one look informed Carma that she was used to being in charge.

Carma would break her of that.

She fired another burst of automatic fire into the ceiling. It rained plaster. "You heard him, where's Rose?"

"On the forty-second floor," Wellford cringed.

"How do we get to him?" Kirk asked.

Wellford regarded him like a single offensive hair in her soup. "Get to him?"

Carma stuck her gun in Wellford's face.

"Around the corner," the businesswoman spat, her hands curling into fists. "Back there. There's a private elevator. It'll take you straight to him."

Ezekiel peered around the indicated corner and gave Carma and Kirk a thumbs-up.

"So what is this place?" Kirk asked, glancing around.

"Security check point," Wellford explained, attempting to compose herself. "Mr. Rose's personal elevator starts here. No one goes up without an appointment."

"What's at the top? More guards?"

Wellford hesitated. "No."

Carma pushed the gun's black mouth closer to her nose.

Wellford swallowed. "An assistant went up there. Not ten minutes ago, but no one else. No guards."

"You got any duct tape?" Carma asked her.

That confused the woman. "What? No."

"Too bad," she gestured with her gun. "Lead the way."

The notion shocked Wellford.

"Get your ass moving," Carma ordered and that got the business-type going. Carma followed. Kirk and Ezekiel joined them at the private elevator. The businesswoman pressed a white button centered in a gold-plated interface.

Carma frowned at the New Brunswick warden. He looked away in embarrassment.

"Wasn't expecting it," Ezekiel muttered.

"What's this?" Kirk asked.

"Ezekiel got his ass karate-tossed," Carma explained with a disdainful shake of her head.

That put a little smile on Kirk's face. "That so?"

Ezekiel cleared his throat.

The ding of the arriving elevator saved the warden from answering.

39

They crowded into the elevator, facing a glass wall and a horizon where ominous clouds smothered the skyline. When the lift ascended, the overhead lights dimmed, only to be replaced by thousands of city lights twinkling to life outside, illuminating the snowy metropolis in a universe of stars. Vehicles streaked up and down grid-perfect highways, aiming cones of light. Kirk gazed at the awakening city and the clouds hanging above it all. He drank in the sight, marveled at it, knowing he might not see another ever again.

Carma stood between him and Wellford, not a foot away.

"Noticed you killed those guards back there," Kirk said to Carma as the elevator whisked them to higher levels.

"Us or them," Carma explained. "I have a feeling whoever's up here has an idea of what's going on, but the corporate ladder is just too good to give up. That right, Tracy?"

Wellford didn't answer, but she shivered at the accusation.

"Thought so," Carma said. "So who's up there again? You said an assistant?"

Wellford nodded.

The soft thump of passing floors filled the ensuing silence, as haunting as a heartbeat.

"The elders are rich," Kirk murmured.

Wellford didn't comment. He didn't worry about her. He'd get his answers from Rose.

Lights marking each individual floor flashed by, running across their features. The city glowed beyond the shatterproof walls, and for a moment Kirk had the odd feeling of standing within a brilliant glass of champagne, bubbles and all. He noticed his reflection in the clear surface. Carma regarded the city, her face reflected as a heavenly constellation.

And as they rose higher, her eyes drifted to his.

The elevator slowed to a stop. The doors parted with a whisper, exposing a wide corridor. Bright overhead lights shone and flashed like lens flares upon polished walls of copper. The metal surfaces were cut into careful quarters and framed in thick slabs of elegant oak. A collection of white and gold Ming vases surrounded a redwood desk, the furniture's lines and points highlighted by gold trim. The accompanying chair resembled something better suited to a cockpit. On one corner of the desk rested a brass leaf, where a single strand of incense burned, the smoke a thin wire to the ceiling. Calcutta spice, exotic and calming, lingered and thickened the air.

"Jesus," Carma muttered, gawking at the colorful Xuande ceramics.

Her nerve returning, Wellford cast a disdained look at the barbarous lot of them. Carma pushed her off the elevator. Kirk and Ezekiel followed, attracted to the mesmerizing entrance at the end of the corridor.

The copper walls, stretching from ceiling to baseboards, ended in a closed set of double doors that might've been taken from a medieval castle. An actual spiked mace decorated one half of the portal while a curved sword adorned the other.

"You're the receptionist?" Carma asked as she turned to Wellford.

She drew herself up. "*I'm* a personal assistant."

"Then move your personal ass," she said, pushing Wellford.

As they walked by the desk, Ezekiel traced a finger across the cobalt pigmentation decorating the nearest vase. "These things—"

"Worth millions, yeah, I know," Carma cut him off. "Tongue in, Ezekiel."

"This is how they're able to keep us in money," an equally awed Kirk whispered, nudging a stalled-out Ezekiel. "They can afford to."

"You know what's interesting?" Carma asked as they approached the magnificent double doors.

"What?" Kirk asked.

"Ms. Wellford hasn't asked one question about who we are or why we're here." Carma grabbed the woman's arm and turned her around. "And I find that pretty goddamn peculiar."

"I…" Wellford's eyes batted like a slot machine taking a kick. "I'm in shock. You have guns—"

"Move," Carma said, twisting her around and keeping a hand on her shoulder.

At that instant, a near overwhelming sense of doom crashed down upon Kirk. Infiltrating the elders' lair—if Rose was indeed an elder—had been exceedingly easy.

Far too easy.

His heightened senses tingled a warning, stopping him not ten feet from the majestic ferociousness of the double doors. Carma noticed and stopped Wellford. A puzzled Ezekiel halted and cocked that hard face that might've once been a soccer ball.

"What?" Carma asked.

"It's too easy," Kirk told her and gestured with his gun. "All of this."

Ezekiel regarded the corridor as if it were a trap.

"We've been careful," Carma said.

"They're waiting for us."

"You think it's a trap?"

"Has to be."

Carma pulled on Wellford's arm, summoning a grimace. "No one knows," the businesswoman said. "I swear. As far as I know, you're supposed to be—"

"Dead?" Carma finished.

Wellford nodded, fearful of the warden's wrath.

"See," Carma declared to the others.

But Kirk wasn't so sure. He expected ninjas to drop from the ceiling any goddamn minute. Or laser beams to erupt from the walls to cut them all to pieces. Maybe even the floor dropping out and dumping them into a spiked punji pit.

"Just keep that gun ready, okay?" Carma instructed him. "And if it is a trap, then get behind me. I'll protect you."

Ezekiel smirked. Kirk kept his smartass comments to himself.

Discussion over, they went to the door.

And opened it.

Despite the combined strength of Ezekiel and Kirk, the twin slabs of hardwood swung open with all the unhurried elegance of a melting glacier. The sprawling room beyond was an extension of the corridor, except far more extravagant. The wardens zeroed in upon the two figures inside, one of whom stood with an incredulous expression. The standing man was dressed for winter, with heavy boots and open coat, revealing a thick sweater. A fur hat rested on the only desk in the room, a piece of furniture so dense and large that it could've been a coffin for an ogre. Behind him was a bank of windows where dark snow fell, obscuring the heavens.

The man—carrying considerable meat on his frame—regarded Wellford first and the gun-toting invaders second.

"Sit down, chunky-soup," Carma warned.

The extra-large individual balked at the command, frowned, and finally regarded the other figure in the room.

Christopher Rose himself.

Rose sat behind a mahogany bunker of a desk, elbows resting on the arms of a chair reserved for high-salaried CEOs. His features were fair, long, and angular to the point of commercially enhanced. Rose's full head of blonde hair was parted on the side, every strand accounted for and combed to the right in a glaze that shone in the room's soft lighting. His tailored suit was of a material unavailable to mere mortals. Even though he was sitting, it was evident he was in exceptional physical shape.

But the surprising thing was, Rose wasn't the aged corporate curmudgeon hooked up to his own private dialysis machine and blood supply.

Rose couldn't have been any older than twenty-five.

Kirk kept his MP5 trained on the boy-king.

Rose looked from his unexpected guests to the man standing before his desk, still refusing Carma's orders.

"She said sit," Kirk repeated, hefting his weapon to his shoulder while fanning out to the right. Ezekiel skirted left, past a bright corridor with a series of closed doors. Carma remained in the center and placed her gun's barrel to Wellford's ear.

Neither Rose nor his bulky man-servant seemed concerned.

"Sit, Blacksmith," the boy-king eventually said.

And Kirk's mind blazed with recognition.

That voice.

Rose was the voice on the cellphone. Rose was an elder. One of *the* elders. The final, damning revelation momentarily rooted the Halifax warden to the spot.

Blacksmith reluctantly sat, his hands clawing into plush armrests, and glared missile-fire at the three hostile arrivals.

"You're the elder," Kirk said.

Rose switched his cold-blooded attention from Blacksmith to the warden. "*An* elder. And you're Douglas Kirk."

Kirk nodded.

"Well," Rose stated softly, remaining seated. "I wasn't expecting you to be so… alive."

The elder's eyes flickered to each warden in turn. The doors to the private chamber had closed without a sound. Carma sat Wellford down in a lavish chair identical to Blacksmith's.

"Carma Jones," Rose said, the words carrying the authoritative quality of a judge. "I'm disappointed in you. And you, Ezekiel Allen."

"Surprised to see us alive?" Carma asked, her UMP-9 positioned at her hip, just behind Wellford's head.

"Yes," Rose admitted. "But mostly disappointed. Especially you, Carma. You had potential. Vast potential. I admit I had plans for you. You would have risen very high in our organization."

"Never was one for kissing the boss's ass," Carma said.

"Evidently."

The conversation lulled. Kirk approached the desk, weapon pointed at the elder. A phone set rested upon the wood's surface, next to a leather-bound day planner and a computer terminal in the shape of a church steeple. The warden stopped when there was no way he could miss, short of an earthquake toppling the building.

"So then," Rose said. He folded his hands in his lap and pushed himself back into his chair. "You're here. You made it. Despite our best attempts to kill you. Congratulations."

"Call off the hunt," Kirk ordered. "Right now."

"Call off the hunt," Rose repeated with an astonished chuckle. "Just like that."

Kirk nodded.

"That will take some time."

"To make a couple phone calls? Best start now."

"And afterwards?"

"I have questions."

Rose hadn't blinked in a very long time. "I suppose you do." He made no move for the phone, however.

That irritated Kirk. "Make the call."

"Oh, I will, but before I do I have some questions of my own."

"Make the call," Kirk insisted, his voice rising.

"Or you'll shoot me?" Rose smirked. "You'll shoot an elder. With that?"

"You didn't seem to mind having folks shoot us," Carma answered. "Regular people, too."

"They were private contractors," Rose explained with an uninterested shrug. "Mostly human, granted, but hardly regular. We use them when necessary, when the task is considered beneath the regular wardens. When we do use them, naturally we arm them. Hardly seems fair to send someone after such dangerous game without properly outfitting them first, doesn't it?"

The elder smiled, displaying a perfect set of teeth, and refocused upon Kirk. "The police reports I've read described Barronni had been partially eaten. You've been feeding, haven't you, Douglas?"

Rose *tsked*. "Naughty, naughty."

Kirk adjusted his grip on the MP5, but no longer felt confident in the weapon.

"I haven't received any reports yet regarding Bryce and his pack at Ezekiel's home," Rose continued. "That was a short-lived fire. Intense, but short lived. I would wager, however, that when I do see a report, bodies will have missing pieces. Am I correct?"

Kirk didn't answer.

Rose watched him with subdued delight. "There's feeding, Douglas, and then there's gluttony. You'll have to learn to control that, somehow."

"Yeah," Kirk said, "that's one thing that's been bothering me."

Rose smiled. "*One* thing."

"Yeah, one." Kirk indicated his gun. "Then there's this. And all that other stuff. Why did you kill Morris and Ross? And why are you trying to kill me? I'm not sick. I'm stronger, faster, and I heal quicker now. Even from silver wounds. That has to be of some value to you, to find out what's going on with me. Maybe to even offer, I dunno, treatment?"

"Treatment," Rose's smile stayed in place. "There's so much you don't understand."

"Why don't you enlighten me?"

"Very well," Rose said, blinking as if incredibly weary. "But that will require me to start at the beginning. Are you willing to listen?"

"We got time."

Rose raised an eyebrow. "We'll see, won't we? Do you know where the earliest werewolves appeared?"

"No."

"Of course not. The neophytes rarely bother with their history. Let me educate you. Ours is an ancient species, Douglas. Ancient. Spawned from the blackest magic. By witches, for reasons time forbids me to explain. The first werewolf was cursed, doomed to hunt the night as a beast. A man becomes a monster during a full moon, craves human meat, and never is able to marry his beloved. To age at a trickle, while his friends and family wither, die, and become dust. Mere words don't adequately describe the horror of such a fate. One has to live it to fully appreciate it. Isn't that right?"

Kirk didn't answer.

"It is," Rose continued. "Most certainly is. Ah, of course there are individuals today who would embrace such a condition, but back then it was indeed a curse. Not even the witches fully understood the sorcerous power they'd unleashed. Those bitches never expected their magic to work so *well*. The power they uncorked twisted the first man in unpredictable ways. They also never expected the first *were* to *adapt* to the curse over time. To *embrace* the curse. The passing of centuries can twist one's moral values. It can make one question one's existence and what lurks beyond death. It changes a person. Loneliness? Well, no witch foresaw werewolves being able to propagate their species with a single bite, enabling that first *were* to form a new family. Feasting upon human flesh? There are innumerable accounts of survival in the wild or at sea, where the survivors devoured *anything* that would appease their hunger. Raw fish. Worms. Blood. Grass. The bark stripped off a tree. Anything, really. The hunger eventually eclipses the horror of repeat feedings, desensitizes one, until our chosen sustenance becomes nothing more than… food, needed to maintain one's abilities, which are wondrous, indeed.

"When one realizes that the curse is, in reality, a *gift*, one gladly adheres to the rules. It can take years, you understand, but it happens even to the most resistant. Faster, if you witness your peers committing the acts. Those first werewolves eventually embraced the curse, revelled in it, but they realized that, after hundreds of years, they would still grow old and perish. That obviously became a concern. Once you embrace such a life, it's impossible to relinquish it. But the werewolves suspected that, since their very existence originated in black magic, could there not be a way to further extend their life? Perhaps by using the very magic that spawned them in the first place?"

Revulsion surfaced upon Kirk's face. Carma and Ezekiel shifted with unease.

"What did you do?" Kirk asked, dreading the answer.

Rose chuckled. "What the human race is attempting to do now. We studied immortality. Using very un-scientific laboratories and methodology. No stem cell research back then. No test tubes or control groups. We conducted experiments of a different kind. Much more primitive. You would call them bizarre. We even decided not to eat people at all. That didn't work. It weakened us. We've since learned a *were* can still function as a *were* if they subsist on any meat, just not to full potential. We ate herbs and spices with believed mystic properties to no effect. We concocted elixirs of youth that failed miserably. We hunted down witches and forced them to do our bidding, devouring them when they failed. We even appealed to the dark gods called upon by the witches themselves, who originally smote us. All to no avail."

Blacksmith no longer watched Carma and Ezekiel. The big man listened to the elder's history session. The room's air became oppressive, heavy with secrets being revealed. The incense from Wellford's desk penetrated the double doors and wafted through the office chamber, its fragrance thick on the air.

Rose gathered his thoughts, remembering things perhaps best left forgotten. "Those were dark times, indeed. Desperate times. You have no idea. When you've outlived everything around you and your aging bones become a prison, well, you'll do anything to prolong the inevitable. Anything. At night, there were those amongst us who swore they could hear those old spellcasters cackle at our dilemma, dancing jigs beyond the grave. Their curse had worked after all, or so it seemed. Despite our best attempts, we were still, ultimately, doomed.

"Until one day. As cliché as it might sound, the first *were*, well into his years and close to dying, decided to climb a mountain, to sip from a spring purported to have magical properties. Utter bullshit, as you can imagine, but then, well, we were still a superstitious lot. He selected one other *were* to accompany him, the first person he'd bitten and turned.

So they went, and disappeared for days. *Weeks.*"

"When the pair finally came back down the mountain, it wasn't a pair at all. It was only the first victim of the creator's bite. A *were* called Rodin. Rodin told us a horror story, of how he and the creator scaled a mountain, hand over hand without any aid, higher and higher. Of how the creator's handhold failed, resulting in a fall, and how the creator reached out at the last moment and clutched Rodin's ankle, dragging him down into a deep chasm. They landed upon a bed of rocks, breaking their bodies. With nothing to eat, their healing abilities were severely tested. They changed into wolves so that their bones would mend, their cuts would heal, but that only prolonged the torture. The chasm was deep. Far too deep for either to simply climb out. They doubted anyone would find them before they finally perished, shriveled into desiccated skin and bones. In those days, we believed only time and fire could end a *were*'s existence. Just those two. But a new way was about to be discovered. So, there they were, Rodin and the creator, at the very bottom of the mountain's throat. In the dark. Starving. Stricken with thirst. And, above all, *angry*. Rodin was angry at the creator for clutching his ankle and pulling him down. In a very short time they were two trapped rats. They slung threats at each other. The threats became claws. Fights ensued, each one more serious than the last. Three, I believe, the final one being to the death, where it was discovered a werewolf's jaws could slay another of its kind by ripping out its throat. These days, on the rare occasion that a werewolf kills another, it's impossible not to consume some of the meat and blood, but the effects aren't really noticeable and soon subside. That day, however, Rodin killed the creator and, being so utterly famished, ate his flesh. Drank his blood. And when a pair of human shepherds stumbled upon him, he'd already consumed all of the creator over the span of twelve days. Right down to the very bones, which he cracked open for the marrow. During that time, he found himself revitalized, energized. He believed it was from feeding, and not what he was feeding upon. When the shepherds pulled him out with their ropes, Rodin devoured them as reward, but the taste of man did nothing for him. He came down from the mountain, craving *were*. And shortly after, he shared that knowledge with a few selected others. Those who weren't part of that group were the first to be eaten, and when they were consumed, Rodin and his *weres* experienced increased strength, endurance, and speed. Even healing. And, most importantly, youth. Aging had been arrested after the consumption of *weres*, but eventually, they realized they had to eat again. And once a regular pattern was established, it was discovered that appearances could actually be reversed to a more youthful hue. To a point, of course."

"Oh my god," Carma said softly.

In the elder's eerie pause, the words equaled a thunderclap.

"God had revealed one of the great mysteries of the ages to us," Rose smiled at Carma. "It wasn't a mistake. We'd discovered immortality. We weren't... cannibals. In our minds, we were consuming a lesser species. A sub-species.

One that would become entirely domesticated. We'd become an apex predator, and we once again laughed at those believing they'd cursed us."

"You mean..." Kirk lowered his weapon and stared. "That I..."

"You're an elder," Rose stated, watching for a reaction.

The others looked to Kirk with expressions of horrified wonder.

The knowledge staggered the Halifax warden. "This is insane."

"Is it?" Rose glared back. "Not in the least. From that time on, a select few, the eldest of us, worked out the conditions for our survival going through the centuries. Humanity could never know about our existence, of course, that was a given, but neither could the regular *were* populace. And as the humans fed the lesser werewolves, selected *weres* would, in turn, feed us. Of course, a herd of werewolves has to be carefully managed to avoid any unpleasant uprisings. So we established the warden system. Assigned certain werewolves to function as sheriffs. When in fact..."

Rose paused for effect.

"...you're nothing more than sheepdogs. Guarding and later killing the ones we deem ready for the slaughter, ringing the dinner bell once done. Of course, there are times when we cannot wait for a *were* to be culled from the packs, so certain elders within our inner circle were assigned covert hunts, unknown to the general *were* populace. To fill the larders when necessary."

"I can't believe it," Kirk whispered.

"Wait," Carma said. "Does this happen around the Harvest Moon?"

"Every dog needs to be walked," Rose said. "The Harvest Moon allows all *weres* one night of unrestricted hunting. We believe they need it. Allow them to scratch that itch. Free range, if you will. And if some happen to disappear during that time…"

Rose shrugged, his meaning clear.

"Now, regarding the usage of guns," the elder suddenly resumed. "Do you know how we discovered silver could cause us harm?"

The three wardens didn't answer.

"Of course you don't," the elder said. "I'll tell you. During the Harvest Moon in the year 1136, a Pisan woman grabbed a crude silver knife and stabbed a *were* invading her kitchen, just before she died. That poor beast nearly bled to death before finally putting fire to the wound. Even then, the *were* almost perished. After that, we avoided silver entirely, until we realized the potential of that metal. As a weapon. And as a warden's badge. Give them *something*, we realized. Something to distinguish the wardens from the rest. Something dangerous. Forbidden. Even coveted. Admired."

"Why knives?" Carma cut in. "Why not guns?"

"Carma," Rose addressed her softly. "You were on my list, you know."

"What's the truth, then?" Kirk interrupted. "Knives for us but guns for you, just because it's unwise to arm the peasants?"

"Come now, Douglas," Rose chided. "It's positively

stupid to arm the peasants."

The admission stunned the wardens.

"So Borland was an elder, too?" Kirk asked, regaining his composure and trying to understand.

"No," Rose answered.

"Were the dogs the reason you wanted him dead?"

"Ahhh, the dogs. No, they were unexpected. No, Borland is dead because he refused our invitation. He was on the cusp of becoming an elder and, like you, had the pleasure of being lectured on our history. Unfortunately, after learning about the necessary dietary measures and our true nature, Borland decided he had no wish to partake."

Kirk shook his head. "You said he had dementia. That he was insane."

Rose frowned. "After refusing eternal youth, immortality, and the absolute power and wealth we enjoy? Yes, from our point of view, he was insane."

"He knew about the tracking. The silver?"

"He knew everything."

A gust of wind spattered snow against the darkened windows.

"So I'm an elder," Kirk said slowly. "Because I ate another *were*."

"You're obviously experiencing the benefits," Rose acknowledged. "But, not quite. Not until we permit it. No one expected you and Morris to do what you did after executing Borland, but those kinds of transgressions do occur from time to time. When they do, we dispatch them the best way we know how. Send in a designated agent.

Which was Bailey in this case. And if the agent fails, we use secondary measures. Kill teams. Armed to the teeth, of course. Or wardens. What or who we utilize depends upon several factors."

"So that's why you wanted to kill us?" Kirk licked his lips. "Me and Morris, and Ross Kelly?"

"Ross Kelly?" the slightest knot of puzzlement upon the elder's forehead.

"The Newfoundlander. The one I changed."

"Ah. Him. The man you turned without permission. Douglas. One of your duties is to prevent lesser werewolves from expanding their pack without permission. You know that. We didn't think a chosen warden would ever do such a thing. I know you believed you were saving the man's life, but seriously, what do we care about… them?"

Rose chuckled.

"You bastard," Kirk said quietly.

The elder grew serious. "But you had to be put down. All of you. You doomed yourself with that first forbidden bite. I understand the circumstances, but you must realize, ultimately, ours is a very exclusive club. We have strict rules. A stringent selection process."

"So," Carma began, "we're weaker if we don't eat people, but we can still function. We operate at full strength if we do eat people. But if we eat another *were*, we become you."

Rose nodded.

"So why were we bugged?" Carma asked.

The elder smiled. "Even cattle are tagged. From a logistics point, it's easier to keep track of small herds rather than large ones. In time, however, we plan to tag all of you. It's best that way. You can't imagine how delighted I've been with recent developments in surveillance applications."

"The knives were a surprise," Kirk said.

"I know they were," Rose agreed with a flicker of sympathy. "I know. But you were never supposed to know about them, you see. Never. And we never expected any of this to happen. Or you to be without your phone or knife. How did you discover the devices, by the way?"

"Doesn't matter," Kirk said. "As long as we solved that mystery. Right?"

Rose nodded with grim approval. "Yes, Douglas. I believe we were wrong about you. You're one of us. Truly one of us. I see that now. You killed Borland. You survived Bailey and his unfortunate resurrection. You even survived the human contractors sent to kill you and managed not only to elude the werewolf packs on your trail but also discover the various tracking devices we utilize. All of that culminated in your unexpected arrival here. I must say... we admire that level of tenacity. People refer to us as fictional monsters, but they're sorely mistaken. We're *survivors*, you see. We've taken curses and willed them into gifts, transformed disadvantages into advantages, flipped defeat into victory. As you have done."

"You making me an offer?" Kirk asked, cocking an eyebrow.

"I am," Rose acknowledged. "But I will have to discuss your admission into the order with the others. As I've mentioned, there's a selection process we observe. No one is simply admitted, and we must keep our numbers down. To preserve the werewolf herds, you understand. But every few hundred years or so, because of duty rendered, or as a reward, or simply injecting new blood into the fold, we will admit a new elder."

"Like Borland?" Kirk asked.

Rose hesitated. "Yes. Like Borland."

"Let me get this straight," Carma interjected. "Borland knew everything. Everything you just told us, and he still said no to you."

"Borland was a fool," Rose scoffed. "He had his opportunity and cast it away. He's been dealt with. Those infected dogs were a surprise, as I've mentioned, and something of an insult to what we are. I don't know what he intended to do with such a force, but we were right in putting him down. Thanks to you, Douglas."

"Me and Morris you mean."

"That's right."

"But Morris wasn't elder material."

"Obviously not."

Rose studied the three wardens in turn, but returned his gaze to Kirk.

"You *know* what power surges through you, Douglas," the elder said. "You know. There's no going back to what you were. Not after tasting it. There was one elder who refrained from eating *were* flesh and she was seized by violent bouts of hunger that nearly drove her mad. That episode even threatened the veil shielding our existence. The cravings left her in the end, though I remember it taking months. It was a hellish experience for her. Not unlike a person attempting to cure himself of an opiate addiction."

"You mean I can go back?"

The question perplexed Rose, and he frowned with incomprehension. "To what? To being just a werewolf? A servant? Why would you? Look at me. My physical appearance. My obvious position and wealth. I'm offering you the very *same,* Douglas. Truthfully, how old do you think I am?"

Kirk stared, refusing to chance a guess.

"You are one of us," Rose said, but then his expression hardened.

"There is one issue, however."

"Yeah? What's that?"

The elder took his time, studying the newest prospect, before he finally nodded at Ezekiel and Carma. "Execute them."

Kirk's mouth dropped open.

"We have a *very* stringent selection process," Rose explained smoothly as if Ezekiel and Carma weren't present at all. "And rarely accept new blood into the fold. It's a carefully balanced pyramid of power, you understand. Resources must be limited and managed. When we do choose an elder, it's only one. Now that you know everything, it shouldn't be a difficult choice. Kill them. It's not hard. Wouldn't you rather join us at the table rather than continue feeding at the trough?"

The Halifax warden had no answer.

"Kill them," Rose said curtly. "Or as hell as my witness,

I'll muster every level of law enforcement to track you down, from the federal police to the security intelligence service and every country cop in between. I'll employ every last assassin and kill team at my disposal to hunt you down. I'll mobilize every last *were* on the continent and charge them with bringing in your head. You won't have a moment's peace. Not an hour's rest. And in the end, when the hounds finally close in on you, you'll probably be grateful for your approaching death. And if you shoot me, that will only harden the resolve of the remaining elders to hunt you down. We'll make it our life's existence to stomp out the sickened blight that is Douglas Kirk and his companions."

Kirk frowned at the threat.

"Shoot them," Rose insisted, perhaps tired with Kirk's hesitation. "Shoot them now, Douglas. Empty that weapon into their hides and join—"

Kirk and Carma jumped when Ezekiel fired his MP5.

A burst of light cut into Rose's chest, shredding him in a burst of expensive silk and spurting scarlet. The fur hat and computer jumped off the desk. The elder jerked and bucked before he toppled from his chair.

An outraged Blacksmith rose, his hands clenching.

Wellford screamed.

Carma stepped away from the businesswoman and shot the man across the knees. Meat and bone blew apart, dropping Blacksmith's face forward onto the floor. A bald spot flashed as he fell. Blood splashed the floor as Wellford screamed even louder. Carma switched her off with a slap to her head.

Ezekiel rushed to the fallen Blacksmith, aimed, and rattled off a burst into the back of his skull. Fragments skittered. Ezekiel altered his aim and emptied the last of the magazine into the corpse's chest, seeking the heart. The weapon eventually ceased firing and he studied it with disdain. After a moment, he allowed the gun to fall from his hands.

The clatter echoed in the room.

In the aftermath, Kirk's nerves unlocked themselves. He realized he still had his own weapon, unfired. He studied the corpses littering the room before meeting Carma's eyes. She set her jaw and held Wellford's quivering shoulder, keeping the businesswoman in check.

Ezekiel stood over Blacksmith's unmoving body, MP5 at his feet. Smoke wafted from the hot barrel.

"The hell was *that*?" Kirk demanded.

Ezekiel shrugged. "Fucker talked too much."

"Douglas," Carma said and indicated the desk, behind which Rose had fallen.

Kirk went to the elder, halting at the expanding pool of blood. Rose was on his chest, face down, and attempting to crawl towards the wall. Blood oozed and filled the smears he left upon the floor. He stopped upon sensing Kirk's approach and looked over his shoulder. A wretched giggle escaped him. Rose achingly rolled himself over, onto his back, and raised a set of red hands in surrender.

Blood traced his smile. His eyes glowed with insane hurt.

"Maybe…" Rose whispered and stopped for a rusty cough. Blood speckled his skin and lips. "Maybe… *he's* one of us."

He cackled softly, a dying man's chug.

The elder might've had a point, but Kirk didn't agree. He hefted his MP5 and placed it on the desk. He extracted a silver knife from his boot, the blade that once belonged to Bryce.

Kirk hunkered down and gripped Rose's chin. The blood made the jawline slippery.

"This is for Morris and Ross," the warden said.

And stabbed the elder through the eye.

For seconds, Kirk wielded that silver blade with bad intentions, making certain there would be no regenerating, no second life, for the thing called Rose. He inflicted so much damage that not even the elder's superior healing ability and resistance to silver would matter. When he was done, he left the weapon straight up in the elder's chest. Kirk sat on the corner of the desk, shaking his head at Carma.

"Don't come up here," he warned her.

"Messy?"

"Yeah."

"You okay?"

Kirk took a few seconds before nodding. His hands trembled so he grasped them in a double fist. Rose's voice haunted his head. An unsmiling Ezekiel stood near Blacksmith's corpse. Wellford shivered in her chair, sniffling and moaning in a low pitch. Kirk silenced her with a look.

The dead continued to bleed.

For long moments, none of the wardens moved.

"Are you there?" the telephone's loudspeaker asked.

40

The three wardens traded surprised expressions before focusing on the desk's telephone set.

"We're here," a wary Kirk answered.

"Douglas," the voice greeted. A different voice. Not so deep, but gruff. One used to giving orders. "I'm surprised at you."

"Thanks," Kirk said, eying the telephone with distrust. He quickly scanned the office, searching for any cameras they might have missed.

"You're probably thinking you're done," the voice stated. "That you've lopped off the dragon's head and the villagers are saved. Not quite."

"Oh. Great."

"I think you and I and your companions have some unfinished business to attend to, don't you agree?"

Kirk looked to Carma. "What kind of business?"

"The killing kind," the voice emphasized. "I'll explain in greater detail once you arrive here. Our meeting isn't one of violence, you understand. It's one of business. Are you willing to meet with me under a flag of temporary truce?"

Needles of ice stabbed at Kirk. He looked to the other wardens. Carma and Ezekiel nodded.

"Sure," he said. "Where are you?"

"I'll make arrangements. Have you killed Rose's bodyguard?"

Kirk glanced at Blacksmith's bleeding carcass. "Uh, the assistant? Yeah, he's dead."

"He's not Rose's assistant. Blacksmith was Rose's bodyguard."

Ezekiel shrugged once again.

"Her name is Wellford," the voice said.

The wardens looked to the woman in the chair.

"I'm... I'm here," Wellford said, her eyes wet and red.

"Wellford, take them to the flight lounge. Allow them every courtesy. See to it that no harm befalls them."

A shocked Wellford gasped. "What? But they—"

"They are traveling to me," the voice cut her off. "Clean up whatever mess they've made there. Business continues. Do you understand?"

A sulky pause. "Yes."

"As of now, you are the acting chief executive of Atticus Yor, until I decide upon a replacement."

"Who are you?" she asked.

"I'm the owner."

That bit of news visibly shocked Wellford, but she composed herself almost immediately upon realizing her promotion.

"Douglas," the voice said.

"Yeah?"

"I don't think I need to remind you, but I will anyway. Don't kill anyone else. Don't kill the pilots. From here on in, your fight is with me. Is that understood?"

Kirk nodded. "It is."

The voice paused, then, "I'll be waiting."

Snow pattered the glass and blotted out the city. Ezekiel took his knife to the dead Blacksmith, ensuring that the man remained deceased. Once he was finished, Kirk picked up the discarded MP5 and offered it to him.

"Take it easy with this thing, Tex," Kirk cautioned.

Ezekiel snatched the weapon away.

Kirk briefly smiled at his companion's reaction. He then saw the corridor across from Rose's desk. The idea of leaving it alone struck him, but the curious part of his mind wanted him to investigate.

He walked towards the hall.

"Where you going?" Carma asked.

"Just checking things out," he answered.

"Wait then," she said and asked Ezekiel to watch the woman.

Carma joined Kirk at the corridor's mouth. They counted two closed doors.

"This place is nicer than my apartment," Kirk observed as he stopped at the first, a heavy slab of custom-fitted oak.

"I'd say."

"Cheeky."

"You said it, not me," she smiled. "Don't put it out there next time."

Kirk opened the door, flicked on a light and, with a whistle, placed one shoulder to the frame. Carma pursed her lips at the opulent spread before her. A king-size mattress covered in maroon comforters was decorated with pulled down sheets of black silk. Matching reading chairs guarded the foot of the bed. A stone fireplace graced the left wall, near a sumptuous cherry wood desk with gleaming brass knobs. The bright cave of a walk-in closet was just past the fireplace. Surrounding it all were a series of oil paintings, some surreal, some not. All depicted the wolf packs prowling the open wild.

The bathroom was located to the right, with an adjoining sauna. Gold fixtures shone under the light, while polished black marble tiling twinkled.

"This wasn't built in a day," Kirk whispered.

"Not even a year," Carma added.

He went to the bed and sat down, dazed by the extravagance. A huge television sat on a coffin-sized stand and was positioned back from the bed. He touched the comforter and was sorely tempted to flop back onto it.

Then he remembered who had slept there.

Carma wandered over and ran a hand over the sheets. "Egyptian. I'd say a thread count around a thousand."

"Nothing but the best," Kirk commented.

"This shit's worth a ridiculous amount of money."

"Money they got."

"Yeah."

"There's nothing here. Let's check out the other rooms."

"Hey," Carma stopped Kirk with a hand. She stepped before him and stared into his eyes.

"What's up?" he asked quietly.

"You really mean to meet him?" she asked.

"Yeah, I do."

"Think that's wise?"

Kirk shrugged. "The way I look at it, we're after the elders. I'm willing to go as far as I have to settle this. I can't go back. If I do, every time I answer my door I'll wonder if it's a trap."

Carma nodded.

"You don't have to go, though," he said.

She smirked. "Yeah, and then wonder what happened to you? Sooner or later, they're going to find out you bit me."

"Tit for tat," Kirk smiled gently.

"I think I prefer to be there. See what he has to say. Don't want to break your ass out of a basement cell a second time."

"I ever thank you for that?"

"Yeah, you did," Carma said. "You saved my life."

For a moment they remained silent, studying each other's eyes.

"Wanna check those other rooms?" he asked her.

"Is there a need?"

"I don't think so," he admitted. "But just to make sure. Someone could be lurking."

That hardened her features.

They went to the second door in the corridor and opened it. Cold air swept past them, and for a moment, Kirk thought a window had been left open. He gazed upon a dining room, one that matched its cousin across the hall, filled with striking décor and colors. A set of silverware covered the tablecloth.

Then he saw the kitchen.

His gut twisted and clenched, acting as a warning not to go any further.

"Dining room for six, easy," Carma said and stepped past him. "And kitchen."

"Yeah," he said from the threshold.

She wandered past the long table. "Looks like a chef's wet dream."

Kirk followed her past the spotless scullery, and saw the freezer door. His blood ran cold at the sight, and it had nothing to do with the temperature.

"You okay?" Carma asked.

"No."

She studied him before glancing at the freezer. Her face grew stern. She lifted her gun, more for confidence than caution, and approached the steel door. Kirk shadowed her, and every step forward felt like edging toward a precipice.

Carma gripped the handle.

"Carma?"

"Yeah?" she asked.

"Maybe… we should leave that."

"You serious?"

"Yeah," he nodded. "I'm serious."

"Might be something in there."

"I don't think there's anything in there."

She considered him for a few heartbeats, then contemplated the door. "We gotta look."

Kirk's heart sank. "Okay."

"You ready then?"

He nodded.

She opened the freezer door, releasing a plume of frozen air.

All thought left Kirk. He stared, his mind reproaching him for ever letting her do such a thing. Carma peered inside and stopped, gawking at what lay at the back of that chilling ice cavern, refusing to look away.

Foodstuffs lined the shelving units on either side of the freezer, but that wasn't what horrified the wardens.

Twinkling in the scant light near the back was a naked torso, hanging from low rafters. Wire bound wrists to a steel bar, suspending the body five feet above the floor, where the legs would've been if they were present. They were not. There was nothing below the hips except a clean butcher's cut. The body's face was destroyed, and a ring of bullet holes riddled the pale blue flesh around the heart. But Kirk recognized one feature.

Recognized it right away, in fact.

Whoever had hung Moses Morris up hadn't bothered to shave off the warden's beard.

They closed the door to the frozen tomb and left Morris where they found him, unable to do anything.

Kirk and Carma returned to Ezekiel and Wellford,

informing them both of what they discovered. Ezekiel's face dropped with shock. Wellford trembled visibly, and Kirk believed her terror was sincere.

Carma directed Wellford to lead them back to the reception area. Once away from the horrors of the main office, Kirk felt a little better.

He'd have to return to that freezer, however, and properly take care of Morris's remains.

Back in the reception area, Wellford grabbed a box of tissues off her desk while the wardens stood in solemn silence.

"Over there," she gasped, her eyes red. "There's an elevator to a flight lounge. You'll find a selection of winter gear. Choose your sizes."

"Winter gear?" Kirk asked. "Where are we going, exactly?"

Wellford cleared her throat and smoothed out the lower parts of her jacket. "I don't really know. Mr. Rose never disclosed the location, but it's north. I've already summoned the pilots."

"Pilots?" Carma asked. "Rose could afford his own pilots?"

Wellford regarded her as though just witnessing a cockroach speak. "Rose has his own airline."

"*Had* his own airline," Kirk corrected.

The new head of Atticus Yor sniffled. She ignored the remark, her hands shaking, and picked up the phone on the desk.

Carma hoisted her UMP-9 to her shoulder.

"I'm just calling the flight staff," Wellford explained. "The helicopter needs to be prepped. Fueled."

Ezekiel stood off to one side, struggling to reload his MP5. "Goddamn piece of—"

"Here," Carma said and took the weapon from him. She replaced the magazine, primed it, and handed it back. Ezekiel muttered his thanks.

"I have to go," Wellford informed them. "I have other duties to attend to."

"You sit the fuck down right there, sister," Carma warned.

Wellford promptly did as she was told, watching the warden with uncertainty.

Carma eventually looked from her to Ezekiel. "You heard everything back there, Ezekiel. Any of that tempt you?"

"What? That immortality shit?"

"Yeah," she said and shared a smile with Kirk. "That immortality shit."

"That's only if I go full cannibal, right?"

"Right again," Kirk said.

The New Brunswick warden screwed up his face. "Don't think so. Think I'll stick to hamburger. Don't need to live past my expiry date."

Kirk looked at Carma. "What about you?"

She took her time answering, but in the end, she shook her head and lowered her eyes.

*

The snow continued to fall under darkening skies.

The helicopter, an AgustaWestland according to one of

the pilots, lifted off from its helipad on the forty-sixth floor of the building. There'd been a few numbers and letters after the name of the machine, but Kirk had soon forgotten those. The bird was a flying executive suite, a penthouse of the skies. He sat facing the cockpit's closed doors and chanced a glance outside his window, taking in the glowing helipad below. When the lights faded out of view, he looked out at the twinkling city and admired its charms.

Wealth, Kirk thought, remembering his concrete pit back in Halifax.

Carma sat across from him, her back to the cockpit. She leaned towards the window, her knees almost touching his. Ezekiel filled a seat on the left side of the helicopter, facing the rear. They wore winter parkas over their Kevlar vests, snow pants, wool hats, and boots, all taken from a small changing room on the building's forty-sixth floor. The helicopter's cabin temperature was comfortable, adjusted for their heavy coats. Wellford, who had recovered quite nicely from the massacre in Rose's office, had explained that during the winter, the CEO would entertain guests by flying them out to private ski resorts. Often, the bigwig business types didn't prepare for such jaunts, so Rose had outerwear of all sizes brought in and stowed away. Rose sometimes flew off to the north himself, disappearing for weeks.

Wellford didn't object to the wardens bringing their automatic weapons onto the flight. Neither did the pilots. The elder on the telephone didn't mention it either.

That was both comforting and worrying.

Kirk tore his attention away from the city below and

marveled at the helicopter's interior once again. The bird wasn't some refitted search-and-rescue two-seater meant to jump between cities. It was the absolute pinnacle of luxury. The cabin was both an immaculate design and an ergonomic delight. The armrests of their leather seats offered all manner of comfort, even controls to activate built-in massage rollers. There were flip-out tables, built-in notebook computers, and individual pull-down screens for movies and TV. An additional eight seats were separated from the first class by a polished redwood partition. A small kitchenette was located behind it all, along with a full bathroom.

Whatever Rose might've been, he certainly wasn't one to spare expense.

"Ladies and gentlemen," a pilot's voice issued through the speakers. "Our course is plotted and we have a long trip ahead, so I'd suggest you get comfortable. We'll be traveling at about three hundred kilometers an hour, or about one-ninety miles. Don't worry about fuel as we've topped off the main tanks and reserves. I've been told to extend to you every hospitality, but because of the late hour, there will be no in-flight service. If you do need a drink or snack, feel free to raid the kitchenette at the back of the plane. I believe it was fully stocked. That's all."

Kirk undid his belt buckle and stood on uneven feet. He went to the cockpit door and opened it.

A clean-shaven man in uniform turned his attention away from an assortment of back-lit instruments.

"Where're we going?" Kirk asked.

"North," the pilot answered.

"Where north?"

"Atticus Y has a remote chateau up there. The CEO heads up there for hunting. Nice spot. Just past a park reserve."

"How far away is it?"

The pilot smiled. "Get some sleep. It's a three-hour flight."

"Three…" Kirk faltered, surprised by the distance. He couldn't do the numbers in his head but figured sleep would be in order. He closed the door and returned to his seat.

"How far are we going?" Carma asked.

"Far. Three hours."

"There's nothing up there," Ezekiel said.

"There's something," Kirk told him. "'Cause we're heading there."

"I'm still wondering why no one tried to gun us down in that changing room," Carma mused. The three of them were very much aware of the possibility before getting decked out in winter outwear. To their surprise, however, no one had attempted to kill them.

Which magnified Kirk's suspicion about the meeting.

"This is better," he admitted. "Like the main event."

He patted the locked and freshly loaded MP5. Whatever waited for them up north, Kirk felt confident they could handle themselves. He looked forward to confronting the voice on the telephone.

"I think he just didn't want us ripping the hell out of his building," Carma said, not caring if the pilots heard or not.

Ezekiel grunted agreement.

"Well," Kirk said, "we'll find out soon enough. Maybe he wasn't behind the hunt. Or Morris's and Ross's deaths. Maybe Rose was operating alone."

Ezekiel didn't appear to buy it. Neither did Carma.

"Not that it matters," Kirk said. "We go up there, hear what he has to say, then kill the bastard—"

"Kill the bastard," Carma cut in. "My, my, Douglas. What big teeth you have."

Kirk didn't react. "And then we spend a year in rehab."

"Rehab."

"Been thinking. The hunger isn't as strong when in wolf form. I don't know if the elders know that or not. Doesn't really matter if they do. They said that the cravings leave after some months. Maybe being in wolf form is the key. Anyway, I'm tired of the city. Spending some time up north might be the thing to do. Detox. From all of this. What do you think? You interested?"

Carma was surprised. "You're asking me to spend a year with you in the bush?"

"Well…" Kirk gently smiled. "A few months at least. Until we're all better."

To his surprise, Carma smiled back. "Sounds good."

"Fuck that," Ezekiel snorted, effectively shattering the moment. "I'm not hanging out here for a few months."

"Not one for the country?" she asked him.

"Not for a year," Ezekiel said. "I like both worlds. Once this is all done, I'm getting back to my territory and finding a new apartment."

"Might not be so easy," a pensive Kirk said.

"Gonna try anyway."

Kirk cocked an eyebrow at Carma.

She didn't look away. After a few seconds she leaned forward, studying Kirk's face. "You know something?"

"What?"

"The lines. Around your eyes. The crow's feet?"

"What about them?"

"They're finer," she said. "Not as noticeable."

Kirk touched his face. "You sure?"

Carma sat back and smiled.

"I'm sure," she said.

One hour into the flight, Ezekiel snarked in his sleep, shifted, and turned towards his window. The startling snore roused Kirk from his own doze. He never could truly rest while sitting up. It was too uncomfortable for him.

He looked up and saw Carma eyeing him.

"Hi," he said.

"Hi," she said back. "Couldn't sleep?"

"Not like this. No."

"He's having a pretty good snooze there."

"I just have a hard time sleeping while sitting upright."

"Yeah, I remember."

"You do, huh?"

"Yeah."

Kirk was very aware of how quiet it was in the cabin and unsure of what to say next.

To his surprise, Carma took care of that for him.

"Douglas… do you ever wonder why I changed you all those years ago?"

The question took him completely off-guard. Of course he wondered. He wondered for a long time until he forced himself to stop wondering, because wondering was driving him insane.

But to her question, his voice failed him, so he shook his head.

"Because I didn't want to be alone," she said, peering into his eyes. "Not through all those years. And you know why I left?"

Kirk could barely breathe, remembering his dreams. He shook his head again.

"It wasn't about that thing," she said softly. "About you not knowing who you were. Not really. That was just… smoke. I knew what you were. Who you were. I left because of my own guilt. Because I realized what I had done to you. How I'd… cursed… a good person. It took me a while to figure that out. Took me a little longer to get up the guts to tell you, that what I did was wrong. And if you remember, I'm not the best at admitting when I'm wrong."

Kirk smiled. He didn't remember that in the least, nor did it bother him.

"And now, well," Carma shrugged. "Now I realize I've missed you all those years. How's that for flip-flopping?"

Kirk couldn't respond right away. After a second's flutter, he managed to whisper, "That is something."

"It is pretty big." She smiled and took a breath. "Sorry I left."

Kirk was about to respond when Ezekiel's snore cut through their conversation like a buzz saw.

"I'm glad you're here," Kirk whispered close to Carma's ear.

"Me too."

"I never forgot you."

"You never forget your first one," she murmured.

Kirk couldn't agree more.

Then, deciding upon something, she leaned towards him.

And somewhere over the Manitoba wilderness, they kissed.

*

The helicopter descended, whipping the night into a blizzard that sought to rip the skin from the mechanical bird's hide. Kirk awoke with a start, met Carma's drawn expression, and immediately looked out the window. He couldn't see shit.

"I think we're here," Ezekiel muttered over the noticeable whine of the engines.

A short time later, the helicopter bumped and wobbled before settling down upon a solid platform. One of the pilots emerged from the cockpit.

"Last stop," he announced, bright-eyed and far too supercharged. He immediately started unlocking the outer door. When he opened it, a powerful blast of snow shoved its way through.

"Just backwash from the rotors," the pilot shouted as the

meager heat in the cabin was sucked out into the night. "Nothing serious. Step out and walk straight ahead. Someone will meet you."

Kirk and Carma exchanged looks. They both wondered if they needed a hostage. In the end, she shook his head. Message received, Kirk undid his seatbelt and headed toward the hatch.

"Have a good night," the pilot said pleasantly.

Kirk wondered if the man was high. He faced the open hatch as the others lined up behind him. Snow peppered his face as he took his first step onto the landing pad.

And dropped into a blizzard.

Freezing winds battered his face and quickly frosted his beard and eyebrows. He lowered his head into the gusts, cringing at the stinging ice. Landing lights turned the world into a screaming curtain of white. A blast of wind staggered him as Carma bumped him from behind. She grabbed his shoulder, and they shambled away from the heart of the storm. A clatter of metal indicated that the pilot had resealed the helicopter's door. The rotor blades' whine heightened in pitch.

Glowing moons outlined the periphery of the landing zone, flickering in and out of sight through the raging snow. Kirk fought against the helicopter's rotor wash and stomped towards the ghostly outer ring.

A figure materialized, tall and broad and unmoving in the mounting tempest, blocking the way. Kirk stopped at the sudden appearance and squinted at the stranger. A parka hood was pulled tight over the figure's head, hiding his face against the blowing snow.

Kirk raised his MP5 and hoped to God the weapon hadn't somehow frozen.

The figure didn't move at all.

"You the owner?" he barked over the howl of the ascending helicopter. The landing pad was a blinding smear.

The stranger didn't reply.

"Hey! I said—"

The stranger turned around and leisurely walked ahead into the flurry. The snow obscured the figure's wide back. Only two steps and he almost vanished into the white night.

"Follow him," Carma said, urging Kirk. Ezekiel appeared on his left and the three of them got moving. Overhead, the helicopter lifted into the night sky, showing an underbelly alive with festive lights of red and green. It turned and swooped to the south, thundering over a black wilderness. Kirk shivered despite his winter outerwear and turned his attention back to his mysterious guide.

The stranger led them along a wide path choked with knee-deep snow, plodding farther into the dark without a word. Coniferous trees covered in white rose up on either side of the little party and prevented them from losing their way. The lights of the landing pad disappeared behind them at some point and the snow and wind increased until Kirk thought he was walking along the back of a moving freight train. At times, a bough reached out of the dark and grazed his forehead, and he flinched from the contact.

"Where are we going?" Kirk shouted toward the eerie golem on the trail ahead.

And got no answer.

Where the hell are we? Kirk thought. The idea that they'd been dropped into the unchartered wild of northern Manitoba in the dead of night, with a snowstorm coming on, no less, left him with a feeling of rising dread.

Growing impatient with the lack of answers, Kirk sped his pace, cutting down the distance between him and the silent guide. The stranger's back came into view, broad and bowed and several inches taller than Kirk. He grabbed an arm just above the elbow. The action stopped the larger man and he turned around.

A face of bone peered out from underneath the parka's drawn hood, the empty eye sockets black and staring and implying a question. Shadow cloaked half the skull's features while snow clung to bone. A sinister smile missed its upper right incisor.

Kirk faltered and retreated a step. Snow blasted through that space, but the stranger remained.

Kirk remembered his gun and lifted it enough to aim at the guide's knees.

The blizzard whipped them with icy gales and screamed for action, yet the towering guide made no move.

Neither did Kirk.

The skeletal face turned back to its path and the figure resumed its march.

Not exactly sure what he'd just seen, it took a nudge from Carma to get Kirk moving.

Onward the little band slogged, through white drifts and freezing winds. The cold air feasted on Kirk's bare skin. He wasn't tired, but he worried about the frost gathering on his

MP5 and frequently rubbed the barrel clean. Every gust brought back memories of a fearsome blizzard bent on scrubbing an island off the face of the planet. Kirk checked every so often to make sure Carma and Ezekiel followed.

Some twenty minutes later, the trees on either side of the path vanished, and the wind slammed into the three wardens, bending them at the hips. The guide lumbered towards a wall of snow-spattered pitch, and it took Kirk a second to realize what he was looking at, just as the blackness split at the edges. A door opened and light spilled out, casting a fiery hue over the stranger's deep tracks. The man kicked his boots clean and, with a thick arm, motioned for the wardens to hurry.

The storm raged as the stranger closed the heavy door, cutting off all wind as if sealing them within a vast tomb. A single electric lamp shimmered on a wall, stretching the wardens' shadows beneath a vaulted ceiling. Stacked cedar surrounded them, while irregular stone tiles covered the floor. The wardens pulled back their hoods in awe of the grand entryway. Kirk's ears buzzed with the absence of the howling wind, but heard the storm's fury from the far side of that door.

"Whoa," Carma whispered.

The stranger threw back his hood, uncovering a sweaty shock of hair. The skull came off next, and the mask dangled from the man's hand. Kirk stared at a round face, the skin weather-browned and dark. Scars crisscrossed the ogre's complexion, some more gruesome than others. Deep grooves that might've been dug out by a crow's beak.

The man pulled off his coat and hooked it on a high wooden peg set into one of several metal racks. He wore a sweater underneath, along with faded jeans. He bent over and removed his boots, placing them on a wide vent cut into the floor.

Then he directed his attention at the three visitors.

"Your boots," the man grunted. He waited.

The wardens hesitated, unsure of what to do, then Carma put one foot to the other and pulled hers off. "What the hell. He's not asking for the guns, right?"

Kirk supposed she was right.

Kirk got his own boots off and when he did, the guide placed them with the other footwear on the floor vent.

"Coats, too?" she asked.

But the large man didn't answer her question.

"This way," the ogre growled, beckoning with a finger before heading through an open church-like archway, into a log hallway where his head barely cleared the ceiling. His socks whispered on the stone floor, the flat surfaces gleamed within pockets of incandescent candlelight.

The wardens watched the figure shamble along the hallway. Carma went first, and the others followed, shuffling along warm tiles.

"In-floor heating," Carma noted. "Nice."

"No expense spared," Kirk commented.

"Guess not."

The wardens passed a row of floor-to-ceiling windows, their reflections captured in the thick glass. Storm winds whispered beyond while snow gathered at the base, rising to lower thighs. If Kirk didn't know better, he would've thought he was peering out at the moon's surface.

The hallway ended in an immense living room, the far wall constructed of thick logs and storm-proofed glass. Fire crackled and burned in an enormous stone hearth to the left, a stack of cut wood piled near its mouth. A stout man, his thick frame outlined in a red hue, studied the flames with his hands clasped behind his back. A long, greasy slick of a ponytail reached his waist. He wore a forest-green silk shirt and blue jeans. He turned when the wardens entered the chamber, showing a prominent widow's peak and an aristocratic nose that might've been half of an isosceles triangle.

"Thank you, Nickolas," the man said to his servant, and faced the wardens, his hands still clasped behind his back. "Wardens."

He was youthful, though not quite as Rose had been. Stocky, even stout, but not as much as, say, the recently deceased Blacksmith. His clean-shaven jawline revealed features hinting at an East European ancestry.

The three wardens aimed their weapons at the two men, but Kirk was somewhat distracted. A pungent scent laced the air, suppressed somewhat by faint wood smoke, and emanating from one of four darkened archways. Puzzling over the smell, Kirk adjusted his grip on his MP5.

Despite the gesture, the elder didn't appear the least bit threatened. Nickolas stood against a wall-length book case, his intimidating shadow cast across several thick tomes.

"My name is Warren Vidal," the elder said in an odd, yet

smooth, blend of English and French accents. "By tomorrow afternoon, you will be referring to me as Warren. Or you will be dead. The choice will be yours."

Kirk's gaze flickered from Vidal to his leveled MP5 and back again. "All right. If you say so."

"I do say so," Vidal growled and arched his head. "You're in my realm, now. My world. This place has been my residence for the last twenty-seven years. I decide who ventures inside these walls. Just as I decide who lives. Or dies. So, yes, I say so."

Big balls, Kirk thought, since the elder had a gun pointed at him. Kirk checked on Nickolas. The big man remained motionless, but a thin smile crossed his unpleasant features, as if he expected violence and looked forward to it.

Carma stepped away from Kirk and took aim at the silent Nickolas. Ezekiel also spread out, pointing his weapon at Vidal.

"Twenty-seven years," Kirk repeated, fingers flexing on the MP5. "Why so long?"

"It was my time," Vidal answered, chin held high, his permanent scowl a mask of concentration. "In your case, it might be twenty to twenty-five years until you move, to ensure the herds don't grow too suspicious of your youth. For me, it's a little longer, give or take a few years."

"And you own Atticus Yor?" Kirk asked.

Vidal didn't bother answering that question. "How is it you managed to kill Rose?"

"Luck."

"Unfortunate. For Rose. I've been asking myself that very

question since your conversations with him. In his private chambers, no less. It's amazing that you even located him. We… take pride at how we distance ourselves from the lesser *weres*."

"Rose wasn't expecting us," Kirk said. "At all."

"No," Vidal drew out. "I suppose not."

Kirk considered the range, which was less than fifteen feet, with no cover except for some plush furniture in front of Vidal. The ancient *were* simply had no place to go if Kirk opened fired. He had to admit, Vidal didn't flinch easily. And that made him uneasy.

"I apologize," Vidal said and frowned. "My… grief over losing an old friend has frayed my sense of hospitality. Drinks?"

Fire crackled.

"No thanks," Kirk said. Carma shook her head.

Ezekiel, however, wavered at the offer.

"Would you permit me, then?" Vidal asked and snapped his finger before anyone could react.

"I don't think now's the time," Kirk said.

"Nonsense," Vidal scoffed in distaste. "Now's a very good time. I may die this very instant. You've made your intentions clear by killing Rose, and I don't resent that in the least. He did try very hard to kill you. And, let me be clear, I was *not* the one who authorized the hunt or any other initiatives aimed at your deaths. That was all Rose."

Kirk was about to comment, when, through one of the room's four archways, another large man appeared. Carma spun at the abrupt appearance, dividing her attention between the unmoving Nickolas and the new arrival, who halted on the threshold the second she aimed at him. Fat-faced and smelling of musk, the newcomer carried a tray of chrome or some such shiny metal other than silver, with a white cloth draped over its surface. An upright bottle of fancy crystal sat in the center, rising above a fence of elegant glasses.

Time stopped.

"He moves and I'll shoot," she warned, the UMP-9 steady.

"Of course," Vidal said in that strange blend of accents. "I expect no less."

"Anyone else hiding in here?"

"No," the elder quietly assured her, eyeing her down the length of his nose. "We are all present, now."

"Good," Carma said. "Quicker that way."

The winds blew somewhere overhead, rushing over the house's thick shell.

"May I?" Vidal asked, indicating the bottle with a nod.

"Go ahead," Kirk said. "Just be careful about it."

"Thank you," the elder said and motioned to the new man. "Elias."

Without a care in the world, the man approached Vidal and presented the tray at arm's length. The elder inspected the goods and took the bottle into his hands. He unscrewed the top and poured, the soft gurgle pleasant to the ears. Kirk smelled the whiskey and the one called Elias. The strong, mystery odor remained as well, though somewhat overpowered by the nearness of the other scents.

Vidal filled his glass halfway before placing the bottle back upon the tray.

"Thank you," the elder said.

"Smells good," Kirk remarked.

Vidal swished the drink around before sipping, draining a third of the whiskey as if it were cold tea. "Twenty-five-year-old scotch. Would you like some?"

"Got any cola to mix with it?" Kirk deadpanned.

The unimpressed scowl deepened on the elder's face. "To business then," he said, as if unwilling to waste any more time with his guests.

"I heard your conversation with Rose and I agree with him, to a point," Vidal said, swishing his remaining scotch in his glass. "I know he tried to sway you, but I believe he could have done better. He made a mistake and paid for it with his life. I'm not about to repeat that mistake. You are one of us, Kirk. And I'm willing to extend to you the same offer he did, without consulting the other elders. I'm also willing to extend the same offer to your companions here."

Neither Carma nor Ezekiel reacted to the elder's words.

"You sure you can do that?" Kirk asked.

"I can," Vidal deadpanned. "But I have something else in mind. A position. Better suited for your talents. And determination."

Kirk couldn't believe the elder was trying a second time. And that mysterious smell once again divided his attention.

Vidal stopped swishing his drink. "You've killed an elder. That's not an easy feat. Allow me to be frank. I have need of *weres* like you. Agents, if you will, to impose my will upon the rebellious. The troublesome. Rivals, even. Does this appeal to you?"

A dismayed Kirk shook his head. "Rivals. You mean other elders?"

"I do."

"You kill other elders?"

Vidal looked into his glass. "In reality, our order isn't as united as you might believe. Time has a way of fragmenting even bedrock. We're a factious group, with some elders occasionally unifying against others over tiny matters. Personal slights. In the past I had semi-regular dealings with, say, our cousins to the south or in Europe. Perhaps once or twice every century. There would be disagreements, but nothing that couldn't be discussed and resolved. These days, with the world connected on so many levels, with borders overlapping borders, differences are becoming increasingly more commonplace. And more complex. Territorial matters. Herd management. Breeding issues. Even wealth distribution. Sometimes these matters can be resolved through dialogue. Sometimes not. In those impasses, violence has become an accepted recourse. A recourse that requires a qualified agent to... conduct operations."

"Holy shit," Carma exclaimed softly.

Vidal didn't bat an eye. Instead, he took a long sip and watched Kirk over the rim of his glass. "Consider it. We both want the same thing, you and I. Rose is dead. There is only one elder remaining in this territory. Me. And I'm willing to negotiate. There are invaluable benefits with the position. Riches. Property, status amongst the ruling body. Power in decision-making. Freedom."

"Like holing yourself up in a shack in the middle of nowhere?" Carma asked, the question loud in the cavernous living room.

Vidal didn't dignify that with a response.

"The lady asked you a question," Kirk said, glancing at a darkened archway near the southern corner of the room. "Better answer."

"This is hardly a shack," Vidal said with the slightest curl to his lips. "We all must retreat from the world from time to time. Finishing a term amongst the herds isn't a prison sentence, however. You still have access to all the amenities. You are free to roam, and in luxury I might add, provided it isn't in the same circles of your recent stationing. Thirteen years ago I hunted in the hills of my ancestral Armorica. I prefer the solitude of the north, however. I enjoy the cold."

"How many elders are there?" Kirk asked.

"That doesn't matter," Vidal said, dismissing the question. "Think about what I'm offering. Take the night. Rose is gone and I need a replacement. In time, I'll appoint you or one of your friends as CEO of the company. You don't need knowledge of corporate affairs. Rose didn't. Wellford oversees all operations. Estates befitting royalty will be made available to you, anywhere in this territory. Generous bank accounts will be assigned to your identities. Your finances will explode overnight. Companionship will also be made available. And all you have to do is swear allegiance and… do my bidding when called upon."

Windows thrummed and rattled overhead, straining

against the growing wind of the northern Manitoba wild. The temperature dropped in the room despite the popping fire. That mysterious smell grew stronger, pushing through the other layers of scents in the room.

"There's my offer," Vidal said. "Will you reconsider?"

Kirk took his time answering, long enough to draw looks from Carma and Ezekiel.

"No," the Halifax warden finally said. "In fact, I'm thinking that, once I'm done with you, I just might go on a hunt of my own."

A thin smile spread across Vidal's face, lighting up his shadowed complexion. "We're already thinking alike. Join me, Douglas. I'll happily provide you with directions on how to find them and much more."

"You'd do that? To the other elders?"

"Certainly. In this age? Without hesitation."

"No," Kirk said finally. "I won't be your killer."

The elder's smile vanished. In the chilling silence that ensued, Vidal sighed. "You would have been an adept agent, Douglas Kirk. And you *are* a killer. Reluctant, yes, but a killer. You just need motivation, is all. Is 'no' your final answer?"

"Yeah. Pretty much. Thanks, anyway."

An impassive Vidal watched him for heartbeats.

Carma and Ezekiel looked to that darkened archway, their noses twitching.

"Then our business is concluded," Vidal announced. "And the flag of truce is no more."

Upon the utterance of that final word, a grizzly, the

largest bear Kirk had ever laid eyes upon, burst from a darkened archway and raged into the living room. Chairs flew in the wake of the animal's snarling, charging mass. Vidal's man-servants Nickolas and Elias dove for the shadowy sidelines of the room, while Vidal was suddenly in Kirk's face, attempting to wrestle the MP5 away. The blinding speed shocked the Halifax warden. Vidal yanked at the weapon, and Kirk refused to relinquish it, matching the elder's strength. There they stood, toe-to-toe, while Carma and Ezekiel fired at the monstrous bear in their midst, the light from their automatic weapons striking the beast in a blaze. Meat and fur exploded from the creature's hide.

But the *were* grizzly didn't falter. The supernatural behemoth took the barrage head on, absorbing the silver, taking the pain. It charged Carma.

Except Carma was no longer there.

Vidal gave up tugging on the weapon, and rammed his aristocratic forehead into Kirk's nose. Cartilage flattened and blood burst from Kirk's face. Strands of hair hanging in disarray over his features, Vidal pulled on the weapon once more, but Kirk still wouldn't release it. The last pull tightened the Halifax warden's finger on the trigger, and the weapon fired between the pair, sewing a line of spider webs up the middle of the room's picture window. Power chords of terror cut the air, with the underlying spatter of gunfire crackling underneath.

Vidal took advantage of the distraction and smiled while he rammed his noble head into Kirk's face twice more.

The second time, Kirk smiled back.

And let the *were*blood flow.

Vidal sensed the change immediately, and it showed on his face. What was once a look of predatory glee distorted into a mask of undisguised horror.

Just before Kirk threw him through the picture window in an explosion of glass.

Wind and snow rushed into the room, and Kirk whirled his MP5 around just as Elias leaped at him over the sofa, arms cocked with silver sickles. The automatic blast struck the manservant's navel and ripped up the front of his chest in a bloody burst of meat. Elias stopped in midair as if connecting with an invisible wall, and as he fell Kirk had only a heartbeat to decide his next course of action, knowing full well Vidal was outside in the wintry dark.

The Halifax warden dropped to a knee and fired at the bear, the tracers blinding in the fireplace glow of the room. The blast shredded the grizzly's shoulder in an inky geyser, distracting the animal from pursuing a bobbing and weaving Carma. Despite the damage, the creature still closed the distance swung for her head. She threw herself to the side, narrowly ducking under flashing claws.

Ezekiel righted himself and shot at the bear, blowing away pieces of its mighty back. The monster wailed, and glowered at the newest attacker.

Then the shadowy outline of Nickolas rose and hurled an axe at the New Brunswick warden. The weapon flew across the room like a spinning firework, cleaving Ezekiel's upper chest and dropping him to the floor.

Nickolas readied a second axe as the grizzly pawed for

Carma once again.

Kirk shifted and placed a *sonnavabitch* burst into Nickolas's head, shattering it. The *were* dropped as if stepping into a bottomless pit, and Kirk resumed firing at the rampaging bear.

Carma ducked and rolled, eventually taking herself out the same archway they originally entered. The bear clawed for her at every step, but her frantic gymnastics kept her from harm until she tumbled through the archway.

Which was the exact moment Kirk shot a load of silver into the bear's furry ass.

The grizzly whipped itself around, speckling the walls with dark matter.

Kirk fired at the thing's head, scalping it in a second, the silver ricocheting off a skull plate as thick as battleship armor. And underneath the crackling impacts, the bear hunched down with a terrible grin, took the best the warden had, and charged.

The warden rolled out of the way of the monster, but its claws sheared through his sweater and grazed his protective vest. Kirk righted himself, exhaled a spray of blood, and continued firing at the beast, destroying one of its eight-ball eyes. The eye exploded in a pop of jelly, but the bear lined the warden up once again.

Kirk continued firing, squeezing the trigger until his finger went numb. Bullets peppered the bear's head and bounced off into the walls, the light dying in the deflections. The beast continued to smile until Kirk sent a silver volley into its teeth, chipping six-inch fangs into white needles.

The animal's snout disintegrated, shoving the beast back a foot.

That got the monster's attention.

Just as the MP5 clicked dry.

Shit, Kirk thought and fumbled to swap out the spent magazine.

The grizzly barreled into him, knocking him flat. Jaws snapped for his face. Kirk bared his own fangs, holding the monster back by the length of the MP5, pressing the weapon up under the bear's considerable jawbone. Blood pattered Kirk's arms and face. Foul breath wrinkled his nose.

The bear wheezed, its maw a frothy red, and by sheer power alone, steadily bore down on the trapped warden, overpowering the lesser breed.

Kirk groaned, realizing the thing was far too strong for him, even in his altered state. Only seconds remained before the thing ate his face.

An automatic volley slammed into the bear's head, shoving it to the left, causing the supernatural monstrosity to cringe as if it were being doused with cold water.

Carma continued firing until the bear shied away. A rear leg kicked a sofa in her direction, crushing her against a wall in a screech of wood.

Ezekiel rose unsteadily on his feet, firing from the opposite side. His bullets ripped up the left side of the beast until a deluge of gore resembling coffee grounds spattered the floor.

Distracted by the newest attack, the grizzly wavered, determined where the stinging beams of light were coming from, and jumped for Ezekiel. The warden held his ground, head hunched into his shoulders until he screamed at the beast. Bear claws flashed downward, tearing the warden to the floor in a violent slap of meat and metal.

The gun went silent.

But the grizzly wasn't quite finished with Ezekiel.

It chomped into the warden's arm, breaking it in multiple places. Ezekiel shouted and clawed at the animal's bleeding face, but the bear merely shook its head, lifting and smearing its victim across the stone face of the fireplace.

Kirk rolled onto his side and extended his claws. Ezekiel's agonized mewling urged him to hurry.

A screech of wood and Carma was free of the sofa. She didn't wait for Kirk. She shouldered her UMP-9, sighted her near invincible target, and fired. Tracers slammed into the bear's belly, perforating it with soppy explosions.

The bear released Ezekiel. It howled at the latest pain and spotted Carma across the room. The entire face of the animal resembled a bloody rose of meat, but somewhere in that mass of bullet-wrought petals, an eye beheld the *were*-female. It lumbered towards her, nowhere near as fast as before, but picking up ramming steam.

Carma held her ground, firing at the monster as it charged—

—just as Kirk reached out and grabbed a fistful of fur, using the beast's forward momentum to leap onto the creature's back. He landed in a precarious straddle, his balls sending him a nauseated memo never to do such a thing again. Gunfire crackled. Bear bits jumped and whizzed through the air. Holding onto a blood-slippery scruff, Kirk pressed his head against a pumping shoulder blade and looked up to glimpse Carma mottled in shadow and firelight. She unloaded her weapon from the hip.

Narrow-eyed and fearless.

Kirk reached down and sunk the claws of his weaponized hand deep into the thing's throat.

And squeezed.

Carma winked out of sight an instant before the creature slammed into the wall behind her with all the force of a tank. The house trembled, absorbing the impact. Pictures dropped and unseen crystal shattered on the floor.

Kirk kept squeezing, even when the bear moaned underneath him and blood erupted around the curved daggers of his fingers.

Carma screamed somewhere underneath the *were* behemoth.

That single note tripled Kirk's effort. He ripped, with every bit of strength in his being.

Until he touched bone.

The bear ceased wailing, its massive bulk shuddered, and with a dying hiss it settled down onto the drenched sofa.

His claws deep into the thing's throat, Kirk waited three heartbeats before pulling his hand free. The bear didn't move as he slid off its back, splashing down on a drenched floor.

"Shit," he whispered, and made the mental note to burn the beast, just to be sure it was dead.

Carma's legs poked out from underneath the creature's massive paw.

Kirk rounded the dead thing and spotted her, half hidden under a heavy foreleg.

"Oh shit," he panted and pulled at the thing's paw. It came free, and Carma yelped, her head snapping forward as if doing a sudden stomach crunch. Her hands went to her side, staunching an ominous flow from where the bear's claws had raked her down, tearing her Kevlar vest asunder. In the firelight and shadow, Carma looked very pale, but she controlled herself, pressed down on her horrible wound, and smiled crazily at Kirk.

"I'm okay," she said in a puff of breath.

"Carma—" Kirk protested.

"Get Vidal," she spat as if stricken with hypothermia.

"He's outside."

"Get him," she said through clenched teeth. Her eyes moistened.

"Carma."

"*Get him*," she shrieked, then, "before... he changes."

That bullet of information took Kirk straight between the eyes. He glanced over his shoulder, across the wreckage of the living room, to that jagged maw where he'd heaved Vidal's cultured ass into the night.

"I'll be back," he said.

And left her.

He crossed the living room floor, his shadow enormous against the far wall, and stopped.

There, lying on at the foot of the fireplace, beneath a shocking bar code of shredded clothing and blood, Ezekiel Allen watched Kirk and giggled. His right ear and half of his cheek had been ripped away, and most of the skin covering his lower jaw. The fire's orange glow rendered the other half insane, and the picture oddly reminded Kirk of the first time he laid eyes on the New Brunswick warden, back in his Halifax apartment.

Baxter had been alive then. And Morris. And several others.

"Here," Ezekiel released in a smoker's wheeze that clicked on the intake. He held up his MP5.

Kirk stopped, horrified at the bear's handiwork and how deep that thrown axe had cut the *were*. Red bone glistened in the firelight, underneath a stream of scarlet. The protective vest lay skewed to one side, baring part of Ezekiel's untouched midriff.

"Don't you... don't you worry," Ezekiel whispered and giggled again. "Not... not silver."

"Help Carma," Kirk said as he grabbed the weapon from his companion's hand.

Mad with pain, Ezekiel's expression lightened in a ghastly affirmative. He reached for the fireplace's poker.

Kirk backed away from the warden, recognizing the *were's* intention. Ezekiel hooked a glowing log from the fireplace depths. Red embers flared. The log's end shimmered and glowed, resembling the shifting surface of the sun.

Ezekiel pulled himself toward the log.

Kirk turned away from the scene, not needing to see what came next. He reloaded the MP5 with a fresh clip. Readying the weapon with a slap, he crossed the floor and leaped

through the shattered window.
 Into the hoary northern Manitoba night.
 Ezekiel's screams followed him.

41

How long? Kirk thought to himself as he followed bloody footprints through the gathered snow.

No more than two minutes and counting. No more than that. If he hurried, he could catch Vidal in the mid-phase of his transformation. If he was lucky, and if Vidal, being an elder and all, hadn't somehow mastered the quick change, Kirk could gun him down at his most vulnerable.

The warden suspected Vidal didn't know about Borland's quick change, however. If he did, Vidal certainly wasn't aware Kirk had mastered that half-state. He recalled the elder's expression when he attempted to pull Kirk's gun away and discovered he couldn't. Vidal hadn't counted on that, and he'd been surprised by Kirk's sudden flash of fangs and all the *were* trimmings.

Vidal had been *surprised*.

That rang true in Kirk's mind.

Wind-sculpted drifts filled the gaps between trees, creating elegant white mesas and gullies. Vidal's tracks cut through and ruined the chilling splendor of the gathered snow. Kirk cricked his right shoulder and hefted his MP5. A strong breeze fanned wisps off the drifts, flinging it across his face. He welcomed the chill, needed it. The cold forest spice filled his nose but he could smell Vidal as easily as following his tracks.

A structure loomed up ahead, a small church of some kind, materializing out of the frigid dark like a tomb's entrance. Vidal's tracks led to a doorway flung open. Kirk's claw clicked against the MP5 as he awkwardly tried to insert it through the trigger guard. When he'd blown out the window, his clawed finger had already been in place, but now, it annoyed him. He finally got his digit on the trigger and hissed through a mouthful of teeth.

Kirk shouldered the weapon and approached the darkened entrance. The *were* blood flowed through him at a controlled rate. A high wall covered in snow rose on his left, and it took him a second to realize it was a complete cord of stacked firewood. The small building was a wood shed.

A wary Kirk proceeded, swearing under his breath that Vidal had better not fire up a chainsaw.

He crept forward, smelling the air, detecting wood and cold and the unmistakable scent of Vidal's aristocratic ass. Kirk reached the shed and placed his back to the right of the doorway.

And spun into the darkness.

A chunk of firewood came down on the MP5's barrel, eliciting a frightful burst of gunfire that lit up the dark. A second length of firewood smashed across Kirk's forehead, knocking him flat in a splash of fine powder.

Kirk willed his senses back, and rolled over onto an elbow in time to witness Vidal emerging from the woodshed. The elder held two lengths of cut firewood in each hand, swinging them lazily like a pair of chainless nunchucks.

Kirk sprang to his feet, much to Vidal's disdain.

"I was wrong," the elder whispered as snow fell. "You're *not* one of us. I can smell Borland's taint all over you."

"Yeah," Kirk crouched, his fingers flexing.

"What have you done to yourself?" Vidal asked, bewildered.

"Upgraded," Kirk snarled.

And lunged.

But the elder matched the warden's blurring speed. He cracked one firewood club off Kirk's skull, stopping the charge in midflight. Then he followed up with a crushing blow to the temple, a mallet-strike to the cheek, and a finishing uppercut to the jaw. Three solid connections that blurred into the warden and took him off his feet.

The gathered snow failed to lessen Kirk's fall. He lay there, stunned, and attempted to roll over.

Vidal cracked a club off the *were's* skull, splitting the skin in a burst of blood.

Kirk drove a foot into the elder's knee, buckling it backwards. Vidal dropped without a sound. Kirk recovered, claws extended and bloody jaws snapping. He rushed in, seeking his adversary's throat.

Vidal kicked him squarely in the balls.

That solid heel contact drove Kirk to his knees with a

shocked grunt. He writhed there, caught in a gasping, nauseated swoon.

Somewhere, around the periphery of his pain, the elder struggled to his feet.

"You're an abomination," Vidal declared with venom. "Rose was right to unleash the kill teams on the likes of you."

The elder straightened, considered the pained warden still cradling his nether regions. He took his time retrieving a piece of firewood. He shook the snow off the weapon and considered the building storm.

"I'll feast on the others instead," Vidal vowed, "starting with the woma—"

Kirk blasted off the ground, tackling the elder about the waist and driving forward. Vidal's head clapped off the upper beam of the woodshed entrance, the blunt impact breaking bone. Wood fibers crackled. The elder toppled over Kirk's shoulders and crashed into a heap.

But that last charge was all Kirk could muster, and he crumpled to the dusty floor. Groaning, he crawled about the interior of the shed, fingers scrambling in the cold dark, very much aware that Vidal was still outside. His guts screamed at him to stay still, to not move, so that repairs could be made.

He touched the warm barrel of his MP5 and relief fired through him. Kirk grabbed the weapon and rolled over, the gun sights fixed on the open doorway. Snow fell at a slant, filling the entrance. The wind raged, swallowing all other sound. Kirk waited, the sickening grief in his balls lessened.

"Vidal?" Kirk finally called out and received no reply. "Vidal?"

Beyond the opening, nothing moved. Kirk listened, smelled.

The elder's scent had diminished.

Bastard's gone, Kirk realized and struggled to his feet.

42

Snow clung to Warren Vidal's open wounds. He ran a hand over his head, smoothing his hair back, and flicked the residual blood away. That would throw the breed off his tail and buy him a few seconds more. In his mind, the fight was over. Nickolas, Elias, and Sebastian had certainly killed the other wardens. Sebastian's true form, the bear, was a truly impressive beast to behold. Borland hadn't been the only one dabbling in magic best left in the dark, and Sebastian, as well as Elias, were the results of several years of sorcerous experimentation.

Kirk, however, had proved to be an even greater surprise.

Ignoring the sting of his wounds, Vidal forced his damaged knee to work by sheer will. Every footfall pained him, but no matter. Whatever Kirk had become truly disturbed him. Repulsed him even, like maggots in a hamburger. The warden's strength surpassed his own in his human suit, but Vidal dismissed that. He had no further intention of engaging in fist fights with that one, for fear of becoming infected with whatever pulsed through Kirk's veins.

Besides, Vidal considered himself royalty, and royalty did not risk exposure to the diseased.

Through the snow-glutted forest Vidal marched, grimacing at times, but driven. Black specks dappled his tracks. In short time the manor loomed in the dark, a long and angular derelict moored to the wilderness and set against the surrounding night. In the summertime, the whole area would be awash in exploding flowerbeds and well-manicured lawns.

Vidal approached a wall interspersed with long windows. The encroaching cold annoyed him, so when he stopped before a glass doorway and discovered it locked, Vidal lost a drop of control.

He put his left elbow through the stormproof glass, shattering it with effort. Vidal groped at the inner lock and opened the door, the heat thawing him.

Muttering curses in a foreign tongue, Vidal entered his home. The hallway bled heat and was silent. He glanced to his right, in the direction of the living room—a good five-minute stroll away—and listened. Smelled.

The foul stink of wolverine musk reached his face and soured his nose. Vidal frowned at the odor, which overpowered and effectively masked the scent of a transformed *were*. In this case, rendering Sebastian invisible to the wardens. Sebastian had been Vidal's surprise, knowing full well the *were* bear could absorb a punishing amount of damage before succumbing to its wounds, including those inflicted by silver.

But there wasn't a rustle or a whiff, or anything else in

the direction of the living room. That didn't bode well on the elder's mind, and he wondered if his servants failed him. He lingered, thinking, before turning left and hobbling down a darkened corridor. More windows lay on his left while open doors remained on his right. Vidal ran his hand over his bleeding wounds, the most recent being his left elbow, and flicked his noble blood into rooms as he passed them, hoping the trail might delay the warden a little.

The corridor ended in a grand library where the original works of literary titans adorned the walls. Old paper and leather spiced the air. The few windows cut into the wall cast gray shards of light upon an oak table and a pair of baroque chairs fitted with soft cushions. The elder crossed the floor, passing an aged globe suspended in a worn but polished wooden stand. He stopped at a desk and pulled open the top drawer.

A stainless-steel hand cannon lay inside, along with a box of shells.

Vidal gripped the custom-made pearl grip and pulled out the sidearm, a seven-and-a-half-inch barrel Super Redhawk revolver, one of the most powerful handguns ever manufactured. He opened the six-shot cylinder and checked the rounds out of habit. Vidal always kept the weapon loaded with some special, hand-crafted, .480 hollow point silver bullets.

He had bears in the house, after all.

If needed, the Redhawk would put one of them down.

In fact, the Redhawk would rip their heads off.

Vidal brought the fearsome weapon up to his face and

bared his teeth in a snarl. His eyes flickered to the open doorway of the library, a void in an otherwise hoary gray quarter-light permitted by the study's bare windows.

Footsteps. The barest whisper of socked feet on hardwood floors came from the corridor. The warden's fragrant sweat followed, faint but growing stronger, as did a scent of spilled blood.

Kirk had entered his home.

Without another thought, Vidal gathered up the box of spare shells and placed it on the table before him. He considered his surroundings, decided nothing amiss, and faced the doorway. He turned sideways, assumed a duelist's pose, and took a deep, calming breath.

He aimed.

Sooner or later, Douglas Kirk would appear in that tall rectangular frame.

And when he did, Vidal intended to blow his head off.

43

The heat washed over Kirk's battered form as he followed Vidal's trail into the house. He slouched against the wall and regarded the lightless corridor. *Big place*, Kirk thought, and considered both ends of the hallway before slinking off in the direction of the blood.

Vidal was bleeding, badly. Kirk noted the smashed glass and the stains coloring the shards and knew, with each passing second, the elder was healing. The smell of rosined wood, stale air, and blood surrounded him, and the near absolute dark slowed him to a careful walk. He placed a hand to the wall, feeling the curve of a log, and proceeded with his MP5 pointed forward, the scent of fresh blood leading him along. The house was quiet, and though he didn't know where Carma and Ezekiel were exactly, he figured they were somewhere behind him. Kirk focused on the corridor ahead, his senses coming alive. His socks made no sound on the floor, and for that he was grateful. Snow covered him, however, and the warm air would soon leave him dripping.

The blood trail deviated to the right, through a dark

doorway. Kirk studied it for a second before edging up to the portal.

Kirk couldn't pass by the door without first ensuring Vidal wasn't hiding within, so he saddled up to the doorway's edge and spun into the room.

Empty. Only a pair of computers rested on elaborate workstations, complete with headsets and webcams. Technical manuals and other books lined a shelving unit. An inner door led to an empty bathroom.

No Vidal, however.

Sniffing, Kirk returned to the corridor and lingered, getting his bearings. He slunk along the hall, feeling more and more as if he were exploring the pipe-laden bulkheads of some vast interstellar vessel. Door-sized windows appeared on the left and lit the dark to a point. Snow piles pressed against the glass. He couldn't hear much beyond the thick shell of the elder's extravagant fortress, just the wind cutting itself on the mansion's heights. There was an undercurrent as well, a deep, earthy hum that traversed the entire length of the passageway. Wealth, Rose had said, and Vidal had mentioned the same. The elders had plenty of that. Kirk thought of his own concrete shithole back in Halifax.

Sweat ran down his face and he scrubbed it away with a sleeve. He placed his back to the wall and checked forward and aft. He waited, ears straining, and didn't hear anything else. Winter buffeted and sprayed the nearby glass, the winds intensifying. Fresh blood beckoned while that deep, earthy humming swelled in his ears. He wondered if it was a nearby generator of some kind.

He hoped Carma and Ezekiel were still alive.

Something adorned to the ceiling boards above the windows caught his attention. Dark spheres that resembled squished basketballs. Kirk studied the odd globes on the walls where the light didn't reach.

He gasped in horror.

Heads.

In an unholy display of taxidermy, decapitated heads lined the upper shadows of the walls, their grimaces preserved in a glaze of waxy resin. A dreadful collection of murder, studded to the support beams along the corridor, just beneath the ceiling. Some had their mouths open in a permanent scream, as if their jaws had locked upon feeling the guillotine's bite. The ones above Kirk thankfully had their eyes closed, but some did not, and those bothered him the most.

His heart rate increased and his skin prickled. He swallowed, uncomfortably aware of the click in his throat. He tore his eyes away from the gruesome sight and checked left and right. He swung the gun back, aiming it down the corridor, down the gullet of something that stretched out forever in the nightmare dark. Smelling nothing but blood, Kirk stalked on, refusing to look at those terrible trophies. Another window and another open doorway loomed ahead, and again the scent split in puzzling fashion. He peered inside the room and saw a selection of tightly packed washers and dryers.

Composing himself, Kirk continued farther down the vaulted passage, running a hand along the bare ribs of the walls. An energy crackled upon the air as he neared the corridor's end.

Kirk stopped. There was something else puzzling his nose. Then he recognized it, of all things, the hint of twenty-five-year-old whiskey.

Vidal was close.

Wiping his forehead, Kirk lifted his MP5 and crept forward. Not twenty feet ahead was a rectangular doorway capturing the midnight glow from an unseen window.

The warden approached.

Footsteps sounded behind him, and the air currents shifted ever so slightly. Kirk glanced back and spotted shadows bobbing in the dismal dark, far behind, but hurrying towards him. He studied them for a moment, straining to hear, and was rewarded with a set of huffing.

Two sets, in fact.

Kirk regarded the open doorway just ahead. Rows of shelves materialized against the far wall. A library, perhaps. And with every creeping step, the sweet scent of the whiskey beckoned.

"*Douglas!*" Carma hissed in a loud whisper, her voice speeding along that massive cedar pipe and blowing past his ears.

Kirk cringed at his name.

The elder would have heard.

And the whiskey scent was growing stronger.

44

"*Douglas!*" the word reached Vidal's ears, caressing them like the breath of a ghost.

Reinforcements. On their way.

Vidal realized he'd slightly erred. He knew his home well, that the long hallway to the library was bereft of lighting save for whatever night radiance the windows allowed. It was, in effect, a near perfect shooting gallery. Kirk was *inside* that shooting gallery, past the open doorways and with no cover to speak of. Nowhere to escape.

Now was the time to strike.

Vidal arrested his aim in a ninety-degree pause and rounded the corner of his desk. He walked swiftly and with purpose towards the doorway, his features set. His soaked feet scuffed over the polished floor, but he didn't care.

There, at the very edge of the frame, he paused and listened. Smelled. *Blood. Were blood*, tangy and yet corrupted by elements unknown to him. His fingers tightened around the pistol grip of his private howitzer.

A scent came to him, as did the barest breath straining to be unheard.

Kirk was in the pipe.

And very close indeed. Vidal smiled with satisfaction.

Strike first, strike hard, the elder thought.

He whirled around the doorway, stepping into full view and bringing his hand cannon to bear with a click of its hammer.

And there, dead center in the corridor, was Douglas Kirk.

45

Vidal's dark outline appeared in the doorway, a gun pointed directly at Kirk.

Instead of firing his own weapon, Kirk flinched and flung himself to the wall just as Vidal's gun discharged with a fiery boom. In that small confined space, the shot sounded like the first of a battleship salvo. A thunderbolt blasted Kirk off his feet and skidded him ten feet along the stacked logs of the wall, until the force dropped him like a flap of dead meat. His finger jerked the MP5's trigger and fired a short but vocal retort into the corridor's base, just before his MP5 skittered away. Wood chips scattered.

Time stopped. Kirk attempted to breathe, but his entire chest felt half-crushed despite his protective vest. He rolled onto his side, intending to sit up, but a second blast slammed into him, leaving him gasping. He attempted to lift the MP5 but saw that he no longer had a hand, and that his wrist bubbled and frothed like a freshly spudded oil well.

Then a third and fourth blast struck him, bucking him off the floor with a force so hard Kirk believed he was back in Alice's underground cell, frying on that electrified floor. His lower extremities conveyed the sensation of something falling out of him, just below the waist.

A shadow stood over him, its arm extended and ending in a void that smelled of cordite and scorched metal.

Stars suddenly flashed across the ceiling. Low-flying meteors that blazed over Kirk's vision in slow-motion, lighting up the man standing over him with planet-killing force. Vidal's shadow erupted into pieces. A chunk of shoulder, a piece of neck, a jagged U around his lower ribs. But the most spectacular and gruesome sight of all resulted from the few shots that exploded into Vidal's face, warping those aristocratic features as if his entire skull were being slurped into a very personal black hole.

Vidal collapsed into a deep, nightmarish ocean polluted with bloody chum.

Or so it appeared to Kirk.

A disturbing wailing pierced the ringing of the warden's ears, but he was unsure of the direction and the source. He still couldn't breathe correctly, and he was aware of a deep penetrating pain just below his head. His arms wouldn't move, nor his legs. He cringed from the silver, an involuntary reaction he was well acquainted with, but that was okay.

He was an elder now. Silver was no problem. No problem at all.

Then the pain seized him.

Absolute agony grabbed him in a freezing clutch of steel claws that sunk into his upper body and pried the muscle apart in bursting, protesting sinews. The hurt clenched his vocal chords and left him squeaking, wheezy, sputtering lung matter and blood. He squeezed his eyes shut while his ears and chest screamed. Nothing responded, his limbs trapped under immobilizing weights.

Dark. The world was so dark.

But then a flawless glowing moon appeared above him, white and pleasing and distracting him from the wreck of his body. It lifted him above the terrible suction of his wounds and the mind-eating agony. That coin-shaped light held his face, drawing him up close so that he could discern its features. A woman.

Carma.

And Carma was speaking to him.

No. That wasn't right at all.

Carma was *shouting* at him.

"*Sttttaaaaay* with me, Douglas. Stay with me. Look at my face, okay? Look here. Right here. There you go. There you go. See, I'm here now. Don't think about anything else, okay? Don't think. No, don't look down there. Don't. Hey, *hey* I said *don't LOOK. Okay?* Look at me! Don't you piss me off. I'll jack slap you again if you do. You know I hate that shit. Now, show me how tough you are. Show me how tough you are. That's a fucking order, dumbass, an *order*. You think you're tough, well then show me. Right now. You show me and then—and then we'll go running in the forest like before. Just like before. You wanna catch me? Huh? Out there? Under the moon? 'Course you do. Well then show me how tough you are and—and I'll let you catch me, okay?

Show me how tough you are and I'll let you catch me. I'll let you catch me…"

Her voice drifted, lessening in force, though he could still see she was edging towards panic. Something had tipped her off. Kirk preferred to just as soon slink off into some dark corner until she got whatever was bothering her out of her system. Carma's mouth worked, he could see it just fine, but no sound came from it.

Kirk relaxed in her arms, as limp as a boneless fish. He'd take his time. A feeling of wellness spread throughout his person. His heart rate slowed, thudding in his chest and temples, the sound like a single taiko drum being pounded on by an exhausted performer.

He stared at Carma's face.

And stared.

And somewhere at the far end of a darkening, collapsing tunnel, he heard her scream.

46

Six months later.

"We're about to land, sir."

The words, spoken by the pilot, stirred Ezekiel from his nap. It had been a long flight from the city, and the engine drone had put him out minutes after takeoff. He grunted at the pilot, who straightened and returned to the cockpit.

His senses returning, Ezekiel scratched his face, stretched, pulled on the untucked ends of his black shirt. He leaned into the nearby window. The afternoon sun blazed through the portal, and he squinted against the glare. Below him, the forest resembled a green maze of landscaped trails and glades. Ponds dotted the terrain like unpolished silver. The helicopter, the same luxurious AgustaWestland model that had carried him up here six months ago, slowed to a hover over a landing pad of asphalt that covered a wide patch of cleared timberland. A single trail snaked through the trees, towards a wooden structure some hundred meters away. The size of the elders' retreat amazed Ezekiel. It had been a while since he last saw the log castle, and the sheer size and scope of that extravagant mansion set his head into a wag of disbelief. He didn't know much about construction, so he could only stare and marvel at the effort needed to erect such a fortress in the middle of nowhere. Wellford might know. The CEO knew pretty much everything else about the elders' operations.

The thought of Wellford brought a smile to his face. He'd formally appointed the woman to CEO upon returning to civilization and, in retrospect, it was the smartest thing Ezekiel had done in his capacity as the new president of the company. He knew nothing about running a multinational firm with offices in sixteen different countries, but he didn't have to, not with her running the show. All that was required of him was to let her do her thing and then find something to occupy his time. And he occupied it very well, thank you—by sitting back in the shadows, preferably in the company headquarters' upper two-level suite, a magnificent abode with a stunning view of Winnipeg's cityscape.

Especially at night, when the city lights came alive like thousands of lit candles spread across an elegant table. Beer not only helped his city-gazing, but enhanced it, along with his own personal collection of music blaring in the background.

Wellford had been key in the transition of power at Atticus Y. Like a true capitalist, she didn't care about who ran the company, as long as daily operations continued and profits were reaped. And she certainly didn't mind the increase in her salary, as well as her overall compensation package, which included a bonus structure and retirement award that left Ezekiel dazed and speechless. Was she worth it? These days, she certainly was. Wellford also didn't know much about the affairs of *weres* south of the border, or to the east, which wasn't an issue. There was no reason for Rose to ever disclose the particulars of the *were* society to her. She was, in effect, the front, and a very efficient one at that.

She did know a few things, however.

She showed Ezekiel the leather-bound address book filled with Rose's penned uppercase writing, where he'd kept the names, addresses, and, most importantly, the phone numbers of every warden in his territory, which was essentially everything north of the forty-ninth parallel. She also showed him the surveillance room and introduced him to the sixteen-person team that maintained a twenty-four-seven surveillance on every warden in the northern territory. Every aspect of their lives that could be monitored was observed, from email and internet sites to phone calls, credit card usage, right on down to the electronic funds transfers all wardens received every two weeks, directly into a bank account.

Everything was already set up and fully functioning, and didn't lose a beat when Ezekiel helmed operations in a strictly figurehead capacity. He had a disposal crew remove Moses Morris's half-eaten corpse from that horrifying freezer just off Rose's private office. Ezekiel was even surprised to learn that Hale reported in for his scheduled shift following his ordeal. The man was even part of the disposal team that cleaned up the mess in the head office and the freezer, though Hale had paled and struggled to keep a low profile when passing by Ezekiel, much to the *were's* amusement. Ezekiel didn't have anything against Hale, and made a note of doing something nice for the guy in the future. Just to erase that unpleasant time in the truck.

In the end, the only thing Ezekiel had to do was lord over it all. And maybe infuse a little fear into those beneath him from time to time. Word on the street was that he'd died, and the techs could electronically disguise his voice if he ever had to call up some of the wardens he knew. What the techs could accomplish with their computers was damn-near sorcerous.

Ezekiel, however, wouldn't worry about contacting anyone in the foreseeable future. He knew firsthand how often the elders reached out to the wardens, and because Rose had officially closed the hunt with the deaths of the Ezekiel, Carma, and Kirk, the once New Brunswick warden didn't have to call anyone at all. Vidal had spoken about cousins to the south, but Ezekiel didn't worry about them either. In time, maybe other elders would contact him, which made him wonder how he'd explain the usurping of Rose and Vidal.

But he would worry about that another day.

Today, he had other things to do.

Namely, delivering supplies. Much-needed supplies. *Six months.* Ezekiel shook his head. How his fortunes had changed, from a semi-drunken dog living in a little shit hole of an apartment to this, head of a multinational corporate empire. A figurehead, of course, but Ezekiel didn't give a damn about that part.

Outside his window, trees and brush violently bucked and bent over as the majestic helicopter descended. *Bow to the king*, Ezekiel chuckled and scratched at an ear fully regenerated, the same ear the *were*bear (how fucked up was *that*?) had raked from his skull. After Kirk had ripped the monster's throat out and ran off after Vidal, Ezekiel applied fire to his bleeding bits, a sensation he hadn't suffered for years. After he'd finished cauterizing his wounds, Ezekiel had staggered to Carma's side with a hot poker and fused the gaping slivers left by claws that nearly disembowelled her. The damn bear had actually managed to shred her protective vest. Ezekiel didn't mind burning himself, but he hated doing it to Carma, hated putting her through that scorching misery. She got through it, even directed him to seal up a few gashes on her back.

After that short but intense battlefield surgery, Carma and Zeke had gone to find Kirk.

The image of a mighty fire filled Ezekiel's head then. After the fight, he'd been tasked with disposing of the bodies, and he recalled the stink of the *were* bear as it cooked in that grim funeral pyre.

He shook his head at the memory and ran his fingers over the plush leather of the armrest. He loved the chopper, loved the tripped-out speaker system that blared his mix of seventies rock and a few select club tunes, and adored the fact that the kitchenette in the back could be outfitted to be a serious bar. His old partner in crime, Baxter Ryan, not so long gone and certainly not forgotten, would've had seriously enjoyed the ride. Morris too, for that matter.

A gentle bump marked the landing. Ezekiel undid his seatbelt with a guitar cord flick of his hand. The pilots—Perry and Jonah—emerged from the cockpit and opened the outside door. It was only early summer, but the day promised to be an unusually warm one. Warm, moist air flooded the cabin, tinged with the smell of forest and hidden streams. That one snort lifted Ezekiel from his melancholy reflection.

"I'll help," he said and stood, turning the heads of both pilots.

"We can manage the unloading, sir," Perry informed him.

"Yeah," Ezekiel drew out and smoothed out the black dress shirt he'd worn. The jeans he left alone, along with the biker boots. "I need the exercise."

The pilots could understand that. It was a long flight over the stunning Manitoba wild.

So the three of them unloaded the supplies Ezekiel had been asked to bring. Foodstuffs, condiments, even magazines and pocket novels. Ezekiel cocked an eyebrow at the packages of condiments, and he wondered just how much cooking was getting done up here. Beyond that, the company retreat had a satellite dish for television programming, but he doubted it was used much.

The helicopter's dying rotorwash had kept most of the mosquitos at bay, but when the blades finally stilled, the annoying bugs took to wing.

Ezekiel waved a hand before his face.

Though trees hid the pathway and most of the lower level, the mansion's peak was visible through the treetops. He looked around and saw no other wildlife.

"Everything's unloaded, Mr. Allen," Jonah reported after a time.

Mr. Allen. Ezekiel had told the guys to call him by his first name when in private. Or just Zeke. Not that it bothered him being addressed with the honorific. He was getting to like it, even.

"Good," he nodded and glanced to the edge of the landing pad, where a low wall of boxes resembled a castle's battlements. "Good."

Silence then, for a few seconds, precious and serene. A hidden brook gurgled somewhere to Ezekiel's right. The birds hadn't resumed chirping yet, but they would. The trees murmured amongst themselves, disturbed by a westerly breeze.

"I don't see a trolley anywhere," Perry began. "Should we carry all this to the house?"

Ezekiel took a deep, gentle breath through his nose, sifting through the different scents riding the air, identifying what he could. When he was done, he said, "You really want to lug all that shit up there? In this heat?"

Neither pilot commented.

They'd do it if he'd asked them to, but it wasn't in their job description.

"Not really," Jonah admitted, the more vocal of the pair. "Unless you don't mind returning to the city while it's dark."

Ezekiel didn't mind that at all. Winnipeg was glorious after dark, but he held his wide stance and didn't answer right away.

The wild. The beautiful, wonderful wild. Its colors charmed him, tugged at his very core.

A familiar scent caught his nose and he recognized it immediately. He took it in, savored it, and a little smile tugged at one corner of his mouth.

"Changed my mind, boys," he announced. "Think I'll hang around here for a while. Get back to nature for a bit. You head on back. I'll contact Ms. Wellford when I'm ready to come back."

The men didn't react right away. "You sure, sir?" Jonah asked.

Ezekiel took another sniff of the clean air. As an afterthought, he gestured for them to be off.

Orders received, Perry and Jonah boarded the helicopter. Ezekiel shielded his eyes with a hand as the machine powered up, the rotor blades' slow, powerful swoops swirling into a monstrous gale. Sound and wind hammered at Ezekiel's ears. The powerful upsurge buffeted his stance, staggered him. Trees bent over as if inspecting their roots. The helicopter's undercarriage winked its lights as it rose.

When the flying machine cleared the forest heights, it smoothly banked to the right, and headed south. The chopper disappeared in seconds, the beat of its rotors diminishing into nothing.

The trees relaxed as Ezekiel wandered to the center of the landing pad. He looked to the south, listening, smelling.

The mid-afternoon sun beat down and he wiped the flowing sweat from his face. He unconsciously undid the three top buttons of his untucked shirt.

Underbrush crackled. He stopped and turned.

Nothing appeared, even though he knew he was looking in the right direction.

"C'mon, now," Ezekiel coaxed. "The hell you waiting for?"

But still nothing emerged from the forest depths.

"You best come out," he muttered. "'Cause I'm not about to lug all this shit up there alone."

The wind blew by him in response.

Then, at the edge of the landing pad, a wolf emerged from the surrounding woods. A huge wolf, larger than any of the species needed to be. It sniffed the ground, then the air, and lifted its regal head. Bright yellow eyes regarded Ezekiel with solemn attention.

"Hello, Carma," he greeted softly, happy to see her.

Another snapping of underbrush and a second, larger wolf slunk tentatively from the woods. It also sniffed at the ground and followed Carma's trail until it stopped beside her. The animal sampled the air, deemed it good, and yawned.

A short yowl summoned a smile to Ezekiel's hard features.

"Hello, Kirk," he said.

Epilogue

Snow covered the marshland, right up to a distant wall of fir trees, whose Christmas peaks stood out against the deep blackening-blue of the horizon. Somewhere over the hills, a snow machine rattled, probably heading home. Nothing replaced the sound of the diminishing engine. The forest was silent, save for the chuffing of boots through deep white banks of powder.

The cold air nipped at Alvin Peters' jovial cheeks, turning his chubby face into a healthy red. He didn't mind. He stopped in his snowsuit and boots, the snow rising as high as his knees, and took in the sight before him. An open expanse where a few stunted trees rose above the white plain like crooked sign posts, marking a hinterland highway that Alvin now knew by heart. Ross would have known it too, and a moment's sadness took Alvin then, fully understanding what his friend felt when he went hiking in the woods.

It was tough trekking over a path hidden by deep snow, but Alvin did it, without the aid of any portable oxygen tanks or inhalers. He didn't rely on any devices or medicine those days, and his garbage can-sized oxygen concentrator, affectionately called C-Cup, kept him company. His inanimate roommate occupied one corner of his computer room in his new home—a house which formerly belonged to recently-departed Harry Shea. The inhabitants of Amherst Cove marveled at Alvin's complete recovery from his respiratory problems. Even his own doctor wondered how he did it and wanted him to head into St. John's for tests, just to see if what was happening to Alvin could be analyzed, replicated, and applied to the thousands of others living with severe breathing problems.

Alvin told him he'd consider it, but wasn't sure if he ever would. One of the last things Ross told him, after he'd bitten Alvin and brought him over to the other side, was that he had to keep the bite a secret, that no one was supposed to know about it, at least not until Ross contacted Douglas Kirk and explained the situation to him.

Mum was the word. That included any hospital tests.

Ross never got that chance to inform Kirk, sadly enough. And despite frequent phone calls to the numbers Alvin had access to, no one answered, leaving him without guidance. He kept trying until one day Dougie Kirk called him out of the blue, from a number he didn't recognize. Alvin tried calling that phone number back, but it had gone silent. He even tried the new number Dougie had given him, but still no one answered. After a while, Alvin stopped trying to call altogether. So he kept a low profile, for the immediate future at least.

That was a year ago.

He still hoped that one morning he'd answer his phone and hear Dougie's voice on the other end, telling him what to do. Where to go. Something. Anything.

But it hadn't happened yet.

Alvin was, in effect, on his own.

Ross and he used to talk. Long talks. Ross couldn't see his friend suffer so, especially since he knew he had a solution to Alvin's deteriorating health. An alternate lifestyle, so to speak. Alvin knew the basics about lycanthropy from watching movies and reading books. But the nice thing about being a werewolf was that he didn't necessarily have to eat a person, which was great as Alvin had no desire at all to chow down on someone. The very thought of biting into someone's unwashed ass sent him into dry heaves. He'd stick to burgers, or if he really got a hankering, squirrels, the saucy little bloodsabitches that they were. Even those were no fun choking down. The very thought turned his stomach.

Alvin suspected his dietary choices limited him somehow physically, but, in all honesty, he didn't care. When he filled his lungs to capacity, tasting air clean enough to make him high on life, he felt so good, so damned *thankful*, that he didn't care in the least. He still could eat all the nachos and pizza he liked. Those dishes didn't really help in his weight loss (he was still a stout lad) but it certainly didn't slow him down either.

The sky continued to darken and Alvin walked across the frozen marshland, struggling with the snow, but chugging along without any difficulty in breathing. A glorious, wonderful gift.

Alvin stopped in his tracks, arched his back, and regarded the deepening hue of the sky. The evening star twinkled back at him.

Minutes later, he halted at the forest's edge and located a hidden cleaning amongst the trees. Alvin had discovered the little place months earlier. He cut boughs wider than Egyptian fans and used them to cover up his clothing, not that anyone was out here at night. And he was well away from the usual snow mobile trails.

He stomped his feet, punching deep recesses in the snowy floor. Once finished, he stopped, took another hit off the pure air, and looked up. The sky was almost black. And over the hills, the white pearl that was the moon peeked into view. Alvin felt its seductive tug.

Life is good, he thought. He missed his friends, but he was sure he'd make new ones in time. Maybe even marry that little Estonia honey he flirted with online. That would be something. He wondered if his little soldiers could still hit the target, if pups were a possibility.

Thoughts for another day.

The moon rose a little higher over the hills, its face brilliant. With the fallen snow, the night would be positively glowing.

He shrugged off his snowsuit and carefully placed it on a snow bank. The cold enveloped him then and he welcomed it. He lifted one leg across the other and pulled off his boots, then removed his sweater and undershirt. When he finished shimmying out of his jeans, he concealed his clothing with the cut boughs.

Rubbing his hands together, Alvin checked on the moon. Still rising, and watching, a white glaring iris in the sky.

The naked man stood in the deepening shadows and filled his healthy lungs. Alvin thumped his chest and grinned fiercely. His eyes moistened just a little. His eyes watered every time, it seemed, just before the change.

Thanks, buddy, Alvin sent off heavenward, beaming his gratitude once more to his dear departed friend, Ross Kelly.

The moon rose higher, calling him.

And Alvin answered.

About the Author

Keith C. Blackmore is the author of the Mountain Man, 131 Days, and Breeds series, among other horror, heroic fantasy, and crime novels. He lives on the island of Newfoundland in Canada. Visit his website at www.keithcblackmore.com.

www.ingramcontent.com/pod-product-compliance
Ingram Content Group UK Ltd.
Pitfield, Milton Keynes, MK11 3LW, UK
UKHW041300180426
11947UKWH00009B/591